The
Judas
Flower

First published by Bastei Lübbe 2017

This edition, Long Midnight Publishing, 2023

copyright © 2017 Douglas Lindsay

ISBN: 979-8386568009

THE
JUDAS
FLOWER

DOUGLAS
LINDSAY

LMP

prologue

Tuesday evening, mid-March, top end of Hope Street, Glasgow.
Cold air, rain falling. Just after eight, there were a few people on
the street. A short queue outside a nightclub, two smokers
standing at the door of a pub in t-shirts, oblivious to the weather.
Here, a couple staying at the DoubleTree, out for an after-dinner
walk beneath a large umbrella with the Jaguar motif. Passing
them by was a young woman, clutching a newborn like a
running back who'd fumbled his last possession. Further down
the street, loudly, three older men, their conversation switching
from politics to football, having turned, with a barked expletive,
on a sixpence. On the wet ground, leaning against the walls of
buildings, one beggar, two beggars, three beggars, four, in quick
succession. Two huddled and cold, drunk, asleep; one, with a
dog, playing a desultory guitar; one nodding a bitter greeting to
all who passed.

   Into this age-old mix walked Archie Wilson, out through
the doors of the Garland, in need of some fresh air. A sudden
world of riches had left Archie stuffed and struggling for life,
exacerbated by the excesses of wine, women and food.

   He had the weight of all the worlds on his shoulders,
feeling a sense of loss for his old life. His former self. Late
nights, getting up at six thirty, long days working on the golf
course in all weather, the treat of a bottle of wine, saving up
weeks in advance for a trip to the cinema, barely any money in
his pocket, but at least no credit card debt either. The simple life,
little beyond existing day to day. No choices to be made, other
than whether to have pasta and tinned tomatoes for dinner, or no
dinner at all.

Now there was no limit. *The world's your oyster*, was what the man from the company had said. What did that even mean anyway? Why was anyone's world ever an oyster?

Archie took out his phone, brought up Google and started to type, the couple beneath the umbrella passing in the opposite direction.

Falstaff: I will not lend thee a penny.

Pistol: Why then the world's mine oyster, Which I with sword will open.

Ha! thought, Archie Wilson. *Fucking Shakespeare. Should have known.*

"Probably says on the Internet somewhere that Shakespeare wrote *all your base are belong to us*," said Archie to himself, smiling as he went, returning the phone to his pocket.

"Talking to yourself, again, Arch?" he said. The smile became rueful, and he shook his head.

He stopped and looked back up the road. Suddenly the street seemed quieter than it had a minute earlier. The three men had turned down a side street, the sound of their conversation retreating into the rain, the nightclub queue had disappeared, the smokers had tossed a pair of cigarette butts onto the wet ground.

The city dwellers and their lives, thought Archie, *all with somewhere to go.*

The movement continued around him. Cars and pedestrians, the city at night. And here he was, richer than any of them, and he had no idea what his next step would be.

Money, money, money, that was all he seemed to think about these days. The sooner he was able to get rid of it the better.

He shivered at the cold and the damp. And that was another thing. Why was he still here? Why hadn't he got off his backside, submitted his passport application, and got on a plane away from this place? Who in their right mind, with the size of bank balance that he now possessed, would be walking down Hope Street at this time on a Tuesday evening, when he could be literally anywhere on earth?

A Street named Hope. There was a fucking joke, in this town, in this life, on this doomed planet.

He looked down at the beggar at his feet, the guy with the guitar, strumming his way through the chords for *Hallelujah*, the strings out of tune. Reached into his pocket, pulled out a few notes, fives and tens and twenties, bent down and dropped them

—

into the flat cap that lay on the pavement.

"Cheers, mate," said Archie, as though thanking him for the guitar playing, and walked on.

"Fuck. Thanks," came the voice behind him, and Archie acknowledged him with a wave.

Further down Hope Street. No particular destination in mind. This very moment a metaphor for the way his new life was going. A car passed on the road, travelling in the opposite direction, slowed, then came to a stop. Archie kept walking on. The driver checked in the mirror, nothing coming up behind, and then reversed quickly, coming to a stop opposite Archie.

Window down, Archie still hadn't noticed.

"Archie!"

The voice called out across the damp road, through the cold, dank, dreich night air.

Sometimes these days people spoke to Archie in the street and he ignored them. If the mood took him, he'd put his head down and ignore everyone.

This evening, he automatically lifted his head. He looked across the road. He didn't smile, he didn't feel any lifting of the gloom that surrounded him, but fatefully, fatally, he decided to engage.

There would be no more mornings in the life of Archie Wilson.

WEDNESDAY

1

Just after ten in the morning. Detective Sergeant Marc Bain watched Cooper walk into the open-plan and look around. The detective chief inspector looked agitated, but then he always looked agitated. Bain stared at him long enough that he caught his eye, and then Cooper walked over.

"Marc," he said, "where's the Inspector?"

Bain glanced back at the folder he was rifling quickly through. Documents from an accountancy firm that had granted them access to old paperwork, but not computer files. He was hoping he'd find what he was looking for without having to go through the hassle of warrant procedures, knowing that the firm had the connections and the money to put up a fight. So far he'd come up empty.

A second, then he turned back. He knew Cooper would be angry, but Pereira wouldn't want him lying.

"She had to go into school to pick up Anais," he said. "Some problem or other. She'll be back as soon as she's sorted it out."

"Seriously?"

It was a rhetorical question, and Bain didn't bother to answer. It wasn't the first time.

"I thought the inspector's mum was on-point for emergency pick-up?"

"You'll have to ask her," said Bain.

Cooper turned away and looked over the office, thrusting his hands in his pockets as he did so. There was a look about him that suggested he wanted people to notice him. So they could see how pissed off he was.

A moment, he seemed to acknowledge to himself that that was exactly what he was doing, then he turned back to Bain, his voice heavy with resignation.

"We have a classic dead-body-in-the-cemetery situation," he said. "The Necropolis, of all places."

"Presumably not one that's supposed to be there?"

"Yes, Marc, that's why you're going. On your way, contact the inspector and get her to join you there."

"Foul play, I presume?" said Bain, already getting to his feet.

He wouldn't have been going if there hadn't been.

"Oh, yes," said Cooper, "this one's a ripper."

*

Aliya Pereira sat absolutely still in the small chair, staring out the window. Her daughter sat next to her, head down, equally still, bar the small movement of her left foot scraping back and forth over the carpet.

The Headmistress had yet to join them, but for some reason Pereira was reminded of Tom Wilkinson in *The Full Monty*, sitting in an office while the lads played with gnomes through the window behind the heads of the company suits. The thought of it didn't bring a smile to her face, however.

She was, in fact, trying not to think about anything. Work was piling up, she was supposed to be at the office, supposed to be doing a job, yet here she was, called in to see the headmistress for the second time this term, and every person in her office who thought she shouldn't be where she was would be nodding to themselves and passing comments of self-justification.

The door behind opened, and the headmistress entered. Pereira didn't turn, although Anais couldn't help herself. Her head quickly dropped again as she made eye contact with Mrs. Walkey.

Walkey sat down behind her desk, didn't bother with any artifice involving the paperwork around her, and looked across the desk at Pereira.

"You've been informed of the incident?" she said.

The headmistress was in her early fifties. Something of the Imelda Staunton about her, Pereira usually thought.

—

5

"The details seem sketchy," Pereira said. "Perhaps you could fill me in."

Walkey pursed her lips, her eyes settling on Anais. The girl did not look up.

"Anais punched Jack Grey. Second time this month, as you'll know. We have zero tolerance for fighting in this school. This is a seat of learning. There's no place for this kind of behaviour, especially from a young girl. It's bad enough when it's the sixth year boys, but this…"

"I'm sure it won't happen again," said Pereira, and even as the sentence was leaving her mouth, she was aware that she sounded like one of her own clients.

"You said that three weeks ago," Walkey shot back.

Pereira did not have a reply. She glanced down at Anais, wondering if this time she might have something to say for herself, but she was as resolutely silent as she always was when brought into this situation.

"We're sending her home," said the headmistress. "She can come back–"

"You can't!"

"Yes, yes I can. And we are," said Walkey, alternating between taking responsibility herself and sharing it with unseen others.

"There's nowhere for her to go."

"I thought her grandmother looked after her? That's what happened last time."

Pereira's mother wasn't due to collect Anais until three that afternoon. She would already be on the train to Perth, meeting a friend for a few hours. Pereira wasn't going to get into explanations with the headmistress, however.

"She can't today."

"There must be someone else," said the headmistress, "and if there's not, you'll have to take her with you. That's all."

The two women stared across the desk at each other, the child silent and forgotten for the moment. As though this argument was about something other than her.

"What about Jack Grey?" asked Pereira.

"What about him?"

"Have you established his part in this? Is he also being sent home?"

"No!" said Walkey, seemingly exasperated. "He absolutely is not. I wouldn't be surprised if we both, you and the school,

—

6

end up at the wrong end of a lawsuit out of this. Your daughter cannot, and I repeat, cannot go around punching people for no reason."

"There's always a reason," said Pereira, her voice cold, her tone giving no quarter.

The headmistress paused a second, and then turned her eyes on Anais.

"And will you tell us the reason, Anais, please?"

Pereira barely expected her daughter to look up, never mind answer, and she was getting ready to give her a nudge when Anais slowly lifted her head and held the headmistress's gaze across the desk.

"He's an asshole," she said.

*

They sat in the car, parked on a double yellow line outside the school.

Silence.

Pereira stared straight ahead, lips set firm, teeth pressed together. Anais stared at her hands, swallowing occasionally, waiting for her mother to speak.

An uncomfortable silence that was Pereira's to break, a silence with which she was no more at ease than her daughter. Her certainty and authority at the police station, and in her day-to-day duties, so often disappeared when faced with her own thirteen-year-old. How often did they find themselves sitting like this, trapped in an endless deathly hush?

"Why?" Pereira finally forced from her lips.

"I said why," replied Anais.

Pereira placed her hands on the steering wheel, gripping tightly. The engine wasn't running, they weren't going anywhere.

"What did he do?"

Even though they'd started talking, the silence between words was still thick.

Maybe, thought Pereira, one day the silence would become so great it would form into an actual, physical entity. It would envelope them, the way silence enveloped people in books. But this silence wouldn't just envelope them in the metaphorical sense, it would swallow them up, eat them whole, and they would disappear.

—

7

"If you don't tell me what he did, the Internet's going off for the rest of the week."

"I need it for school."

"I don't care."

The silence returned, thick and dark. Pereira gripped the steering wheel, Anais stared at the dashboard. Finally Pereira turned to look at her daughter.

"Tell me, or the Internet goes off."

"He called me a Muslim," Anais said quickly.

Immediately there was a slight change in the colour of Pereira's knuckles, the grip on the steering wheel slightly relaxed.

"And a terrorist."

"And you punched him?"

"Yes."

"You didn't want to explain that you weren't a Muslim, and that even if you were–"

"He knows I'm not a Muslim, Mum. He's an asshole."

A beat. A further relaxing of the fingers, until she lowered her hands. And here she was, again, finding herself in the parenting quandary, of when to be the authoritarian and when to be the friend. Did she too frequently lean towards the latter because of their family situation? Anais wouldn't be the only thirteen-year-old girl to struggle to adapt to having a half-brother nine years younger than her in the house.

Perhaps it was what everyone did these days. Or maybe it was because that was what she wanted. Pereira wanted her thirteen-year-old daughter to be her friend.

"You know how many people are assholes in the world?"

Anais shook her head.

"Practically everyone," Pereira continued. "Even people who aren't generally assholes will, at some point, act like an asshole, even if they don't particularly mean to. You'll see it many, many times in your life, and you can't go punching someone every time it happens. You just can't."

"But he was an asshole *to me*."

Pereira reached over and took her daughter's hand.

"I know. I know. But punching isn't going to sort anything out. It's not going to make anyone else look at you and think you've been wronged. You make him the victim, when he's not. He's the asshole."

Anais giggled, while Pereira had the usual feeling of guilt

—

8

about using bad language in conversation with her daughter. No wonder Anais had used the word in front of the headmistress.

"Next time, can you try talking to him about it? Try explaining your heritage."

"Have you, like, been in a school playground?"

"Yes."

"It's not the eighties anymore, Mum."

The phone rang. Pereira squeezed Anais's hand, gave her a last comforting smile, then lifted the phone.

"Marc?"

"You OK to talk?" asked Bain.

"Just leaving the school."

"Can you meet me at the Necropolis?"

Pereira hesitated, glanced at Anais.

"What's up?" Pereira asked.

"Dead guy," said Bain.

The street stretched away, a few parked cars, no other traffic. A couple walking a dog, arguing, or just talking animatedly. The newsagents up the road. The shuttered windows of the old dry cleaners next to it in the small block.

Pereira had been intending taking Anais back to her office, putting her in one of the interview rooms. That was her only option. Cooper was hardly likely to be impressed, but as long as it didn't interfere.

Taking her to a potential murder scene, however, was in a different league.

"K," she said, making her decision, and clicked the phone off. She would find out the details when she got there.

Picked a bad day to take my daughter to work, she thought, and started the car.

2

The rain was steady, but not too heavy, as Pereira walked quickly up the hill, across the grass. Over the bodies of the dead.

The murder scene hadn't been hard to spot, the group of police officers congregated around one grave. There had already been a perimeter area set up, and she nodded at one of the officers on duty as she ducked beneath the tape and approached the crowd.

Bain was in attendance, turning to watch his inspector approach, nodding as she came alongside, slightly out of breath.

"Sorry," she said.

"It's fine. Victim's still dead."

She lifted her eyes, then walked past him to look at the cadaver.

The deceased was a man in his mid-thirties. He was sitting down, his back resting against the headstone, the body propped up by a thin piece of rope tied around the neck and knotted behind the stone. He had been stabbed, lightly, in the corner of each eye, so that two lines of blood had dried on his face. On the top of his head, a small metal cross had been hammered into his skull. This was the only obvious sign of what would have killed him. Blood had dried, dark red, on his hair.

His hands were folded together in his lap, and a small branch with pink blossom had been inserted in the fingers, as though the hands were being used as a graveside vase.

"There are marks on his wrists," said Pereira. "Bound and killed elsewhere, and then brought here."

"Yes, that's what we're thinking. Although it could be he was killed here, and then the bonds were removed so that the killer could… create the artwork."

"Yep, that's what it's like. As though the killer has meticulously recreated a work of art. But the cross hammered into the head…," and she let the thought drift away. "Any ID?"

Bain glanced at her, and then looked back at the victim. Didn't immediately answer. Pereira waited a few moments, then said, "What am I missing?"

"You don't read the tabloids," he said. He wasn't asking the question, he knew she didn't.

"Help me out."

"His name's Archie Wilson. Lottery winner from a couple of months ago."

"How much?"

"Hundred and thirty million."

"Pounds?"

"As opposed to what?"

"Euros?"

"Pounds, I think," said Bain. "Doesn't really matter, though, does it? It was a shedload, whichever way you look at it."

She took another step, and finally bent down beside the body. She leaned forward and smelled around his mouth, studied the marks on his wrists, the entry wound of the cross into the head, then pressed her fingers lightly against his cheek to get the feel of the corpse, before looking over the rest of his body, across the abdomen and down his legs to the bottom of his trousers and shoes.

Bain watched her as she made her intimate, precise examination, quickly processing and taking everything in.

"Bound by the ankles too," she said after a couple of minutes. "You can see where the fabric has been marked, the tape torn off. Been dead ten to twelve hours, I'd say. He'd been drinking, maybe something else there too."

She got to her feet and looked around. There were five other police officers in immediate attendance, and at the bottom of the hill she could see the first couple of Scenes of Crime Officers arrive, Corkin and Gayle, laughing about something as they walked round the winding path, pulling on gloves as they came. They were both wearing rain jackets. No one else seemed to have come properly prepared, as though they were all surprised that it would rain in Scotland in March.

She looked south, across what she could see of the city

—

11

between the great memorials and stone crosses from their vantage point on the hill. Glasgow stretched away before them, the buildings anonymous pale greys and browns, towards the grey-green hills in the distance. To her right, the Cathedral and the Royal Infirmary. Then she looked up at the sky, low grey cloud, no sign of the rain easing, no hint of blue.

"What did the tabloids say?" she asked, finally turning back to Bain.

"I don't think they know he's dead yet."

"Sergeant, just because your buddies are on their way up here, don't be getting all glib with me. What were they saying about him after he won the money? Any idea yet what he was doing with it?"

"Not much. The tabs were doing their best to make out he was splashing his money and being a bit of a dick, but when you read the stories… there was nothing there. There was some suggestion he might buy Albion Rovers."

"Are they for sale?"

"Don't know. They would be for the amount of money he's got. He'd been seen around town with a few women. Younger than him, and way better looking. Classic… A couple of stories about him throwing money around, but still small-time stuff compared to what he actually won. As for his long-term plans, I'm not sure."

"Any ex's or unhappy relatives pitching in to the media scrum?"

He shook his head, and said, "I'll check it out."

"Archie Wilson, you said."

"Yep."

They turned as Corkin and Gayle came alongside them, stopping to look down at the corpse. A moment, then Gayle nodded.

"Definitely dead then," he said.

"You people are hilarious," said Pereira. "We'll leave you to it. Take care of the flowers, we'll need them."

"Hmm," said Gayle, disinterestedly. "Pansies, are they?"

"Seriously, Henry? Pansies? They're from a tree. Blossom from a tree. You can't see that?"

"Now that you mention it," he said. "Cherry? Apple?"

"*Cercis siliquastrum*. The Judas Tree, as it's more commonly known."

"Shit," said Corkin, shaking his head. "You're something

—

12

else, Inspector. How d'you know this stuff?"

"Sounds like a message," said Bain. "Never good when people leave messages. What's the significance of the Judas Tree?"

"Rumoured to be the tree from which Judas hung himself," said Pereira. "The Mediterranean redbud. It's said that the flowers of the tree had always been white, but when Judas used it to commit suicide, the tree felt shame and its white flowers turned blood red. They've been red ever since."

The three men looked down at the small branch, propped in the folded hands of the body.

"Load of pish," said Corkin.

"Those leaves are pink," said Gayle. "If the tree was aiming for blood red, it made an arse of it."

"Do we get them in Scotland?" asked Bain. "If it's a native Mediterranean plant?"

"Good question," said Pereira. "We need to find out. And while we may get them, the chances of them flowering this early in March are slim. Well, nil, I'd have thought, particularly given the weather the last couple of months. Someone went out of their way to get these... You think you'll be able to get any footprints out from all of this lot?"

"Aye," said Corkin, "we can give it a go. And here," he continued, pointing back slightly down the hill, "you can see a wheelbarrow track. Two tracks, in fact, one heavier than the other. The barrow was laden on the way up, empty going back down."

"Right. OK, gentlemen, you should get on with the job."

She nodded at them, and took a step or two away, Bain falling in beside her.

"No sign of Edgars?" she asked.

Bain shook his head.

"On her way, far as I know."

"Right. Who found the body?"

Bain looked around, and then pointed to a man standing on his own, a spade in his hand, looking down over the city.

"Do we have a next of kin?" asked Pereira.

"Not yet," said Bain. "I think there were parents in the tabloid coverage, but I'm not sure."

"'K. You get into that. I'll speak to the grave guy, then we'll go and see the mum or the dad, or whoever. And make sure you get the name and details from the headstone, just in case the choice of stone wasn't random."

"Yes, ma'am," said Bain. Moving past her to kneel by the stone, he missed the look of consternation she gave him, then she took a last look down at the cadaver, stepped around the police photographer and approached the man standing alone, leaning on the end of the shovel.

"Mr....?" she said.

He glanced at her. "Who are you?"

She took the ID from the inside pocket of her jacket and held it towards him, the words, "DI Pereira," automatically spoken to accompany the movement.

He looked at the card, then at her, and then let his eyes go up and down her body. When he'd finished the examination he made a small gesture of acknowledgement, then looked away again.

"Going to be raining for a while," he said, pointing south. "Unusual to see it come up from there, but it happens sometimes. Youse lot'll be gone soon enough, I expect."

He was wearing overalls, but nothing waterproof, the wet patches on his shoulders beginning to spread.

"Mr....?" asked Pereira again.

"Underhill," said the groundsman.

Pereira gave him a slightly raised eyebrow. "Really?"

"What?" he said.

"That's the fake name Frodo Baggins uses. It's a well-known fake name."

The groundsman looked quizzically at her, then at the small crowd around the headstone, then back to Pereira. "Fuck's Frodo Baggins?"

A moment. Did it matter what his name was? And easy enough to check in any case.

"You found the body," she said, moving on, no question in her voice. She wouldn't be talking to him if he hadn't.

"Aye. Pissed off about it 'n' all."

"Why?"

He glanced round at her.

"Why? Would you like it if the first thing you found when you got into work in the morning was some dead cunt?"

He held her gaze for a moment, then turned away. She smiled once he was no longer looking at her.

"You're the groundsman?"

"You can always tell when you're speaking to a detective,

eh?" said Underhill. "Seeing the things everyone else misses."

"And you're pissed off?" said Pereira, ignoring the sarcasm, Underhill's words high up on the lists of those she'd heard many times before.

"Aye, I am," he said, turning back to her. "I mean, seriously? Why'd they have to bring the bastard here? A cross in the head and body tied to a headstone? Seriously? How many shite films has that guy been watching? Jesus."

"How d'you know it was a guy?"

He held her gaze for a while longer, then finally turned and looked away again.

"Usually women wouldn't be that stupid. I'm not crediting *you* with fuck all, though."

"What time d'you arrive this morning? Was there any sign of disturbance? I presume the gates are locked at night."

He took a moment, and she let him have it. He was going to answer, but he just didn't want to appear too ready with the information. Wanted to retain some control over the interview, let her know that any information he passed on was because of his good grace.

"Got in at eight thirty. Made a cup of tea, read the paper."

"Which one?"

"What?"

"Which newspaper were you reading?"

He didn't turn, thought for a moment on whether or not he was going to reply.

"The Scotsman. I know, there's only me and about three people left, but I like it, so you can piss off."

"I'll just stay here for the moment."

"Don't see what that's got to do with it. Anyway, went out just after nine, that's when I found him. Never seen him before, so I know, I know it's nothing actually to do with the cemetery. I know it's likely just some arsehole killer who's read too many books. Then I called you lot, made sure the front gate was locked, and had a look around. Found the lock on the gate down at Ladywell had been chibbed."

"Can you take me down there?"

"Suppose," he said.

"Let's get to it."

The groundsman grunted, hesitated a while longer until he felt as though he had established some influence on proceedings, propped the shovel against the back of a headstone, and then

---

walked away, heading down the hill.

"Come on, I've not got all day," he threw over his shoulder, even though Pereira was right behind him.

*

When they got to Pereira's car, she was relieved to find Anais sitting where she'd left her. Leaving the graveyard and thinking about her daughter for the first time in an hour, she'd suddenly become nervous that she would have wandered off.

They got into the car, Anais already having moved into the back seat.

"Anais," said Bain, nodding.

"Hello."

"Everything all right?" asked Pereira.

Anais was looking at her phone, *playing BB-Tan probably*, thought Pereira, and hadn't looked up.

"I need to go to the toilet," she said. "And I'm hungry."

Pereira stared straight ahead, her hands automatically finding the steering wheel, thinking about where they were going next.

3

Pereira and Bain were sitting at the kitchen table in a small house near Bellahouston Park. Archie Wilson's father was staring at them from the across the table. Or, more accurately, staring at Pereira. The mother was fussing around the kettle, getting the teapot, cups and saucers together.

Neither Pereira nor Bain wanted tea, but this wasn't about taking a drink. It was letting the mother deal with the news of her son's death by whatever means she felt necessary. If that was making a cup of tea for the messengers of bad news, then so be it.

The light was on in the kitchen, the day outside dark, the sound of rain against the window.

"Where're you from?" asked Wilson.

His wife glanced over her shoulder, but her eyes dropped and she decided not to get involved.

"Cathcart," said Pereira.

"I don't mean that. Pakistan or India, something like that?"

"I was born in Rottenrow. Lived in Glasgow all my life."

He held her gaze for a moment, then finally he gave up and lowered his eyes to the table.

"We're going to need to ask you some questions," said Bain, kicking himself for allowing Wilson to make the usual queries of the boss. "Are you all right with us doing it now, or would you—"

"Now's fine," said Wilson.

The kettle had rumbled to a conclusion, and once the noise of the water being poured into the teapot had gone, they could tell from the sound of Mrs. Wilson's breathing that she had

—

17

started crying.

"Get on with it," said Wilson.

"If you're sure it's all right."

"I keep telling you it is."

Mrs. Wilson turned, a tray held not particularly securely in her hands and placed it on the table. There was a small plate of Jammie Dodgers. One each. Four cups, a jug of milk, the teapot, a bowl of white sugar. She stood for a moment, her hands still gripping the side of the tray, as though contemplating taking it away again, then she straightened up, swallowing loudly.

She looked at the two detectives, wanting to say something, wanting to excuse herself, but she couldn't speak. There were no words, not even for that. And then she turned, quickly, as the first sob broke on her lips, and then she was out of the kitchen, door closing, and they heard the sound of her footsteps on the stairs.

"Like I said, get on with it."

The teapot sat untouched, a silent witness to the conversation.

"Your son won the lottery six weeks ago?"

"Six and a half."

"Was he living with you before then?"

"Did you do any research before you got here?"

"We came straight here, Mr. Wilson. Given that Archie has been in the news, when word gets out, it's going to be spread quickly. We didn't want–"

"Aye, fine. He'd been living in a two-bed with a mate of his. One of they… I don't know what you call them. Dresses up in… cross dresser, that's what he is. Dresses in women's clothes. Up Great Western Road. Archie said it was for the shorter bus journey to the golf club in the morning. Anyway, he quit his job and moved out after he won the money. Been looking at houses, staying at the Grand, the hotel further out of town, out past Knightswood. Flushing the damned money down the toilet if you ask me, but he wouldn't listen."

"Can you give us the person's name? The one he lived–"

"Naw. I can give you the address, you can go and check for yourself."

"The lottery ticket, he bought it himself? He wasn't part of a syndicate? There was no dispute over who'd actually bought the ticket, or whether someone had lent him the money? Or someone actually bought it for Archie, anything like that?"

"Aye," he said, and his eyebrow moved to accompany a slight nod. He looked past Bain, in between the two of them, out of the window.

"And…?"

"The guy. The cross dresser. I think he might have been wanting his share. Or something. Archibald had hardly spoken to us, but he said the queer was looking for something, said there'd been a gentleman's agreement. I mean, gentlemen's agreement with someone like that… That's a laugh."

"Had there been any legal action started?"

"Don't know."

"And what about you, Mr. Wilson?" asked Pereira. "Had Archie promised you anything?"

Wilson did not immediately reply, then he glanced at the pot of tea without making any move towards it.

"There's fresh paint in the kitchen," she said.

He didn't answer.

"Like, in the last week fresh."

"What of it?"

"You do it yourself?"

A quick glance at the coving showed a not entirely professional job where the magnolia of the walls met the white of the ceiling.

"What's your point, caller?" said Wilson.

"Presumably with the money your son had, you could have been in a new house by now. If you didn't want to move, you could've had a new kitchen installed. The units you have here, they must be at least fifteen years old."

"There's nothing wrong with them. They're cupboards. They hold things. They'll still be holding things a hundred years from now."

"Did you paint the kitchen yourself to make a point? You didn't need his money. You could improve your life without asking your son for a handout. I mean, it's not much, but that doesn't mean the point isn't made?"

"Are we finished?"

"Did you expect your son to give you a share of the money, or were you repulsed by it and didn't want to know?"

"If I say we argued, are you going to arrest me?"

"Probably not."

Wilson snorted quietly, shook his head.

"Go and speak to the queer," he said after a moment.

—

"Are there any other friends or family members that might have contacted Archie since the lottery winnings?" asked Bain.

Another snort from Wilson, and now finally he lifted the teapot. Swirled it round, then poured out one mug, added milk, set it down in front of himself.

"My wife has four brothers and sisters. I have two. Archibald had at least fifteen cousins. First cousins, that is. God knows how many second cousins and removed cousins or whatever you call it. As for friends?" He shook his head. "Probably. I mean, every bastard has friends, don't they?"

"Fifteen cousins?" asked Pereira. She knew about cousins. "How many of them were looking for money?"

"You'd have to ask them," he said.

He looked harshly across the table, his eyes moving from one to the other, then said, "Are we finished? I've got my tea."

*

Again, to her relief, they found Anais where they'd left her, at a Costa Coffee two blocks away from Wilson's house.

"Hey," Pereira said, "everything all right?"

"I'm bored," said Anais.

"Don't punch the other kid next time and this won't happen," said Pereira. Anais rolled her eyes. "We're just getting a coffee, but we'll sit at another table. We need to talk about the case."

"What is it?"

"Someone's been killed."

"Cool. Can I have a panini? It's lunchtime."

"Sure. Chicken and tomato? Salt and vinegar crisps?"

Anais nodded. "Phone's almost out of charge," she said. She hadn't looked up from it the entire time.

"We're going back to the station after this," said Pereira. "Someone'll have a charger."

"Cool."

Pereira went to the counter and stood in the short queue. She wasn't thinking about the curious case of the lottery winner with a cross embedded in his head. There was far too much she didn't know, therefore it was far too early to think about it. All she'd have now was needless conjecture.

She looked at Bain, still standing outside in the rain, talking on the phone. A dreary few minutes passed. The queue, the

---

order, the food slowly assembled on the tray, the noise of the coffee machine, the flair of the barista, trying to inject some life into a dismal early Wednesday afternoon in Glasgow.

She took the food to Anais, who acknowledged it with a nod, and then took the two coffees to a table by the window, where she sat with Bain, who'd finished his call a couple of minutes earlier.

"How are we doing?" she said.

"OK," said Bain. He had a small notebook out and was still writing down what he'd been told over the phone.

"The headstone was chosen for a reason, it seems. It was the grave of a William Craven, died in November 1893. There's nothing recorded of his life until sometime in his twenties, when he received a large amount of money upon the death of his aunt. It's not clear what he did with the money, if indeed he had the time to do anything with it. He died aged twenty-eight."

"The killer had done his research."

"Yes. And I've got the name of the person Archie Wilson shared a flat with. He's called Frank Henderson, likes to be known as Fran apparently."

"OK. I think we'll go back to the station after this, check in, I'm going to need to leave Anais there, then we'll head over to see Fran. And we should get out to the Grand Hotel."

"Maybe we should go to see Fran now. Then, since we'll be heading out that way, go on to the Grand."

"Why?"

Bain looked over at Anais, then lifted his eyebrows at Pereira. *Better to avoid the boss seeing Anais all day*, he was thinking.

"He'll just have to live with it," she said. "I can handle him."

"If we get tied up back at the station for a while, then head over to the other side of the city to see Fran, sit in traffic both ways, by the time you get back to the station it's going to be way after three. We'd be as well just getting on with it. Anais's been sitting around for two hours already. And really, what she's going to do at the station. She'll still be on that thing."

Pereira looked past him at her daughter, head down, phone in one hand, panini in the other. It was hardly the time to think about it, but when was there ever time?

She wanted there to be a better way. Something else she could do. This was terrible, sitting here looking at her kid, stuck on a mobile device for the day, doing who knew what. And what *did* she know about her daughter's activities on the phone?

"Her phone's almost out of charge," said Pereira.

As usual, Pereira's guilt meant that she worried about how to make things easier for Anais, rather than making her daughter accept that she'd just have to sit and be bored, for a reason of her own making.

Bain looked round at Anais, then glanced around the shop, looking for electrical sockets.

"She doesn't have a charger with her?"

Pereira shook her head.

"There was a phone shop just down the road," said Bain. "We could nip in, get something we can use in the car."

Pereira looked out the window, looked along the road. Couldn't see the shop from where she was sitting. Raindrops ran down the windowpane.

4

The sitting room of the flat was small. One insubstantial two-seat sofa, and a single comfy chair, a two-seat dining table with only one chair, lamp with a table, a low wooden unit designed for a television, but covered with various pieces of life's detritus, newspapers and dirty plates, a couple of glasses. The television, at least twenty inches too big for the size of the room, was attached to the wall. The furniture, despite being meagre in quantity and size, was all squeezed tightly into too small a space, like an overweight man still dressing in last year's t-shirt. In the middle of it all was an old, fake-Persian rug, crumpled at the edges, too big for the small space.

Fran Henderson sat on the sofa, legs crossed, hands clasped together. Bain had taken the seat opposite. Pereira was standing at the window. From her position she could see the car, she could see Anais, head down over her phone, in the same position she'd been in for the previous few hours.

"Total bunfight, by the way."

Henderson was wearing a skirt and a halter-neck top, lipstick, some foundation and mascara, but no wig; hair shaved short, chest hair obvious, the voice regular, deep and rough, with a thick Glasgow accent.

"I mean, I'm like that, why wouldn't it be? I said to him, get the fuck out of Dodge, man. Fuck out of Dodge. Every bastard's going to want a piece of you. Family, friends, people you meet down the boozer, people you've never heard of, people who seen you on the news. Jesus. Every bastard going. I'm like that, take the money and run, my friend. See if it'd been me, I'd've moved to the Caribbean by now, some shit like that. To some island full of rich wankers who weren't interested in the money."

"He didn't take your advice," said Bain.

"Aye well, see what you get. Imagine what it's going to be like now, man. Every bastard in that family's going to be fighting over it. The fucking government'll probably end up getting it. Ha! It's probably them that killed him. Youse'll be getting close to making a breakthrough, then you'll get visited by some kind of James Bond cunt telling you to keep your noses out and to shut down the investigation. That's what'll happen, man, count on it."

"Did you buy the ticket for Mr. Wilson?" asked Pereira. She didn't look round as she said it. Listening to Henderson, worrying about Anais at the same time.

"Aye, I did. Who told you that?"

Neither Bain nor Pereira answered, and finally Henderson nodded.

"Right. His old man, eh? Classic. Aye, I bought the ticket. I mean, that's what we did. We spent two quid each, every damned week, on that crap. Sometimes I bought them, sometimes Archie did. Didn't matter. He had his numbers, I had mine."

Pereira finally turned.

"How'd you and Archie first start sharing?"

"Just sort of happened. I was working at the golf club when Archie started. He was looking for a room, I was needing a bit of money. He moved in, never left. Well, not until…"

"You don't work at the golf club anymore?" asked Bain.

"Chucked it after Archie started paying me rent. Thought I could live on that and the social. Some chance. Fucking social. Got a job at M&S, but that didn't last. Too posh for the likes of me."

"Is the place usually so untidy?" asked Pereira.

Henderson looked around, turned back with a curious look. "What…?"

"Is the place usually so untidy?" repeated Pereira.

"Seriously? You're looking at me, and you're like, here's a bloke identifies as a woman, you'd think he'd be out with the fucking Pledge every day? That it?"

"We're just trying to get a measure of Mr. Wilson's character," said Bain.

"There was a study last year from the Humboldt University,

Berlin," said Pereira. "Demonstrated that men identifying as women have a higher incidence of OCD, one of the results being a tendency towards order and cleanliness."

"That right?" said Henderson.

"Interesting that you don't show the tendency."

"And did it say that all such men have an OCD?"

Pereira didn't answer.

"Didn't fucking think so, by the way."

"Had you discussed with Archie whether you were going to get any of the money?"

Henderson stared at Pereira, the lips pursed for a moment, the fingers working together.

"Are youse suspecting me, here? I mean, that's what youse lot do, isn't it? I've seen the shows. The killer's usually close to the victim."

"Just answer the question, please," said Bain.

"Aye, whatever. We had an agreement. If I won, I was paying for him to take a year off work and go round the world, some shite like that. Like he was ever going to go round the world. If he won... Well..."

Henderson gestured to the skirt, looked back up at Pereira.

"Can't get it done on the NHS?" asked Bain.

"Aye, in about fifteen year."

"When was the last time you saw Mr. Wilson," asked Pereira.

"About a week ago," said Henderson. "Met up for a drink. He was paying."

"And? Was he going to honour his commitment?"

"So he says," said Henderson. "Told me to pick a place and he'd get the money to me quick as he could."

"Had you found anywhere?" asked Bain.

Henderson looked at him, the shoulders moved slowly.

"Suppose I had."

The doorbell rang. Henderson sighed heavily, glancing at the clock.

"Fucking postie again."

Henderson got up, opened the door. The postman was standing in the short corridor, smiling, a large sack of letters in his hand.

"Fran," he said.

"Mingus."

The bag was handed over, no further words exchanged.

Henderson carried the bag through the small sitting room, opened one of the doors off – a bedroom that was becoming filled with similar mailbags – tossed it onto the pile, and closed the door.

The twice-daily ritual completed, Henderson returned to the sofa and sat down.

"Either one person's writing a fuck-tonne of begging letters, or else every single bampot in Scotland's having a go."

"Did Archie ever read any of them?" asked Bain.

"Never. Very sensible. You start going down that road, you are so screwed, man. Seriously."

"Why was he keeping them?"

"Don't know. I guess he was stuck in the middle there. Didn't want to get into the nightmare of looking at them, but felt bad about binning them. Some shite like that."

"We'll send someone round to pick them up, if you don't mind. Shouldn't be any longer than half an hour."

"Can youse do that? I mean, just turn up, steal some bastard's mail and open it all?"

"You want to stop us?" said Pereira.

"Don't give a fu–"

"Good," said Pereira, "we'll send someone round." She then added quickly, "Where were you last night, around midnight?"

A moment, Henderson looked unimpressed, then the head shake.

"Jesus. We come to it at last, eh? The great question of our times. I was here on my own, watching the tele. *The Hobbit*, all three films, extended editions, back to back. Don't judge me."

"There's no one can vouch for you?"

"Fuck should I know? There was no one else here, if that's what you mean. Went to get a carry out around six. Just down the road to the chinky. You can ask them, they know me. If Archie was killed at midnight, then Jesus, I was onto *The Battle of the Five Armies* by then."

Henderson looked at Pereira, waiting to see if there was another question coming.

"I can tell you what happens in the film, that should exonerate me, right?" Henderson laughed again, then added, "Fuck's sake, man," head shaking.

*

Walking across the road to the car, the sun behind high cloud.

"How d'you know about that study?" asked Bain. "I mean, the study from Humboldt University in Berlin. D'you read *everything*? I mean, apart from the tabloids."

"On the one hand, yes, I do read everything," she said, unlocking the door. "On the other, that particular piece of information I made up."

Bain laughed. Pereira's phone rang as she was getting back to the car. Anais didn't look up as they got in.

"What are you playing?" asked Bain, glancing behind.

"Wonderworld," she replied without lifting her head.

Bain watched her for a moment, but decided not to ask. Little point in having a one-sided conversation.

"Sir," said Pereira, phone placed on the dashboard on speaker, as she started the car and drove off.

"Where are you?" asked Cooper.

His voice sounded flat. At first he'd often seemed to be annoyed when talking to her, then Pereira had had the conversation with him, had been strong enough to let him know how he came across. It had been hard to know whether it had made him self-aware, whether it had made any difference to him. In any case, now it seemed that he flattened his tone, tried to give nothing away.

She still thought about DCI Parker, still felt the loss of his departure whenever they bumped into each other in a corridor or in the canteen. DCI Parker had been great. DCI Parker who had done so much for her. Just a good boss, that was all. Good at his job, good with his people, had run a good team. Four months now, since Parker had been kicked upstairs, and she hadn't yet got used to the new guy. And he, obviously, hadn't got used to her.

"Just been to see the victim's flatmate, on our way to the Grand," said Pereira. "Trying to establish Archie Wilson's whereabouts yesterday evening."

"OK. There's an officer at the hotel," said Cooper, "but not one of ours. Just standing on the door making sure no one gets in. Go there, come straight back afterwards."

"And we're going to call in and see Edgars," said Pereira.

A pause from the other end of the phone. The part of the conversation when she knew that Cooper would have to be forcing the disinterested tone.

"What happened with your daughter?" he asked, which Pereira hadn't been expecting. She glanced in the mirror. Anais's head stayed down. Maybe she hadn't even heard. Zoned out, in that netherworld that children now inhabited.

"I dropped her off with a friend. She's fine. We'll go to the Grand, speak to Edgars, and we'll come in."

"Make it quick," said Cooper.

The phone clicked off.

Pereira stared straight ahead, letting the conversation evaporate into the air. Nevertheless, no matter how much she wanted to ignore it, she couldn't really. It wasn't just about her.

"If he asks you," she said, glancing quickly at Bain, "tell the truth. You don't have to lie for me."

Bain nodded, didn't reply.

"Why does that man not like you?" came the voice from the back.

Pereira glanced in the mirror. Anais hadn't looked up, but of course she'd heard everything. Not so immersed as she seemed.

"He likes me just fine," said Pereira. "He's just stressed. Someone's been murdered, and the buck stops at him. Or, at least, that's what he feels."

She looked in the mirror again. Anais was still looking at her phone.

5

Parking outside the Grand, they could see that the media had already arrived. Two TV trucks, several other signs of obvious journalistic activity. They glanced at each other, and then Pereira looked behind her.

"Come on, kid, you're coming with us. You can sit in the bar and eat peanuts."

"I'm staying here," said Anais. Didn't take her eyes off the phone.

"I need you to come."

"Why?"

"Because if you don't, the Sergeant and I are going to walk in there, the press will see us, and they'll realise we're the police. We look like the police. Some of them might even just plain recognise me. I don't want to go there. So the sergeant is going to take off his jacket and tie, I'm going to take off my jacket, and we're going to walk in holding your hand, like a happy family of three, straight past the media who aren't going to recognise us."

Anais was looking up now, staring at the hotel. "Is this thing you're investigating famous?"

"Yes."

"Aren't you worried you get caught on film with Anais?" said Bain. "The boss might see it."

"If we're really unlucky. I don't want to speak to these people, not now. Haven't a clue where we are with this, and I don't want them catching us out. They may well know far more than we do. Come on, Sergeant, jacket off. And you," she said, looking behind, "no funny business."

29

"You'll look stupid walking in the rain with no jacket," said Anais, reluctant to move.

"It's not far. Come on."

*

Ten minutes later they were sitting in a small office on the first floor. The deputy manager of the hotel, Condon – *absurdly young for the position*, thought Pereira – was sitting behind his desk, Bain and Pereira, feeling underdressed without their jackets in a work situation, sitting across from him.

"I'm frankly surprised you didn't get here sooner," said Condon. "Strange to just have someone on the door of the room, when the media people have been here since before twelve."

"The investigation's just getting going," said Bain. "There are always a lot of people to talk to in the first few hours."

"What can you tell us about Mr. Wilson's time here at the hotel, and about last night specifically?" asked Pereira. She'd have to have a word to the sergeant about justifying himself to outside parties.

"I don't know how much use I'm going to be in terms of last night," said Condon. "He wasn't here. We know he left the hotel at around four in the afternoon, and then we never saw him again. Nor will we now," he added.

"Was he alone?"

"No, no, he wasn't. He was with two young women and another man."

"You've got footage of them?"

"Yes, we do. We've looked through everything from the last couple of days already. We've been waiting for you. As I said."

"You've got footage of the others arriving at the hotel as well?"

"Yes. Monday evening... or, rather, Tuesday morning, at around three a.m. They then stayed in Mr. Wilson's suite until four p.m. yesterday afternoon, at which time they all departed. There's been no sign of Mr. Wilson, or anyone else from his party, since then."

"How far back do your CCTV tapes go?" asked Bain.

"One month."

"We'd like to see them all."

Condon hesitated a moment and then nodded. "Of course."

30

"Can we see his room now?" asked Pereira.

"Certainly."

"Has anyone else been in today? A cleaner?"

"I'm afraid so. Your officer wasn't quick enough to arrive. The suite was tidied and the sheets changed, the bathroom cleaned, at around ten o'clock this morning, before news had reached us of Mr. Wilson's unfortunate demise."

*

They stood in silence for a few moments in the sitting room of the suite. There were three doors off, all closed. The large windows, which had the net curtains pulled to the sides, looked out over fields towards the Campsies.

Condon stood with his hands behind his back, head down. Waiting. Bain walked over to the window and looked out, thinking that while the view was nice, there was much better to be had, especially when money was no option.

"Did he always leave the place immaculate like this?" asked Pereira.

"Like I say," said Condon, "the cleaner had been through. I don't believe Mr. Wilson ever left the suite especially tidy, no."

"We're going to need to speak to the cleaner."

"Of course."

"Now."

Condon had the look of being torn, as though he didn't like the notion of the police being left alone in one of his hotel suites.

"We're not going to raid the minibar," said Pereira.

Condon hesitated for another second, then nodded and left the room.

"Damn it," muttered Pereira, when the door was closed. "We should have split up, you should have come round earlier. Not that it matters, if this place was cleaned as we were just discovering the body."

"We didn't find out he was here until we spoke to his dad," said Bain.

"Everyone else seemed to know," said Pereira, indicating with a thumb in the vague direction of the out-of-sight press corps. "We need to look at all their footage, establish if there's a way in or out of the hotel in case he, I don't know, snuck back in. I don't know why he would sneak back in, but let's check. So, the likelihood is that he wasn't killed here, but…"

She finished the sentence with a dismissive wave, then started walking around the room, gloves on, opening and closing drawers. Bain watched for a moment, and then started circling the room from the other direction.

All through the sitting room, throughout the two bedrooms and the two en-suite bathrooms and the toilet off the sitting room, everything they found was brand new and expensive. Clothes and jewellery, toiletries and cosmetics, shoes, tech, on and on. Archie Wilson had been spending his money, but he had so much of it, he could probably have lived like this for the rest of his life.

In one bedside drawer, Pereira found two small bags of white powder, one of them sealed, the other open and dumped, spilling some of the contents into the drawer. No spliffs, no pipes, no needles. She dabbed her finger into the powder to taste, though she hardly needed to. She left the bags where they were. There would be others along soon enough to bag and tag.

Back into the sitting room, Bain already there, standing at the window, looking out on the hills across the fields.

"Anything?" asked Pereira.

"He's spending his money," said Bain, with a nod at a gold iPad which he'd looked at, been unable to get into, and placed beside the TV, "and there's certainly sign of the women that were here for the night."

"More than just them. His female visitors are likely legion, I should say. What would you do if you had all that money?"

Bain turned and looked at her.

"What d'you mean?"

"For women?"

"Well, he could take his pick, couldn't he?"

"Yes, he could. But I wonder. If you walk into a bar, showing off your money, every single woman you pick up is going to be looking for something as a result. And those women won't want to think of themselves as whores. They don't want five hundred quid stuck down their bra on the way out. You pick up women on the back of being rich like that, you'd better be prepared to either pay up, or get the grief."

"Prostitutes on the other hand…"

"Exactly. You can get the best, and there are no expectations on the part of the woman, other than payment."

"Everyone's a winner."

"Yes, Marc, everyone's a winner. Ask around, there might

be someone at the hotel who knows where he got them. Do it now, don't go through Condon. I'll wait for the cleaner."

"Yes, ma'am."

"I also found this," she said, holding up a bright red lipstick she'd found in the bathroom. "Recognise the colour?"

He stared at it, then looked back at her.

"Blood red, the colour of the flowers of the Judas Tree?" he said.

"I thought we'd all agreed they were pink?"

"I don't recognise the colour," said Bain drily, as she had ignored his joke.

"Same as worn by Frank, or Fran, Henderson."

Bain took the lipstick from Pereira, removed the lid, unscrewed it – it was well-used – then put it away and placed the lid back on.

"Looks like red lipstick to me, boss," he said.

"I'll give you that. And yes, there are a million red lipsticks out there, but so far we've spoken to one acquaintance of Mr. Wilson, he – or she – wore this specific lipstick and now we find it amongst Wilson's possessions."

"But it's red lipstick. How can you tell it apart from all the other red lipsticks?"

She blinked. Bain recognised the hesitation, thought immediately that he knew the answer, felt awkward for pushing her on it.

"I recognise lipstick, Sergeant. I'm a woman, we all can," she lied. Making it about her gender, rather than her own particular talents. The fact that she had obsessively taken the time to catalogue lipsticks, just in case it was needed at some point. Just like she'd obsessively taken the time to acquire so much apparently useless knowledge. "Men can tell the difference between the off-side trap and a putter, women know lipstick."

He laughed and shook his head.

"Funny," he said, relieved that the slight awkwardness had passed.

There was a knock at the door, then it opened and a young woman dressed in grey entered.

"You asked to see me?"

"Thanks for coming," said Pereira, as Bain left the room, nodding at the cleaner as he went. "What's your name?"

"Magda."

"Polish?"

"Yes, ma'am."

"You're all right talking in English?"

"Yes."

"That's good, thank you. You've heard what's happened to Mr. Wilson?"

She nodded.

"So, I know under other circumstances it might be wrong to discuss things you find in a guest's bedroom, but given that we are now in the middle of a murder investigation, I must ask that you tell me everything you can."

"Of course."

Pereira opened her arms in an on-you-go gesture, then added, "Start with what you found when you came in this morning."

*

Pereira walked down to the hotel bar, found Bain already there, sitting with Anais. They were both on their phones. She was going to take a seat, then thought better of it. They really did need to get on. She'd allowed herself to be much too slow in the take-up of the investigation, and although it didn't look they'd missed anything by being tardy in coming to the hotel, it felt like they were still playing catch-up.

"Come on, we need to pull the happy family routine. Actually, doesn't matter whether or not we're happy. You all right, kid?"

"Sure," said Anais, not looking away from the phone, as she got down from her seat.

"I'm just going to call gran and drop you there, on our way to pathology."

"Wait, what? You're going to pathology? Can I come?"

Now she looked away from her phone.

"No, madam, you cannot. And keep your voice down, the press are just the other side of that door. Now shh, until we're in the car."

She got the disapproving eyebrow, and then the head was lowered to the screen.

And so they walked past the media, across the carpark, and into the car. As she was closing the car door, Pereira heard a voice from the media crowd standing outside the hotel say,

"Shit, there's that Paki police bird," then there was the sound of the approaching hurried footsteps and there were the shouted questions, and they were lost as she started the engine and drove quickly off without looking round.

6

"Drugged. Bound and gagged. No sign of torture. Then the spike with the cross on top was hammered into his head. Specially made for the purpose, perhaps. Don't know."

The cross, which had been used to kill Archie Wilson, had been placed on a small trolley to the side of where Wilson's body was lying. The full body was exposed, showing where he'd already been opened and sealed back up. The pathologist, Dr. Edgars, was gently tapping her finger on Wilson's upper arm as she spoke. She delivered every word as if it annoyed her.

As ever, in Edgars' place of work, there was music playing. Always film soundtracks. She was talking to the background of the love theme from *Romeo and Juliet.*

"He'd used cocaine, marijuana, nothing else. Looks like it was pure, high quality. No crap, other than the fact, obviously, that you're an idiot if you're putting either of those things in your body in the first place. I suppose if you're going to do it, you might as well do it with good stuff. When was the last time you had eyes on him?"

"Left his hotel just under twenty-four hours ago," said Pereira. "We've yet to trace his further movements. Time of death?"

"Midnight. Thereabouts. I'm going to say the killer didn't know what they were doing, was worried that he might wake up, so they drugged him, tied him up, stabbed the eyes to get the blood going, and then hammered in the cross."

"Why d'you think they didn't know what they–" began Bain.

"I'm guessing," said Edgars. "Bite me. Unless you've

hammered a metal cross through someone's skull before, you're not going to know how long it'll take. You might be a bit nervous. Much easier just to knock them out, make sure they're sitting still, can't do anything about it."

There seemed to Pereira several reasons why you might drug a potential murder victim, but that was as good as any.

"What was the drug?"

"Sodium thiopental. Massive dose. Might well have killed him itself by the time it'd worked its way through his system, but it never got the chance."

"So the killer was taking no chances."

"None."

"Anything else?"

Edgars looked up and down the body.

"He'd had sex, but I guess that's not a surprise. Most men in their thirties are going to start having sex every day the minute they win that much money. So unimaginative."

Bain said nothing. He also didn't think it was unimaginative.

"Any idea how long the drug had been in his body before he was killed?"

"Decent," said Edgars, as though she rated all the questions that investigating officers asked of her. "Hard to say, but at least half an hour. That's all I've got. Long enough that Wilson was well gone."

"And how was it delivered?"

"Spiked drink."

"How much notice will he have had of it coming?"

"Interesting. Given the method of delivery, and for him to have had so much of it in his body, he must have downed a lot of alcohol. Maybe someone got him to play a drinking game. Maybe he just downed his drinks anyway. Maybe they were shots. It would kick in, though, kick in damn fast. Given the money he'd won, he really ought to have been being careful, but he was obviously an idiot."

They all stared at the body, Edgars' fingers now resting on the upper arm.

"Dead now," she said. "Didn't live to regret his stupidity."

*

There were six of them in the small room, sitting around a long table. There was no obvious hierarchy from the way they were seated, as Cooper didn't believe in standing at the front, or sitting at the head of the table.

He did, nevertheless, lead the discussion. As well as Pereira and Cooper, there were Tobin, Parks and Somerville. They'd all spent the afternoon on the murder of Archie Wilson, and were getting together to share information.

Pereira, nominally leading the investigation, would have preferred Cooper not to be there. She considered it micro-management. Yet he considered that he himself was leading the investigation, even though all he was doing was coordinating, allocating and cajoling.

"We've identified the two women who left the hotel on Tuesday afternoon with Wilson. Escort girls from the Madison Avenue Agency," said Bain. "Made a quick call to their office, but someone'll need to go round there to have a chat. I didn't get information on whether or not these girls were hired through into Tuesday evening."

"We know this agency?" asked Cooper. "Presume it's not actually New York based."

A couple of them nodded.

"It's run by some crowd through in Edinburgh," said Bain. "As respectable as these things get, I guess. We've come across them once or twice, but it's always the clients causing the trouble. Generally they've got as much class as people in this business are going to have."

"And the guy?" asked Cooper.

Bain nodded at Pereira.

"We already spoke to Wilson's flatmate, a transsexual named Frank, or Fran, Henderson. She's waiting for the operation, said that-"

"She?" said Cooper, casually.

Pereira held his gaze for a moment, and then decided to let it go. As it was with one's children, there were times to pick an argument.

"Henderson said that Wilson had promised him the money. Anyway, we recognised that a lipstick left in Wilson's suite was the same as the lipstick Fran was wearing, and sure enough... He's wearing jeans and a baseball cap, so it's not definite from the images on the screen, but best we know, the guy with the two hookers and Wilson is Henderson. There's certainly nothing feminine about what he's wearing. And he'd already told us he hadn't seen Wilson in about a week, so we need to get back there."

"You think this is our guy?" asked Cooper. "I mean, Jesus that would be straightforward, but there's no reason why it wouldn't be."

"We'll bring him in," said Pereira.

"Please. And really, if the guy's on TV wandering around with no trace of any femininity about him, let's just all ditch the transsexual crap, shall we? That whole thing might well just be some sort of bullshit. The minute we start enabling the guy... Jesus."

Hands on his hips, he looked round the table, before nodding at Parks.

That little rant, thought Pereira, hadn't really been aimed at Henderson and the notion of transsexuality. Nevertheless, she did, on this occasion, completely agree with him. That was why it wasn't the right time for the argument, and it probably was time to stop paying lip service to the possibility of Henderson being transsexual. He was a man who'd stuck on a dress, that was all, and there was likely some reason behind it other than any notion that he might feel trapped in the wrong body.

"Wilson had started managing his money through a Glasgow accountant, Cobalt & Greys," said Detective Sergeant Parks. Mid-thirties, didn't usually work with this team, but she'd been drafted in by Cooper because of the media. This was going to be all-hands for a short period, and hopefully they could come to a quick conclusion. The media wouldn't be caring about any other crime in Glasgow this week, and Cooper's part of the Serious Crime Unit would, at least, follow their lead. "I spoke to Cobalt, who wasn't especially forthcoming. Sounded like he had better things to do than talk to the police."

"We'll go round and have a word," said Pereira.

"You need to go to Madison Avenue," said Cooper.

"We can do both," said Pereira.

She liked to talk to everyone. She liked to look into their eyes. She didn't think it meant that she didn't trust her colleagues, but it wasn't something she thought about too often.

"We need to get on with this," said Cooper, his voice flat, yet allowing no argument. "The press are going to be on our backsides until we get a result. You go to see Madison, Marc can speak to the accountant."

Bain nodded, casting a glance at Pereira as he did so.

Pereira was staring at the table.

Cooper looked along the table, catching the eye of Detective Constable Somerville.

Somerville had been substantive in the post for less than six months, and he was already unsure of whether he would be staying. Committed for another two and a half years or there would be a financial penalty in leaving, but he was contemplating taking the hit.

"The party of four," he began, "Wilson, Henderson, if it was him, and the women, were taken by limo to a private club in town. The Garland. They arrived there at some time after four-thirty, the women left around six, Henderson shortly afterwards. Wilson left the establishment at just after eight. He wasn't met by a car, and he appears not to have told anyone where he was going, least not anyone we've spoken to."

"That's the club at the top end of Hope?" said Pereira.

"Yep."

"Do we know if he came down the hill or headed–"

"He came down the hill, ma'am," said Somerville. "So he could have been heading for Central, but he could obviously have been heading for several hundred other places."

"Would he normally have been picked up?" she asked.

"His driver lives in a small apartment in Merchant City. Kept the limo in a lock up behind Candleriggs. It was a business he'd had going for a couple of years, but he said it hadn't really been working. He'd been happy to be taken on as the full-time driver for Wilson. Basically had to be available to him twenty-four-seven, but that he wasn't especially demanding. Last night, he dropped the party off at the Garland, and said he'd wait. Wilson told him he could go home. Said he'd probably call him later. No more contact."

"Did he have anything to say about what kind of client Wilson was, if there was ever anything going on in the back of the limo?"

Pereira was aware of Cooper's fingertip-tapping on the desk. This was why he oughtn't to have been there. He wasn't interested in the investigation, wasn't interested in talking about it, listening and learning. His approach was entirely results-focussed, as though results could be achieved by just telling people to make them happen.

"We didn't get into that," said Somerville.

"Can you go back to him, please? In fact, get him to come

in if you can. The driver's likely to know more than anyone."

"Yep," said Somerville.

Pereira held his gaze for a moment, realised he was slightly uncomfortable, then looked back at Cooper. She could tell Somerville recognised he'd done an incomplete job. He hadn't asked half the questions he should have done. She knew that every day for Somerville brought a reason for insecurity and a lack of confidence, and she was going to have manage him carefully if she wasn't to lose him.

Cooper nodded at the last round the table, DC Tobin.

"Bernie," he said.

Detective Constable Bernie Tobin was Cooper's man. Everyone knew it, some talked about it. It didn't matter, though, he was just another detective constable in the branch and got on with the job same as everyone else.

"I've got nothing, sir," said Tobin. "Got tied up with the Strangways robbery."

"Of course," said Cooper, then said, "Anyone got anything else?" as he placed his hands flat on the table.

Nothing. Cooper glanced at the clock, nodding to himself, then said, "Right, everyone knows what they're doing? I need you to spread out and get on with it. Aliya, Madison Avenue, Marc, speak to the accountant, Rhonda, I'm going to need you to track down the murder weapon, but first, get round to Henderson's flat, bring him in. He might have pegged we're onto him, and leg it if he sees either of these two. Colin, get back to the driver, we need everything he's got from the last six weeks. And Bernie, round to the club, get everything you can on what went on with Wilson yesterday evening before he left. Who he talked to, what he drank, what kind of mood he was in."

"Boss," said Tobin, nodding.

"We'll get people looking at CCTV in the town centre after eight. See if we can identify where Wilson might've gone. And the will… is there any sign of a will? Because, you know, whoever's standing to benefit from over a hundred million smackeroos has some kind of motive right there."

"Nothing," said Pereira.

"Right," said Cooper, and he clapped his hands sharply. "Add it to the list. Come on, head out, let's do this. We'll meet back here at 18:30."

Chairs were pushed back, the meeting began to rise. Cooper was the only one not to move.

"Inspector," he said, as they began to file out the door.

Pereira stopped, let the others leave, closed the door behind them and stood by the table. There was a silence in the room that she couldn't quite fathom, and she really had no idea why he'd asked her to stay back.

"Everything all right?" she asked, when Cooper wasn't immediately forthcoming. He was holding her gaze, seemingly thinking over what he had to say. It never occurred to her that he might be attempting to assert some authority over her with what he thought to be an intimidating silence.

"I saw the footage of you driving away from the hotel," he said. "Your child was in the back of the car."

She didn't reply. Caught red-handed. Bain had warned her, after all. She'd said they'd have to be extremely unlucky. Maybe it had been inevitable.

"Was she with you all day?" he asked.

He noticed the tensing in the jaw line, the grip on the back of the seat she was standing behind.

"Was she with you all day, Inspector?" he repeated.

"I dropped her off at Mum's after the hotel."

Cooper reverted to silence. He wasn't trying to be intimidating, as it equally never occurred to him that he might be. He was trying not to say what he thought, that was all. Saying what he thought out loud would leave him open to an official complaint, and give her some sort of advantage.

"You took her to the murder scene?"

"She stayed in the car."

"Did she?"

"She stayed in the car."

"You took her when you went to interview a witness?"

"She stayed in the car."

How many times had Cooper kept her back to talk about some slight or other he felt she'd brought to the station? So often trivial in the past, now she knew he was absolutely right. She had nothing.

"We don't run bring-your-daughter-to-work days," he said. "We don't do lessons in murder inquiries for young girls. We don't take family members, children, to bloody murder scenes…"

"She stayed in the car."

"It's not the point, Inspector! Jesus. You know how much of my life is spent dealing with the media? You know how much time they spend criticising us? I don't have to answer that, do I, because I know you know. You know what these people are like. We can't do a bloody thing. Any opportunity and they are so far up my arse they're spewing their anti-police bilge out of my damned mouth."

The platitude was on the tip of her tongue, but she let it go. The *it won't happen again* or the *I'll try to make sure I have better plans in place for the next time*. There was no point. It wasn't going to ameliorate the situation, and he was too annoyed for pointless assurances.

Those words were for herself, not him.

"Go," he said.

She hadn't been expecting such an abrupt dismissal. No warning, no talk of disciplinary action, no *this is your last chance*. She didn't imagine it was over, but perhaps this was all there was for the moment. The anger, and then the incident would be filed away. At some point this, and others, would be brought forth together to make his point.

She turned and walked quickly from the room.

—

43

7

Pereira was sitting in a comfortable office reception in an old building, a block away from the Mitchell Library. There had been seven business names on the buzzer plaque, and the Madison Avenue Agency had fitted in nicely alongside the other six, perfectly in its place amongst the business consultants and marketing operations. Pereira wondered how many others were not as they seemed.

She'd only been sitting in reception for a couple of minutes, and she knew she was being kept waiting, just so the woman she was here to meet, Alison Lindberg, could make the point that she didn't jump at seeing the police. For the moment, and as long as the few minutes didn't drag out too long, Pereira was happy for Lindberg to get to make her point.

There was a woman behind a counter, looking at a screen that completely held her attention. Like everyone she saw in this position, Pereira wondered if the woman was scrolling idly through the Internet or playing solitaire or involved in some other frivolous activity of the ages. Maybe she was actually working.

The reception area was designed in elegant, sleek lines, hung with simple artworks – modern art, of shapes and designs, which worked perfectly to enhance the area – a light beige carpet, two long sofas of warm orange along the walls. In the corner, on a low table, there was a Japanese peace lily, perfect in form, with a single white flower at the top of the plant.

There was such an air of cleanliness about it, it seemed like the reception area of an expensive spa. *For all your disease-free prostitute needs*, thought Pereira, the rueful smile not finding its

way to her lips. Or, *Madison Avenue, Clean Prostitute Solutions.*
Maybe that was their slogan.

The door to reception opened and two women entered. Both
dressed casually, jeans and a t-shirt on one, jeans and a long-
sleeved, grey sweatshirt with *Property of USC, 1947*
emblazoned on it, on the other. The receptionist smiled.

"Hey," she said. "All good?"

"All good," said one of them. The blonde.

"Couldn't be better," said USC 1947.

Pereira recognised them as the two who had left the hotel
with Wilson. Seeing them in the flesh she also recognised them
as possibly the two most attractive women she'd ever seen in her
life. The kind of women that would make most other women feel
remarkably plain in their presence. It was certainly how Pereira
felt, sitting there, looking up at them.

"You can go in," said the receptionist, "she's waiting for
you."

As she said it, she glanced over at Pereira, then quickly
looked away again. Pereira watched the two women for a
moment, and then made the decision. Those few minutes that
she'd allowed Lindberg were over. She didn't want the three of
them sitting in the office sorting out some story or other, while
she waited in reception.

As they knocked and opened the door to Lindberg's office,
Pereira was quickly up off her feet, and then walking in behind
the blonde as they entered.

"Wait!" came the voice from behind, and then the door was
closed, and Pereira was standing just inside the door, with the
other three women staring at her.

This office was of a similar size to the reception area, and
decorated in the same style, with just an air of greater expense
about it. To the right there was a unit with a jug of water and
four glasses. Lindberg's desk was by the window, so that
Lindberg sat with her back to the restricted view out onto
Berkeley Street.

There were two chairs to this side of the desk, another two
against the opposite wall to the unit with the water glasses.

"Can you wait, please?" said Lindberg, her voice edgy.

Pereira walked round the two women to take a position in
the middle of the room.

"I need you ladies to sit down. We've got a lot going on
here, so this won't take–"

"I asked you to wait," said Lindberg, getting to her feet. Neither of the other two moved.

You owned the room, or you got out. If she was going to get anything from them, it would be right now or else she'd be lost.

"We can do this here, or you can come down to the station," said Pereira, the words so well used they were said without thinking. She had no idea how many times she'd said them over the years. Only in the rarest of circumstances did they end up taking the discussion anywhere.

The two women waited for instruction. Lindberg stared angrily at Pereira, but they both knew which way it was going to go. A business like this lived on the edge of the law, and while it was uncomfortable having the police in the office, the harder they made it for the police, the harder the police could make it for them.

She nodded, her eyes still on Pereira, and the women sat down.

"Thank you," said Pereira. "Right, ladies, names please, and a quick recap of what happened between you and Mr. Wilson on Monday evening and Tuesday."

They looked at each other, they hesitated, they looked at Lindberg.

"We just need to get on here," said Pereira. "We already found drugs in the hotel room. We're not interested in that. We want to find out who killed Mr. Wilson, that's all. Tell me everything, you've got nothing to worry about."

"Can we trust you?" said the blonde. If she had an accent, thought Pereira, it was educated, east coast.

Educated, she thought to herself? Everyone's educated.

"What's your name?"

"Hermione," she said.

"Right. Nice name."

"My mother thought so."

"You don't look young enough."

"It's nothing to do with Harry Potter."

"And you?"

"Lydia," she said. "After Mrs. Bennett's youngest. Mum always said she could tell I'd be a flirt right from the moment I was born."

She smiled at Pereira, the smile she gave her clients. Pereira held the look for a moment, turned back to the other.

"Hermione, if you would," and she indicated for her to talk.

Picking up on the look she'd seen in Pereira's eyes, Hermione crossed her legs, clasped her hands in her lap, smiled.

Oh, for God's sake, thought Pereira. Whatever she thought she was doing, it wasn't working.

"We've been with Archie a few times. Always the two of us together. We're a team."

"Are you a couple? I mean, are you together out of working hours?"

"No," she said. "But we could be. Just hasn't happened yet."

"Good to know," said Pereira sharply, not pausing to take any interest in Hermione's slightly dipped chin, eyes running over Pereira's body. "Tell me about Monday."

"Lydia was round at mine, the limo picked us up. What's the driver called?"

"Tomasz," said USC 1947.

"Tomasz, right. He's Polish. Everyone's Polish these days, have you noticed?"

"No," said Pereira. "What then?"

"He took us to the hotel. Sometimes… we never knew until we got there what the set-up was going to be. Sometimes it was just Archie, sometimes there might be someone else. Another guy. There was someone there on Monday. His name was Frank. Hadn't seen him before. Archie said they used to share. A flat, I mean. Share a flat."

"Did you have sex with Frank?"

"No," said USC 1947. "We discussed dialectical materialism. We sat up until, I don't know, four in the morning, talking about Engels."

"Hilarious," said Pereira. "Tell me about Frank."

"What about him?" asked Hermione, the smile still on her face from USC 1947's interjection.

"When we spoke to him earlier he was dressed in women's clothing. Was that something you witnessed?"

"Sure. He seemed to love that shit. Wore my crotchless half the night."

"But you had sex?"

"Yes. We had sex. That's what happens."

"And did Frank and Archie have sex?"

"You mean, did they fuck each other?"

"That's what I mean."

47

"No."

"And did Frank strike you, or say anything to you, that suggested he was transgender, or did he just look like a guy who wanted to stick on women's clothes?"

Hermione and USC 1947 looked at each other, then turned back to Pereira and shrugged.

"Just a guy. Why? You think Archie was killed by a queer?"

"We *know* Archie spent his last morning and afternoon alive with you two and Frank, that's all. Why did you leave the hotel at around four yesterday afternoon?"

Another glance between the women, then they returned to Pereira with a shake of the head. They seemed to have lost interest in flirting with her, having picked up on her disdain.

"It was getting pretty boring. We'd been there for God knows how long. We'd done everything we were going to do, several times. Everyone needed a break."

"Felt a bit claustrophobic," said USC 1947.

"Yeah."

"And you went to the Garland?"

"There was talk of taking off for Gleneagles, somewhere like that. He said we might go this weekend. Guess that won't be happening now. In the end, we went to the Garland. Again."

"Usual spot?"

"Always the same. A few weeks, and he'd fallen into a routine. People do, don't they? More drinking, more listening to him and his plans. Going to change the country. If he hadn't died, he'd likely have been sitting in the same place a year from now."

"Five years," said USC 1947.

"Or until he'd spent all his money," said Hermione.

"Apart from changing the country, did he have specific plans?" asked Pereira. "Was he lavish, did he give you far more than you were owed, did you see him toss the money around elsewhere?"

"He was cagey, all right," said Hermione. "On the one hand he seemed to be happy spending the money, but then there was a limit. Like he'd decided what age he was going to die, and he'd calculated how much he'd have for each day. It was still a lot, though."

"Sensible and wanton at the same time," said USC 1947.

"And you left at six?"

"Bang on. Couldn't get out fast enough in the end. Just needed the air."

"You know the movie *Eureka*?" asked USC 1947, and Pereira nodded. "That felt like him. Suddenly he had nothing to live for other than having fun, and maybe he was going to think of something, maybe he really was just living it up before settling down into some sort of plan, but we could see him stuck there forever. There was something hanging over him. Something…" and she jabbed a finger into the side of her head.

"You never answered the detective's question," said Lindberg. "Did he give you extra?"

There was bound to have been the odd issue with interviewing the women in front of their boss, but if this was all it turned out to be, it was hardly important.

"No," said USC 1947, and Hermione joined her with a shake of the head.

"Did he tell you what he was intending to do last night?" asked Pereira. "Or did you see him at the Garland talking to anyone in particular?"

"We sat in a group. The main room of the club, people sit around in these big armchairs. We've been there and you end up in a room, upstairs, fucking, or whatever. But we'd done that back at the hotel, so yesterday we just sat around, Archie pretending to be this thing. The people in there, MSPs and councillors and business types, they don't give a shit. They know who we are, but they're happy to have women who look like us in. Archie was talking to some guy."

She looked round at USC 1947.

"Were you paying attention?"

"Yeah. He was a minister. Something in the Glasgow church. Or maybe he was a bishop. He, for one, didn't like the look of us."

"If he was a minister, then he'd likely be Presbyterian, therefore wouldn't be a bishop. So…?"

"Don't know. He was talking about churches."

"Rather than chapels?"

"Yes."

"What about the churches?"

"Don't know. When it came down to it, it was about money, of course. That was all anyone ever talked to Archie about. Whoever Archie was before, he was gone. Archie had become his money, that was all. Kind of sad. But what do we care?"

"Did you get the minister's name?"

"No."

"You?"

Hermione shook her head.

"I was falling asleep, to be honest."

"Can you describe him?"

"Bald."

"Bald? Completely bald? Or did he have–"

"Completely bald. Like that guy in… whatever movie. I can't remember the name."

USC 1947 laughed.

"There are lots of bald guys in lots of movies," she said, and Hermione laughed with her.

Pereira watched them for a moment, and then turned to Lindberg.

"Did he have someone booked for last night?" she asked. "The girls went at six, was that it for the day?"

"Nuh-huh," said Lindberg. "Daisy and Riley, two of our other girls, were due to meet him at 21:30. Went to his hotel, he wasn't there. They waited until midnight, then they got in touch and I told them to go home and wait for the phone to ring."

Pereira nodded. That tied in with the two women reported to have been sitting in the hotel bar for much of the late evening.

"It never did," added Lindberg.

*

USC 1947 and Hermione were gone, Pereira was still in the office with Lindberg. The door had closed silently behind them, Pereira hadn't sat down.

The two women held a long gaze across the desk, then Lindberg smiled.

"You like what you see, Detective Inspector?"

Pereira didn't respond.

"They're expensive, but I'm sure we can do you a deal."

8

While Pereira sat with the prostitutes, Bain sat with the accountant and financial advisor.

Eston Cobalt. That was the name on the door.

The office, at the top end of St. Vincent Street, was no more than a few hundred yards away from where Pereira was conducting her interview, separated by the late afternoon wall of traffic on the M8.

Cobalt's office was on the top floor of a new office block, looking down over the motorway towards the river. Spacious, bright, silent, not a sound sneaking in from the road.

Bain was standing with his hands in his pockets, waiting for Cobalt to get off the phone, watching the world fifteen floors below. Would he ever get anything done if he worked up here? Likely not. He would sit at his desk and look below, and his mind would wander.

This is the place for an imagination, he thought. Maybe the view could be better. The motorway was the motorway, and he could see little of the river bar the bridges, but there was something hypnotic about looking down on any scene, no matter how mundane.

He remembered reading *The Secret Life of Walter Mitty* when he was at school, and wondering why it was a thing. What was it that was at all remarkable about Walter Mitty? Didn't everyone think like that? Didn't everyone's thoughts wander at the slightest sound of a siren, the ringing of the phone?

And this was where his dreams had led him. Detective Sergeant in the Serious Crime Unit in Glasgow.

He turned, aware that the voice had stopped talking behind him. Eston Cobalt walked round from behind his desk, and came to stand beside Bain.

"Sergeant," he said, "sorry about that. Excuse the language."

"That's all right," said Bain, although he hadn't been listening.

"Sure I can't get you a drink?"

"I'm good, thanks."

Cobalt nodded, then turned to the window and looked down over the motorway. Cars solid in both directions, moving marginally faster westbound than east. The day still grey, the evening closing in earlier than usual as a result.

"Pity the poor bastards who have to sit in that every night," he said.

"You don't?" said Bain.

"Live in the west end. Just get my guy to take me along Argyle Street. I work in the car, doesn't matter what the traffic's like. Bugger about poor Archie," he added, shaking his head.

"Yes," said Bain. "Did you see it on the news, or were–"

"Maggie told me," he said, indicating with his thumb to the door. "I think someone had called her. Guess the whole city's talking about it."

"You know who you're going to deal with now?"

With the darkness coming, Bain could still see Cobalt's face reflected in the window. His expression showed he didn't know.

"We'll wait to hear from the lawyers or next of kin. I guess that'll be his dad. He hasn't been in touch, but even then, we'll need to wait for the legal stuff to get sorted out before progressing. The account'll take care of itself in the meantime."

"Archie had employed a lawyer already?"

"We're associated with a legal firm, he was using them."

"Was there a will?"

"There was. Drawn up last week."

He raised an eyebrow at Bain's reflection.

"Classic," he added. "One week he makes a will, the next week…" and he made a strange sound, his thumb drawn across the neck.

"You can give me the details of the law firm?"

"Of course. They're just over there," he said, pointing at the building across the street.

Bain nodded, then they looked down as their eyes were diverted by a Ferrari, in regulation bright red, that was inching

—

52

its way into view, coming off the bridge. Start, stop. Start, stop. Start, stop.

"Poor bastard," said Cobalt. "What a waste."

"I expect you won't want to give too many details, but would you be able to say how much of his money Archie had spent already? Hardly made a dent, I presume."

"Seriously? He hadn't spent *any* of the money. You know, the actual money."

"What d'you mean?"

"The man was loaded. Overnight, loaded. You don't spend that kind of money when you get it, not unless you're an idiot. Soon as you start spending money, it disappears. He'd invested the money. Or, more accurately, we'd invested the money for him. Started earning from day one."

"How much?"

"Somewhere between fifteen and twenty grand."

Bain let out a low whistle.

"Nice. Just in the six weeks since he won the lottery?"

Cobalt turned and looked curiously at Bain.

"What?" asked Bain.

"Do you know *anything* about the finance industry?"

"No," said Bain.

"No," said Cobalt, nodding, "doesn't sound like it. Since we took control of his portfolio, he has averaged earnings something in the region of seventeen thousand pounds a day."

"*A day*? You're shitting me?"

"No, Sergeant. A day. The man has a hundred and thirty million pounds. Well, had. Not anymore. You don't even have to invest that kind of money with any particular risk in order to have an exceptionally high daily return."

"Jesus."

"Yeah," said Cobalt. "Jesus. So, we weren't taking chances. Not at this stage. He was just living it up, enjoying himself."

"D'you know if he was doing anything other than drugs, alcohol and women?"

Cobalt shook his head.

"Had he even left Glasgow?"

"Don't think so. He had plans, but he hadn't gone yet. Seems he'd fallen quickly into a routine. He'd have got himself out there eventually."

Bain finally took himself away from the window and sat down in the chair opposite the desk. Cobalt followed, round to his own side, the view from this window looking down to the Hilton hotel.

"You understand where we are, Mr. Cobalt," said Bain. "Someone killed Archie, and we're just at the beginning of trying to understand why it happened. Did he discuss any of those plans with you? Was there anyone else involved in making those plans? Was there anyone out there who expected to see some of that money?"

"He had a pretty big family, so I understand. You know, Archie was all right. I'm going to say he was limited. That's the way to put it. It was like, at first he just didn't know what to do with it. He talked about setting up some sort of fund to pay the family, give them a bit each, but it was a pretty big fucking family, and you know how it is… once you start, phhht, there's never a place to comfortably draw the line. There's always some third cousin lurking out there you've forgotten about. He was waiting, that's all. The family would've got their money eventually."

"What about friends, charities, hangers on, the desperate letter writers?"

"He'd been told not to even look at the letters. So he didn't. Never read them, not from day one."

"Was there anything of particular interest to him, something or somewhere that he might have looked to spend his money?"

"Only heard him seriously mention two things. One was Albion Rovers, and I really don't think he was that serious. And anyway, we said, if you're looking to do something with your money, don't go anywhere near a football club. Absolute definition of a money pit. Jesus."

"And the other?"

"His local church," said Cobalt, making a small gesture to express his curiosity.

"Why?"

"Said he'd gone there when he'd grown up. Don't think he'd even gone to church in a while, it was just somewhere that reminded him of his home town."

"Which was?"

"This side of Mosspark."

"And how far down that road had he gone?"

Cobalt tossed an unknowing hand.

"Couldn't tell you. Not so far that he'd come to me looking for the money. He'd shown me the building on the Church of

---

54

Scotland website, but that aside, I don't know if he'd spoken to anyone there, or if he'd gone to look at it."

"Can you show me? You remember where it was?"

"Hmm," he said, and then he nodded, reached into his desk drawer and took out a gold-plated iPad, identical to the one in Wilson's hotel room.

"Just searching through the history," he said. "Haven't watched porn on this thing, so haven't had to clear it yet."

Then he held the iPad up, so that Bain could better see the back of it.

"Archie bought me this," he said. "Typical. Searching around for something to spend his money on. Nice guy."

Then he turned the tablet and held it across the table.

Bain reached forward and took the tablet from him.

Bellahouston Old Parish, building in excellent repair, £175,000.

He studied the photograph for a moment, and then passed the tablet back across the desk.

"I know," said Cobalt nodding. "Know what you're thinking. It just adds a layer of religion to the mix. Can't beat it, eh?"

9

Pereira looked at the time, then quickly swung her car into the side of the road, seeing that the florist was still open. Parker & Sons. An old shop, not part of a chain. She'd never shopped in there before, but she'd driven past if often enough.

She was due back at the station in under ten minutes, but there was something else which had slipped her mind earlier. Seeing the flower shop had reawakened the thought.

She hoped it would be Mr. Parker, or at least someone who'd worked in the business for a long time, rather than an eighteen-year-old earning after-school money. Even if she didn't get anywhere, it was in her mind now, and she could make some calls the following morning.

The bell above the door pinged as she entered, and a man in his sixties turned at the sound. He looked at Pereira for a few moments, taking the measure of her and then turned away again. He was at the back of the shop, by a table, potting a series of small plants.

"I'll be with you in a minute," he said.

"I'm not here to buy anything," said Pereira.

She could see that he stopped what he was doing, just for a second, and then started up again.

"What then?" he asked. "You're not from Schilling's mob?"

"Who's Schilling?" she asked.

Another hesitation, and finally he accepted he was going to have to engage her, and he turned, wiping his hands on his waistcoat.

"What d'you want?" he asked.

"D'you know anything about the Judas Tree? More

56

specifically the flower of the Judas Tree."

He grunted, his shoulders moved slightly.

"What d'you think I can tell you?" he said.

"How likely is it to grow in Scotland?"

He stood absolutely still in response, staring at her.

"Who wants to know?" he said eventually.

Typical, thought Pereira.

He was acting as though he was a suspect, or as though there was a reason for him to be questioned by the police, when she was just there completely off the cuff. And the details of the flowers had not yet been released to the media, so there was no way that he could have heard about it, and have formed a conclusion that the police might have decided to come looking for him.

She held forward her ID card.

"DI Pereira," she said.

"You don't look like a police officer," he said.

"Mr. Parker, is it? Or are you–"

"Yes, Parker."

"Can you grow the Judas Tree in Scotland?" said Pereira, now just wanting to get on with it.

"Why d'you think I'd know?"

"Do florists ever sell the flowers?"

"I don't," he said. "Never have. Don't last for shit the minute you take them off the tree. Short enough when they're on it. I mean, florists don't sell cherry blossom or apple blossom, do they? Why would they sell–"

"I don't need the commentary, Mr. Parker. All I wanted to know was where someone, in Scotland, would get hold of some Judas flowers."

The hands were unconsciously rubbed gently against the waistcoat again.

"You mean now?"

"Yes, now. In the middle of March."

"Well, not from a tree growing naturally in Scotland, that's for sure. I mean, they're becoming more common, especially since every halfwit started going to a garden centre on a Sunday afternoon. You can buy the Judas Tree easily enough. Will it flourish?" and he shrugged. "Most people couldn't grow weeds if they tried. They're not great up here, but with all this global warming that's going on, it's hardly the weirdest thing in the world."

"But since it's too early to see the flowers in Scotland...?"

He shrugged.

"You ever heard of the Internet? It's this thing, a big thing, that exists in a place that no one really quite understands."

"You're hilarious. Will the trees be flowering in the south of England already?"

"Unlikely, but I don't live there."

"Look, Mr. Parker, can we just cut the attitude, please?" she said, her voice quiet and expressionless. Tired already, gone six o'clock, not dark yet, although getting there quickly enough. "You're not in any trouble, no one's arresting you, I just stopped by to see if you could help me. Answer the–"

"Yes, all right, if it'll get rid of you," he muttered, like he was doing her an enormous favour. "Look, they're just the same as anything. You'll get them easily enough from somewhere. So if you're thinking, I need to find out where someone got his hands on the flower of the Judas Tree, forget it. I mean it. Go online, you'll find a hundred sites you can buy them from. Good luck with that.

"Are they flowering already in the south of England? Maybe, if it's been a mild winter, and a bit of sun the last few weeks. Seems like the end times sometimes. Weather's so screwed up. Daffodils in November a couple of years ago, I remember that. On the news. But even if you can't source them from Englandshire, you'll be able to get them from the Channel Islands or France or Italy or somewhere. Can't think why you'd want to..."

He shrugged. A moment, nothing else to be asked, then she nodded, said, "Thanks for your help," and turned quickly from the shop, the bell tinkling on her way out.

"Aye, right, love," he said to her back. "No need to be so grateful."

She stood on the pavement, while the cars passed, headlights picking up the last of the rain, and she waited to cross the road. It had just been a thought. She couldn't remember ever seeing a Judas Tree anywhere in Scotland, but it didn't mean there weren't thousands of them. It would have been too easy if there'd only been one supplier for the whole of the UK. Worth the asking.

She looked at her watch. Two minutes late, still five minutes to get to the station. The last meeting for the day, they could discuss how they would move forward in the morning,

—

58

then hopefully she could get home. Not too much of a stretch to believe she could be in by seven-thirty, eight at the latest.

*

They were all back around the table, the same six as before, outlining where they'd got to. There was a common thread. Pereira had the prostitutes saying that Wilson had been speaking to a minister. The accountant had told Bain that Wilson had been considering buying his old church. While the driver had not been of a lot of use, he had told Parks that Wilson had, on several occasions, asked him to slow down as they passed church buildings. Tobin was able to report the name of the man Wilson had been speaking to, Reverend Doctor Thomas Melville, the Church of Scotland's principle convener on the property committee.

It was a thread, if a slender one in relation to Wilson being murdered, but they had someone to talk to at least. One person they didn't have to talk to was Fran Henderson, who had not been at the flat.

Cooper was sitting back, arms folded.

"We got anything else for this evening?" he said, receiving a few head shakes from around the room. "The press are baying, of course, so we need a quick result. We've got the shout out for information on Wilson's whereabouts last night, we can start collating responses in the morning. We've got the team looking at them as they come in, discarding the obvious trash, of which there will be more than the usual fair share, given Wilson's sudden recent celebrity. We can split the promising ones between you first thing tomorrow. I've got to do the media again in twenty minutes, but I can bat them aside for now. Early days, but I don't want it dragging on."

"Are we putting out a call for Henderson?" asked Pereira.

She wasn't sure herself, and was happy to defer to Cooper on it.

"What d'you think?" he said, batting it back at her.

"Too early," she said. "There's some merit in it, but it could be he's just out for the evening. If we go out officially, he might run."

"Yeah, right," said Cooper nodding. "We'll stick with that. Anything else?"

Blank looks around the room, then Cooper banged his fist

—

pointlessly on the table and got to his feet.

They left the room at just after seven-thirteen. Not too bad, she thought. She couldn't leave straight away, but it wouldn't take too long to wrap up everything that needed to be done. Thought about texting her mum, but decided to leave it until she was walking out the door.

Sat at her desk, brought the computer up, quick check of her e-mails. Bain sat opposite, doing the same.

"You heading off?" she said, without looking over the desk.

"No rush," he said. "Might stay a bit yet, put in another hour or two."

She nodded. She wanted everyone else who should have been gone to leave. She hated them all staying when she had to go home, she hated being the one who didn't put in the extra time.

But how could she? Not today. It was bad enough most days, but today when her daughter had been dragged round the houses, all the while staring at the stupid three-inch screen?

"It's all right," said Bain. "You should head. Really, it's fine. I've got nothing to get home to, and it's not like there's anything major going to develop this evening."

"No, no, it's not that," she lied. "You shouldn't work too long. You'll get no thanks for it in this place."

"I won't be too late," said Bain.

"Good night," said Parks, waving from across the office. "Sorry, got to dash."

"Course," said Pereira, waving back. "See you tomorrow."

Back to work, she thought. Focus. She was tired though, and the information on screen just seemed a jumble of words and figures. Fifty-seven unread e-mails. She could at least zip through them and get rid of the crap she didn't need to know. Leave the rest, drop the kids off sharp at school in the morning, then get in and get through them before the investigation really kicked back into life.

Five minutes. Ten minutes.

"Parks!" called Cooper, walking from his office, and shouting across the open plan. The open plan wasn't that large, he'd barely needed to shout, and it was instantly apparent that she wasn't there.

"She's gone, sir," said Bain.

"Dammit," said Cooper. "We've got a report on Frank Henderson. He's working at some fairground at the far end of

Glasgow Green."

A moment, that was all, but Pereira knew what was required. It should have been her who was bringing Henderson in anyway. It was no attempt to curry favour, no attempt to make amends to Cooper for having dragged Anais around all day. He wouldn't care, and she was far more concerned about the opposite effect, the ill effect it had on her family. It wasn't about any of that. It was her job, that was all, and she had to go and get on with it.

"I'll go," she said, already getting up from her desk.

"You want me to come?" asked Bain.

"Yes," said Cooper, answering for her. "Small fairground, one of these pop-up ones that moves every couple of days, just off Greendyke Street. Let me know that you get him. Bring him in. Stick him in a cell, leave him there overnight, we can deal with him in the morning. If things get ugly, call for back-up."

He turned back into his office and closed the door. Bain and Pereira shared a look, and then had their jackets back on and were heading out the door.

10

The evening had come, dark and cold and damp. Colder than it had been for a while. Cold for March, even in Scotland. They parked the car a block away, wary of Henderson having become aware of their renewed interest, and approached the fairground.

It was a small and sad little affair, squeezed into a space no bigger than about four tennis courts. A merry-go-round, dodgems for under-8s, a Ferris wheel of no great size, a couple of stalls, a yellow rollercoaster that would not have set the heart rate of a three-year-old going.

The train of four carts on the rollercoaster was trundling round the looping figure of eight. All the carts were empty. There were yellow and white and red lights flashing, and music playing – *Celebrate* by Kool & The Gang – but even that was at an unusually subdued volume, and the song itself seemed overcome by the weight of melancholy that hung over the fair.

It wasn't just the rollercoaster that was empty. There wasn't a single child in the entire place.

Henderson was easy to find, standing by the entrance, arms folded, his back to the path that led to the fairground, watching the trundling yellow cars on the yellow rollercoaster, rolling round and round and round, never going anywhere, never stopping.

They stood behind him for a few moments, watching. He hadn't seen them. He was wearing an old green parka, zipped shut, hood down. Below the waist he had on a long, flowing dress, down to his ankles and his Doc Martens.

As far as they could see, there were five other people in the fairground, standing by unused rides, chatting in empty stalls.

Just like the scene of Archie Wilson's death, this was like a painting, Pereira thought. You could capture the moment. What was the guy's name? The *Nighthawks* painter? Hopper. It could be one of his. Edward Hopper. The sad lives of people, just trying to get by. Doing what they do.

Noticing the look in his direction from a woman at one of the stalls, Henderson finally turned. Bain and Pereira were standing a few paces back. He looked at them for a moment, then turned back, as the two officers walked up alongside him.

"Archie still dead?"

"Why's the 'coaster running?" asked Bain.

"Attract customers," said Henderson.

Bain glanced around. The entire park seemed deserted. The entire city, in fact. Too damp, too cold, as though Glasgow had packed itself away for the evening, hoping the morning might be a little brighter.

"I thought the people who worked these places travelled with the fair?" said Pereira.

"I'm security," said Henderson.

"Really?"

"What does it look like I'm doing?" said Henderson. "They don't have permanent security, because when they go to shitty little places like, I don't know, Fairlie or Drymen, some shite wee town like that, they don't need it. You come to Glasgow Green, there's a good chance you get a bunch of neds showing up."

"You employed by an agency?"

Henderson snorted.

"I know Mal, the owner. From way back. Just do the odd thing for him when he's in town. You want to speak to me about that? Arrest me because I've known someone for twenty-five year?"

Kool & The Gang came to an end. There was a moment of perfect silence, and then Sinatra started up, singing *Fly Me to the Moon*. A cold, bleak evening, a deserted fairground, the incessant trundle of the four connected yellow trucks.

They stood for a while, watching the rollercoaster, strangely spellbound, Sinatra playing away, now seemingly a little too loud, over it all.

"My dad used to sing this song all the time," said Bain. "*Fly me to Dunoon...* that's what he sang."

"My dad used to sing that too," said Pereira, momentarily forgetting, in the peculiar nostalgia of the moment, that she was

---

63

in a hurry. Just wanted to get this over with and get home. That *was* what she wanted, wasn't it?

If the kids fell asleep without seeing her before bedtime, would they even notice? Would it make any difference to them whatsoever, apart from some reminder of the often-fleeting nature of her relationship with them?

"Yeah, same here," said Henderson. "Think everyone's dad sang that when they were a kid."

Suddenly there was some strange kind of bond between them, which was enough to have Pereira snapping out of the moment. She shook her head, a positive movement to break the spell.

"You lied to us, Frank," she said.

"Did I? Which one did you work out?"

He turned and looked at her, smirking, as though trying to cover what he'd said. That he hadn't really been lying.

"You said you hadn't seen Archie for a week."

Henderson didn't reply. They waited, gave him a few moments. Sometimes interviewees needed to fill the silence, and it was just a matter of offering it to them. However, they'd been standing here already in a silence that could have gone on for a long time, and she suspected that Henderson would be quite happy to return to it.

"You were at the hotel with him on Monday evening, left there mid-afternoon yesterday. You then went to the Garland Club. Curious, Frank, really. It wasn't as though you'd been alone at the flat with Archie, and therefore could easily deny it. You were out, in two different very public places. With CCTV. What did you think was going to happen?"

"I didn't kill him."

"Why did you lie, then?" asked Bain.

Henderson kept his eyes on the rollercoaster.

"You weren't wearing women's clothes either," said Pereira. "Why was that?"

"Didn't need to," he said. "Didn't feel the urge. I get urges."

"Just urges? Getting the operation seems a bit excessive if you're feeling urges."

"You can't tell me what I feel," said Henderson.

"No, but you just told us what you feel," said Bain.

"I'm going to make a suggestion to you, Frank, but first I need you to tell us why you lied to us. If you don't, and I need to

---

64

explain it to you, you're spending the night at the station."

"I'm not going anywhere. I'll lose my job."

"You've known Mal since way back," said Pereira, "he'll understand. Why did you lie to us, Frank?"

Sinatra came to an end. Another moment, when the only sound was the clunking of the yellow carts on the track, and then *Whiter Shade of Pale* started up, the organ a seemingly perfect complement to the evening.

"Last chance."

Henderson stared straight ahead, eyes open, mouth closed.

"I suspect, Frank, that you're no more transsexual than anyone else," said Pereira, making the decision to follow through on what she'd just threatened. She would explain it to him, and then he'd be accompanying them back to the station. "From what I understand from the ladies with whom you spent the night, you might like to dress in women's clothing, and why not? But that's as far as it goes. I think you've got some scam in the works, possibly involving benefits. People are taking ownership of themselves these days, you can claim what you damn well please and think the authorities have to respect it."

She paused, briefly wondering what Cooper would think if he heard her make this speech, the expletive that would escape his lips.

"You lied to us because you were doing something that undermines whatever scam you've got going on. And although the scam might not involve us, it hardly matters. It could come back and bite you, that's all. So we turned up at your door, you didn't think clearly. Or worse, you'd actually planned it and decided it was a good idea, and you lied. You're a genius, Frank, you really are. And you're coming with us."

"Really, all right," said Henderson, turning at last. "You've got me. I've got an unfair dismissal claim going from my last job, all right?"

"M&S?" asked Bain.

"Aye. So, that's it. I need to wear the clothes. You happy?"

"I look forward to hearing the details tomorrow morning," said Pereira. "You can make your excuses to Mal if you like, then we're leaving."

"Aw, fuck," muttered Henderson, head shaking. "Bollocks."

"Why weren't you wearing the clothes last night leaving the hotel, then?" asked Bain. "Surely…" and he finished the

---

65

question with a movement of the shoulders.

Henderson looked at him, then over his shoulder at Pereira, shaking his head.

"The girls were laughing at him," said Pereira.

He shot her a glance, then trudged off towards two men who were leaning against a stall, a defensive air about them, waiting to see what the two obvious coppers were after.

11

Pereira opened the front door at just after ten. Stood for a moment in the hall, gauging the state of play in the house. The low sound of the television came from the sitting room; the small light was on in the hall upstairs, but there was no one talking. Hopefully Robin would be asleep, but she hardly needed to wonder what Anais would be doing.

The sound of the television disappeared, and then the door to the sitting room opened and her mother appeared, already putting on her heavy winter coat, an item of clothing she would likely wear until the middle of June. She stood just in front of her daughter, and then reached out and touched her face.

"You look tired," she said. "You shouldn't sit up too late."

"I need to decompress, but I'll try."

"You need your sleep."

"Yes."

Her mother nodded, knowing that Aliya wouldn't listen, much the same as she'd never listened in the past, much the same as she herself had never listened to her mother.

"Everything all right?" asked Pereira.

"Yes, they're fine. Robin was still awake twenty minutes ago. He wanted to see you. So..."

There was no point in mentioning Anais. She was the same every day, after all.

Her mother squeezed her arm and moved towards the door.

"Have you eaten anything?" she asked, as she walked past.

No answer.

"You should eat something. I'm surprised those clothes still fit you."

"I'm fine."

"I'll see you tomorrow. And get some sleep."

"Yes, Mum," said Pereira behind a weak smile.

The door opened. Her mother was gone with a wave. The door closed again. Pereira stood for a moment, once more in silence, and looked at the kitchen door, looked up the stairs. Cup of tea or glass of wine? Either way, it would have to wait.

She removed her jacket, placed it on the coat hanger by the front door and walked up the stairs, soft steps in case Robin was already asleep. Into the bedroom that the children had been sharing since they'd had to find this house, the small bedside light on, Robin lying in bed looking at a book, Anais on the other side of the small room, sitting up, looking at her phone.

"Hey," said Pereira. "Sorry I'm so late. Everything all right?"

She smiled at Anais who glanced back, then she knelt down beside Robin's bed, kissing him on the forehead.

"All right, big man, how are you?"

"What time is it?"

"After ten, I'm afraid. I'm sorry. Had a very busy day."

"Anais said someone was killed."

A moment, she thought of glancing over her shoulder at her daughter, but managed to stop herself.

"Yes," she said, "but it's nothing for you to worry about."

Robin looked at his mum for a moment, gauging whether she was just saying that, or whether he really ought to be worried.

"Are they dead now? The person who was killed?"

"Yes."

"That's sad."

"Yes."

"When someone dies it's wrong to put them in the garbage."

Pereira nodded, ignoring the quiet, mocking snort of laughter from behind.

"Yes, yes it is."

"People should be recycled," said Robin. "I want to be recycled."

"You can't recycle people, you spacktard," came from across the room.

"Please don't call your brother that," said Pereira, looking over her shoulder.

"He's not my brother, he's just your bastard lesbian love

child."

"What's a spacktard?"

Pereira closed her eyes, stopped herself turning again, shouting. Deep breath. The positive effort to stay calm, to ignore being baited. She'd risen to that taunt the first time, and that was why it had been thrown at her several times since.

"It's not anything," said Pereira. She squeezed Robin's hand. "Anyway, people can be recycled, or at least, bits of them can. Like the heart and the kidneys. When someone dies, sometimes they can take a part from that body and give it to someone else who's otherwise healthy, but needs a new heart or a new liver."

"How do they do that?"

"Doctors do it. It's very complicated."

Another moment while Robin processed the information. Pereira held his hand throughout, her fingers lightly caressing the soft skin.

"How was school?" she asked.

"When I die, I want my heart to go to a dog."

Another snort from across the room.

"That's very thoughtful of you," said Pereira. "I'm not sure that would be possible, though. I think it might have to go to another person."

"Oh. Maybe you can have my heart, Mummy."

Pereira squeezed his hand a little tighter.

"Oh, please. Pass the sick bag."

"Thank you," said Pereira, "but my heart's fine. Now, tell me about school."

"Sally Jenkins swallowed a bee and it stung her tongue. She nearly died."

*

Twenty-five minutes later Pereira finally walked into the kitchen after Robin had talked himself to sleep. She had been close to leaving several times, but just as her guilt at not spending enough time with her children meant that she enabled Anais's phone addiction, she invariably allowed Robin to stay up later than she knew was good for him.

He stayed up later, he was more difficult in the morning, tired even before going to school, she got annoyed at him, she felt guilty as they so often parted on bad terms, at the end of the day she would spend as long as possible with him to compensate, and he would invariably end up being too late getting to sleep.

The clock on the hob blinked on and off in red, 00:00. There must have been a power cut at some point during the day. Her mother hadn't said. Looked at her watch, 22:37, then fixed the clock.

Straightened up, stood for a moment savouring the peace. Cup of tea or glass of wine? There was barely a decision to be made.

Glass from the cupboard, into the fridge, filled the glass almost to the top from the bottle of Pinot Grigio she'd opened the night before, closed the fridge door and walked through to the sitting room.

There were two table lamps on. She turned off the larger, brighter one, sat down in the single comfy chair by the fireplace. The light of the electric heater still softly glowed. The heat had been turned off, but the room still felt warm from her mother having had it on all evening. She'd likely turned it off when Pereira had texted to let her know she was on her way home.

She took a drink, rested her head back against the seat. Stared at the television. There would be news on some channel or another. Someone would be talking about Archie Wilson, but she wasn't interested. Others could watch the news. She needed to switch off.

Switching off, of course, was always an aspiration, rarely a reality. There were only two more weeks of school before the Easter holidays. Two and a half weeks to plan and worry over, and only a few days off work. And then that would be out the way, and summer would loom large and long. Seven weeks, and her with two weeks leave. And where could they afford to go in those two weeks? Some small cottage in the Highlands or down the Clyde or on the east coast. That was all. She couldn't conceive of being able to afford to go anywhere else. And did it matter anyway? Robin was young enough he'd be happy anywhere by the sea, Anais would just want to know there was Internet.

Perhaps she could book somewhere for a week with no WiFi. Not tell Anais. Face the wrath when she got there. Would a week be long enough to get past it, for them to be able to spend some decent time together?

Every decision she made regarding her children, it felt like

Cooper was watching her, waiting for the slightest mistake, to insert it into his own personal narrative of Pereira's career.

And then there was Lena. There was always Lena, still in her head, impossible to shift. Martin, she rarely thought about. He was gone, long gone. Anais might cling on to some idea of him, but he was so infrequently in Pereira's thoughts. The wounds from the break-up with Lena, however, were far fresher. They didn't feel like they'd be going anywhere any time soon.

She had to learn to say no when Lena asked her to come with Robin for those Sunday afternoons. She had to learn to say to Lena that that was her time with their child. She herself should have been finding something to do with Anais. It was four hours, that was all, and it could be for her and her daughter. Instead, Lena would invariably ask if she wanted to join her and Robin, and Pereira could never refuse.

And when Lena didn't ask, the hurt was crushing, like the moment she'd walked out, repeated over and over.

She took another sip of wine, and now she closed her eyes. Peace would come eventually. Lena would some day no longer be in her head. That's what happened. People got over people. People moved on. People found other people. It happened to everyone.

She opened her eyes again and looked at the swirling orange light of the fake logs in the fire.

THURSDAY

12

Pereira couldn't recall exactly what it was like going into work before she'd had kids, but in her mind she remembered workdays starting with at least some sense of optimism. You got out of bed, you showered and cleaned your teeth, you ate breakfast or not, you got into work while things were still quiet, and there it was. A new day. Everything was fresh. Like the first snowfall of winter.

She knew it hadn't been that rosy, but still, there'd been something about it. Every day had been a new start.

Now? She was regularly worn down before she even got into work. Anais's daily indifference could do it to her within five minutes. Robin was exhausting, in turn endlessly talkative, the voice constant, demanding she pay attention and engage – something that was sometimes wonderful, sometimes a battering ram of sound – in turn, difficult and complaining, not wanting to get dressed, not wanting to go to school.

That morning it had been the latter. She'd known it would be the case. Not enough sleep. Anais, also, looked like she'd finally fallen asleep with her phone in front of her face at four a.m.

And so Pereira had arrived at work, as relieved to part from her kids as she had been guilty the night before for being late, and already worn down by the day. The school run also meant that she never once got into work early, she never had the chance to take the first few minutes of the day, silence at her desk, a cup of coffee and time to ease her way into business.

She always walked into a busy and bustling office, with a feeling of being behind the curve and needing to get straight on

72

with the grind.

She stopped just inside the door and surveyed the scene. The usual weekday morning. Everyone at their desks, the bustle of noise.

There were fourteen desks in the open plan, one office, Cooper's, with windows out over the open plan, and two small conference rooms off to the side. The office and part of the open plan had windows looking out onto the river.

At the far end of the open plan, windows looked out over the bank, facing upriver. On the wall beside the entrance, there was a coffee machine, which the union had lobbied – and failed – to be paid for by the service, a water cooler and a vending machine with assorted snacks.

Bain brushed past Pereira on his way into the office, a piece of paper in his hand.

"Boss," he said. "All well?"

"Sure," she said. Time to engage. "What have we got?"

"We should get down to talk to Henderson. You want me to grab you a coffee while you get settled in, then we'll head."

"Thanks," she said.

And they were off.

*

"Why did you leave?"

Henderson shook his head, but more as an indication of pointlessness than an unwillingness to answer.

He had a cup of coffee, Pereira and Bain had their coffee. The small room smelled of it. There was a constable standing at the door. The constable didn't have a coffee, although she was partial to one.

When she was younger, Pereira had loved the police interrogation scenes in the old movies, especially the part where the detective jumped up out of his seat, leaned across the desk, grabbed the crook by the collar and snarled in his face.

That didn't happen so often these days. In fact, if it ever did, chances are the crook in question would be able to walk free, tossing a lawsuit for police harassment into the mix along the way.

Not that Henderson was the type who needed grabbing by the scruff of the neck. The dress he was still wearing didn't have a collar in any case.

73

"It was just a bit shite. The women had buggered off, and what was left? A bunch of guys sitting round a poncy club drinking champagne. Give us a break."

"Who was there?"

"Fuck do I know who they were?"

She held his gaze across the desk until he lowered his eyes.

"Let's start at the beginning," she said. "How many times had you been at the club?"

"Three or four," he said.

"That's not so many as to lose count," said Pereira. "Was it three or was it four?"

"Three. Tuesday was the third."

"Did Archie go to the club with anyone else?"

A moment, while Henderson considered whether or not he was going to talk. However, he'd spent one night in a cell and he didn't really want to stay any longer. He had no one to harm by talking, and Wilson certainly wasn't going to be complaining.

"Naw. He didn't have any friends. Not, you know, not in the time leading up to winning the cash. He had friends from the old days, maybe, but he wasn't really a going out kind of bloke. Stayed in the flat most nights. And course, lots of the old friends came out the woodwork soon as he got the money, but he didn't respond to any of them, far as I know."

"So no friends at the club?" Pereira was asking the questions, Bain sitting silently at her side, watching.

"He was starting to know people, and they were recognising him 'n' that. Couple of folk, I suppose. Don't know their names though. If you ask me, they were a bunch of snooty fuckers. Looked down at him, especially when he brought the women in. And really especially when he brought me. Fuck's sake, man. Looked at us like I was someone else's shite floating in the bog."

There was little to be gained pushing for more, as Tobin already had the names of people who were used to talking to Wilson.

"Did you have any idea what Archie was going to be doing on Tuesday evening?"

"You kidding?" he said, laughing. "He did the same thing every night, man. It was like... I don't know, there must be more than this, right? You win all that money, and fine, a few days of parties and women, maybe a week or two, but at some point, very soon, you're going to start using your imagination. You're going to dream big, man, right? Because you can afford to dream big. Archie didn't have a big fucking dream in his whole body. There was just something. I don't know…" Another shake of the head. "So, on Tuesday evening he was going to be doing exactly the same as he did every other night. Dinner at the club, get hammered, get a couple of hookers, go back to his hotel and fuck. Whatever, man, you know. That was his life."

"And if he wasn't giving you money for an operation, was he going to do anything for you? Apart from get you laid."

He scowled, as though he had been discomfited by the use of the word coming from Pereira.

"Said he was taking his time. Fair enough. I mean, you get enough of these bampots who squander all their shite in the first few months. He was waiting for everything to settle down. Said he was making shed loads in interest every day, which sounded like pish to me, but that's what he says. That's what he was spending."

"Where'd he get the drugs?"

Henderson lowered his eyes again. The fingers of his right hand, lightly gripping the coffee cup, began to tap against the Styrofoam. The silence continued.

"God, Frank, would you just get on with it? Archie's dead. No one thinks you killed him. Literally no one." Bain glanced at her, stopped the smile coming to his face. He remembered how she'd once relaxed the killer Jenkins with the same words, the same tone. "You're not a suspect. You're not even, as everyone says these days because of American TV shows, a person of interest. If Wilson had dealings with a drug dealer, *then* we have a person of interest. If it was you, then get it out there and be done with it. I'm not even, necessarily, at this stage going to ask who your dealer is. We just need to know where Archie–"

"It was me," said Henderson, voice low.

"Thank you. Who?"

"What?"

"Who'd you get the drugs from?"

"You just said…"

"Come on, Frank, we're all adults here."

Henderson shook his head, and now he lifted the coffee cup for the first time in several minutes and took a drink. Grimaced, set it back down on the table.

"Fuck's sake," he said.

"Did Archie ever talk to you about churches?"

75

Henderson breathed out heavily through his nose, stared off to the side. *Classic*, he thought. *Fucking classic. The easy one now. The harmless question. The seemingly harmless question.*

"Aye," he said, without looking at her. "Always. Always banging on about it. He loved churches. I mean, he didn't believe in God, any of that shite. Nothing like that, so he said. But he liked churches, especially when they were empty. Said he liked to sit in them. Enjoyed the peace and quiet."

"And did he mention that he might buy one?"

"One? Jesus. I can tell you, because he showed me often enough. You go on the Church of Scotland website. Look at it. At the moment they have, I don't know, like fifteen churches for sale, least they did the last time I looked, which was on Tuesday, believe it or not. I mean, the last time I was shown. He was thinking of buying the job lot."

"What was he going to do with them?"

"Fuck should I know?"

"Because you were his only friend, and he talked to you. Come on, Frank, we can do this."

Henderson shook his head, lifted the coffee again. Another drink, another grimace.

"He had some cockamamie plan or other. He was going to start, like, little missions or something. Food kitchens and food banks, drug clinics, AA meetings, a hodgepodge of do-gooding pish. And he liked yon music, you know choirs, what d'you call it…?"

"Choral."

"Aye, fucking choral. He liked choirboys." He laughed. "So he had some shite or other about having a choir in some church, and they'd be practicing every day, and this and that and whatever. It'd be his way to give back to the community, he said, which is fair enough, right, because there's no' a community in the whole of fucking Glasgow that's no' wanting for a male boys' choir."

*

They walked back up the stairs to the office, empty cups in hand. Behind them, Henderson was taken away in the opposite direction, back down the road to the cells at Dalmarnock station.

"You think he killed Wilson?" asked Bain.

"Don't get any sense of it," she said, "but let's not get

carried away with my innate ability to pick a murderer out of a line up. At the moment he's pretty much alone on the suspect list, so let's leave him there. Nevertheless, we are going to let him go. What about you?"

"Not feeling it," said Bain. "Maybe if Wilson had been kicked to death in a brawl or something. But what we saw, the artfully staged revenge, I don't see that coming from Frank. Or Fran either, for that matter."

Pereira smiled, then stopped on the stairs.

"Artfully staged revenge," she said. "Nice. I like that." And she walked on.

"Beginning to sound like an interesting guy, Wilson," said Bain, a step or two behind.

"You think?"

"There's always interest in juxtaposition," he said. "On the one hand the only thing he could think to do at the moment, while everything settled down, was take drugs, sleep with prostitutes and get hammered. Yet, the only thing we know he was thinking of doing long-term was this weird civic notion, like a modern-day mission."

Up to the top of the stairs, along the corridor.

"I wish I could see how this interest in empty churches might have led someone to put a cross in his head. Although at least the religious aspect of it ties in."

Into the office, and Pereira automatically stopped beside the coffee machine.

"I feel we don't have a picture of who he was before he won the money. We're very focused on that, but we shouldn't let the first thirty-five years of his life just slide away."

"I'll put together a profile."

"Thanks. I'm going to see the parents again, though, so I'll take the immediate family side of it. We can collate after. Want another coffee?"

"Thanks, boss, that'd be great."

The open-plan buzzed around Pereira as Bain walked back to his desk. She glanced into Cooper's office. The door was closed, his head down. Reading a report, on paper, rather than on screen, his elbow on the table, his hand rubbing his forehead.

She turned back to the machine and started off the first coffee. When the machine had originally arrived, there had been seven different options, none of which had been a straightforward coffee with milk. Complaints had been passed along to the relevant people, and finally, six months later, someone had come to remove the decaf latte macchiato option, and add the plain old coffee with milk option.

Glanced at her watch. Already after ten. She'd been called to the school to take Anais home by this time yesterday. Then she cursed herself for having had the thought, looked around, couldn't see any wood to touch in the immediate area, and tapped her head instead.

13

Just before midday, back at Mr. and Mrs. Wilson's kitchen table. The stage in the investigation when this kind of repeat visit would become more of a feature. The initial conversations had been conducted, now there was time to come back and re-examine. Rarely did anyone completely open up to the police, regardless of the circumstances.

"Church?" said the father.

"Yes," said Pereira. "More specifically, the Old Parish at Bellahouston. It was where he attended when he was young, is that correct?"

The old man scoffed, shook his head.

"Yes," said the mum. "When he was young."

Mrs. Wilson had been medicated. Valium or Prozac or both or something else, anything else, just to get her through these few awful days, until the funeral. A funeral that would be inevitably delayed, given the circumstances surrounding the death.

"How young?"

Mrs. Wilson initially deferred to her husband, lifting her cup of tea with a slightly unsteady hand, then finally restarted the narrative when it became apparent that her husband wasn't talking.

"John was an elder at the kirk back then. Was so for a long time. Archibald came with us, every Sunday. Went to Sunday school until he was eleven, then he joined the Youth Fellowship, but he was never that interested. Not in the Bible study side of it, at any rate. He sat with us in the kirk every week for a while, but by the time he was fourteen... teenagers, you know how it is, they move on."

"You did well to get him to keep going until he was fourteen," said Pereira.

"What would the likes of you know about it?" asked Mr. Wilson. He didn't look up though, just delivered the line with what he considered the appropriate level of scorn, and then lifted his cup, his hand much steadier than that of his wife.

"Please, go on," said Pereira. "He never went back?"

She shook her head, then said, "Well, once, just the once. It all went to pot at that place, several years later. The minister retired. Reverend Smith, lovely man, had been there for close on thirty-five years. Didn't want to go, and we didn't want him to go either, and fit as a fiddle…"

"What happened after he left?"

"He was always going to be a hard act to follow."

"Bloody woman," said Wilson.

"We got our first female minister. Young. She wasn't popular. Wanted to make changes, and you couldn't blame her, the congregation was falling." She talked on, through the husband's repeated dismissive snorts. "She brought in the Praise Band, more modern hymns, she introduced the new Lord's prayer… most of the hymns came from Mission Praise, she kept the children in church for ten minutes longer every week, she had a family service once a month."

His head was shaking almost continually by now.

"John left the session, as did several others. Anyway, none of it worked, and gradually, over time, numbers dwindled away to practically nothing. In the end we were told to merge with St. Malcolm's and St. Andrew's, and there you are. The congregation went off to St. Andrew's, and our dear old building was put up for sale. That's quite recent, I have to admit, but there's no one buying it. Who would?"

"And you said Archibald went back one more time?"

"Yes. Four years ago. They held the final ever church service in the building. That was nice. A nice evening. The church was full then."

"Like bloody *Songs of Praise*," muttered Wilson.

"Archibald had been living up in Inverness then, had been for a while. Not sure why he came back down for the service. He did always ask about the church, I'll say that."

"A nostalgia thing," said Pereira.

"Yes."

"One of the consistencies of childhood," said Pereira. "If its

---

80

worst crime was that it was boring at the time, that'll be forgotten. You remember the feeling and the people, the atmosphere. And you're going to remember Christmas services far more than a dull service, some rainy October morning."

"Ach! What am I thinking?" said Mrs. Wilson, but her voice didn't rise and fall with the words. There was still that evenness of tone, the tone that said her emotional functions had been shut down for the day. For the duration. All she had at the moment was some pleasure in talking about her boy, and about a part of his past that was not painful. "There's me saying he only ever went once more. He went every Christmas, to the Watch Night service. For years before he left home, and then whenever he was back here for Christmas. Not that that happened so often."

She lightly tapped her husband's elbow. "Why didn't you think of that?"

"I knew you'd remember eventually," he said dryly.

"So, nothing more than a happy childhood memory," said Pereira.

"Yes, now that I think about it," said Mrs. Wilson, nodding. "And he was thinking of buying the building?"

"So we understand. He obviously hadn't discussed it with you?"

She shook her head. Mr. Wilson wasn't for responding.

"What was he going to do with it, I wonder?"

Mrs. Wilson asked the question, and stared away across the kitchen, eyes drifting to the window, and the chill day outside.

I'm likely losing her again, thought Pereira, but she had what she needed. The connection had been made, a simple one at that.

"He was going to turn it into a mission for the community," she said. "A soup kitchen and a food bank, drug and alcohol counselling, that kind of thing."

"Archibald was going to do that?"

Her hand was resting on the table, Mr. Wilson glanced up, an untrusting look in his eyes, at Pereira. Pereira nodded at the mum and smiled, finding herself reaching across the table squeezing her fingers.

*

Bain stood at the door of the old, large house in Rutherglen. On

81

Rodger Drive, overlooking that end of the old Overtoun Park, where once there'd been football pitches. Didn't come out this way very often, didn't know the area. He stood with his back to the door, looking at the retirement home across the road.

Not a sign of life.

Maybe they were all inside, doing their gymnastics or aerobics. Maybe they were all already set for the day, breakfast slurped, now slumped silently in front of the television, their peace disturbed every now and again by a woman in a white coat coming round, asking loudly if they were ready for a cup of tea.

They should be outside, he thought. *Like kids. Outside as long as possible, even if it is bleak. There should be a great horde of the aged on the lawn behind the home, doing tai chi, like one of those parks in Beijing, where great lines of people moved together.*

In his head he started to form the movements.

The door was opened by a woman in her thirties, casually dressed, long sleeve t-shirt, jeans, long hair, with a fringe down over her eyes, which she constantly moved away with her wrist, as though her hands were covered in paint or flour.

"Kal Ritchie?"

"Sergeant Bain," she said. "Come in. But look, I'm absolutely crunched for time, so you're just going to have to bear with." She talked quickly, the words a stream, as he entered the house and she closed the door behind him. "Mary can get you a cup of tea, if you'd like one. Would you like a cup of tea?" Bain shook his head. "OK, cool. Well look, come in, but as I said, please don't mind me, I need to get on, but I can answer your questions, although like I said on the phone, I hadn't seen Archie in so long, like five years or something, but never mind. Come in, come in."

They entered a room behind the sitting room at the front of the house, a place that might once have been a dining room. It was, instead, a dumping room, a clutter of papers and musical equipment.

Three of the walls were covered in film posters, mostly of the classics – *A Day at the Races*, *Sabrina*, *It Happened One Night* – but some were for more recent films that Bain didn't recognise. *The Monkfish Cowboy*. *A Winter Night*. *The Girl in Socks*.

The wall backing on to the sitting room, however, was kept blank, as it was obviously used as a screen for projected films.

—

At that moment, a film had been paused, with a woman in mid-scream, a strange, nebulous green creature towering over her from behind.

"You're watching a movie?" said Bain. "You a critic?"

"I'm scoring the film," said Ritchie, and as she said it she sat down behind a keyboard that was lined up directly before the wall. "Just on my initial run through, trying to get an idea, formulate a few basic motifs. Just ask as we go along, don't worry, I can multi-task."

She set the movie going, the volume down low, as the girl screamed and the green monster trailed her from behind. A moment, and then the sweep of strings started from the keyboard. A brief burst, then it stopped, and Ritchie pressed a few keys on the computer that was built into the keyboard. Finally, Bain looked away from the screen and down at the piece of kit on which she was working.

"That's like something out of Star Trek," he said.

"This? It's pretty old. The guys doing what I'm doing out in Hollywood, they'd laugh at me."

"What's the movie?" asked Bain.

The thing had the woman by the feet. She kicked out at it, imbedding a six-inch heel in its eye. It didn't seem to mind. Music came in bursts from the keyboard.

"A 1950s B-movie spoof. *The Creature from Black Gulch.*"

"Anyone in it?"

"A lot of Scottish guys. McEvoy, Ewan Macgregor, Gerard Butler, people like that. Think Johnny Depp's got a bit-part, but I haven't seen him yet. Course, it might just turn out that he's the creature."

Bain looked back at the screen.

"Seriously? This looks shit."

"It's supposed to. It's a spoof. Anyway, ours is not to reason why, ours is just to write the soundtrack. You always get these things… sorry, Sergeant, I know the movie business fascinates people. I could talk about it all day myself, but I really could do with getting on."

The green creature suddenly froze, a pained look on its face, and then turned slowly. There, behind it, was Gerard Butler, having just deposited a samurai sword in its back.

"Fuck you, you slimebag, green-ass piece of shit," said Butler.

Ritchie stopped the film again.

"I don't think they said stuff like that in 50s B-movies," said Bain.

Ritchie laughed, shook her head.

"Look, I'm sorry, Sergeant, this isn't working. Perhaps we could just have a quick chat and you could leave me to it. That thing about multi-tasking I just said," and she dismissed the notion with a wave of the hand and rolling of the eyes.

"Archie Wilson," said Bain. "You've been following the news the last few weeks?"

"Well, I heard about it, of course," she began, and once again her speech began to pick up pace, like the words were being squeezed from a balloon. "Not at first. I never pay any attention to lottery winners. I'm not really a people person. I watch the news, but I'm never interested in stories about people, as such. Lottery winners? Good for them, but I'm not interested. Anyway, Beth called me one day to mention it, so I read about it online. But I was due in Berlin round about then, or something, can't remember, and I had another thing to do in LA for a week, so I was just getting on with my shit. I thought about calling Archie, congratulating him, you know… well, not call, would probably just have e-mailed, but then, you know, I'm sure everyone and their gran was getting in touch with him, and a lot of them would've been asking for money, or at least, establishing contact with the hope that the possibility of money would arise, and I really didn't want Archie to think I was interested in any of his easily-gotten gains. And then, of course, you know when Archie and I split up it wasn't really a mutual thing, more on me, so I hated the thought of him thinking that I might want to get back together with him just because he was suddenly loaded."

Gerard Butler continued to look down on them, mid-snarl.

"But don't get me wrong, I didn't think he'd come looking, or want me even if I'd offered myself. I expect he was going to have his pick now. Had he found anyone in the last six weeks?"

Bain was a little surprised, suddenly being invited to talk.

"Not that he hadn't paid for," he said.

"Ah. Well, at this stage, that makes sense. No point in lumbering yourself with a relationship right from the off, and you might as well get the sex in while you can, eh?"

Bain glanced over his shoulder at Butler, felt like he was being watched.

"I'm just looking for some background on Archie," said

Bain, turning back to Ritchie.

"Of course. We met at Aberdeen uni. Both did biology. We were teamed together in a laboratory for the year. I was the fastidious student, Archie was the rogue. Opposites attract and all that. Nothing happened that year, but eventually we fell in together and by the time uni finished we were a thing. And that thing became an on-and-off thing for the next ten years, including an engagement. That was wrong. But he asked, and I, in a moment of dumb romantic stupidity, agreed. We got jobs in Inverness, he played football at the weekend, I played music. He lurched from one thing to another, no great ability, no great interest, I eventually fell into this. Hobby became full-time. We never did get married. Eventually I left him, came back down here."

"Did he go to church when he was at uni, or in Inverness?"

A moment. That was unusual, thought Bain. The first time she'd naturally broken the stride of conversation.

"That's interesting," she said. "I hadn't really thought about that. I mean, he didn't, not as a thing. But every now and again... And if ever we went anywhere, you know, visited a town or a city, he always wanted to go and look at the churches. Hmm... he always went at Christmas, of course. The Watch Night service."

"Did he believe in God?"

"Don't think so. Never said, never acted like it."

"Drugs?"

"Smoked weed occasionally. There was one time one of the guys he played fives with got some coke. We had that."

"And?"

"It was awesome," she said, then she stared off into the corner of the room for a moment, before quickly bringing it back. "That was all. Didn't become a regular thing."

"Why did you end it?"

"We'd become stuck," she said, the voice beginning to pick up pace. Obviously something she'd answered many times before. "You know, same old thing every night, every weekend. Archie... he was lovely, but he didn't like change. Hated trying new things. He could have eaten the same thing for dinner every night, he always wanted to go to the same restaurant, never varied from more than three things on the menu. Watched the same shows. I mean... I don't know how many times he'd watched *Blake's 7* and *Twin Peaks* and *The West Wing*. Holy crappoli… I'd want to watch something new, and he'd just leave me to it. We ended up rarely doing anything together. Then I started getting into this, and I'd have to travel to London or LA or wherever, and I'd say come with me, and he'd be like, I don't want to get on a plane, I hate airports, I hate flying… So, it was time, that's all. Time to split."

"Would you say he had no imagination?" Bain managed to squeeze in.

"Hmm… I'm not sure. He could be a fantasist, I'll give him that. He liked his lesbian fantasies for a kick-off. Always on at me to get another woman into bed. Funny, given how much he hated meeting new people, he'd have been quite happy getting into bed with one of them, as long as I did the work. Men and lesbians, what are you going to do? I hope at least he managed to buy that in the last few weeks."

Bain nodded, smiled ruefully.

"Well, good luck to him."

"He was living back in Glasgow, you knew that?"

"Sure," she said. "Came down a couple of years ago. Wasn't working for a while, then got a job as a greenkeeper at Dalmuir Municipal. No idea how he got that. At least he wouldn't have had to talk to people."

"You saw him since he got here?"

"He contacted me. I put it off at first, then eventually I thought, what the hell. He wasn't bugging me or anything, nothing like that. He e-mailed one night, and I was feeling maudlin or something, maybe I'd just watched some movie or other, it happens. We went out for dinner. It was nice, but the spark was long gone. For him too, I could tell. We talked and ate, and by the end of the evening we'd just run out of things to say. Everything we'd ever needed to say to each other had been said, everything we'd ever have to talk about was finished. Funny that, huh? You can talk to someone every day for the whole of your life and never run out of conversation. I remember hearing an interview where Kirk Douglas said that about Burt Lancaster. They'd be making a movie together, and at the end of the day they'd just sit outside, having a drink, talking until the small hours of the morning. Every night. Friendships like that are kind of nice. Not me and Archie, though. We'd had our thing, and it ran its course. We should have got out much earlier, but that's how it goes."

"You know if he hung around with anyone in Glasgow?"

"I remember he was sharing a flat with some guy back then, but I don't know any more. He never mentioned anyone else."

"Any idea why someone might have wanted to have had him killed?"

"You mean, apart from the fact he'd just won over a hundred million pounds?"

"Yes," said Bain, "apart from that."

"Really?"

"Obviously we're already looking at that," he said. "Just covering the bases. We could get focused on one thing, then it's something from his past that comes and bites him. And anyway, even if it's as a result of the money, it's still likely to be someone with a history with Archie who did this to him. The chances of someone seeing Archie on the news, then deciding to kill him just out of badness, are pretty slim, legion though the numbers of horrible people out there are."

"Fair point," she said. "But sorry, I have no idea why anyone would want to kill him. He was kind of dull, that's all."

She glanced back at Gerard, still stuck in his suspended grimace. Bain took the hint. He was done for the moment in any case.

"Thank you," he said. "You'll be around if I've got any other questions? Not heading off to Hollywood or anything?"

"I'll be attached to this for the next few days, then I've got another few projects to work on. Look, you never know in this business. Things seem pretty flat, then suddenly someone calls you out of the blue. It's always a rush job, always an emergency."

"You seem to be doing all right," said Bain, indicating Gerard on the wall.

"This is super low budget. First time director, been around the film business in various roles, got lots of mates. They all did it for biscuits. As am I. Leave me your card. I'll call if I think of anything, or to let you know if I need to go away."

Bain reached into his pocket, took out the simple card with his name, mobile number and e-mail address. No rank, nothing to suggest he was in the Police Service.

"Thanks," she said. "Sorry, I should…"

"Yeah, of course," said Bain. "I'll see myself out."

He nodded, she smiled, he turned. As he was walking out the door, he heard the movie hiss back into life, then Butler said, "I'm thirsty as fuck. Let's do this, so I can get a fucking beer."

14

There was a bitter wind at the top of the Necropolis, making the day even colder and more inhospitable. Low cloud, no rain, but still a draining, awful bleakness about the day. The headstone was still taped off, two police officers on duty stopping people getting too close. They were both dressed for winter.

Pereira was already standing over the headstone looking down upon it when Bain arrived. They stood together for a while, reading the details of the life and death of William Craven, such as they were.

Born 27th May 1865. Died 13th November 1893. Son of Gilbert and Agnes. Sorely missed by sections of society.

"That's a funny line," said Bain eventually.

"Yes," said Pereira. "Do we get down to the particulars of Craven's life I wonder? I mean, other than that he earned a sudden windfall, but didn't really get to enjoy it."

"We could get Somerville or Tobin to have a look."

"Yep, you're right. You never know."

Bain studied the headstone for another few moments and then turned away, looking down across the graveyard and out across the city. Glasgow beneath a low, grey cover of cloud. The word blanket came into his head. How dull, he thought. Cloud cover like this was always a blanket. Like the first snowfall of the winter, if there even was a first snowfall of the winter. The blanket of snow.

"You haven't found a book of matches with the name of a nightclub on it, have you?" asked Bain. Suddenly the cold had begun to work its way inside him, as if looking out on the bleakness of the day had finally woken him up.

"No," she said, prosaically. "I wasn't looking for the

metaphorical book of matches. Just wanted to get the feel for the place again. The last resting place of Archibald Wilson, looking out over the headstones of the dead."

She turned fully now, following Bain's look out and down across what they could see of the rest of the cemetery.

"So we've got Wilson leaving the club at some time after eight. He was killed around midnight. The body was discovered here at around eight thirty the following morning. So there's a twelve-hour period we need to fill in, and at the moment it's all blank. All of it. We've no obvious motive, and no suspects – bar the cross-dressing fraudster, of course."

"We have the murder weapon, and we have the drugs used to sedate him," said Bain.

"Yes. A metal cross, fashioned into a spike. That needs investigating. Maybe it was bought off the shelf, although I don't know why someone would make it in the first place."

"Have they been running facial recognition through the CCTV cameras in town for Tuesday night?"

"Sure. Already done and dusted. Nothing."

"And Henderson? Have we got his movements on film?"

She shook her head.

"Every time we try to do this, every damn time, we come across just how many of these cameras have been turned off, either for cost purposes, or because someone somewhere started wetting their pants about surveillance. Makes it so bloody difficult."

Bain nodded in agreement. Silence came to them again, a silence that somehow felt like a luxury. An indulgence. As though they had time to stand in silence, looking over the city.

"Look at all this," said Bain. "How many graves are there?"

"I know. You're thinking what I'm thinking. How did this person, this killer, know to put Wilson on Craven's grave? How did they identify Craven out of all those people as a man who had come by chance upon a fortune? When you speak to Somerville, or Tobin, or whoever, get them to look into that too. Is the story of Craven well known, or at least, easy to find by anyone who started looking?"

"Yes, boss."

Another break in the conversation. They were no nearer finding the killer of Archie Wilson than they had been at this point the previous day, but the investigation was still in its infancy. There were still numerous strands of inquiry, still numerous people to talk to, many of whom were yet to be unearthed.

The media might cry about lack of progress after twenty-four hours, but no one at the SCU would be doing that just yet.

The moment grabbed them. The melancholy of it, a grey early afternoon on a cold day in a graveyard, the city and the west of Scotland stretching bleakly out before them. Away to their left they could see Underhill the groundsman pushing a wheelbarrow along a path – not the barrow that had been used to wheel Archie Wilson's body –his movements inaudible from this distance.

One of the duty police officers, Constable Jeffers, stood silently a few yards away. Time stopped for a while, the only sound the general rumble of the city, with even the cars on the M8, barely more than a hundred yards behind them, blending into the same single white noise.

"What's next on your list?" asked Pereira at some point, breaking the moment.

"Lawyer," said Bain. "Find out about the will. You?"

"Going to see the Church of Scotland property convenor," she said. "Agreed to meet him at the cathedral. Convenient for us both. Want to come in before you go to St. Vincent Street? You can head off if it looks like he's a talker."

"Sure," said Bain.

She nodded, but didn't move. Not yet. A few more moments of peace.

And then there, out of nowhere, Lena was in her head. Like she'd just walked in, unexpectedly, for lunch or a cup of tea and a chat.

Lena didn't like graveyards. Lena thought everyone should be cremated, and that the bodies of those who were already dead should be dug up, cremated, a single memorial erected, and the cemeteries turned into parks for the living.

Lena liked grey days. Lena liked silence. Lena liked melancholy, in a strange kind of a way.

"Come on," said Pereira, "let's go and see the vicar."

*

"The church is dying, I'm afraid, and I don't think there's anything anyone can do to stop it. We're good at either end of the scale, of course, for numbers, I mean. The old still come. It's what they've always done. And the young, the mothers still bring the young ones. The mothers come along – invariably the mothers – and it's like a social group. Ten minutes in the church, then off to sit and chat and let their babies and toddlers crawl around. Some places might have a mums and toddlers service at ten. We do try. But really, most of those babies and toddlers will be gone by the time they're ten. The chances of hanging on to them through the teenage years are next to zero."

The Reverend Dr. Thomas Melville slowly moved his shoulders. There was a hardness about him, about the face and the small, round glasses and the completely bald head, that was at odds with the softness of his voice.

As so often happened, Pereira felt his words personally. Hadn't that been her? Taking Anais along to church on a Sunday morning for the respite of it, then letting her off the hook as soon as she'd begun questioning the Bible stories and the legitimacy of the message.

Now, Sunday mornings sitting beside her mum in church, with Robin, Anais left at home to play her games. How long would it last with Robin? And how much longer would she keep going herself, once Robin had started questioning why he had to go when his sister didn't?

"I'd say it was the same with faiths the world over, but that's not the case, is it? Islam flourishes. The Russian Orthodox Church flourishes. All sorts of religions and faiths and sects are burgeoning around the globe. And what do we do here in Scotland? We've become secular in stages, and the will of the people must have its way. No one designed it or planned for it, it just happened. An organic dying of the light. Little to be done, the situation quite beyond saving, I fear."

"The church was dying out in the mid-nineteenth century," said Pereira, "and it came back. You never know. People may find something in it yet."

"In the nineteenth century it didn't have to compete with the Internet," said Melville, smiling. "And you, yourself, if you don't mind me asking. You practice religion? Hinduism?"

"Christian," she said. "Church of Scotland."

"Good grief," said Melville, smiling. "A convert! We must enshrine you in a stained-glass window at once!"

To her right, Bain smiled and shook his head.

"My parents were members of the Presbyterian Church in Mumbai. They joined the Church of Scotland when they came here in the early 1960s. I've been going all my life."

"Well, I do apologise," said Melville. "An old man seeing just what's in front of him and nothing else. To which parish do you belong?"

"I think maybe we should talk about Archie Wilson, if you don't mind," said Pereira.

"Of course, of course."

He laughed, waving away the previous question, waving at himself.

There was a sharp noise behind them, the sound loud in the choir of the cathedral, and they turned. A visitor had dropped a walking stick, that was all, and a couple of people were fussing around the man, making sure he was all right, that the stick was quickly back in his hand.

Pereira, Melville and Bain were seated in a pew near the front, by one of the thick square pillars, smaller rounded columns built into each one. The great, wooden ceiling was far above them, and they spoke in quiet voices.

Around them a few visitors walked. There were two officials of the church, dressed in flowing blue robes, around the altar at the front of the choir, talking quietly.

"Mr. Wilson was interested in buying church property?" asked Pereira.

"Oh yes, he certainly was. Very interested. Indeed, we were just discussing it on Tuesday evening…"

He let the sentence go as his mind drifted to what must have happened to Archie Wilson not long after they'd had their conversation.

"We understand you have as many as fifteen properties for sale at the moment," she said, and as the words crossed her lips she kicked herself for having not checked. Where had she got that information from? Henderson. She was asking questions based on the word of a small-time, phony cross-dressing fraudster.

"We have fifteen on the site at the moment, but another five being prepared. Further to that, we know of at least eleven more that are likely to come up in the next year. After that…" and he shrugged. "Like I say, congregations are dying out, quite literally, and every year there are more and more buildings put out to grass."

"And how many do you think Mr. Wilson would have been interested in buying?"

—

"All of them."

"All?"

"Yes. This wasn't just going to be an instance of him offering to buy the church in which he'd been Christened. Nor, indeed, of buying those churches currently on offer. We talked of a long-term, permanently funded trust, where every church that went out of service, Archibald would buy from us to create a network of mission houses, helping the local community in whichever way was best required. If it was a poor area, and a food bank was needed, then that's what there would be. If drugs were a problem, then the same again. If the area didn't suffer from such afflictions, then it could be that the church would be transformed into a library or a community centre or a sports facility. It would have been a very noble cause. Of course, we did discuss the fact that communities often argue about what exactly it is that they need, but ultimately Archibald wouldn't have had to answer to them. He could have been the judge of what would work best. Or, as he put it, his people could be the judge."

"Did he already have the people?" asked Bain. Beginning to think that it was time for him to leave. The doctor was indeed a talker, and he himself was contributing nothing. On the plus side, he had never been into Glasgow Cathedral before, which felt something of an oversight.

"I don't believe he did," said Melville, then he looked between the two of them and made a small gesture, his hands open to the heavens. "Job 1:21, the Lord gave, and the Lord hath taken away…"

"Did you have an agreement in place?"

"Oh no."

"Nothing in writing?"

"I would be pushed to say that we even had a verbal agreement. We were in discussion. It was very exciting, and I felt sure that it would happen, but Archibald was quite clear. He was going to take his time with his money, consider all his options."

"Do you know of any other options he was considering?" asked Bain.

Melville shook his head, then turned, as a voice began to sing behind him. Pereira and Bain looked round, and for a few moments they watched as one of the young men they'd seen walking around in the blue robe sang a solo piece, his voice high, the words, in Latin, clear and precise.

The voice echoed perfectly up and around the clearstory and the high, vaulted ceiling, crisp and bright. The few moments turned into another few. *What a beautiful sound*, thought Pereira. Bain, at first distracted by it, had quickly had enough. If they were going to be just sitting here listening to someone singing, then he really did have to be getting on.

He tapped Pereira on the shoulder, leant forward.

"Need to head, boss," he said. "I'll see you back at the ranch."

"Sure," she said. "Be careful walking out. This is the kind of music people get killed to."

He smiled, nodded a goodbye at the minister, and walked quickly, and quietly down the central aisle.

"Thomas Tallis," said Melville. "*Miserere nostri.*"

"It's beautiful," she said.

"Yes."

She meant to stop listening and ask further questions, but as the singing continued she found that she could not take her attention from it. And so they listened until the song was over, and at the end she had to stop herself applauding.

They sat in silence, watching the young man as he discussed his performance with the other older man in blue.

"Rehearsing for a performance at the weekend," said Melville, then he exhaled a breath and shook his head. "Perhaps there's hope for us yet."

Pereira nodded.

"You never know, Dr. Melville, you never know. Now, I'm afraid, we come to the awkward part of the conversation."

"Yes?"

"Archie is dead, that's why we're sitting here. You won't have heard the method of his murder."

"Stabbed, I believe it said in the newspapers, his body placed…" and he let the sentence drift away, indicating the direction of the Necropolis, not far from where they were currently sitting, across the old Molendinar Burn, which had long ago been covered by Wishart Street.

"Yes. He was stabbed," said Pereira, "however, not in any conventional means. He was killed using a metal cross, the end of which had been sharpened into a slender spike."

"Good God!"

"Yes, Doctor," said Pereira, marvelling at just how old-

———

94

fashioned he sounded. "In addition, his body was deposited against a very specific headstone in the cemetery, and in his lap were placed flowers from the Judas Tree. There are very clear religious aspects to his murder."

"Well I never…" was all he managed.

She watched him closely. The first moment that you came to it, that was always the point when you could tell. Had they the slightest reason to suppose that Dr. Melville might have had something to do with Wilson's murder? None whatsoever. However, at this stage of a completely open investigation, you just had to be wary of everyone. Not necessarily suspect everyone, but wariness was called for.

"We're in the early stages of the investigation, but at the moment the only lead we have is that Archie was considering spending some of his money on the church. There's a clear tie-in with the nature of his death."

"Wait," he said, "you don't think… Wait, you think I might have had something to do with it?"

"No," said Pereira, "I don't. I'm not saying that. In fact, I'm not really saying anything. We're at the beginning, Doctor, that's all. We need to speak to everyone. We need to ask everyone questions. You don't need to get defensive."

"I wasn't getting defensive!"

"You folded your arms," said Pereira, and Melville looked down at his arms as though just realising what he'd done. He shook his head, relaxed them again.

"Believe me," she said, "I cannot begin to think how Archibald's interest in the church would have led someone to murder him. I just wanted to know if you could think of anything."

"Well, I really can't. I mean, it's quite extraordinary."

"Very well," said Pereira. "You were at the Garland on Tuesday evening."

"Yes," he said, and the arms folded again.

"Strange place to meet?"

"Not at all," he said. "It's a very respectable club. Very respectable. Some of the finest men in Glasgow attend that club."

"They let Archie in with two prostitutes."

"They were no such thing!"

Well, thought Pereira, *I'm just going to let that one go.*

"How long did you speak to Archie?"

95

"Oh, I don't know. An hour, maybe two. Time," he said, dismissing the notion, as if it were immeasurable.

"Did you just talk about the churches?"

"Yes. The churches, those that were available, those that would become available in the future, what Archibald's plans might be for them."

"Was there any hint that there might've been some outside party interested or involved?"

"With whom? It was us that was selling them. There was no one else involved."

"Archie didn't have a partner?"

"He'd become one of the richest men in Scotland! He didn't need a partner. And if there was someone, why kill the man with the money?"

"Was there someone else at your end? Someone else who might have been thinking of buying the churches, who might've thought Archie was getting in the way?"

"Really?" said Melville, his brow furrowing, a look of scorn finally coming to his face. "What do you think this is, Inspector? It's not some high stakes game. There really wasn't that much money involved, not in property terms. And no, several times no, there was no one else involved, and even if there had been, I had not mentioned to anyone else that Archibald and I were talking."

"Archie had, though," said Pereira.

He stared at her, the curious contempt still on his face, and then he turned away as the vocalist began singing again, a long, clear note suddenly filling the space of the cathedral choir.

15

To Bain, it seemed the lawyer in charge of Archibald Wilson's affairs could not have been more than twenty-five, which would have been very young to be the one tasked with the control and distribution of over one hundred million pounds. She probably wasn't quite as young as she looked.

Lucy Hilton's office, while smaller than that of Cobalt, the financial and accounts man, was similarly decorated in what Bain presumed must be this year's style. Sleek, simple, pale blues and greys, which also, as it happened, described her clothing.

They were sitting at her desk, each with a cup of tea in front of them.

"You understand, of course, that at this stage we're under no obligation to supply you with any information on Mr. Wilson's will?"

"I know," said Bain. "Ultimately, however, we both want the same thing…"

"Do we?"

Lucy Hilton did not sound like she wanted to be talking to the police.

"We both want to find Archie's killer. You can let me know details of the will, or I can go away and spend some of the time I should be devoting to finding the killer filling out paperwork, and you're going to have to show me the will anyway."

"Nice speech," she said, "but you're still not getting the information."

"Really?"

"I know what the police are like, Sergeant Bain, and you don't go giving them something for nothing. That's all."

"This isn't a *something for nothing* situation," said Bain. "This is a *common cause* kind of a thing."

He tried smiling, but Lucy Hilton did not look amused, and the smile quickly left his face.

"Sergeant, I respect your need to do your job, but at the moment we do not have need for the police."

"It's not about *need*," said Bain.

She answered with a harsh silence.

"Can you tell me if you've already contacted the executor or the executors of the will?" asked Bain, having given her a few seconds before accepting that she wasn't about to volunteer anything else.

"Yes," she replied coldly, "we've notified the executor of the will. That should hardly be a surprise, under any circumstances, never mind this particular one, when the details of the will are going to be of interest to very many people."

"And you can tell me who the executor is?"

"I can, yes, but I'm not going to."

Bain breathed deeply, trying to rein in his frustration.

"Really?" he said, unable to rein it in as much as he'd have liked. "Don't you want us to find out who killed Archie Wilson?"

"What *is* that? Are you seriously trying to make me feel guilty? *Don't you want us to find out who killed Archie Wilson?* Really? Please. Of course I want you to find who killed Mr. Wilson, but don't try to make me feel guilty just because you want to shortcut your job."

Bain was silent. Yes, she was right, he had been trying to guilt her into it. But if she was trying, in turn, to make him feel bad about it, that wasn't working either.

"When was the last time you spoke to Mr. Wilson?" he asked, tone levelling out. Get through the questions, squeeze as much information from her as he could, then get out without giving her the opportunity to lodge a complaint for harassment. Lawyers never did need much of an excuse.

"Friday."

"Last Friday?"

"Yes. Last Friday."

"His will had been completed by then?"

"Yes."

"You were still conducting legal business, though?" he asked.

98

Another pause. "I saw him privately."

That was unexpected. Bain took a moment, having not really thought they would be going there.

"A date?" he asked eventually.

"If that's what you want to call it."

"Well, you were there," he said. "Would you call it a date?"

Another slight hesitation, and then she said, "Yes, all right. Yes. It was a date."

"That's interesting," he began, and then he himself hesitated, unsure how to introduce the subject of prostitutes to the conversation.

"Is it?" she said. "It's interesting that a woman went out with a man, or that a man went out with a woman?"

"He seemed to be spending most of his evenings with prostitutes," said Bain bluntly.

"Yes."

"So, where did you fit in?"

"Maybe he just wanted to talk to someone," she said.

"Did you sleep with him?"

She replied with a dismissive face aimed across the desk.

"What did you do?" asked Bain.

"Really, Sergeant? Am I a suspect all of a sudden?"

Oh, please, thought Bain. The police did not treat everyone as a suspect; sometimes, however, it seemed that everyone treated the police like the police were treating them as a suspect.

"Archie Wilson was murdered," he said, his voice completely dry. "We're just trying to get a picture of his life in the last few weeks before that happened. Anything you can tell us, no matter how trivial or unimportant it might–"

"Yes, all right, Sergeant, I know the spiel."

An image flashed into Bain's head. Maybe it came from sitting in these high office blocks with huge windows. Perhaps they were much lower than their American cousins, but sitting inside, he thought, the effect would be the same. And didn't people in movies smash in through those windows sometimes. Action heroes and superheroes. And the image came to him of a man in black crashing through the window behind Hilton, grabbing her to whisk her away, and he could either sit here and let it happen, in which case she would be thankfully gone, or he could fight for her, and win her favour.

Oh, I'd let him take her, he thought.

"Sergeant?"

"So, what have you got, Ms. Hilton?" he asked.

"What d'you mean?"

"If you're so familiar with our practices... Let's accept that you're not a suspect, so really there's no chance of incriminating yourself. Can you just let me know if there was anything he said or did, when you were together, that might be of use to us in the investigation? Any plans, anyone who'd been in–"

"Yes," she said, cutting him off again. "Archibald was... it was very dry. What did he talk about? He said he'd been getting hundreds, thousands of begging letters, but that he wasn't looking at them. He talked about the money, the kinds of things he might do. But it was all, you know, it was largely mundane. Go and see the Taj Mahal. Book a flight into space. And he had this idea about buying his old church. Worthy, I suppose," she said, and for the first time there was a softening in her voice. "So lacking in imagination, though. With the amount of money he had, it seemed to me he could have been doing something big. He just had no idea what that was."

"He said just the one church?" asked Bain.

"I wasn't really paying attention," she answered. "Might have been more."

"And was there anything else specific? Any names, any ideas, any hint that there was unhappiness in his family, or that people were forcefully looking for money?"

"No," she said. "He knew people were circling. Families do, don't they? But he didn't talk about it, was trying to just keep himself above it all until he had some idea where he stood."

"What was he waiting for? I mean, it's not like the money hadn't cleared."

"I don't think he was waiting for anything. He was just giving himself time, because he was a bit frightened by it all. Maybe it doesn't seem like it, given the prostitutes and the drugs and the whatever else he was doing. But suddenly he was a thing, and he didn't really know what to do with that."

"Were you going to see him again?"

A beat, but he didn't think it indicated what it often could; the quickly-worked-through thought process to cover the lie.

"He asked me again for this Friday. Well, yes, he asked me for any night I was available. I didn't just say no. I said I was away all weekend, and no, I wasn't. I also told him I don't go out during the week, and yes, I do. So I deferred until this

Friday, but I probably hadn't intended going."

"Not interested in the money?" said Bain, regretting the question as soon as it had left his lips.

"I think we're done, Sergeant," she said. "I've got work to do, I presume you do too.

"Last chance," he said, getting to his feet, feeling a strange sense of relief that the interview was over, "to give me any details of the will."

"Sergeant," she said, bowing her head formally, and then she turned to her left and brought up her computer screen.

Class dismissed.

Bain smiled to himself, thinking as he left the office, that he probably would rescue her from the masked man in black crashing through the window after all, just because she wouldn't want him to.

There was a smaller outer office, with its own huge window looking directly across at another office block. Bain nodded and smiled at Hilton's personal assistant as he walked through, then he was out into the reception area, another bright room, with a view up St. Vincent Street, a water cooler, a magazine rack that Bain had noticed featuring this week's magazines, and one person sitting waiting.

Bain stopped, took a moment, then started walking on. "Mr. Wilson," he said to Archibald Wilson's father.

"Sergeant," said Wilson.

Bain stopped again, just as he was getting to the door. "How's your wife?" he asked.

Wilson looked up, face as expressionless as ever. "Not good," he said. "Thank you for asking."

There was little gratitude in the voice.

Bain nodded, opened the door to the corridor and left the office.

16

"So, we need to go back and see Mr. Wilson?" said Cooper.

They were back at the station, the first round table of the day, early afternoon.

"I guess there could have been other reasons he was there," said Bain, "but being executor of the will has to be at the top of the list, given Hilton's position."

"Right, makes sense. You all right with that?" he asked, looking at Pereira.

"Of course. I doubt we'll find him very forthcoming, but obviously yes, we'll ask."

"What else have we got?" asked Cooper, looking round the room.

"I found the murder weapon," said Sergeant Parks, and she held up a page that she'd printed off the Internet. "Well, at least, where it came from, given that we already have the weapon. We'd been thinking that it was a bespoke thing, but sadly, no, it's not that easy."

She then pushed out the sheet, a copy each for everyone around the table.

"This comes from a website named Dedicated2Pets.com. They sell metal crosses of various sizes to put in your garden when you've buried your pet. The one used to kill Archie Wilson is their smallest model."

Parks paused for a moment, letting the others read the page, not wasting words by telling them what they were looking at.

There was a picture of a cross, exactly the type that had killed Wilson. There was wording to attest to the quality of the cross and to its long-lasting, all-weather durability. It was suggested that it was the perfect memorial to use for smaller pets, such as voles, stick insects or spiders. The RRP was $29.99, but you could get it from the website for only $7.99.

"Dear God," said Cooper, breaking the short silence. "Where are these people based?"

"Wyoming," said Parks.

Cooper looked back at the cross, noticed for the first time the dollar sign rather than sterling, shook his head.

"Right," he said. "Any sign that they're available in the UK?"

"Can't find any. And this is the only place I've found them."

"You speak to them?"

She shook her head. "Too early. Seven hours behind in Wyoming," and she looked at her watch. "I'll give them a call in an hour. The chances of them happily just turning over information on customers, however... I'll speak to them first, it could be they've never sold to the UK, and they just tell us that. If not, I'll give the police guys at our embassy in Washington a call, see if they can help."

Cooper was shaking his head. "This is nuts. Who'd buy this crap?"

"Kids," said Pereira. "They love doing stuff like that. Burying their pets. Going in for some sort of proper service. Stupid we hadn't thought of this being where the cross came from, seems kind of obvious now."

"You've done this?" asked Cooper.

Pereira looked round the room, waiting to see if anyone was going to back her up, but they were all looking at her expectantly. She smiled and shrugged. "Sure. Back when Anais was young and cute. We made the cross out of lollipop sticks, though. I'm sure if she'd known there was such a thing as a pet-specific cross for the bottom of the garden..."

Cooper heard her out, waited to see if there was actually going to be anything of use – ignoring the fact that he had asked her about it in the first place – then turned back to Parks.

"Jesus," he said. "Anyway, let us know if you make any progress. Sounds too much to ask, but you never know. Bernie?" he said, turning to Tobin.

"Nada," said Tobin. "We've run everything we can on the CCTV, and nothing's come up. Vanished off the face."

"Right. And you had the wheelbarrow?"

"Even more of a non-starter than the cross, sir," said Tobin.

103

"Taken the tyre-track, the width, the groove. It doesn't precisely fit any model currently available in the stores. Been around a couple, made some calls to the manufactures. They're mostly like, what the fuck? So, can't say for definite that the guy didn't just go out and buy a new wheelbarrow, but there's nowhere to go on it. And let's face it, wheelbarrows last forever. My dad's still using the same one he had in 1960. Can't be the only one."

"OK," said Cooper, and he drummed his fingers. "So, we have Wilson leaving The Garland at just after eight and then disappearing, to be killed around midnight. Still no nearer filling in his movements within that time frame."

"The possibility is that there's just a single moment to be captured," said Pereira, "where he got into a car, or walked into a building. Thereafter he was under the control of the person who eventually killed him, and he could have been moved around the city in a boot or on the floor of the back seat."

"Yes," said Cooper, nodding. "We just need to keep looking," he added, although it was not entirely clear who was supposed to be doing that, and where they should be looking. "And beyond him being a bit dull, enjoying expensive sex, and planning to buy up unused churches from around Scotland, we've got nothing on the man himself?"

A few head shakes around the room.

"Any possible idea on how the church thing could have led to him being murdered?"

"Nothing so far," said Pereira. "Didn't really like the cut of the jib of the Church's property convener, and he got a bit chippy with me, but let's not go suggesting the Church of Scotland have anything to do with it. And anyway, they were the ones benefitting from what Wilson was doing, I can't see why they would've wanted the arrangements changed."

"Someone else wanting to buy them?" said Somerville, who had been quiet throughout the meeting.

Pereira shook her head.

"Not according to Dr. Melville anyway. And it's true, if you look at the website, some of these places have been listed for months. Two, at least, for over a year. They're empty shells with stained-glass windows. If someone had wanted them, they could have had them at any point."

"What if it was a specific building?" said Cooper. "There might have been one that had just come up for sale, or that someone has been planning to buy for a while, then along comes moneybags, and phhht, all this other guy's plans are toast."

Pereira thought it over. She had, in any case, already thought about that very point.

"Sure," she said. "It's possible. We can speak to Melville, maybe see him at his office, get details of all enquiries about the properties."

"Where did you see him today?"

"At the cathedral," she said.

"He pullsh a gun," said Parks, and Pereira smiled at the *Untouchables* reference.

"Maybe someone knows something specific about one of the churches," said Bain. "They want to own the building because they know there's a body buried in the grounds, or there's something in the building that's worth a lot of money that people don't know about, or there's a map of buried treasure hidden in a secret compartment in the vestry, something like that."

Pereira smiled, recognising a fine example of her sergeant's occasionally fantastical imagination.

"Nice, thought, Marc," said Cooper. "Nevertheless, if we take away the boys own adventure aspect of everything you just said, you might have a point. You can have that one."

Bain smiled, nodded.

"Right, what else...? How are we getting on with Wilson's tech?"

"Still nothing," said Pereira. She'd checked with Technical Support before coming in. They'd all been here before, however. These things usually took a while. "No sign of the phone, obviously he'd have had that on him. The iPad, I don't know, reckon we might just have to forget that. We're not equipped. The Acer laptop they're a little more optimistic about. Nothing yet though, so, you know..."

"OK, keep on at them, we're going to need that," said Cooper. "I'll speak to someone about the iPad, see if we can get help. What about the queer, Henderson? What happened to him?"

"You can't use that term, sir," said Pereira.

He gave her a steady, unyieldingly unimpressed stare.

"Can't I though?" he said.

"You just can't, sir," Pereira insisted. "It's not the 1970s."

"Yes, Inspector, thank you for that. Is Mr. Henderson, who likes to dress in ladies clothing, still in the cells?"

"No, we released him shortly after we spoke to him this morning. We're going to keep tabs on him, although I stopped short of deciding to have him tailed. However, we had no reason to hold him."

"Right," said Cooper. "And how are we getting on with the bags of begging letters?"

"It needs to be staffed, sir," said Pereira. "We've got them set up in Room 4, and we've each taken a turn, but there are a lot of letters."

"OK, I'll try to get another couple of bodies on it. I'll get them to speak to you, you can tell them what we're looking for. But all of you, please, try to fit in sometime today. Or, I don't know, take a bag home with you if you like. Careful with it, because you never know when you might find the thing we're looking for, and if we do, we're going to need to forensics the shit out of it. Nevertheless, it might be a less soul-destroying way to do it. Room 4 would turn anyone into a basket case."

He let out a long sigh, took one last look around the assembled company, hands laid flat on the desk.

"Anyone got anything else?" he asked, receiving a lot of blank looks and shaken heads in response. "Right, get to it."

17

Another phone call to Mr. Wilson, gruffly answered. He did not want to see Pereira again that day, but reluctantly agreed she could visit him at their house at the same time the following morning. Another phone call to Reverend Dr. Melville, and Bain too had an appointment for the following morning.

And so the afternoon went. It felt to Pereira as though they had come to the end of the initial stage of the investigation. They had thrown everything into it, spoken to as many people as they could fit into the first couple of days. Often, usually, in fact, while they may not have had the guilty person in custody by this stage of an investigation, they would certainly have an idea of where they were going.

This was one of other ones, however. No clear road ahead, and the only lead they were working on – the religious aspect of the killing – not even remotely suggesting any possible motive or potential culprit.

She needed to stand back, take a break. Despite the five hours sleep she'd managed to squeeze in before she'd been woken by Robin at five thirty, she felt quickly exhausted by the case, the better part of thirty hours concentrating on one thing. Trying to think a breakthrough into existence.

She left work at six, taking two bags of letters with her. She intended leaving them in the car until the children were in their rooms. She didn't want Anais asking if she could help look through the dead man's mail. It seemed the kind of thing that would appeal to her daughter.

Texted her mother as she was on her way out of the office, as usual, and arrived home twenty-three minutes later.

She walked in, quietly closed the door behind her. Stood for a few moments in the hall. She could hear the television in the sitting room, the sound of her mother in the kitchen.

Twenty-three minutes hadn't been long enough to decompress. Not long enough to wind down and make the adjustment. One life to the other. There was no switch to be thrown, no magic potion. It was like coming up from deep water, or entering the air lock in a space station. You needed time. And maybe your head didn't explode or your ears start bleeding, but it could be just as painful in its own, humbling, crushing, stressful way.

Her mother's face appeared at the door. The moment snapped. Pereira had managed to turn the twenty-three minutes into twenty-four. That was it for small victories.

"Dinner's ready, I'm just putting it out. Can you call the children? Anais is in her room."

Pereira answered with a nod, and then she was on her own again. Another two seconds, then she heard the quick series of thumps, the door to the sitting room opened and Robin emerged, full force, top gear, maximum volume.

"Mum! Did you catch anyone yet?"

And he threw himself at her and was in her arms.

*

Pereira sat by the fireplace, glass of white wine in her right hand. Drinking slowly. Didn't want to have another glass. Trying to remember to savour the taste of each sip. Hold it in her mouth for a little longer.

A regular evening, her mother having stayed for dinner, before leaving around nine. Anais had actually put down her phone to have a chat at bedtime, and Pereira had promised her they would go shopping together on Sunday afternoon. The case, if it was still ongoing, could wait. And Lena... if Lena called and invited Pereira to go out with her and Robin, then Lena would just have to wait too.

Ella Fitzgerald was playing. *I love Paris in the springtime...* Slow and melancholic, then major chords and uplifting. She and Lena had never been to Paris. This was safe ground. Lena hadn't even liked Ella, so that made it easier. Pereira could now listen to her when she wanted, let the warm voice roll over her in waves, sometimes mournful, sometimes joyful. And then, just when you'd forgotten it was there, a track featuring Louis Armstrong would begin, and there would be the delicious contrast in voices, and there would be the trumpet and the playfulness.

Head back, eyes closed. Trying to clear her mind. But she had nowhere to go, that was the trouble. She had no happy place, no respite, nowhere to travel to in her mind, no one to be with. The only person she wanted, didn't want her, and the fantasy was ruined. She had nothing. And so, when she wanted to concentrate on something to take her mind off the pressing duties of the moment – and there were always duties, always pressing – she failed to do so. Like now.

Two yards away from her, on the small two-man sofa, were the two bags of mail she'd brought home with her. She'd brought a knife through from the kitchen, and those envelopes wouldn't be opening themselves, the letters weren't going to be read by anyone else.

Another drink of wine, then she opened her eyes, laid the glass down, tensed slightly and acknowledged that this was it. Time to get on with it. Enough of a break, the sooner she began, the sooner she'd be in bed.

She got up, lifted one of the bags, sat down in the spot, opened the bag, tipped the contents onto the seat beside her, and lifted the first envelope.

"And please don't get sucked into reading the sob stories, for God's sake," she said quietly.

First letter.

Fuck you, Wilson, you greedy cunt. Hope you choke on your fucking money.

She paused for a moment, taking pleasure in the best that several thousand years of civilisation had to offer, then placed the letter back in the envelope and moved on.

Next up. This one was written on the notepaper of a well-known Edinburgh charity.

Dear Mr. Archibald Wilson, Congratulations on your stunning lottery win. I'm sure by now… et cetera, et cetera.

She folded it and placed it in the envelope, envelope back in the bag.

Next up.

*

She got to the end of the first bag, made a start on the second.

Put it all away, decided she'd set an earlier alarm than usual and see if she was awake enough to do some more in the morning before the school run.

She had kept out just one letter. The first two had been a fair overture of what was to come. There was the occasional letter of congratulation, though only one from someone who had obviously known Wilson, but the bulk of the correspondence was split into either the begging or the abuse category, the former marginally outweighing the latter.

The one piece of correspondence she kept separate was in a small envelope, a page from a letter-writing notepad. Glasgow and the date were written in the top right-hand corner – it had been sent two weeks previously – with a very short accompanying text.

Remember Taynuilt, you Son of Simon.

No signature.

She obviously had no idea what the reference to Taynuilt meant, but it would be worth asking around. Perhaps his father would have some idea, although she had no particular thought that he would choose to tell her, even if he knew.

It was the Son of Simon that stood out. A particular phrase. Judas had been the son of Simon, and Wilson's body had been dumped with the flowers from the Judas Tree.

Maybe it wasn't much, but it certainly made the letter feel different, and hadn't that been what she'd been looking for? There was no point in sifting out the obnoxious "*you're a retard*" letters; they weren't going to lead to anything. Archibald Wilson was unlikely to have been killed by jealousy. There would be something else.

Sometime between twelve and one she finally packed it in for the day, put the envelopes in a cupboard, closed the door over, turned out the lights, did not have to turn off the music as Ella had naturally come to an end more than an hour earlier, and walked slowly up the stairs, hoping that sleep would come as quickly as her brain was demanding it.

FRIDAY

18

First coffee of the day, the office already busy, a few moments to acclimatise to the morning and the working environment.

Robin had been classically difficult. As though he'd decided that he was going to be tired and in a bad mood in order to test his mum. And so the idea of looking through more of the letters that morning had proven completely futile, and she'd had to deal with Robin in as restrained a way as possible. This, naturally, had meant that Robin had reacted, as he often did, even more badly, so that ill-temper got close to an all-out tantrum, and there'd been a major battle just getting him into the car for the drive to school.

By the time she'd got him successfully strapped in, she was too angry to be stressed. Door closed, fists opening and closing, barely breathing, she stood for a moment.

Anais had finally emerged once the screaming had been confined to the car – much too embarrassing to be seen with a kid having that kind of meltdown – locked the door behind her, and then handed the keys over to her mum.

"All right?" she asked.

"They don't call them the Fucking Fours for nothing," said Pereira. Anais laughed, and Pereira had immediately felt guilty for swearing in conversation with her daughter, and for making a joke to one of her kids at the expense of the other.

Would that she could go five minutes in the family without doing something that gave her pause.

A deep breath, and she'd moved on, as much as she ever moved on.

She placed the bags down by the side of the desk, nodded

across at Bain.

"Hey," she said. "How'd you get on with the letters?"

"Nothing much," he said. "Kept out one that was pretty nasty, but really most of what was there was just generic resentment."

"If this drags on, I mean, if we're still nowhere in a week or two weeks, then we're actually going to have to take the time to log every one of these, cross referencing as we go."

"Yep," said Bain, nodding. "'Cross' being the operative word. Anyway, the boss is downstairs at the moment. Nothing to do with this, actually, think it's on the Eilenberg–Ganea business…"

"We're staying well out of that."

"So I thought we'd just get everyone together, talk it through, see if we've got anything that matches, or whether there's a one-off of sufficient strength to warrant further investigation."

She was nodding long before he had finished.

"Yep," she said. "Let's do it now. And grab Payne and Cleveland. They were looking at some of them too. Tell them all just to bring anything of interest."

*

The door closed, Pereira acknowledged Constable Cleveland, the last person into the room.

"Thanks for coming in. I'm not asking, or expecting you to have got through everything you were allocated. It doesn't matter anyway, as it'll be a task that'll continue for quite some time yet. There'll be more, that's for sure. So, I'll start it off. It was mostly begging letters, some filth in there too, but nothing that I didn't consider petty jealousy. I did pick out this one. Six words. *Remember Taynuilt, you Son of Simon.* That's all. Stood out for a couple of reasons, but the big red light is the name. Judas was the son of Simon, which obviously ties in here with the flowers placed in Archie's lap. Anyone get anything addressed to the Son of Simon, or any kind of reference to Taynuilt?"

A mixture of blank faces and heads shaking. Pereira nodded. Long way to go yet, still plenty of letters to be looked at. Disappointing, nevertheless.

"All right," she said. "Who's first? Marc?"

"This one's pretty focused and verging on specific, so I thought I'd keep it out, see if there are others like it. It's made easier, though, by the fact that the guy's supplied his name and address, so you know..."

A couple of the others laughed.

"*Wilson, see youse bastards with your money. Doesn't matter who you were last month, see now, you're one of them. And we're coming for you. Head on a fucking spike, my friend.* And, I should add, that the *head on a spike* line is actually written in the modern fashion with a full-stop after each word..." Another couple of laughs. "*We know where you live. We know where your parents live. We know your passwords. We know when you will die. Enjoy the fruits of your so-called triumph. You won't see us, but we'll see you.*"

Bain lifted his eyes to look around the room, then said, "*Your friend, Jack Torrance.*"

"*The Shining*," said Pereira.

"Sorry?"

"Jack Torrance was Nicholson's character in *The Shining*. Did you check the address out yet?"

"Yep, it exists, at least."

Pereira looked around the room. Constable Cleveland was nodding, and Pereira nodded at her to talk.

"I got a similar one," she said. "This was signed Travis Bickle, which was Robert De Niro's character in *Taxi Driver*," someone else saying *Taxi Driver* at the same time. "Was yours from Castlemilk, sir?"

Bain nodded.

"Dates?" asked Pereira.

"Ten days ago," said Bain.

"A week," said Cleveland.

Pereira puffed out her cheeks, shook her head. "Who puts their address if they're actually going to do it? Either the address is false, or it's just some nut wanting to attract attention to himself. He'll probably film us as we arrive and stick it on YouTube. He can get his fifteen seconds."

"We can bust his balls for wasting police time," said Parks.

"Yes, we can. Presumably he doesn't care. Constable, can you do a background on the guy, try to check him out without actually going round there. If we need to talk to him, we can, but let's try to avoid it. Anyone else?"

"I got a couple from the same Wilson family member," said

Parks. "The first one wasn't particularly remarkable, the second much more insistent. It just felt like there would be others."

"What was the name?"

"Alice. His cousin, by the sound of it."

Pereira looked at Bain, who nodded. Bain was on top of the family connections.

"Yep, Alice. I've got one of hers too, didn't keep it out though."

"Me too," said Pereira, and she looked round the room.

A *not sure* from Cleveland and Somerville, nods of affirmation from Payne and Tobin.

"Yes," said Tobin, "I singled her out too. Got three in my lot, and the last one… just had a feel to it, particularly after the others. She'd started off chatty, friendly, just writing to make contact. The tone shifts quickly through the three letters, so I presumed there'd be more."

"Read out the third one," said Pereira.

Tobin unfolded the letters he was holding, sorted them into order.

"Pretty short, by this stage. It was dated last Thursday. *Archie, what the fuck man? Is this what money does to you? Is this who you've become? What's next? Voting Tory and getting your fucking ermines for the House of Lords? Can't believe you're doing this. Life is about family, Archie, you little shit. Family! We share. We always shared. Some of that money's mine, and you'd better give it to me. You listening to me, Archie? You know what I can do. Get in touch. Give me the fucking money. Then we can move on. Alice.*"

He looked up. Payne was nodding.

"That's two days after my second letter, and a bit of a step up from that one," she said. "She was clearly getting wound up. Winding herself up."

"Not as much as she would've been if she'd known he wasn't even reading the damned things," said Pereira.

She paused to see if anyone was going to volunteer anything further, then she looked at Somerville, who was holding a letter. He shook his head at her questioning glance.

"It was a stretch," he said, "because I didn't really have anything. Nothing like those."

"Sure?"

He nodded. Sometimes those were the moments to come and bite you, but she didn't get the sense of it. Not this time.

"Right, thank you everyone, keep at it. I know we're all busy, but try and keep looking through these things as and when. If we can get to the end of today completely up-to-date, that'd be good. If you find anything else, just grab the sergeant or me and flag it up."

Pereira looked around the room, recognised that Parks had something else to say, and asked the question with her eyes.

"I got an answer out of the people at Dedicated2Pets.com," said Parks. "Such as it was, at any rate. A non-answer. They won't give out sales information."

"Would they say whether a retailer imported crosses to Scotland, or whether an individual in Scotland bought one directly from the American website?"

"I asked that specific question, and was not given an answer."

"I'm shocked," said Pereira, drily. "You spoke to the Embassy?"

"Yes. They were helpful, but not necessarily hopeful. They're on it, though. We'll just have to wait it out for the moment."

"K, thanks, Rhonda."

Another look around the room, no one with anyone else, and then with a nod, the meeting broke up.

19

Bain parked his car behind the burned-out shell of a Volkswagen Polo, then got out and stood on the street for a few moments. Taking in the day. Grey sky, a fresh breeze, no sign of rain, the temperature a few degrees higher than the previous day.

On either side of the road there were two-storey terraced homes running into the distance in blocks of four. A quick guess would have been that fifty percent of the windows were boarded up. Cars were parked randomly along the street, all old, some on bricks, the tyres removed. There were a couple of children playing around an old burner in a garden across the street, a hundred yards away a group of four youths were sitting on a wall, tossing small stones at glass bottles on the other side of the street.

In the distance he could hear the M74, but it was a low rumble, the sound of individual cars swallowed up by the day. He stood there long enough to hear the tinkle of a bottle being hit by a stone, and the restrained cheer from the group.

There was a woman sitting on a deckchair in the front yard of the house two doors from where he'd parked, and she'd watched him since he got out the car. She was wearing an orange ski jacket and skin-tight jogging bottoms which would have fitted someone half her size. There was a magazine in her lap, a cigarette in her hand.

Around her a young girl, no more than two or three, was wheeling a small pram, talking to the doll the whole time. The yard would at some point have been covered in grass, but it had worn away and not been replaced, and now it was just hard dirt.

"I'm looking for Alice," said Bain, approaching, hands in pockets.

"You the cops?"

He nodded. "Detective Sergeant Bain."

He almost didn't show his ID card, but caught himself, held it out, albeit too far away for her to be able to read it. Not that she looked, or seemed to care.

"Fuck d'you want?" she asked.

"You're Archie Wilson's cousin?" asked Bain.

She shrugged. "So? Bastard had loads of cousins. Go and speak to one of them."

"I couldn't find your last name. You a Wilson?"

"I don't have a last name. Just Alice."

"Like a Brazilian footballer?"

She smirked and rolled her eyes.

"You'd been writing to Archie," said Bain.

"No' allowed to write to my cousin?"

Bain looked down at the girl, who'd stopped pushing the pram, and stopped talking.

"You're Charlotte?" he said, and she nodded. "Maybe you could just run inside for a moment."

"But I don't want to go inside."

"Has your dolly got a name?"

"Agnes."

"That's a nice name. Has Agnes got—"

"Oh, for Christ's sake, just go inside, Charl. I'll give you a shout in a minute. He's no' staying."

The girl looked round at her mum, then back at Bain.

"Agnes is cold, I'm going to take her inside," she said.

Bain waited until she was gone, looking at Alice the whole time. She was scornfully holding his stare.

"Some of that money's mine," he said, *"and you'd better give it to me. You listening to me, Archie? You know what I can do. Get in touch. Give me the fucking money. Then we can move on."*

She was shaking her head by the time he got to the end.

"Seriously, you're here because of that? You polis must be pretty desperate."

"We have at least nine letters you wrote to Archie," said Bain.

"That all? Thought it was more."

"Getting gradually more threatening as you went along," he said. "Sounds like you were pretty keen to get your hands on some of that money."

She shook her head, and then swept her arm in a great arc, as though she was standing at a cliff top, indicating the vast expanse of country below.

"Look around, Detective. Look at this shit-tip. Look at it. This is our life. You think me and her are going anywhere any time soon? I don't want much, I really don't, but see Archie… Zero point zero one percent of what he had would've got us out of this shithole. I'm his cousin. I'm the first bird he ever shagged. That didn't seem to stand for much."

"He never got your letters."

"What?"

"Someone told him not to look at mail. No one does when they win big on the lottery. Your letters were collecting in sacks, in amongst all the others, in Archie's flat."

"Fuck me…"

"Did you try to contact him by any other means?"

"Aye. I texted. Called his mobile."

"Did he ever reply?"

He got the scornful look.

"You tell me," she said. "You're the one telling me about his letters. You must've checked the bastard's phone."

"No sign of the phone. If we found the phone…" and he let the words go.

"Aye, well, it's no' like the polis to find anything they're actually looking for, is it?"

"Had you tried to go and see him?" asked Bain, ignoring the baiting. The baiting, in fact, very quickly became something that passed invisibly into the ether.

"Couldn't be bothered."

"Really?"

"What? I've got the bairn and all this other shite."

He looked around. It was hard to tell what all the other shite actually was.

"When was the last time you saw him?"

She held his gaze for a moment, and then stared off to the side, looking resentful at the question.

"Don't know. I was about twelve, I think."

"Twelve?"

"Maybe eleven. When was the last time you saw your cousins?"

"You just said you were the first person he'd shagged."

"So I was. Haven't seen him since."

She wasn't looking at him. He kept his eye on her for a moment, and then turned away, staring up the road. Another couple of people had appeared, two young women, dressed for a summer that was still some months away.

"D'you know if he had any contact with your brother?"

"Never speak to that bastard."

"You never speak to your brother?"

"Naw."

"You shag him when you were eleven 'n' all?"

"Fuck off," she said, giving Bain a quick look, and he chided himself. Stupid. Had to be careful about everything you said to people these days. They were only ever one word away from the glib *Dirty Copper in Young Mum Incest Accusation Outrage* on the front of the Daily Record.

"Are you in touch with any other family members? Any of the other cousins?"

"I speak to my mum, if that's worth the words. No' the cousins, couldn't give a shite about them."

"So there was no concerted family effort to get Archie to divvy up the cash?"

"You joking? This family couldn't make a concerted effort to go for a shite."

The young women were approaching, eyeing up Bain as they came. He looked at them for a moment, and then stared past, away up the street. Another stone pinged off another bottle, accompanied by another low, bored cheer.

Bain lifted his head and looked up. A plane was emerging from the clouds, descending towards the airport, and that fantasy he had, of being on a plane that breaks up in mid-air, and of him being thrown from the plane and falling into the sea and somehow surviving, was back in his head.

"You just going to stand there admiring the view? Nothing else to do? Classic polis."

*

Mr. Wilson was in the back garden, kneeling down, knees on a cushion, digging at the earth, removing weeds, placing them in a pile on the grass a few feet to his left. Had grunted at Pereira when she'd arrived, was not offering to move.

His wife had let her in, offered her a cup of tea, and was now standing at the kitchen window, watching, a mug in her

119

hands.

"You going to come here every day?" said Wilson. "You want to have use of a room? You can have Archibald's, he won't be needing it."

He was digging and talking, his words disjointed as though tired out by the effort, even though it didn't seem like that much effort.

"Did you get many, or any, begging letters sent to this address? Either to Archibald, or to you, assuming that people thought you might now have money."

"Hundreds of them," he said, matter-of-factly.

"You didn't want to share that with me?"

He paused, but didn't turn. "This is me, now, sharing. Hundreds of letters."

"Did you read any of them?"

He shook his head, the look on his face unimpressed, and although she couldn't see it properly, she could feel the disdain.

"Mary did in the beginning. Insisted on it. Said it'd be rude not to. Of course, they were all nasty or desperate. Depressing. And, of course, how can you tell if the story of the four-year-old dying of cancer is true? People make these things up, she just doesn't understand that. Thinks too kindly of people. So I started hiding them from her, so she couldn't see them. I'd give her a few a day, keep her happy, but she thinks they've been tailing off."

"Doesn't she get the post some days?"

He glanced round, his eyes not quite meeting Pereira's.

"I get the post," he said.

"Do you still have the letters?"

"They're in my study. Mary knows not to go in there."

"Can you give them to me, please?"

Another pause in the digging. Another big sigh.

"Aye, whatever," he said.

"Do you also have the ones that Mary's already opened?"

"Aye, I do. Anything else? Maybe you could take the electric?"

Pereira stared at him, waiting for him to turn round. He didn't.

I'm trying to find out who killed your son, she thought, but kept the rebuke to herself. People were as they were. In this instance, she'd likely have someone telling her that he would be working his way through the stages of grief, and was indeed still at the early stages, and should therefore be given the utmost leeway. She knew though. She knew the type. He would be like this with everyone, not just the police, all the time.

"Are you the executor of your son's will?"

There was a slight movement of his head, side to side, the head shake of contempt, the small trowel speared again into the earth.

"Yes," he said.

"D'you know when it will be read?"

"Nope."

"You saw the lawyer yesterday? Ms. Hilton?"

"Aye."

"Are you aware of the contents of the will?"

Another pause. Finally he laid down the trowel, rested forward for a second, both hands on the grass, and then slowly pushed himself up, gradually getting to his feet, something that he needed to do in stages.

When he was standing up, looking her at last in the eye, he said, "Yes. I'm the executor. Of course I know the contents of the will."

"Can you help me with that, please?" she said. "We need to find out what Archibald's intentions were."

"Are you going to presume that the biggest benefactor of the will killed Archibald in order to get the money?"

She didn't immediately answer. She knew he would more than likely tell her what she needed to know, but there was always the chance, if she said the wrong thing, that he would just shut down.

"It could be the smallest benefactor," she said. "You never know. It could be the person who's not listed, but thought they might be."

"That could be anyone."

"I don't think it could be just anyone."

A moment. She waited to see if he would answer, but it was as though he needed her to ask the question again.

"I'd be very grateful if you could tell us the names of the benefactors, please," she said, playing the game.

He rubbed his hands on his old, dark blue woollen jumper. Wasn't wearing any overalls. She was reminded of two days earlier, standing at the top of the graveyard, talking to Underhill.

"Me," he said. "He left it all to me."

"Really? All of it?"

121

"Yes. The lassie said it was a quick fix, just in case anything happened. Archie could take his time, slower time she called it, to redo it, make it more detailed."

"*Just in case anything happened.*"

"Aye."

"Yet he hadn't given you any money so far, despite earning nearly seventeen thousand a day."

"What?"

She paused, reading his face, having chosen her moment to drop that piece of information.

"He never told you? He was earning seventeen thousand pounds a day from the interest on his winnings. He was staying at a suite at the Grand, living it up around town, and it was like he wasn't spending a penny." She paused, let that sink in. Perhaps there was a certain brutality about it, when they were talking about his recently deceased son, but you had to come at people from different angles. "And he let you paint your own kitchen," she added.

He squeezed his lips together, then turned away, turned his back on her. She expected him to kneel down, back to the weeding, but he stood still, staring at the wall. Or looking in the direction of the wall, at least.

"He said he'd give me the money for the kitchen, but the advisor, that man in town, the one who works with the lawyer girl, he said he should hold off until things had settled down. It was fine. I mean, it was good advice," he said, half turning his head, so that the words were now at least partially directed her way, "and I would have said it myself. But he knew his mother had been wanting a new kitchen for long enough, he was still eating in it regularly himself, after all… I just wanted… He could have spent some money on his mum, would that have been so damned hard to do? Now you say… seventeen thousand a day? We could have had three kitchens for that."

"Did you argue about it?"

Now he turned fully round. "Are you serious?"

"You painted your own kitchen to what…? Make a point? That sounds like you argued."

"Yes, Detective Inspector, we argued. I argued with my son, who's now dead. Are you happy?"

"Was that the last time you saw him?" she said, not backing off.

"Yes, it was. My son's dead and the last time we talked I

threw him out the house. He didn't even get to see the bloody mess I made of the kitchen…"

His voice was starting to break. He sucked in a breath, lowered his eyes, shook his head as if to rid himself of the oncoming tears. Pereira let him run through the emotions, let him gather himself.

"Is this what you're going to think?" he said eventually. "That I killed my son because of an argument over a new kitchen?"

"No," she said, "I don't think you killed your son."

"That's good," he said, voice beginning to toughen up again, "because I didn't. I just have to live with the guilt of the last time I saw him. You know about guilt, Detective Inspector?"

She didn't answer. There was nothing to say to that.

"No, I don't suppose you do," he said, turning and walking back towards the kitchen. "I'll get those letters."

"I need to ask you about Taynuilt," said Pereira to his back. "Did Archie ever go to Taynuilt? Did anything ever happen there?"

He stopped, but he didn't turn. A moment. She walked up alongside him and looked at his face. Staring at the ground, expression set hard.

"I'm sure lots of things have happened in Taynuilt," he said eventually. "Come on, pick up the letters, then you can take your leave. I think we've talked enough."

20

Bain was standing at a window in the offices of the Glasgow Presbytery, from which he could see, at a stretch, part of the M8, cars flashing by. He was struck by the proximity of these offices to the ones he'd visited previously when talking to the financial advisor and the lawyer, but could see no reason why that would be any more than a coincidence.

"Sergeant," said the voice behind him, as Melville entered the room, carrying with him a couple of folders. "Hasn't taken too long to put together. This folder, the green, are the details of all buildings we currently have for sale, and this, the blue, details of all enquiries, and whether they've been followed up, and to what extent. You will notice that the blue folder is rather light."

"And if I want to go and look at any particular church?"

"The details of how to get the keys are included in the paperwork. For the most part we keep the position of church officer on-going until we no longer own the building, and it will be these people you should contact if you require access. I'm afraid, if you actually want to visit, you will have quite a lot of travelling to do."

"Six are on the islands," said Bain.

"Yes, as are eight of the pending cases, or the very far north mainland. It'll be an enjoyable trip, as long as the weather isn't too horrendous on the ferry trip from Uig. I've brought back my breakfast often-times on that journey, I have to admit."

"I doubt I'll get that far," said Bain, smiling. "I'll look at the Bellahouston church for now, just to get some idea. As for the others, it depends on what we find in the blue folder, and how the investigation's coming along."

"Well, you won't find much in the blue folder, that's for

sure, but you can try."

Bain nodded, tapped his hand on top of the folders.

"I think that's us for now, Doctor. Anything else you can think of that might be of use?"

Melville looked at Bain over the top of his glasses, his polished bald head reflecting the strip light above him.

"I'm not sure there is, Sergeant," he said, "but I'll certainly let you know if anything turns up."

Bain shook his hand and was gone, closing the door behind him. Along the corridor, nodded at the man on reception, then he was down the stairs and out the front door onto Bath Street.

His car had a parking ticket. That wasn't supposed to happen. He shook his head, lifted the ticket from the wipers and got into the driver's seat.

*

Pereira sat back down at her desk. Just gone one o'clock. She'd stopped in at Pret to buy a chicken salad and a vegetable smoothie.

The vegetable smoothie tasted like penance, and she wasn't sure why it was she should have been feeling penitent at that particular moment, especially in relation to vegetables. She drank it quickly as she brought the computer screen up and zipped through the e-mails for the morning.

Regular kind of day so far, nothing that needed to divert her attention. Then she spotted the one-liner from Somerville, asking her to give him a shout when she got in, and she thought that perhaps there'd have been better ways to communicate the information.

She looked over her shoulder, but he wasn't around, so she got to her feet and walked over beside his desk, where Tobin was sitting opposite.

"Bernie, I've got a note from Col, said he had something for me."

Tobin snapped his fingers, looked over at Somerville's desk, searched around, and then saw the letter lying beside the computer monitor.

"He got one for you," he said, and pointed at it.

"Cool," said Pereira, "thanks."

She lifted the letter, and read it as she walked back to her desk. There wasn't much to read.

The sins of Taynuilt, you Son of Simon, they never went away. They never will.

Same writing as before, same paper, same pen. She read the letter, then looked up, around the room.

This felt like something, just as the first one had jumped out of the pile. That there were two such letters, meant even more.

She sat back at the desk, lifted the smoothie, drained it, screwing her face up as she got to the end, and then placed it in the bin. Took a quick glug of water, then opened up the chicken salad.

She should have pushed Wilson on the subject of Taynuilt, but the conversation had got away from her by then. Still, there would be other ways to find out, and probably more informative.

The chair across from her was pulled out, and Bain slumped down into the seat, placing a burger on the desk as he did so. The smell came across the desk to her, and she stared at the wrapped burger, a piece of lettuce halfway to her mouth.

"You're eating that?" she said. "That's just cruel."

"What have you got?"

"Chicken salad, and a vegetable smoothie."

"Dear God, what was in that?"

"Beets. Celery. Something else green."

"Beets? You mean beetroot?"

"Yes. And some other kind of beet."

"What's that? What other kind of beets are there?"

"Yellow beetroot maybe."

"You can get yellow beetroot?"

"Amazing, isn't it?" Then she said, "We've got a thing," to move the conversation on. "But, sorry, you've got the details of the churches?"

"Yep," he said. "Going to look through it now, then head over to the old church at Bellahouston to have a look."

"See if you can find the treasure map?"

He smiled. "What's the thing?"

"Col found another note, similar to mine."

She passed it across the desk, he took a quick look, then passed it back.

"Same paper, same handwriting," he observed.

"Yep. So we need to do some digging on Taynuilt. Tried asking Wilson's old man, but he wasn't talking. If we can find something, well and good, but if we need to ask him again, maybe you can go. I think he's done telling me stuff. You'll get

---

126

on better. And, it turns out, he's the sole beneficiary." Bain let out a low whistle. "He said it was a temporary measure, in case anything happened, and that Archie intended making a more detailed will in the near future."

"In case anything happened, eh?"

"Yes. Anyway, I'll see if I can find anything about Taynuilt, if there are any stories, incidents and accidents… Of course, it could be something that won't have been recorded anywhere. It could be where he dumped his girlfriend for all we know."

Bain shook his head.

"Maybe, but Archie wasn't a dumper. Archie was a cling-on-to-things-for-as-long-as-possible type of guy."

"OK, well I'll start with Taynuilt, and take it from there."

And from there, it didn't take long to find.

21

Pereira and Bain were in with Cooper, who was still on the phone, although he'd waved them in a couple of minutes earlier. She was taking the time to think through what was going to happen next. Bain, standing next to her, was staring out the window. Not concentrating, waiting for the moment when he would have to turn on his brain. Even the fantasist in him was resting. Nothing grabbed his attention. The day, or what he could see of it, passed him by.

Cooper hung up the phone, finished writing a quick note, then nodded at Pereira to go ahead.

Beside her, Bain mentally flicked the switch.

"We've been going through all the mail that was sent to Archie after he won the lottery, and it's the usual mix of jealousy, hatred, begging and desperation."

"I love the public," said Cooper.

"So, there are a few we're looking into, but there was one that really leapt out which read, *Remember Taynuilt, you Son of Simon.* That was all."

"Judas," said Cooper. Pereira nodded.

"Then we found another. *The sins of Taynuilt, you Son of Simon, they never went away. They never will.* No signature, a Glasgow postmark, but no other identifying feature."

"What happened in Taynuilt?" said Cooper. "Remind me exactly where it is," he added quickly.

"East of Oban," said Bain, "by Loch Etive, Ben Cruachan…"

"Right. Of course," and he nodded for Pereira to continue.

"When he was seventeen, Wilson went on an expedition up there with the scouts. Chief Scout award. The River Awe flows nearby, and one of their tasks was to build a raft and paddle across, then down the river. There were four of them, four boys. There was an accident and one of them drowned. It was in the papers at the time, but obviously that was eighteen years ago, and it's kind of drifted out of memory. At least for the people that weren't involved. You remember it?"

Cooper shook his head. "Can't be bothered with these human interest stories," he said. "At least, I presume that's all it was. There was no foul play suspected or found?"

"We're about to go and dig up the inquest, have a look, but there's nothing from the newspapers to suggest it was anything other than an accident."

"The Scout group he was part of," said Bain, "was attached to his local church, the church that now no longer has a congregation and which Archie was talking about buying."

Cooper nodded, as he looked between the two of them. "Hmm," he said. "Not bad. It does stand out when things come together like this. Although, to be honest, I'm not seeing the full picture, or if there even is a full picture."

"There might not be," said Pereira. "But it's worth checking out. There's something about those notes, something more intrinsically threatening than the ones that were promising to put his head on a spike."

Cooper's eyes widened. "Maybe you should be checking up on those as well."

"We're on it, sir. And we'll see where this takes us, try to speak to the other members of the Taynuilt gang."

"Now that we have their names, we should look back through the mail and see if any of them wrote to Archibald," said Bain.

Pereira and Cooper both stared at him. There was a moment of curiosity on his face, and then he nodded ruefully.

"I'll do that," he said.

"Good idea," said Pereira, "you know what you have to do." She turned back to Cooper. "And yes, it could be that someone from back then was sending those notes to Wilson, and it could be that we find the person, but of course it doesn't mean that they killed him."

Cooper nodded, and then indicated the door. Meeting over.

"OK, thanks Inspector. Bring what you've got, when you've got it."

———

129

*

The four boys had camped in a field, half a mile upriver from Loch Etive. At this point the river was some thirty yards across. They had to build a raft and demonstrate that they could traverse the river, and then paddle downstream until they reached the point where the river met the loch. There they had to beach the raft and break it up.

Archie Wilson, Glenn Armstrong, Iain Peters and Mark Randall. Three school friends, and one boy who'd been added to the expedition.

They had camped for two nights, building the raft over the weekend, and were due to be tested by an officer from their troop, James Fforbes, on the Monday afternoon, the second May bank holiday. They decided, fatefully, to try out the raft on the Sunday evening.

The raft was neither well designed nor well-built. They'd found it difficult to control. They intended just crossing the river and coming back to their campsite, not wanting to have to carry the raft back upstream. However, they never made it across to the other side, and immediately started drifting downstream, unable to paddle against the current.

They recalled laughing at the time, that they were having fun.

The river wasn't deep, but in the end, that didn't matter. They hit a number of rocks; eventually the raft began to break apart. Mark Randall, "thoroughly enjoying himself," as they reported, tried to stand up. He fell over, he cracked his head on a rock, he collapsed in the water.

The raft was instantly several yards away from him. The boys all jumped into the water. They had to struggle against the current, walking along the rocks, none of them strong enough swimmers to swim quickly upstream. They all got carried downstream. By the time they got hold of Randall, and had managed to float him to the side, he was dead.

The coroner found that he had been knocked unconscious, then drowned. The inquest found no fault on the part of the other three boys. A tragic accident had occurred. It was up to the Scout Association to carry out an inquiry into their practices to see if any adjustments should be made. However, the general finding was, in essence, that these things happen.

Life, for the three survivors, moved on, to be accompanied

by whatever guilt they chose, or were forced, to carry with them. Life for the family of Mark Randall would never be the same again.

22

Too many strands, thought Pereira. *It felt like too many strands.*
That was always going to be the issue with looking at the letters,
it was always going to open up several cans of worms. Still, it
had led them to this, and it was the kind of incident from
Wilson's past about which they needed to know, and which
Wilson's parents had, perhaps understandably, neglected to
mention.

Neither of the other men who'd been on the raft had left the
Glasgow area, so she elected to go for face-to-face visits, door-
stepping, rather than the quick phone call. They were guaranteed
in any case to get a wary reception, and they had a better chance
of making some sort of progress if they could get past the initial
suspicion.

She had dispatched Bain to see Iain Peters, while she
herself was standing at the door of a small, detached home in a
new development off the Maryhill Road. There'd been traffic
works on the way over, meaning the journey had been longer
than expected, and she was already feeling impatient.

The door was answered by a young boy, maybe nine years
old.

"Who are you?" he said.

"Is your dad in?" asked Pereira.

"Might be. Who are you?" he repeated.

"My name's Aliya Pereira," she said.

He stared at her curiously for a moment, as though making
a decision on whether to let people see his father was something
that he had to do on a regular basis.

"You look foreign but you've got a Glasgow accent," he
said.

Deep breath. Time to lose the impatience.

"That's correct," said Pereira. "My parents are from India, but I was born and brought up here."

"Oh," he said. He didn't seem to understand exactly how that worked, so he thought about it for a moment then said, "Why did your parents come to live in Glasgow? It's shite."

"You should see where they came from in India," said Pereira, with a slight smile.

Immediately she felt bad about the remark. She thought about her aunt's home, and what her aunt would think. As though the line, the aimless, harmless quip had been caught on camera, and would now quickly become a GIF and would go viral, a meme shared around her parents' homeland, and by the time she left this house, she'd already be a pariah in Mumbai, and before this absurd journey into self-reproach had reached its meteoric, and apocalyptic end, she had her mother telling her that she'd insulted her family and her country, and that she could, from now on, look for help elsewhere with her children, meaning a likely end to her police career.

The kid smirked, then said, "I'll get my dad."

And he closed the door.

She turned and looked across the street. Opposite was a tightly packed row of detached homes, identical to the one she was standing in front of. Detached, not terraced, as though there was a huge amount of difference, when there barely seemed enough room to get your wheelie bin down the side. Less likely to hear the thump of the music from next door, the late-night arguments, perhaps, but that was about it.

The door opened behind her, and she turned. Glenn Armstrong, a young face, looked fit, but already prematurely bald, any hair he had, shaved tight, no more than a couple of days previously.

"Hi," he said.

"Glenn Armstrong?"

He nodded.

"DI Pereira," she said, holding out her ID.

He studied the card. His face hardened, then he slowly lifted his gaze and looked unblinkingly at her. They stood in silence for a moment, then Pereira said, "Can I come in?"

"This about Archie?"

"Yes," she said. "You knew I was coming."

He held her gaze for a short time, and then indicated for her

---

133

to come inside.

*

The two letters were the same as the ones Wilson had received.

Remember Taynuilt, you Son of Simon.

The sins of Taynuilt, you Son of Simon, they never went away. They never will.

"When was the last time you saw Archie?"

"Years," said Armstrong, irritation in his voice. Talking about something he didn't want to talk about, to someone he didn't want to talk to. "That was us done with the Scouts. Couldn't go back. Tried a couple of times, but everyone was just so… damned… nice. I couldn't do it. Then I went to uni, Newcastle, and that was me. I was gone. Never went back. As for the others… I think Archie tried, not sure. Iain… don't know."

"You lost touch?"

"Aye. When you're bound by guilt, why would you want to keep seeing each other? We'd been tight enough beforehand, I guess."

"But not Mark?"

"He was drafted in from somewhere else. We didn't know him before that weekend."

"How'd you all get along?"

"Fine. We were wary of him at the start, usual kind of thing, but he fitted in."

"And afterwards with Mark's family, did you get any hassle from them, any blame put on the three of you?"

"None."

"There was never a private prosecution, anything like that?"

He shook his head, his brow furrowing at the suggestion, as though he'd never even considered it a possibility.

"You just had survivor's guilt?"

"Aye," he said.

"How's that been over the years?"

He looked down at the letters, then finally he got up and took a step or two away from the small sofa. The front room was as small as the outside of the house suggested it was going to be, however, and there wasn't far for him to walk. *Little chance of a Jane Austen-esque refreshing turn around the room*, thought Pereira.

"Tough for a while, then I met Jan. Jan sorted me out. Helped me learn to live with myself a bit better. Then Tyler came along. Things seemed to be OK. Won't say I've forgotten it, or forgotten Randall, but you know, getting on. Then Archie was in the news, that started bringing it back, and then these started turning up a couple of weeks ago."

He shook his head, stared out the window at the identikit homes across the street.

"Can you sit down again, please?" she said.

He turned, another sharp look of annoyance, then he reluctantly returned to the seat.

"Do you have any idea who would send the notes?" she asked.

"Must be Randall's family, or someone who knew him, at least. I mean, who else would do it?"

"Can you remember anyone being particularly upset with you at the time? A friend, maybe not someone from Mark's immediate family?"

"No."

She gave him a few moments, but there was nothing else coming. Not without a push.

"Why now?" she asked, a question at least with an obvious answer. Might as well let him give it, however, rather than supplying it to him.

"I presume they saw Archie on the TV. Maybe they thought... I don't know, must have brought it all back, and maybe they thought there was a chance they could get some money out of Archie. I mean, why not? Archie was there when their son died, why not try to get something out of him? I've been thinking about Randall since Archie was in the news, so sure as dammit they would've been. Fuck knows why they'd send the notes to me, though."

"Had you tried speaking to Archie or Iain when you got the note?"

"No way. Didn't want to think about it. Total denial."

"And you haven't contacted Iain Peters, even since Archie died?"

"Thought about that. But I mean, until you showed up, far as I knew I was the only one getting these things. I don't know Iain, I mean, really. Those guys are from a different life."

"You worried whoever did this to Archie will come after you?"

135

Armstrong face darkened further at the suggestion. "Seriously? You think the nutter who sent these notes actually killed Archie?"

"We don't know. The note-sender could just be a joker. Someone who recognised Archie's name, or saw something in a newspaper, then went and read up about the case and decided to have a laugh."

"No one's laughing."

"Someone might be, you never know. Maybe we should put an officer on the door," she said.

"The fuck?" he blurted out, then he shook his head at the vehemence of the reaction. "Sorry, but really? Police protection? You're joking, right?"

"No," she said, "and if I was absolutely sure that these notes and Archie's death were tied together, then I'd already have placed the officer on your door. But this... I just don't know. Is there anything else you can tell us about the day, anything else you can tell us about your relationship with the other boys?"

Eyes dropped. Finally he shook his head, and said, "No," the anger still in his voice.

Angry, and not entirely honest, thought Pereira.

*

Bain did not find Iain Peters quite so talkative, sitting on the grass at the back of his house beneath a grey sky, cleaning a racing bike. Wearing running shorts and a sweatshirt, he viewed Bain with suspicion as he walked round the side of the house, began to get to his feet, and then sat down again, refocusing his attention on the bike when Bain held forward his ID card.

"You know why I'm here?" asked Bain.

Peters was destined to leave gaps in between every question and answer, making sure that Bain knew who was in charge. He would answer when he saw fit, or, indeed, not at all.

"Presumably something to do with Archie," said Peters. "Which means that you lot must be pretty desperate if you're already having to look back this far in his life to try to find a suspect."

"When was the last time you saw him?" asked Bain, hands in pockets, taking the garden in as he looked around.

Large, well maintained. The work of a gardener he decided.

The woman who had answered the door to him – and who he didn't take to be Peters' wife – had said he could either take his shoes off to walk through the house, or go round the back. The cook or the housemaid, he thought. Maybe Peters used her for more personal matters when the mood took him.

"The inquest," he said, then he finally looked back at Bain. "We'd left school by then. You've actually done your research, I take it? You know which inquest I'm talking about?"

"Yes," said Bain, but he couldn't get the next question off before Peters had turned away again. The chain was off the bike, the pedal mechanism had been disassembled. *If that was me,* thought Bain, *I'd never be able to put it all back together.*

"Archie had been receiving threatening notes relating to Taynuilt," he said. "We've no idea at this stage if it's connected to his death, but of all the notes and letters and threats he received following the lottery, these seemed the most intimate and… well, threatening."

Nothing. No break in the methodical way Peters was cleaning the chain, no glance up. Ultimately, Bain realised, there was no answer coming either. Of course, he hadn't actually asked a question.

"Have you received anything like that?" he asked.

Now Peters stopped for a moment, then finally looked up.

"No," he said. "I also haven't received any begging letters or marriage proposals, before you ask."

"Any idea who might have been threatening Archie?"

Peters shrugged, and once more turned to his task. "Can't help you," he said. "There was nothing back in the day. People were upset, that kind of thing, but there was no one who blamed Archie or anything. Nothing like that."

"Did he blame himself?"

Another pause, and again, eventually, he looked up.

"Seriously? We all blamed ourselves, Sergeant Bain. But time goes on. You rationalise these things. You realise. Things just happen. Accidents just happen. There doesn't have to be a reason. There's no God, there's no bullshit. Things just happen in life, that's all. All kinds of shitty, crappy things, and Mark Randall dying was one of them. Is there a day goes by when I don't think about it? Yes, actually, damned right there is. The guilt was there for a while, but some time you just have to accept that you need to move on, or else you might as well just have died in that fucking river at the same time. If Archie was getting

137

notes from someone, it was probably just some arsehole who remembered the story from the news way back, and thought he'd take the piss."

Bain acknowledged him with a slight movement of the head, and looked away over the back garden.

"It's a nice garden," said Bain. "You have help."

"Really? Whatever… Two gardeners, two days a week. Why?"

"No reason. Just like the look of it."

Bain turned back, bringing himself back from some fledging romantic daydream, in a garden such as this, the sun shining. If the sun was ever to shine again.

"You ever have contact with the Randall family after the accident?" he asked.

"Saw them at the inquest," said Peters.

"Things were all right?"

"Yeah, fucking whoop-de-do."

"Nothing since? He had a sister, right? Slightly younger. Sometimes these strange attachments form."

Again, Peters turned a dismissive head towards Bain. "You mean like the *Incredible Journey*, some shit like that? Seriously, Sergeant? Don't you have better questions to ask? Aimed at people who might actually be able to help you?"

"You haven't had any contact with the Randall family since the inquest?" asked Bain, directly. Changed the tone of his voice. Time to wrap it up, get the definite answer from him, and then if they came across anything that contradicted him, they at least had some sort of starting point.

"No," said Peters, quickly following it with, "You know the way out."

Having wished to project the illusion of being in charge throughout, Peters was keen to exert his authority by bringing the interview to an end. Knowing where the real authority lay, Bain was quite happy to leave Peters to his own fantasy of control.

"Mr. Peters," he said. "Thanks for your help. I'll be in touch."

Peters didn't look at him until Bain was walking down the side of the house, his back turned, and almost out of sight.

23

Pereira was sitting in a small café near the Broomielaw, a window seat, with a view down to the river, the traffic somewhat obscuring the view. It'd be nice first thing on a Sunday morning, she thought. Or maybe this was where drunks came to eat breakfast and begin the slow process of sobering up.

She was waiting for Bain, to compare notes on the two remaining survivors of the Taynuilt raft tragedy, before they would go and see the one surviving member of the immediate Randall family, Mark's sister, Laura Kane. The mother and father had both died of cancer in the intervening eighteen years. The mother, three years after her son, and the father ten years, to the day, after that.

Not a lucky family, thought Pereira, and she wondered what the sister would be like. Presumably married, and perhaps she had been able to move on. Perhaps, like Glenn Armstrong, she had put the family tragedies behind her, until the name of Archie Wilson began appearing in the newspapers.

Pereira had an Americano, three sugars, no milk. Still too hot to do anything more than sip. She'd eaten a chocolate croissant, and the empty plate now sat on the table, next to the plate with the croissant she'd bought for Bain. His coffee was in the takeaway cup, the lid on.

Her phone, which was sitting on the table in front of her, started to vibrate. The ringer was turned off. Lena's name flashed up on the screen. The usual feelings of delight and depression and worry and expectation surged through Pereira at seeing the name.

When would she ever be free?

"Hey," she said, as ever feeling like it was an effort to keep her voice on the level.

"Good time?" said Lena.

Pereira automatically glanced out the window, couldn't see Bain approaching.

"Just a minute," she said.

"You're on the Archie Wilson case?" asked Lena.

Why are you asking me about work? she thought. She couldn't have normal conversation with Lena anymore. It all had to be important, it had to be pertinent to their relationship, it had to give her some sign of hope, or else it would bring a fatalistic sense of misery.

"Yes," she said. "Can't really talk about it at the moment."

"Sure," said Lena. "Look, was wondering what you were doing on Sunday?"

Pereira didn't answer. Again, the dual thoughts that always seemed to accompany her when talking to Lena, the hope and the fear, shot through her. Just for a moment she seemed to be making a small breakthrough with Anais. There'd be something there, some unexpected chink of light. They would be spending Sunday afternoon together. Maybe the chink of light could grow.

Don't ask me to do anything, Lena, she thought. *Not this week.*

Except, this week was no different from every other week. She yearned to do something with Lena. She was desperate for Lena. She was obsessed with Lena, and the only way for it to end would be for Lena to leave her life altogether, or for Lena to move back in. This middle ground was torture.

"What's up?" said Pereira, cutting off the line about spending the afternoon with Anais before it even really formed, instantly ashamed for doing so.

"Just felt like talking," said Lena. "Thought it might be a good chance. I mean, nothing like a date or anything, just, you know, kind of a neutral ground thing. We can spend the day with Robin, have pizza maybe, then take him to the park. He can run around, we can have a chat."

Pereira stared across the road, her eyes vaguely registering the vehicles that passed by, somehow listing them off in her head, as though she was talking to Robin. Red car, silver car, motorbike, white van, red car, another red car, that's a lot of red cars.

"You know, you don't have to say now," said Lena, and there it was, in Pereira's gut, the old familiar fear that she'd been given an in and perhaps had blown her chance. What would Lena read into her hesitation? Ambivalence? Jesus, don't let her think that. "Just think it over, I'll give you a call over the weekend."

"Yes," said Pereira. There were words there, something about not being sure what she would be doing work-wise, whether or not she'd be free, but she hadn't even begun to think that far ahead in the investigation. Two days away, so much was happening, so much information flying around.

"OK, Ali," said Lena, "I'll call tomorrow or Sunday morning."

Then Lena hung up before Pereira could respond, and she lowered the phone, looking at it as the name disappeared. Call over, and then there was the familiar photograph of Anais and Robin, hugging on the seafront at Largs.

Lost for a moment, she didn't notice Bain enter the café. He pulled out the seat at the table, and took a bite from the croissant more or less in one motion.

"Thanks, boss," he said. "Everything all right?"

She clicked the phone off and turned it upside down on the table. Let out a long sigh, trying not to think about the uncomfortable feeling in her stomach.

"Girlfriend trouble," she said, somehow those words actually crossing her lips. Like she had anyone else to talk to?

"Know what that's like," said Bain, although it had been a while, and really, he didn't. And certainly not from Pereira's perspective.

"Got any tips?" she asked.

He smiled, dabbing at the corners of his mouth with the napkin, taking a sip of coffee, and then removing the lid to let it cool.

"I always find that burying your head in the sand until it goes away sorts out most problems."

"Yeah, thanks for that," said Pereira. "I'll keep it in mind for future crises. How'd it go with Peters?"

"Not very communicative. Said he hadn't heard from anyone in years, hadn't received any notes, nothing of that sort. He knew soon as I got there what it'd be about, but it's not like Archie hasn't been all over the news. Definitely hiding something, though. You?"

"This guy got the notes. The same two. No other contact, though, so he said. Again, though, there was something there.

He was open enough, but still, there was a mask. Something he's not saying."

"Such as?"

"Another note, maybe. Some part of the story from Taynuilt that he doesn't want to talk about. Maybe just… maybe he has other secrets. I mean, the guy could be having an affair, he could be embezzling his work out of thousands, he could be a paedophile, any or all of the above. He sees the police turn up and he's like, oh shit, they start digging around, maybe they find out I'm sleeping with the fifteen-year-old next door, it's got nothing to do with Archie, but boom, I'm busted. What about your guy?"

"I was wondering the same thing," said Bain, "but certainly now, now that you've said your man got the notes, Peters must have got them as well. Wonder why he lied about it…"

"Hmm," said Pereira, "feels like we're starting to get somewhere with this, the only trouble being that maybe it's got absolutely nothing to do with Wilson's murder."

Bain nodded through another bite of croissant. Pereira looked past him, back out onto the Broomielaw.

Red car, yellow car…

*

They met Laura Kane further along the Clyde, sitting at a table in a small outdoor café, no more than a van with a few seats around it. Somehow, though, the van had an air of mainstream respectability, so that although it wasn't from Starbucks or Costa or Nero, it looked like it could have been.

She wondered how often people actually sat out here, on cold days in March, the dark of evening beginning to encroach.

"Thanks for meeting me here," said Kane. "Work's not really that good for this kind of thing, you know? There's a canteen 'n' that, but you'd have to get through security, and then everyone's going to know what's going on. This all right for youse?"

"Yes, of course," said Pereira. She had a bottle of still water sitting unopened in front of her. Bain had his coffee from earlier, and could see that the guy in the van had thought about saying something, then changed his mind. Kane had a giant cappuccino that would inevitably turn out to be largely froth.

"This about Archie Wilson?" said Kane. "Terrible. I mean,

after he won all that money."

"I think that when the dust settles," said Pereira, "we'll find he was killed, by one means or the other, because of the money."

"Right," said Kane. "Youse just speaking to people that knew him, because to be honest, I hadn't seen him for years. Even then, it wasn't like we all spoke to each other at Marky's inquest. I'd seen him around once, you know, at our place, just before they went away, when they were planning 'n' that, but it wasn't like I spoke to them or nothing."

"How did you feel about the boys after the accident?" asked Bain. "How did your parents feel? Did anyone blame them?"

She took a drink, her face momentarily obscured by the huge cup, then she placed it back on the table, her head shaking.

"I mean, Mum and Dad were greetin' half the time, arguing the other half, but it was like they were mad at each other, you know? They were like that, giving it loads some days. But that's what happens. People get traumatised, don't they? React in different ways. Wait, what does this have to do with Archie? Are you... wait, what? Are you... like, what are you saying?"

"Someone was sending Archie notes in the past couple of weeks," said Pereira. "Threatening notes, after he'd won all the money. Mentioning Taynuilt, saying it wasn't over."

She took this in, her eyes never leaving Pereira's as she spoke, then finally said, "So? You think I was sending weird, threatening shit to Archie?"

"No one's saying anything of the sort," said Pereira, her voice almost teacher-like in its disapproval, "but someone somewhere was invoking what happened at Taynuilt and using it to threaten Archie. It makes sense that it's someone with a vested interested."

"So, given that my mum and dad are dead, youse think I killed him?"

"No, Mrs. Kane," said Pereira, "we don't. It might be that the person who was sending the notes... in fact, not might, more likely probably, the person sending the notes had nothing to do with it. We're just trying to establish who that was, so we can get it out the way and move on to the next thing."

"I'm not married," said Kane, having waited for Pereira to finish before speaking.

"Sorry," said Pereira. "Where'd the name change come from?"

"After dad died..." she said, shaking her head. "I was just

like, this family is cursed, man. I'm like that, I'm changing my name. I mean, I know it doesn't make any sense, like, at all, but here I am, outlived any of them by seven years so far, still going strong."

"Kane?" asked Bain.

"Aye. Took it from Solomon Kane. Used to love those comic books, man. Still do. The movie was crap though. I don't usually fess up to where I got the name from, but since you two are Feds, youse would probably arrest me for lying under oath."

"Presumably you weren't just a family of four," said Pereira, trying to regain the conversation, cutting Bain off from pointing out that no one was currently under oath. "There must've been grans and uncles and cousins. Or other friends at school perhaps. There must have been someone else affected by Mark's death."

Kane looked at Pereira, as though she almost felt sorry for her in her delusion, then shook her head.

"If I think of anyone I'll let you know. Wee Marky was nice, but he was kind of a dweeb. I mean, why'd you think he had to hook up with a bunch of guys he didn't know to do his Chief Scout? None of his so-called mates wanted to do it with him. As for family…" and she shrugged. "Dad was a single child, mum was a single child. Used to say that that was why they got along so well. Huh! They stopped that shite after Marky died, stopped getting on so well. I'll think about it, see if I can think of any other bastard. You got a card or something, I'll give youse a call?"

Bain took the card from his pocket, passed it over. She lifted and pocketed it without looking at it.

"Someone was sending those notes, Ms. Kane," said Pereira. "Someone was minded enough about Archie, once he was in the news, to take the time. If you can think of anyone–"

"Maybe it was Wee Marky himself."

"Sorry?"

Kane lifted her hands, waggled her fingers a little. "Maybe it's Marky. He's come back to wreak vengeance."

"You think?" said Bain.

Pereira would have preferred if he hadn't said anything. It'd only encourage her.

"Why not? Maybe while the rest of them were just a bunch of regular losers for the remainder of their lives, Marky was up there, where he belonged, hanging out with all the other boring-as-shite angels. But when he saw Archie make all his cash, he thought, sod that for a game of soldiers, time to get me some revenge."

We're done here, thought Pereira.

"Was he religious? Mark?" asked Bain.

Kane rolled her eyes. "God, aye. Religious AF. I mean, you don't see it often anymore, do you? We all go to Sunday school, then by the time you hit, I don't five or something, you're just like, this is a load of shite. That's what everyone's like now. But Marky was different, I'll give him that. He loved all that shite, pure into it, by the way. Went to church every week, sang in the choir, helped out at Sunday school."

"We've read the obits," said Pereira. "I don't remember any of that."

"None of us talked to the press about him," said Kane. "Mum, Dad, they hated all that stuff. They refused to do the press conference, refused to release any pictures. They thought it maudlin the way every time some kid dies, the next day they're all over the newspapers. Didn't want any part of it. So what you got in the papers with Marky was just bullshit they'd picked up from people who'd spent the previous five years ignoring him in secondary."

"Was he intending studying theology, was he–"

"God, aye, he was all over it. He was already writing a book about, I don't know, some disciple or other. The, what d'you call it, the bastard one. Judas. Seriously, who writes a book about Judas when they're seventeen?"

She rolled her eyes.

"Any chance the book still exists?" asked Bain.

"Binned it," she said, matter-of-factly. "My dad kept lots of Marky's stuff, but really, by the time it came to it, I was just like that, whatever, man... Who are we keeping it for exactly? Mum's dead, dad's dead, and I'm never going to look at it again."

"Did you actually bin it, or did you give it away to someone?" asked Pereira.

"Stuck it in a skip. There was a guy down the road getting his kitchen done. Bastard never knew anything about it. Job done."

She smiled, looked between the two of them.

"Youse got anything else youse want to know about?"

145

*

"What d'you make of that?" said Bain, as they walked back to where they'd parked their cars.

There was a small cargo vessel, tarpaulin draped across the bulk on its deck, moving past them on the river, upstream, looking like something from a different age. They both glanced in its direction. Pereira barely saw it. Bain wondered where it was going, what it could possibly be carrying in this modern day. Immediately he wondered if it had somehow found itself caught in some strange hole in space/time, and a few seconds earlier had been puttering up the Clyde in 1903.

"It's interesting," she said. "I think we need to find out some more about Mark Randall."

"Wait," said Bain. "You don't really think he's coming back from the dead, ma'am?"

Pereira stopped for a moment, looking at him, making Bain stop to look back, to take the silent rebuke. They continued walking.

"I think that someone from that time, from back then, who knew Mark, who knew his fascination with religion, is now invoking that, and killed Archibald Wilson. Seems to me the mention of Judas is the clincher, given that those details still haven't appeared in the press. If they had, I'd have thought she was just pulling our chain. Under these circumstances, however…"

"So, we're officially ruling out revenge from the dead?" said Bain.

"Yes, Sergeant."

"Pity."

"No," said Pereira, "it's not."

24

Friday evening, final wrap-up of the day. The where they were of it, and the what there was to do next. Issues had been raised and talked through, raised and discarded, raised and parked. Cooper had tapped on the desk throughout.

They had talked it all through, and were coming to the conclusion that they seemed, at least, to be nowhere nearer finding any answers than they'd been that morning.

Wilson's laptop had finally been cracked, but to no great end. It seemed his lack of imagination even extended to the Internet. Searches for sport and news and sex, coupled with extensive viewing of churches for sale in Scotland. "A fine combination," Cooper had said. "Porn and the church. Can't beat it."

It also looked like he'd taken to ignoring his e-mail account, as there were over fifteen thousand e-mails waiting for him, and not all from the previous three days. It was the not-unexpected collection of begging and desperation and marriage proposals. There were the occasional good wishes thrown in, but they were meagre and rare. It was no wonder Wilson had stopped looking.

"So, at the moment, we have nothing concrete on why he was killed," said Cooper. "We have no motive, we have nothing on where he was killed. We have no suspects. Have I missed anything that we don't have?"

"Plenty," said Pereira, although she didn't want to rise to the bait, if indeed he was intending to bait her.

"We're clinging on to this Taynuilt business?"

"I believe it's more than clinging on," said Pereira. "In general, lottery winners aren't murdered. It doesn't happen.

People are killed for all sorts of reasons, but it's almost impossible to find any of those here, in this case. He was a pretty boring guy. Didn't have that much to do with people, didn't seem to be all that interested in things. Anything, really. He was existing, and not much more than that. In his whole life, it's like there's one incident that sparks interest, that stands out. And someone else knew that too, and that someone else definitely seemed interested." She paused, glanced at Bain, then turned back to the boss. "This is it, sir, somehow this story is going to lead us to Archie Wilson's killer."

"And what about Henderson?" asked Cooper. "I preferred him. Just because he's a flagrant abuser of the politically correct bullshit, doesn't mean that he wouldn't also commit murder. The having something-else-to-hide story, would also work if he'd *previously planted* the something-else-to-hide story."

A couple of brows furrowed in the room as people thought about what the previous sentence had actually meant.

"It's not Henderson, sir," said Pereira.

"Why?"

With neither an alibi nor a witness, Pereira was going to struggle to explain her total belief in Henderson's innocence. The fact that she just felt his innocence, wasn't really going to cut it. The only way to completely prove he had nothing to do with it would be to apprehend the real perpetrator.

"I see you're distinctly quiet on that," said Cooper. "Marc, could you write me up everything you have on Henderson, and get me a transcript of the interview you two conducted with him? I'll take a look, decide if we're going to take any further action. Tomorrow morning's fine, but I'll need it first thing."

"Boss," said Bain. He nodded, didn't look at Pereira.

Cooper let out a long breath, cheeks puffed out, slowly deflating.

"All right, Inspector," he said, "I'll give you another day on this. Let's see if you get anywhere, but if it's really a wild goose chase, then it's madness for you to spend so much time on it."

"I agree," said Pereira. "I'll try to get something definite for you by COP tomorrow."

"Yes," said Cooper, "you will."

*

That evening she took a long drive home. Usual situation, her mum at home making dinner for the kids, with the high likelihood of choosing to stay behind to eat with them.

She'd miss her when she was gone – indeed, she couldn't count the ways in which she'd miss her – but sometimes she wished it was just the three of them. And when thinking about Anais, it was one time when she didn't include Lena in her dream of what her life could be like. Anais and Lena had been warring factions more or less from the first day. And never, in all those years, had she been able to blame Anais.

Anais had lost her father over her mother's affair with Lena, and then had had to learn to share the family with, as she called him, *the lesbian bastard love child.*

Pereira drove around, Ella on loud, singing along occasionally, when the mood took her, the CD drowning out her own unmusical voice.

Manhattan… Let's Fall in Love… These Foolish Things… Georgia on My Mind…

Songs came and went, lines and phrases drifted in and out of her head. She sang, she hummed, she listened. When she was about twenty minutes away from home she called her mum. It took thirty-five minutes to get back from there, as she hit traffic on the Aitkenhead Road.

Parked in the driveway at just after seven thirty. Took another few moments. Let the final bars of *Summertime* wend their way woozily off stage, then she clicked the CD player off and got out of the car.

Darkness coming. Dank evening. Stood for a moment, and then, as she turned, the door opened and Anais stormed out. She stared at her mum for a short while, and then said, "Robin's being an asshole," quickly followed by, "and Nanni's enabling him."

Pereira walked forward, reached out and took Anais into her arms. She hadn't known where that had come from. When was the last time she'd hugged her daughter about anything? When was the last time Anais would have wanted to be hugged?

She took it for a few moments, and then pulled back.

"This about the TV?" asked Pereira.

"Check the big brain on Brett," said Anais, and Pereira determinedly rolled her eyes in good humour at the *Pulp Fiction* quote.

"Didn't you mean Brad?" she said.

"Well that depends how pedantic you want to be," said

Anais, and from the slight softening of the voice Pereira wondered if they'd dodged a bullet. Long enough to get in the door, long enough for her mother to put dinner on the table.

"Let's say I want to be very pedantic?"

"The character's name is definitely Brett," said Anais. "Like, definitely. However, Jules sounds like he says Brad, hence the confusion. But if you listen closely, it just *sounds* like he says Brad. He's actually saying Brett, but in a funny, kind of long drawn out way. And anyway, even if he does say Brad, it's just a mistake, and he really should say Brett."

They were in the door, Pereira hanging up her coat. From the kitchen she could hear the tap-tap-tap of a ladle dishing food onto a plate.

"But if he actually says Brad, regardless of whether or not it's a mistake, surely you should say Brad when you're quoting him?"

"No."

"If Orlando Bloom had made a mistake and inadvertently said, *The stars are veiled. Something stirs in the East. A sleepless phallus*, rather than malice," she said, and Anais giggled and hit her mum on the arm, "that'd be the quote. There'd be no point in quoting what was *supposed* to be in the script, would there?"

Into the kitchen, dinner on the table. She smiled at her mum, who returned the smile with the usual look that was a mixture of pity and despair and worry.

"Can you get your brother, please?" asked Pereira.

"Robin!" shouted Anais, as she sat down at the table.

*

Later that evening, kids in bed, Robin asleep, Anais playing a game on her phone. That's what Pereira assumed. That she was playing a game. Maybe, as soon as her mother's back was turned, she was watching porn, or worse, she was chatting to some fifty-seven-year-old guy called Maurice in East Kilbride who was pretending to be a fourteen-year-old girl called Mindy from San Francisco.

She stood in the middle of the sitting room. Silence. The evening had been about as good as it got in the house, but as usual she still arrived at the end of it tired and stressed. An evening when she didn't get to the end and immediately pour herself a glass of wine would be a minor success, but this evening hadn't been it.

She placed the wine on the coaster beside the sofa and looked down at the bag of letters. These were the remaining ones she'd received from Wilson's father, and which the rest of the team hadn't managed to look through yet. A couple of the others had taken home the latest batch that had arrived at the flat shared by Wilson and Henderson. Archie's death didn't seem to have curtailed the flow.

Some days she would allow herself to listen to different music, but tonight wasn't going to be one of them either. She just needed conformity. The familiar sound, the familiar taste on her lips. An hour of looking through letters, and then she could go to bed. And, if it all went to plan, she could delay putting off thinking about Lena until she was lying in the dark and exhausted, and then hopefully she wouldn't think about her for very long before she fell asleep.

She inserted the CD of Ella singing The Cole Porter Songbook, side one. *All Through The Night* started, for a moment she found herself standing still, letting the music wrap its arms around her, could almost imagine that she was dancing in Lena's arms, and then, as the refrain began, she forced herself from the moment, snapped from it, and she was sitting down, taking a drink of wine, and opening up the bag of quiet desperation that held the begging letters that Wilson would never read.

25

Peters had a secret. It was no big deal. No dark secret. Not the kind of secret that would get someone killed. Not even the kind of secret he would have been terribly concerned about people finding out. He just wasn't telling anyone, that was all.

Those who knew him thought he made his money in some sort of online business racket. He was always suitably vague, mentioned stocks and renewables and trading. If he came across someone who might have some idea what he was talking about, he would simply clam up.

It wouldn't have been too difficult for him to spend some time constructing a more rounded story, but he never saw the point. It would have been like learning a few sentences of a foreign language. He might be able to bamboozle people into thinking he was fluent, but an actual speaker of the language would find him out in seconds. Better just not to talk at all, and if anyone thought him rude – as many had – he didn't have to care.

He made his money writing a moderately successful series of pornographic books on Amazon Kindle, under the name J T Conroy. He'd thought of the idea early, right as Kindle was starting to take off, and made a name for himself. Or herself, depending on what you thought of J T Conroy.

Thirty thousand words a book. He would write one in a week, spend the next week editing and proofreading, selecting an image for the cover from available online material, do a final check and then upload it onto the system. Then he would take a week or two off, then go through the process again. In this way, he would churn out twelve to fifteen titles a year, all aimed at the American market. The big one. The one where the real money was.

J T Conroy was now closing in on his/her hundredth title. None of them had been a huge hit. None of them had ever broken into the top one hundred. Indeed, only a couple had even ever entered the top thousand. Nevertheless, with steady sales across the board of so many titles, Peters was taking in five to six hundred pounds a day, and the underlying trend for profit continued to rise.

He was a humourless man, but on occasion even he could see the funny side of it.

No wife, no kids, no responsibilities, mortgage would soon be paid off. Life was all right for Iain Peters. He remembered Archie, of course, he'd always remember Archie, but Archie winning money had meant nothing to him. He'd seen it on the news, then forgotten about it by the next day.

However, when the first note had arrived, the same note received by Archie and Glenn Armstrong, Peters knew straight away. This was because of Archie. It was Archie's fault. Whoever had sent it could have happily existed all their life, with the memory of Taynuilt buried. But Archie was in the news, Archie was rich and Archie was happy, and now someone didn't like it.

And Peters had no idea who that might be.

*

The doorbell rang. Peters' eyes opened; he stared straight ahead.

He'd fallen asleep on the sofa. That wasn't like him, but he'd been for a long bike ride, then there'd been the two beers with dinner. Should have gone to bed when he first thought of it.

Did the doorbell actually ring, he wondered? Or maybe it rang in his dream. That happens sometimes. Perhaps that's all it was. What had he been dreaming about?

There was nothing there. Whatever it was, whatever the narrative had been that was playing out in his head, it had ended abruptly, the minute he'd woken.

It felt late, although it had been dark already when he'd fallen asleep. No lights on in the house.

He closed his eyes again, thinking about the time. Gone eleven. Maybe almost midnight. Had another two days off. Had set himself a target of starting the new book on Monday. That was the plan, even though he had absolutely no idea what it was

---

going to be about. Usually he had something, some theme or some vague storyline around which to hang the erotica. At the moment he had nothing.

Maybe he'd watch some porn over the weekend. That was his usual inspiration. One day the idea for the great erotic novel of our times would come to him. One day. When the mortgage was paid, and there was a new car, and he had everything he needed and money in the bank, he could let the payments from the old titles pour in, and he would take the time to write the ultimate erotica of the age. The one the publishers would actually want to read.

He wouldn't even have to tell anyone he'd been J T Conroy all these years. They would just be amazed at the talent on display for a debut novel.

That year, when it came to needing inspiration, he would watch genuinely erotic cinema. French classics. Old movies, from a time when they could conjure up the power and passion of sex without the need to fill the screen with–

There was a knock at the back door.

It came then. Fleetingly, but it was there. The fear. It came, then it went away again, just as quickly. He was living in Hyndland, for goodness sake. He had nothing to be scared about.

Burglars didn't knock. Killers didn't ring the doorbell.

He finally got up and looked into the kitchen. From where he was standing, he could see through to the window that looked out on to the back garden. Complete darkness.

There was a wooden back door from the kitchen, out into a smaller glass porch. He usually left the door to the porch unlocked. In fact, not unknown for him to leave the kitchen door unlocked too.

Wait.

Had he locked it tonight? He hadn't locked it, he was sure. Usually it was on his list of things to check as he went to bed, and usually that was the point when he actually locked it.

Then the fear came back, and this time it wasn't so fleeting.

Someone had killed Archie. Someone had sent threatening notes to Archie, and then killed him. He'd also received threatening notes. Now it was late at night and someone was trying to get in. The doorbell had been rung, the back door had been knocked. And the back door was unlocked.

He swallowed. He stood in the darkness, the fear creeping, crawling over his body.

He should look behind him, but suddenly he didn't want to turn. If he didn't turn, he wouldn't know. He could walk up the stairs, quickly, then lock himself in the bathroom. Didn't have to look over his shoulder. Emerge when daylight had come. Hope the place was safe, and if it wasn't, if it had been burgled, then he'd call the insurance. Say he had slept through it.

A noise in the kitchen. Was that a noise in the kitchen?

He stopped breathing, stopped all movement, all sound. There was nothing. How could there be a noise in the kitchen? Someone had knocked the door, the wooden back door to the kitchen, but they hadn't opened it.

A quick breath which caught in his throat, he turned, looked over his shoulder. The dark room stared back at him. Swivelled quickly again, back to the kitchen. Nothing. Just the darkness.

A few paces forward. Lights, he should turn the lights on, although that would allow the person outside to see him inside. Shouldn't he just walk around in the dark, try to take charge? How would they know where he was, any more than he would know where they were?

Control the fear, dammit, he thought. Like, whatshername. What was it he'd called her. Jade. That was it. When Jade was scared of the guy who broke into her house, and then she'd turned the tables.

He needed to be the guy who turned the tables. Deep breath. Pause. Walk into the kitchen, quietly pull the bolt on the wooden door. That's all that was needed. Close the curtains. Lights on. Take stock of the situation.

He was telling himself all this. It wasn't working.

Into the kitchen, eyes everywhere, and now making constant quick looks over his shoulder. Hurried breaths. Waiting for the movement outside the window. Someone had knocked the door, they were out there. Even if it was one of the neighbours, even if it was completely harmless, they would still be out there, the body would still pass in the dark by the window. He had to be ready for the shock of it, the inevitable jump scare.

All the way to the back door, footfalls silent on the stone floor. Trying to breathe. Trying to be aware of everything around him. Trying to feel the person on the other side of the door. Trying to see in the dark.

He lifted his hand to the deadbolt. And then, as his fingers lightly touched it, he realised what was odd in the kitchen. The light from the digital clock on the microwave. The green glow. The colour of the kitchen at night. It wasn't there. Neither was the small red light on the cooker. Neither was the comforting hum of the fridge.

Someone had turned off the electricity.

He threw the bolt now, the sound suddenly loud in the dark. He whirled round, pressing his back against the door, to face the kitchen. The dark shape moved in the night.

SATURDAY

26

Pereira was awoken at five thirty, phone ringing. She'd been somewhere in a dream, although, as ever, it was somewhere she couldn't place. Somewhere she didn't remember ever having been before. Her and Martin. That was odd. She didn't think of Martin very often, because when she did, she felt guilty, and she usually ended up thinking of Martin's parents, who hadn't liked her from the start. It had been racism, that was all. Pure and simple racism, which Martin had denied for a while, but had ended up having to concede. And then, of course, in the end she'd given them a damned good reason not to like her.

In the dream she'd been at one of his poetry readings, but he wasn't actually reading poetry. He was standing on stage, lecturing people on car insurance. That old job of his, the one his parents had treasured him having. The good, solid office job.

Back then, he'd been living his parents' dream. Wife, kids, white collar, office manager, three-bedroomed house in Shawlands. *Almost* living their dream. If Pereira hadn't had a job, and if she'd changed her name to his, and if she hadn't been Indian… But when they talked about their son, and told glowing tales of their granddaughter, they didn't have to mention the wife, other than that she existed, and they accepted that for the most part they wouldn't show photographs of Anais unless they were prepared to discuss Pereira's ethnicity.

"Yes," she said into the phone.

Cooper. Cooper at five thirty in the morning. She knew that he rose early, did an hour's prep – reading the news, checking on overnight police reports, planning for the day ahead – before getting ready, eating breakfast and arriving at the office by seven

---

157

thirty. Same routine for twenty years. It worked. Still, it was extremely rare for him to call any of his staff during that first, early morning hour of the day.

"You need to look at the front page of the Sun," he said.

Pereira felt like she'd bolted awake, but wasn't quite thinking straight enough to have a conversation.

"We'll talk about it when you get in," he added, when she hadn't said anything, then he hung up.

She slumped back down onto the pillow, and then lifted the phone. Safari… Google… Scottish Sun… And there it was.

Ghost of Tragic Raft Victim in Lottery Murder Revenge Horror.

She let out a long sigh. Her head seemed to slump even further back, even though it was already on the pillow.

"Crap," she said, voice low.

*

She never made it into the office. Not as early as she was hoping for anyway. Called her mum, got her round an hour earlier than had been planned, huffing and puffing, and she was off out the door before Anais had even got out of bed, kissing Robin on the head as she went. And then the phone rang again, and five minutes away from Riverside, she had to change course and head back into the centre of town.

*

The morning was fresh and dull, a hint of rain. It seemed that the usual troughs and peaks, the zig and zag of Scottish weather, had vanished for a while. The last few days had been unrelentingly grey and dark, the only variance the amount of rain falling at any one time.

Pereira walked across the Bridge of Sighs to the gate of the Necropolis, guarded by a local constable she did not recognise, arriving at almost the same time as Bain.

"Timing," said Bain, as they began to walk up the path together.

"You see the front of the Sun?" she asked.

Bain smiled and nodded. "Pretty funny."

"Yeah, hilarious," said Pereira. "You can deal with the boss when you see him, then."

158

"He knows about it?"

"He called me to let me know. At five thirty."

"Ouch."

"Yeah. Ouch. Any idea on the unnamed police quotes?"

"Made them up, I presume," said Bain. "It was only you and I who spoke to Laura Kane. Unless she just happens to have a friend in the force."

"Even so, they wouldn't know specifics about the investigation into Archie's death."

"There *were* no actual specifics in the report, nothing that hadn't been mentioned before, or wasn't a complete and obvious lie."

"Good point. You're right. They made it all up. Still, we're about to get some sort of answer."

Bain nodded. "Either this latest victim is one of the two men we spoke to yesterday, in which case, Wee Marky's ghost is going balls out, or else it's someone completely different and we've spent the last couple of days playing in the wrong ballpark."

She nodded, then took the note from her back pocket.

"Found this last night, looking through the mail that had been sent to Wilson's home."

Bain took the note from the envelope, unfolded it.

When you lie in bed, can you hear the cries for help? Can you hear yourself laughing? The past is closing in, you Son of Simon. The future is disappearing. The time to forgive and the time to forget are no more.

"Hmm," said Bain. "*Can you hear yourself laughing?*"

Then he handed the note back to Pereira, after he'd read it silently one more time, his lips moving with the words. She placed it in the envelope and returned it to her back pocket.

They walked on up the hill, across the top, past John Knox, on towards William Craven's grave, which was still guarded by a single police officer. They knew where they were heading in the graveyard, but even now they could still not see the group of officers and Scenes of Crime Officers, far down the hill, that would be circled around the latest headstone.

"You go on," said Pereira, and Bain nodded, walking on along the pathway, then she turned back to speak to the duty constable by the headstone that'd been the resting place of Archie Wilson's corpse.

"Constable," she said.

"Ma'am," he said, nodding.

"You were here through the night?"

He nodded. She could tell he was already on the defensive, but then he'd probably already had to answer some questions. Despite the size of the cemetery, and the ease with which someone could have staged another body, it was always going to look bad for the officer on duty. There would be no shortage of newspapers happy to make this look bad for him.

She watched him for a moment, then turned and looked down the hill. Sure enough, the view was obscured by the headstones, and the angle of the hill at this point didn't let you see right down to its base in any case, and that was not to mention the trees, thick at the foot of the hill, despite the lack of leaves.

"Were you asleep?" she asked.

"No, ma'am."

She was still looking down the hill. Nothing to see from here.

"You didn't find the body?"

"No, ma'am, that was the groundsman."

"Mr. Underhill?"

"Yes, ma'am."

She wasn't looking forward to talking to him again.

"He told you, and you called it in?"

"Yes, ma'am."

"I know you don't have sight of it from up here, but this still doesn't look good for you, Constable," she said.

"No, ma'am," he said.

She was forcing the conversation, but she still hated it when she talked to these young constables and the relationship seemed like teacher and pupil.

"You really weren't asleep?"

"No, ma'am."

Finally she turned back to him. "Well, it was dark and it's out of your line of sight, and you're here to make sure this specific site isn't disturbed. There's no reason why you should have seen anything. If you get pushed on it by anyone else, don't try to justify yourself, don't get defensive. You'll be all right."

He held her gaze, unsure how to respond.

"Yes, ma'am," he said finally, uncertainly.

"Not noticing might just have saved your life," she said, and then with a final nod, she was off, heading down the hill.

Did she want this to be Armstrong or Peters? Armstrong, with his regular life, and his kid, and his tiny suburban family home, angry at the intrusion. Or Peters, arrogant and defensive in the face of the police. Did it matter who was dead? Someone was dead, someone would be leaving behind a family. Parents and siblings and partners and children. But did she want it at least to be one of these two men, so that Cooper would have nothing to say when they got in? Her hunch to chase the Taynuilt background story would be proved correct.

Cooper might still be angry about the story of the ghost of Mark Randall, but that story would just have become real. At least, the revenge aspect of it, if not the supernatural part.

She walked to the edge of the escarpment, looking down into the lower half of the graveyard. From here she could see the expected small crowd of law enforcement officers, far away it seemed, amongst the trees.

She watched the scene for a while, could see Bain down below, still short of the crowd, walking towards them, and then she turned to her right and found the steep flight of stairs leading down from the upper level.

*

A few people nodded at her arrival, and then she was standing beside Bain, looking down at the body of a man she did not recognise. He had been bound to the headstone the same way as Wilson, blood weeping from his eyes, and again, a small cross – intended to be a heartfelt remembrance of some child's first pet – imbedded in his head.

As before, held in his hands that had been placed in his lap, was a small branch from the Judas Tree, the pink flowers moving slightly in the gentle breeze.

Corkin and Gayle, standing on the other side of the body, nodded at her arrival.

"Good news and bad news," said Bain. "The good news is that this is Iain Peters, so you know… we know now that we've at least been moving in the right direction. Archie was very probably killed because of the events at Taynuilt, not because of his lottery winnings."

"And the bad news?" she said, aware almost as she said it that she was bizarrely playing the role of comedy straight man.

Bain moved his foot forward, and slowly nudged Peters'

inert right leg.

"He's dead," he said.

Corkin and Gayle both laughed.

"Try not to touch the corpse, Sergeant," said Gayle, and then he laughed loudly at his own line, even though no one was sure why exactly it had been funny.

27

Bain had gone back to the station; Pereira was back where she'd been the day before, the front room of a small family home. This time Armstrong was accompanied by his wife, holding her hand, squeezing her hand. The son was playing outside on the street with a small band of children. A scene, Pereira had thought, from the streets of fifty years ago.

She had watched them for a while, feeling uneasy that this innocent game playing out before her was about to be guarded over by the two constables she had brought with her.

"All right, Mr. Armstrong, we're going to start with everything you didn't tell me yesterday."

"Just wait a minute," said the wife. Pereira let her eyes move slowly to the side. It was usually better when the partner wasn't there. And when they were, it was always better when they kept their mouth shut.

"Saying he lied. Typical police, eh? Two people've been murdered, Glenn might be next and–"

"It's all right," said Armstrong, his eyes lowered, looking at neither of the women. *Wishing he was somewhere else*, thought Pereira. *Or, at least, that he was with someone else.*

"Is it though?"

"Yes," he said, a resigned stiffness to his voice. *Resentment*, thought Pereira. "She's right. I didn't tell her everything."

"What?"

"There was another note?" said Pereira, and he nodded. He removed it from his front pocket, passing it over. Pereira glanced at the note, confirmed it was the same as the one she'd read in the night, and laid it down on the table.

163

Hands detached, Mrs. Armstrong leaned over and lifted the note, then quickly turned to him, the questions in her eyes, the creasing of her brow.

"What does that even mean?" she asked.

He took a deep breath, didn't answer.

For once, thought Pereira, *the partner has actually asked a pertinent question.*

"Glenn," said Pereira, "that's what we need to know. I'm not surprised there was another note, but that's not the question. The question is what does it mean? Archie got the same one, and I'm fairly certain we'll find Iain Peters did too."

Armstrong squeezed his wife's hand again, and Pereira saw the flinch, the moment, the instant she asked herself if she was going to pull her hand away, or be there for him. She stayed, her fingers squeezing back.

"It's all right," she said, then she turned to Pereira. "Can you give us a few moments?"

The face had softened, or at least, there was an open attempt at it. The hair was still pulled harshly back from the forehead, the lips were still drawn too thin.

"No," said Pereira. "I need to hear this, and I need to hear it all, right now."

And there was the harshness again, a flash of anger crossing the wife's eyes, before the hard squeeze of her husband's hand brought her back.

"It's all right, Jan," he said, although his voice was still stiff, nothing in his tone to suggest that he thought anything was right. "I've got to tell her. There's only me left anyway, it's not as though I'm letting anyone else down."

The wife slung the look back at Pereira, who remained deadpan, staring across the coffee table. Waiting for the story. The usual, inevitable, gradual unfolding of truth. The question at the end of this, of course, would be whether he'd actually told everything there was to tell.

"It started… it happened like we said at the inquest, like we told the police. We built this raft, it was a bit shit. Started to fall apart even before we got in the river. Never should have went. But Randall was the only one of us really saying it. He nearly didn't come, but we talked him into it. Then, I don't know, we were all larking about and stuff. Messing about on the river. It didn't seem that deep, that big a deal. Then the raft started to break up. Randall fell off, fell into the river…"

He lowered his eyes, his lip curled, like he resented having to talk. His wife held his hand, her own swallows loud in the quiet of the room. There was a small side window open, and the sound of the children playing outside drifted in. Shouts and laughter.

"It was quite deep where he fell, the water was fast. He struggled in it. I mean, it was shallow enough that he should have been able to stand, that's what we thought, but he couldn't get his feet. We just blithely sailed away from him. We were laughing. Thought it was funny, Mark splashing around like that. Too fucking funny, man. That's what Peters said. I always remember that. *That's too fucking funny, man.* I don't know what we could've done, but we could've tried. We just sailed away, laughing at him as he splattered around in the water, coughing, crying for help... Jesus..."

"When did you–"

"We sailed away," he said. "Really, didn't even see... didn't even see him drown, or die, or anything. We came to the bank on this battered piece of crap not far from the mouth of the river. We were just beginning to pull it up onto the side, still larking about, when down he comes. Mark Randall. But not Mark Randall anymore. Just a body, face down in the water... Oh, we helped him then. Waded out, stopped him before he floated out into the loch, dragged him into the side. We'd all done the first aid course, of course. Scouts... it's like, the first thing you do. But when it came to it..." He shook his head. "Archie ran off to call an ambulance. Me and Peters took turns, trying to bring him back, but like I said... when it came to it, I had nothing. We had nothing. Who the fuck were we, eh? Some bastards off *Casualty*? Really? First aid badge, my arse."

His wife was still holding his hand, though she wasn't looking at him. Staring at the floor.

"Why didn't you tell the truth?" asked Pereira. "It wasn't that you pushed him off."

"We didn't even try to help the bastard," said Armstrong. "We didn't even... we were laughing. He was drowning, we were laughing." Head shaking the whole time, the same angry, bitter look on his face. Finally he detached his hand, got to his feet, took a few steps away from the sofa. It was still a small room though. There wasn't far for him to go.

"I don't know what I'd've done, I really don't. I'd have... Jesus, I don't know. But then by the time Archie's back, the ambulance guys are there, and they're asking us what happened, and there goes Peters. He tells the story, just like it was told at the inquest. Like he'd thought of it, word perfect. After that, I never heard him tell it any other way. And me and Archie were trapped. Stuck in the story…"

He looked at Pereira finally, a moment, then he looked at his wife.

"Sorry," he said, the word delivered with little apology.

She was about to get up, when Pereira indicated with a slight movement of her hand to stay seated, and she shifted her balance and settled back into the seat.

"Have you ever told anyone before?" asked Pereira.

"Jesus," said Armstrong. "Seriously? No!"

"You think one of the others might have?"

"Are you… really, are you taking the piss? No, just no. I mean, you can find someone, I don't even know those guys, whether they were married or anything, but find someone and ask them. Why would any one of us have told anybody about that? I'm…" and he indicated his wife, "I've been married ten years. I tell Jan everything, I really do, but I've never told her this. Why would I? It was done, Mark was dead, there was literally nothing that could be done about it. It was a small page of history in the lives of a bunch of boring people. We agreed. Never talk about it again, not to anyone."

"Well, someone knows," said Pereira.

"I don't know how," said Armstrong.

"Nevertheless, that much at least is apparent, and we need to start thinking about how it happened. So, first of all I have to ask, and please, Mrs. Armstrong, I'm just doing my job, so don't go rising up in outrage."

Mrs. Armstrong looked across the table, an entirely new look of presumptive outrage on her face.

"You knew about it," said Pereira, turning back to Armstrong. "So either someone is going to be out to get you, or else you're behind these two other deaths. Can I ask you what you were doing yesterday evening?"

He looked annoyed, while the wife looked as though she was about to ignite.

"So, what, he's supposed to be sending these notes to himself?" she barked. "Who does that?"

"The kind of person who wants to give himself an alibi," said Pereira drily. "It would hardly be–"

"I don't know," said Armstrong, interrupting. "What time are we talking about?"

"I don't have that yet. At the moment we're looking at a very broad spec–"

"Oh, for God's sake, Glenn. You didn't kill anyone. Jesus. We all had dinner, we sat here and watched an old David Attenborough with Tyler, and then Glenn went out on his bike. End of."

Armstrong glanced at her, looked harshly at Pereira, as though this was all her fault, then lowered his resentful glare to the carpet.

"You went out on your bike?" asked Pereira.

"Yes," he said.

"What time?"

"About nine," he said. "Nine, I went out at nine. Got in about half-ten."

"Late," said Pereira. "Pretty bleak and damp the last few days."

He dismissed the question with scowl. "I've got lights, got, you know, like lime green reflecting shit on my cycling jacket."

What are you hiding, thought Pereira? Why was it people always had something to hide?

As usual, self-reproach was never far away. As if she'd been any different the last year of her marriage.

Still, there was a clear difference between lying about a crime you've committed, and not wanting to say something in front of the wife. There are all sorts of lies, and all sorts of things to lie about.

I tell Jan everything, I really do… That's what he'd said. *I don't think that's true*, thought Pereira, *but it doesn't mean that I need to know this particular lie. There'll be time.*

"You can confirm that?" said Pereira, turning to Mrs. Armstrong.

"Aye," she said. "He came back, we watched Graham Norton, had a cup of tea and some of that millionaire's shortbread my mum dropped off a couple of days ago, then I went to bed. Glenn sat up and watched one of they *Die Hard* films."

"Four," he said. "I watched *Die Hard 4*. Went to bed when it was done, maybe around one-ish."

"Aye," said the wife.

Maybe he went back out, thought Pereira. She was sitting

167

there with her instinct, feeling confident that while there was something implicitly suspicious about the man's behaviour, it was unlikely to be related to the Archie Wilson case. But then, perhaps he went out on his bike, took care of Peters, dumped him somewhere, then went back after dark and moved his body to the graveyard.

She shook her head at the thought. The whole thing, the way for that to have worked out, sounded too contrived. Sadly, predictably, he likely went out and saw another woman, and then after his wife had gone to bed, he texted the other woman for an hour or two. Or sexted, or God knows what, did something by phone.

"Very well," she said. "Until we have a better idea of who's doing this, and exactly what's going on here, we're going to have to consider you under threat. I'm going to station a couple of officers, and you'll have someone front and back twenty-four hours a day. When you go out, I suggest that one of them travels with you, while one stays here."

Mrs. Armstrong was beginning to look outraged again, but Pereira continued to talk through it. She suspected that when pushed, Mrs. Armstrong wouldn't really know why she was outraged, she just likely thought that she should be. It would be the toss of a coin whether she ultimately chose to be incensed by the fact that her husband would have a police escort wherever he went, or because there weren't enough police tasked with his protection. Didn't people on the TV have nine or ten guards?

"I also suggest that you limit going out in the evening, and limit going out on your own."

"How long's this going to go on?" snapped Mrs. Armstrong.

"Can't possibly say," said Pereira. "Wilson and Peters have been killed within four days of each other, so it doesn't look like the killer's hanging around–"

"Wait, you're not using Glenn as bait. Is that your plan?"

"That's not the plan," said Pereira.

"I've seen the films."

"That's not the plan," she repeated. "I'm placing the guards at the current level for the moment. It's still early on in this, now that we know the crimes have a specific direction. I'll need to get back to the station and speak to my colleagues and superiors."

The wife fizzed, but didn't seem to have any further words

———

of wrath to hand.

"Glenn," said Pereira, hoping to refocus the conversation, "as I said before, someone obviously knows about this. Can you think at all, any recollection, of how it might have happened? Was there someone else at the river? Was there a hint at the inquest that something might be going on, that someone had something to say, but for some reason they didn't come forward, or they withdrew their statement before–"

He was shaking his head, long before she'd finished talking, then he cut her off.

"Really, there was nothing at the inquest. It was so... I don't know how, but people seemed to have sympathy for us. I think that was why the three of us never really spoke to each other again. Might've been easier if there'd been suspicion. But there was nothing. No suspicion. Just pity." Head still shaking, staring at the floor, voice still bitter. "Jesus. And really, there was no one by the river. No anglers, nothing. Just the four of us. And then there were three of us. And now..." He lifted his head, looked at his wife, then back at Pereira. "Now there's just me."

28

Another day, another trip to the morgue, standing in the same spot, a cadaver on the table, an identical murder weapon laid on the small table behind the head. Today Vangelis' theme from *1492* was playing, strangely stirring in the background.

"Music sounds like all the corpses are about to rise up," said Bain.

He was already imagining it. Wondering what he would do. Treat them with respect until he established their intentions, or automatically assume they'd have mainstream, flesh-eating zombie objectives.

"But you know, not necessarily in a bad way."

"Sergeant," said Pereira, and he smiled.

"The drawers are all currently empty, Sergeant," said Edgars drily. "There's only Mr. Peters here, and I don't think he's going anywhere, despite the music."

Bain glanced around the room, as though expecting to see some visual contradiction of what she'd said.

"As I was saying," said Edgars, "the only difference we have here is the method used to incapacitate the victim. Cracked with a heavy object to the side of the head. As to what that object was, I can't say. Clean hit, didn't leave anything behind, not that I've found so far."

"So someone came at him from his right," said Pereira, looking at the mark on the head.

"Thereafter, we have the same scenario played out. Bound, gagged, blood weeping from the eyes, and then the cross hammered into the head. And I'm going to give you time of death at around midnight again. Perhaps a little later."

"No chance it was before ten thirty?" asked Pereira.

Edgars smiled. "You want it to be before ten thirty?"

"Just ruling someone out."

"There's no chance it was before ten thirty," said Edgars.

"OK, good, thanks. And what about Peters? Had he been up to anything of interest beforehand?"

Edgars shook her head. "Fit guy."

She pulled back the sheet to display his naked body. Barely an ounce of fat on his torso, strong muscle definition. The women stared at the body appreciatively, Bain with some jealousy. A few moments passed.

"That," said Edgars, "is a loss to the gene pool."

She sighed, shook her head, finally lifted the sheet back over the cadaver.

"What'd he do?" asked Edgars. "Had plenty of time to work out, that's for sure."

Maybe, Pereira found herself mundanely thinking, that's what she needed to get her mind off Lena. A man. A man who looked like that. Alive would be better.

"Not sure exactly," said Bain. "Some sort of online trading, I think."

"We'll get into that," said Pereira, snapping herself back to the moment. "So, apart from being the fittest guy any of us have seen outside of watching the Olympics, was there anything about him?"

"He'd had a beer, maybe a couple of small ones. He'd eaten well that day, nothing else in his system. No drugs, nothing really. Hadn't had sex."

She pursed her lips, looked along the length of the covered sheet, then finally shrugged.

"That's all I've got."

Vangelis came to an end, and there was a brief moment of silence.

"There, Sergeant," said Edgars, "we got to the end of the tune and he didn't come back to life. You can rest easy."

Bain smiled. Pereira looked down on the blue/grey face of the corpse.

*

Peters' house was already busy, a team having been in attendance for the previous hour. Pereira and Bain were met by Detective Sergeant Parks, wearing white gloves, walking from the kitchen into the back garden as they arrived.

"Ma'am," she said, nodding at Pereira. As usual she ignored Bain, and as usual Bain briefly wondered what that might be about.

"What have we got?" asked Pereira.

"We're making headway," said Parks. "No question that this is where the murder took place. There's blood in a couple of spots in the kitchen. The first, there's evidence of spraying. Corkin reckons that was where he was struck across the head."

As she talked, she unconsciously made a movement with her hand, indicating the striking of the blow, her fingers then splaying out to indicate the spreading of the blood.

"That's more or less at the back door. Then against the wall, next to the door in from the sitting room, blood has pooled, although not a great deal. We're thinking that was where he was actually killed."

"Any sign of a struggle?" asked Pereira.

"None. Well, just the blood. We found the same three notes that the others received, in a kitchen drawer. They're bagged already. And the electricity had been cut, just from the master switch in the kitchen."

Pereira nodded, looked in through the kitchen windows, where she could see three white-suited SOCOs.

"Right," she said. "We should go in and have a look."

"And we've got his computer," said Parks. "Logged on already, instant access."

Pereira stopped and let out a low whistle. "That's the Holy Grail these days."

"Yes, ma'am."

"Anything?" she asked. "Apart from the obvious, that if the killer was here he would surely have taken the computer had he thought there might be something incriminating on it."

"Yes," said Parks, "there's that. Seems Peters made his money writing erotica and selling it on Amazon."

Pereira lifted an inquisitive eyebrow. Bain smiled.

"*Alicia's Fifth Gang Bang* looks to have been his latest bestseller," said Parks.

"How much money?"

"Several hundred pounds a day. Like, over five hundred."

"Over a hundred and fifty thousand a year," said Pereira. "Nice. How many books has he written?"

"Ninety-three."

"Ninety-three erotic books?"

"Yes."

"Wow," said Bain. "How many ways are there to describe…" and he let the question vanish into the ether.

"You can read them," said Pereira. "I mean, seriously. Read them. There might be clues."

"Thanks, boss."

"You're welcome. These were under his own name?"

"J T Conroy. We've got into his Amazon account, his Amazon publisher's account I mean, plus we've found several files on the computer itself, so it was definitely him writing it. Again, although it's kind of quirky, if it'd had anything to do with this, you've got to presume the computer would've been taken."

"Yes. It wasn't hidden somewhere?"

"On the sofa, where presumably he'd been sitting before he was accosted."

"Hmm," said Pereira, "wonder how it played out. That everything you've got?"

"For the moment, but we've only been here…" and she finished the sentence with a wave.

Pereira nodded and led the way as the three of them entered the house, using the same door through which Peters' corpse had been removed very early that morning.

29

"What have we got on the headstone this time?" asked Cooper.

"Classic," said Somerville, then shook his head at the use of the word. "Ties in with what we know about Peters. This time it was a Miss Georgiana Grace, who died in 1851. TB. She published several books of poetry under the pseudonym Horace Weltcher."

"Successfully?" asked Pereira.

"Doesn't appear so," said Somerville. "Least ways, they have about three lines on Wikipedia between them, so I don't think she'll be getting a Google doodle on her birthday any time soon."

"Maybe this'll be her catapult to stardom," said Bain.

"We really are dealing with someone who knew what they were doing," said Cooper. "There's some aforethought here, that's for sure. There's no way that we can identify people who've been doing some in-depth digging into the Necropolis archives?"

"A lot of it's online, sir," said Tobin. "But I can get back on to them, see if we can get numbers, any other kind of specifics."

"Yes, do that," said Cooper, then he nodded, looking around the room. Taking a moment. *What's next*, thought Pereira, *that's what he's wondering*.

"I was thinking," she said, "the timing of this. That ridiculous headline in the Sun. It would have gone to press last night, presumably it was up on social media last night. These front pages, they're usually online by about ten pm. Maybe our killer saw that, suddenly realised that we, or someone, was on to the real reason that Archie was killed, and thought they'd better start getting on with it."

"Any sign that this was a rush job?" asked Cooper.

"None," she said. "And the fact that they took the corpse straight to an appropriate grave, if my supposition is correct, would imply that they'd already planned it out. I just thought the timing was interesting. They might not have realised we were onto that old story, might have suddenly thought we'd be looking out for it, looking out for Peters and Armstrong. Took the chance to get rid of one of them while it was still relatively straightforward."

"Hmm," said Cooper. Not looking at her, thinking it over. "Does that help us? I mean, if it meant they made a mistake because it was rushed, then good, but otherwise…"

"Not sure," she said. "Just considering all the angles. And another interesting thing," she continued, not letting him stew in his dismissal of her thought process, "is this headstone the killer selected. It indicates that the killer knew about Peters and this *nom de plume* of his. There's been nothing on the website and in the social media that accompanies the books to suggest Peters ever made his own identity public. So that would suggest it was someone who knew him well."

"Or had hacked his computer," said Bain. "And if they'd hacked his computer, that'd be another reason why they didn't have to steal it. They already knew what was there."

Pereira nodded her agreement.

"Yes," said Cooper, "see if Tech can find anything on that. OK, so what's next?"

"We've definitely got the link to the death of Mark Randall now, so we need to start getting into the nuts and bolts of his life. Who's still going to be upset about it eighteen years later? Who could possibly have known the truth beyond what was told at the inquest?" Cooper was nodding, unusual affirmation in itself. She continued. "And although at the moment we won't know if there's a link back to Randall, and therefore to Wilson, we need to try to establish if Peters' computer was hacked, and if not, who he could possibly have told about his sideline. There's also the major possibility, in fact probability, that one of the three of these men told someone the truth about what happened on the river. We have Armstrong's word that it wasn't him."

"He could be lying," said Cooper, interrupting, his voice deadpan.

"Yes," she said, "but I don't think so. Not about that,

anyway."

Not about that anyway. That was the thing. He was clearly lying about something, and being a married man, a majority of the time the lie would be related to the same thing. And if there was some woman out there to whom he didn't want to admit in front of his wife, wasn't it possible that he'd told that woman things he'd never said to Mrs. Armstrong? And if the other woman knew the old Taynuilt story, while it was unlikely she'd gone about killing the three men, perhaps she'd told someone who had.

Convoluted, convoluted, she thought. Ever-increasing, intricate circles, taking her nowhere, leading her down so many paths. This was one she would check out herself, only bringing it to the room if she thought it was going anywhere.

Cooper waited a moment to see if she was going to voice what was going through her head, then lifted a pair of questioning eyebrows.

"We'll start with the sister," said Pereira. "Bain and I can go and see her again."

"Try not to feed her any more stories she can pass on to the Sun," said Cooper. "If your theory's correct, you got someone killed last night."

Pereira took the hit, held his gaze, and then glanced round at Bain. *Cheap shot, ignore it,* she thought, and wondered if it was something she'd successfully managed to telepathically transfer across the table.

*

They sat in the car in silence, heading out towards Aberfoyle. Ella and Louis were playing, the volume lower than if she'd been alone, yet they weren't talking anyway.

You got someone killed last night.

The kind of line that worms its way inside you, pointless in this case as well. Chances are her theory wasn't correct, and even if it had been, Peters had already been targeted, and it presumably had only been a matter of time.

"It wasn't like we planted the thought in her head," said Pereira, unable to let the slight go, deciding that she needed to air it out in order for that to happen. "And it wasn't as though we called the damned newspaper. The only way to have avoided it would've been to not talk to her. And we had to talk to her, just as we do now…"

"I know," said Bain. "The DCI… he just has to get his dig in, let you know who's boss."

"We didn't get anyone killed," said Pereira.

"I know," repeated Bain. "Anyway, I always hate that, like in movies. You know the thing the terrorist does, like he'll put a gun at someone's head and say, if you don't transfer eight billion dollars into my account by midnight, her brain's getting splattered and her blood will be on your hands. That's just bullshit."

"D'you think anyone actually says that in real life?" asked Pereira, glad of the light relief.

"Didn't the boss just imply it right there? If he'd do it, presumably some ned with a gun at some poor bastard's head would too."

Stopped at lights, the song came to an end, and then *The Nearness of You* started up, the lights changed, and the conversation had drifted away. Pereira's mind moved on, time to focus on Laura Kane and what else there was she could possibly tell them. At the very least, she had to suggest others they could talk to. If not, then it was back to the station, back to the inquest files, and root through the names. Start calling people up, one by one.

Of course, at some point you had to believe that you were calling the right person, and what were the chances of that person readily admitting over the phone that they could be of help? Wouldn't they already have suspected the call was coming? Wouldn't they already have thought through their vague reply, the tone of voice that says, *I'd love to help but wasn't that eighteen years ago? Wait, maybe there's something I can remember…*

That was why the face-to-face meeting was always better. The nuance, the sideways glance, the hesitation, the shadow across the eyes.

"What d'you know about these two?" asked Bain, his voice suddenly out of nowhere, and she realised that she'd been lost in thought, driving on autopilot. How was it she knew the road to Aberfoyle without having to think about it? There must have been signposts at which she'd looked without seeing.

"What d'you mean?" she said, presuming Bain was talking about the case.

"Louis Armstrong and Ella Fitzgerald," said Bain. "I mean,

I don't know anything about them. They always sound like they're having a right laugh. Like it was fun. Even when they sing one of those songs about lost love and whatever else people got upset about in songs back then, they still sound like they're smiling."

She didn't answer. Trying to rediscover her train of thought, but it was gone.

"Expect they hated each other, or they were drunks or drug addicts or something," said Bain.

"I don't know," said Pereira.

He glanced at her, watched her drive for a moment. Aberfoyle no more than a couple of miles away.

"Seriously? I thought you were a big fan?"

"Huge," said Pereira. "But I like the music, that's all. What else is there? Maybe they were happy, maybe they were sad, maybe they had some great relationship... I don't know. Don't want to know. Look them up if you're interested, but don't tell me."

Round a corner, Bain nodding at his boss, unsurprised.

"But you're right. Part of it is that I like to think of them smiling, and if that wasn't the case, I don't want to know otherwise. There are enough Everly Brothers and Simon and Garfunkels in the world."

*

They found her working behind the bar in the golf club clubhouse. Part-time, weekend job. White blouse, top two buttons undone, the clubhouse warm. Five occupied tables, four with men, one ladies group sitting at the back, away from the window, a four-ball recently arrived from the course. Seemed like a reasonably busy afternoon, despite the bleakness of another day in March. At least there had been no rain so far that day.

There was a television showing the final session of the third day of the Dubai Test, England versus Pakistan. Pakistan a sedate 459-3 in reply to England's quick-fire 401 all out by close of day one.

They found Kane drying glasses, in true barkeep style, waiting for her next customer. She laughed as they entered.

"My, my, here come the fuzz," she said.

Pereira had heard that one often enough to neither

appreciate nor be bothered by the quote. They stopped at the bar, looked around the room, the general low noise of chatter and cutlery on plates, drinks being placed on tables, the occasional loud laugh. A waitress walked through, nodded at Bain and Pereira as she passed, went to a table by the window and started to clear away the detritus of lunch, with a, "Was everything all right for youse?"

Beyond the window, the course stretched away, the grass dull green in the grey of early afternoon. A man in his sixties, in yellow trousers and yellow, white and black chequered jumper, was lining up a putt, his playing partners, in similar bright attire, leaning on putters around the green.

"No one seems to be paying much attention to the cricket," said Pereira, glancing at the screen as there was an increase in the noise, and then finally turning to the bar.

"Men can watch sport without watching sport," said Bain, eyes on the TV, looking at the replay of a flowing Azhar Ali drive through the covers for four. "Women usually fail to understand that."

"You're hilarious, Sergeant," said Pereira. "Apologies in advance if I forget to give you a lift back to the office. The walk'll do you good."

He smiled, then he too turned to face the bar.

"So, what have youse got for me today?" asked Kane. "The guy from the Sun keeps calling, asking if there's anything else he can use. They like to build these things. You know, lead with it one day, have a follow-up the next."

"Another man's been murdered, Ms. Kane," said Pereira, "you don't think that'll be enough for him?"

"Aye, I heard about that. Peters, eh? He was a bit of a dick, though, right? It's not like I remember much from the inquest, but him, I remember him. Bit of a dick."

"Was there ever any suggestion, and I don't mean in the inquest, just on the margins, or over the dinner table, or the odd rumour in the press, or just between you and a friend while having coffee one afternoon, anything, was there ever anything to suggest that there was more to the boys' story than they told?"

"Why?"

She'd stopped drying the glass. It was still in her hand, the dishtowel screwed inside it, down to the bottom. Was it because she knew something, or were her ears open to any new facts she could pass on to the Sun?

———

179

"There's got to be something, Ms. Kane," said Pereira. "Two men have been murdered, quite elaborately at that. You don't murder someone eighteen years after the fact just because they happened to be present when there was an accident. You can imagine an impassioned crime at the time, jealousy and anger at the survivors, but all this time later, and to do to these men what was done…"

"Hmm," she said. "I guess. What was done exactly?" she added hopefully.

"Your brother really had no one he was especially close to?" asked Bain.

She thought about it again for a moment and then shrugged, went back into the rhythm of drying the glass.

"Like I said, he was a lonely little dweeb. I really don't think so."

"So, who else took an interest, you, your mum, and your dad aside?" asked Pereira. "Any family, or friends, anyone from school?"

She laughed again. "It was like a ghost town in there, really. Ha! Ghost town. That's a good one after that Sun headline this morning, eh? And by the way, see that line that was in there about youse two being like a short-handed Three Stooges? I never actually said that. He made that up. I mean, it's funny, but I don't want you being mad at me."

"I haven't read it," said Pereira.

Bain shook his head in agreement.

"Any family, or friends, or anyone from school?" Pereira repeated.

Kane smiled.

"Youse are persistent, eh? You think if you ask me the same question often enough, you'll get the answer you're looking for?"

"No," said Pereira, "I hope I'll get an answer that at least gives us somewhere else to look, some other avenue to explore. Someone, somewhere, wants these men dead. Whoever it is, they'd managed to forget about it, and then Archie Wilson got rich, and bang, there's no forgetting, not when Archie's on the front page of the tabloids every day. So, you can help us, or you can come down to the station, because at the moment you're the only person we know with motive to kill these men."

"What the actual fuck? You serious?"

The conversation stopped in the bar, every face turned to

———

180

look at her, at the raising of the voice. She glanced round the room, looked apologetic, turned back finally to Pereira.

"Where were you last night around midnight?" asked Bain.

"What? Really?"

"Where were you around midnight?" he repeated.

She looked slightly panicked, a look that both Pereira and Bain recognised. Classic. Nothing to hide, and put on the spot by the police. Some people reacted angrily, some people looked like they were in imminent danger of arrest.

"I was out with Magret," she said, her explanation, when it came, coming in a rush. "You can call her. Went to Danny's, like at nine or something, then onto the Starlight. Didn't get in until after two."

"Tell us something we don't know about the inquest, or about Mark's life at the time before he died. Who did he know, what did he do?"

"Really, he had nothing, he did nothing. He had his church, that was all. That was the only place he went, the only thing he did. Really, he was that sad of a nerd. A church nerd."

"The same church as Archie Wilson?"

"Aye. That was how they knew each other. I mean, those lads were doing their Chief Scout through the church troop. Marky was doing his through the school, but he'd been left without a group. Like I said," and her voice started to slow, coming down off the panic, "literally no one liked him. He heard about those lads, and managed to join them. But I don't think any of them were regular churchgoers or anything, so they didn't know him really."

"And at the inquest," said Pereira, "was there anyone there in support of the others. Did Wilson, Peters or Armstrong have family, or a girlfriend, or just a friend? Someone they might have confided in?"

"Don't remember. There were various people in and out, different faces on different days. There was one…" she said, then her voice drifted away. She looked down the eighteenth, the most recent fourball shaking hands on the green, walking off, signing cards.

Pereira and Bain watched her, waiting for her memory to kick in.

"She was nice, I'll give her that. Nice looking, I mean, she was nice looking. But I've no idea who she was with, why she was there. Like I say, people came and went."

"You don't remember her name?"

Kane laughed. "Seriously? She was just some girl, that's all, no more important than anyone else. Jeez…"

A moment, and then Pereira detached her gaze and looked round. The scene in the bar was as before, the cricket played on the television. Another interview, and all they had was an attractive woman at an inquest eighteen years previously, who probably was of no interest.

"Thank you," she said, without turning back. A ball, played from far down the fairway, bounced short of the green, and then rolled up, stopping eight to ten feet short of the flag. "I think that'll do for the moment."

"But you know, if youse ask me, it's wee Marky and all that church crap that he was into. I wouldn't be surprised if he'd managed to resurrect himself, you know. Getting his revenge."

Pereira turned away from the bar, acknowledging Kane with the merest of farewell nods.

"Hey, the other guy must be bricking it," added Kane with a laugh. "You must have him under twenty-four hour watch. Just don't give it to G4 or he's fucked. Oops!"

They left the bar, out into the afternoon sun, the last thing they heard being Kane's apology to the bar for once more uttering the word *fuck* a decibel or two too loud.

30

Pereira stood in the grounds of the Old Parish Church, Bellahouston, having arranged to meet the retired Reverend Smith at a little after four. It was only ten to, but she'd wanted to arrive early, take the place in, get a feel for it.

There was an old building – mid-19th century, she knew – surrounded by a graveyard, dating from around the same time. As she looked, she saw no headstones dating from later than the 1890s. She wondered why the killer had not used this graveyard, yet the answer might well be prosaic.

Who would know who any of these people were? There might be a church record somewhere, but then, it might be very obvious if anyone tried to find out.

The Necropolis, on the other hand, with its tens of thousands of graves, and its online records, would have been much easier to access, and much more high profile. That the chosen headstones in some way related to the victims was a small touch, one that the killer likely thought demonstrated an element of panache, but it was hardly worth risking detection for.

In any case, this was not a graveyard tended to in the way that the Necropolis had been all these years. This was a graveyard of neglect. Toppled headstones, grass needing cut, regulation works of graffiti. *Tumshie Ya Bas*, and *Maggie shags like a badger*, and *Eli and Blake 2012*. She looked around the surrounding area, at the six-foot wall and the low houses across the street. It might be a while before a body was even discovered.

No, that was definitely an element of it. The killer was showing off and wanted his work to be discovered.

The phone rang and she took it from her pocket, hoping it wasn't going to be the old vicar cancelling on her.

Lena.

Fear and hope and surprise and nerves and dread came rushing in, as usual, in equal measure.

She'd been avoiding the thought process, the internal argument. Tomorrow afternoon with Lena, talking, really talking for the first time in so long, that was the promise, or the afternoon with Anais, that other promise. Her promise. The one she wanted to keep, if only she could detach herself from her addiction.

"Hey," she said.

"Hey. Saw the news," said Lena. "Guess that's you up to your eyes in it again? I presume tomorrow's going to be off?"

Wait, thought Pereira. Had tomorrow ever been on? Had she agreed to it? She hadn't said anything. But then, perhaps it had all been in her tone. Or perhaps it had been Lena's presumption. When was the last time Pereira had been able to say no to anything she suggested?

"I don't know," she said. She laughed, a peculiar nervousness about her voice. "If someone else gets killed tonight, then we're definitely screwed. Otherwise, I should be all right. We usually get Sunday afternoon, regardless. The dead can wait until Monday morning."

What was she doing? Was this her making an actual, positive arrangement to see Lena? She was supposed to be thinking about it. No! She wasn't even supposed to be giving it any consideration at all. She was spending the afternoon with Anais. She was making the breakthrough with her daughter. She was breaking down all those damned walls that had been building up and up, getting worse all the time, every week it seemed, since she'd taken her away from her dad.

She couldn't possibly see Lena. And yet, as she stood there looking at the gate into the church graveyard, as the old man with silver hair in a warm winter coat closed it behind him, waved a thin hand in her direction and started walking towards her, she knew she would submit to her obsession. Just the same as she had given into it before, when she had broken up her family. Just the same as she always submitted to it, every time Lena came calling.

Now came the guilt. Now came the sunken, depressive feeling. Now came the self-loathing.

_____

"Ali?" said Lena, recognising the silence at the other end of the phone.

"Sorry, got to go," said Pereira. "I'll call in the morning."

"'K. Bye!"

She stood for a moment, staring at the ground, the phone in her hand. And then the flick of the switch, the instantaneous transfer of thought from one part of her brain to the other, from the emotional to the clear-thinking and deductive. She pocketed the phone and watched the old man approach.

"Reverend Smith," she said, "thank you for meeting me here."

He extended his hand.

"Sorry if I'm a little late."

"That's all right. I was just looking around the old graveyard."

Together they took a moment to look at the walls and the faded headstones, the wandering grass and lichen, the graffiti, much of which Pereira found herself embarrassed to be reading, standing next to the minister, as though he'd never have seen the like before.

"A sorry sight," he said. "Come on, let's go inside, you can have a look at the building. Hopefully we'll find that in a better state."

*

There was nothing inside to suggest that the building was not still in use. It was cold and there was a feeling of damp, but the church looked like any other. The pews and the altar and the pulpit were still in place, the lectern holding the giant Bible, the Bible open at the page of the last reading, given several years earlier. That seemed peculiar, but not in any way she thought would impact on why she was here, right now, talking to Reverend Smith. The old stained-glass windows were all intact, the usual jumble of dark colours, frequently impossible to make out exactly what was going on without giving them very close inspection. She could see one small panel broken in one window. The only concession to the fact that the building wasn't used anymore seemed to be that there were no soft furnishings, no cushions on the pews, no runner on the altar, no tapestries or rugs.

"Remind you of something?" said Smith.

185

They were sitting in a pew, second row from the front, as though awaiting the start of the service, Pereira looking around her, taking it all in.

"Could be the church I go to on a Sunday," she said. "St. Andrews, Cathcart."

He nodded.

"I know of it, though I've never been. A thriving congregation?"

She looked at him to see if he was being serious, and there was a slight glint in his eye.

"Could be worse," she said. "We're not currently in danger of having to throw in with anyone else, but you know…"

He nodded sadly. It was the same everywhere, after all.

"Are there a community of… sorry, I feel like I'm being very old and racist and I don't mean to be."

"It's all right," she said, "go on."

"Are there a community of you who go to the church? An Indian community?"

She shook her head.

"No, just me and Mum. Mum and Dad started going there as soon as they arrived in Glasgow. Long time ago now. I've always gone. There was another family for a while, but they moved on. Just Mum and me and Robin now. My son."

"It's good to keep it in the family," said Smith, smiling. "You can't persuade your husband to attend?"

She looked round at him for a moment, then turned away.

She felt so much more comfortable with Reverend Smith than she had, sitting in a similar position, talking to Dr. Melville two days previously. There had definitely been something about him. Melville. Hiding something. Or some other peculiarity, just out of reach of understanding. Something that needed further investigation.

Smith, however, despite blundering like any unthinking old man into a question that was almost too painful to answer, just seemed like a man to trust. She could tell him everything. It was utterly bizarre. She sat there for a moment, the story flying through her head in the way that it had so often, and she imagined laying it all out for him. Her marriage to Martin, safe and secure and ordinary and dull, but the perfect antidote to the Police Service, the perfect thing to come home to. Nine years, nine ordinary, ordered years, and then the fall.

And God, hadn't it been such a desperately sad cliché?

Hadn't it been the kind of stupid, thoughtless evening that Iain Peters would have turned into some trashy erotic novella on sale on Amazon for £0.99? Martin playfully nudging her to sleep with another woman, find someone with whom they could have a threesome. He'd been talking about it for years, and she'd humoured him, as she loved the sound of it. The excitement of it. And then they'd been away, at the small hotel in Fife for the weekend, and there had been Lena. Gorgeous, wonderful Lena, looking so delicious in white, serving them soup and hot bread, chicken in a peppery lime sauce. And Martin had started the conversation when Lena wasn't in the room. *She could be the one.* That was it. Those words. That was exactly how it'd started. *She could be the one.*

Smith gently put his hand on Pereira's arm, spoke with an apologetic smile in his voice.

"I'm sorry, I shouldn't have."

Pereira shook her head, brought herself back. "Sorry," she said. "Yes, sorry. No husband. And yes, you're right, we didn't come here to talk about me. Sadly… you'll have seen the news this morning?"

"Yes," he said, and his eyes automatically drifted up to the large stained-glass window behind the altar at the back of the church. St. Paul, kneeling before the light on the road to Damascus.

"It seems with the two murders this week, that it really brings us to the death of Mark Randall."

"Yes, yes," he said. "Such a sad case. And terrible that we're back here, it really is. I doubt any of us who knew Mark have forgotten, but we had moved on. Life had moved on. His mother and father are dead, of course. Quite lost track of young Laura."

"I spoke to her this morning," said Pereira. "She seems well."

"Well that's good, that really is. Such a tragic family. So sad."

"Tell me about Mark."

"Yes, yes, of course. He was a bight boy, so interested in the church. The history of the church, where it had come from, where it was going. Fascinated by it all."

"Yet he wasn't the type to be interested in the ministry?"

He laughed, a wonderful, gentle sound. *God*, thought Pereira, *I'm sitting next to Burt Lancaster.*

"No," he said, "clever girl. You understand him, yet you couldn't have known him."

"You can't call me clever girl," said Pereira, but she was smiling. "This is not the 1950s, nor are you Bob Peck and I'm a velociraptor."

"I do apologise," he said, and he laughed again, another gentle laugh, "although I'm not entirely sure who Bob Peck is."

There would be those in the Police Service, and in life in general, standing at her shoulder now, outraged that she herself wasn't outraged at the old-fashioned condescension. If it had come from Cooper, yes. But from this old fellow, who'd grown up in that world, the dying breed? They could take their views to the grave. What did it matter? If their views moved on during their lifetime, good on them. If they didn't, well time would do the moving on for them.

"But you're right," said Smith. "Mark wasn't destined for the ministry. If nothing else, he did not believe in God."

"Really?"

"Not many people do, Inspector, I'm afraid."

He shook his head, his gaze still on the window, a view he must have looked upon many times in his life, she thought. How sad it must be for him to see the church fall away to nothing, up for sale, potentially turned into someone's elaborately designed four-bedroomed family home.

"The church was always about community. The sense of that community. That's what's been lost. How many of these people who came along here on a Sunday morning, these serious men and women who gave their time, who helped young ones steer a safe path towards adulthood, how many of them ever truly believed? It didn't matter though, because there was so much else to it. We were bound by our spirit and values and there was a deep faith there, even if the faith wasn't exactly as prescribed in the Bible. Now, it's all just washing away." Again, he quickly shook the thought away. "Young Mark, well that was at the time when people were being more open. More willing to talk. He was quite happy to tell me he didn't believe in God, but it made him no less fascinated by the church and by the idea, the very notion, of Christianity."

He nodded, his gaze now having fallen to the floor, the remembrance of Mark Randall at least a positive one.

"That's who he was. But he was going to be an historian in the end, I think, not a theologian."

188

"And he was really writing a book about Judas?"

"Oh yes. We talked about Judas so often, long chats on Sunday afternoons. Quite remarkable. Teenagers are so wonderful, aren't they? They get bees in their bonnet about the least expected things. He wouldn't have been the first to try, but Mark was quite determined to rehabilitate the rogue disciple. Like he had a mission to save this man whose reputation has been tarnished for so long. You know, I shouldn't bore you with it, but Judas is such an interesting character in the Christian tradition."

"Oh, I know," she said. "Can I ask, do you know if others… was it generally known that he was writing this book?"

"Not at the time, no," said Smith. "He thought it sounded pretentious, although, really, I'm sure the book would have been rather wonderful. I do wonder what happened to it, all that he'd written…"

That was another piece of information Pereira didn't feel the need to relay.

"But he was a modest chap. Yes, modest. Didn't like the idea of calling himself a writer until he'd finished his book and someone had offered to publish it. Decent fellow. Such a shame…"

"So, you aside, who do you think would have known?"

"Oh, well… his Bill and Jean, of course. He had long talks with them, arguments I dare say, when it came to Bill. And I presume Laura knew. Aside from them… He wasn't… he was a peculiar lad. Didn't really have friends. Very self-focused. Not, I should say, not at all narcissistic, I don't mean to say that. Just very inward looking. Liked to challenge himself, was interested in what he was interested in, really. Didn't care, necessarily, what others cared about. I really do wonder what kind of life he would have made for himself, what he would have done in the world. Such a loss…"

She felt it, for a moment. You came across so much loss in the Police Service, so many deaths and disappearances crossed their desks, even if in the end no crime was found to have been committed. So much tragedy in the world. And not just the greater tragedies of the news, of civil wars and countries descending into chaos, of plane crashes and earthquakes, terrorism and random acts of mass violence. There was the everyday tragedy of normal life, the kind of thing that didn't make the news, the kind of incident that might affect just a few people. The type of tragedy that they saw all the time, and which they couldn't allow themselves to be affected by.

Yet, she felt this, right now, the loss of Mark Randall. How strange.

"Oh!" said Smith, and he shook his head. "I'm forgetting things. Such an old fool these days. I remember now. It was mentioned at the inquest. By his mother. Jean would've talked about it. She was so... so moving. She didn't have to speak, but she wanted to say something. She had her say. She talked about it then, and I'm sure most of the people there had never heard that before. Very moving. I can still hear... such fragility in her voice, yet she kept going."

"That is brave," said Pereira.

"Indeed."

"And were there many people there?" she asked.

Is this where they find out Kane to be a liar, she wondered? So often the simple things.

He shook his head.

"Like I said, Mark was not popular. Not unpopular, I should say, but not popular either. There was family, and there were lawyers. Once or twice there were men from the press. Expert witnesses, and the other three boys and whosoever was supporting them on any given day aside, no one."

"Do you remember any of the boys having a girlfriend, or close personal friend there?"

His head was bowed now. At various times she'd begun to think him not so old, not as old as he'd seemed walking in through the gate of the churchyard. In fact, he couldn't be more than in his early seventies, given that he'd had to retire from the full-time ministry around fifteen years previously. Now, though, he looked much older, weighed down by sadness.

He shook his head, eyes open, staring at the floor.

"You know that Archie Wilson had been thinking of buying this building, using it as a kind of mission for the local community?" she said.

He looked up, perked up a little perhaps, smiling.

"Yes," he said. "That would have been wonderful. Community, you see, that's what these buildings have always been about."

He paused, the spark died away once more. "And now the chance of that too has gone."

He bowed his head, his old hands gripping the rear of the

pew in front of them.

*

After Smith and gone, locking the building behind them, Pereira
stayed behind to walk around the headstones. There was nothing
to be found here, no looking for clues to be done. It was purely
breathing space.

Bain called, driving close by, and she asked him to meet
her. The thoughts in her head were usually better formulated
when they were articulated, tossed out and bounced off the wall
of her able sidekick. Her Dr. Watson. Or, as Parks had once
remarked at a drunken office Christmas party, Donkey to
Pereira's Shrek. Pereira had thought that was pretty funny,
whether it was intended to be or not.

The rain started as Bain arrived, as if in some sort of bleak
celebration of the grim conversation to come, amidst the equally
grim surroundings. Not heavy, nothing more than a one or a two
on the scale, just enough to add to the bleak misery of the
afternoon.

"So, the connection we're looking for is there, it's at the
inquest," said Pereira.

They were looking down at one of the oldest headstones,
the name worn away to illegibility, old grass growing more than
halfway up the front of the stone.

"The other side of it, the who knew the truth of what
happened on the river, that could have been relayed by any of
the three survivors at any time. But this thing, this private thing
about Judas that Randall was working on, that seems really only
to have been made public knowledge at the inquest."

"But someone at the inquest could have told someone who
wasn't there, thereby infinitely expanding the list of people who
possibly knew."

Pereira nodded. "Yep. But we have to start somewhere. We
have to start with that inquest, with who was present, who might
still be around today with an interest in the three survivors, and
who might possibly have found out about what really happened.
Then there's the question of why come after them."

"It's surely just revenge," said Bain. "If they'd wanted
money, then why kill Wilson? It was his father who was getting
the money. Unless we suppose his father killed him, and then
killed Peters to make it look like it wasn't just about Archie and

———

191

his money."

Pereira was nodding long before he'd finished talking. "That's where we are. But then, it doesn't just have to be his father, does it? Maybe there's someone else, benefitting in some other way. We can't know what that is at the moment, but yes, we have to be alive to the possibility that it really is all about Wilson, this really is about the money, and the notes to the others and the murder of Peters are some sort of curveball."

"Yep. So, might be about the money, might not. Might be about revenge, might not."

"Yes, Marc, that's about it," she said, nodding. "I'm going to look over the inquest. I want you to speak to Armstrong. Not sure if he'll be at home, but given the armed guard, he shouldn't be hard to find. And I don't care how difficult it is, but you absolutely need to speak to him without the wife."

"Right."

"Find out who he was with last night, if there's a woman, a mistress… If there is such a woman, has he told her anything of his past? We need to get that out of him. Or we might have more chance of getting it out of her, so just get a name."

"You're assuming there's a her? I mean, what I meant was, I'm not implying there's a him, it might just be that he's doing something his wife hates him doing. Going to the dogs, going down the pub, I don't know…"

"You're right. But you get a feeling, don't you? And I got the feeling. There's a woman involved, I'm pretty sure, and I'm not just saying it because there's always a woman involved."

He nodded. "I'll put the call through to the guard, get his whereabouts. I suspect he'll be at home with all the doors locked and a loaded baseball bat beneath his pillow."

Pereira smiled. "Probably. I'm going to start running down the characters from the inquest. Meet you back at the ranch whenever." She looked at her watch. "I really should get home in a couple of hours. Call me if I'm gone by the time you get back."

"Sure. You in tomorrow?"

There was the question. Tomorrow. That thing that was in another compartment in her head.

"Don't know," she said. "Hey, let's try and get this wrapped up tonight, and we don't have to be."

"Sure thing," he said, although neither of them thought for a moment that was likely to happen.

Bain turned away, walking quickly through the churchyard. Pereira watched him for a moment, then looked up at the grey sky, all the while struggling to keep the door closed on that compartment in her brain, the one she didn't want to look inside.

31

The day continued, bleak and grey, as Bain walked through Kelvingrove Park. He'd parked on Kelvin Way, and was walking past the bandstand, heading for an area of grass, where he'd been told he would find Glenn Armstrong, accompanied as he was by the constable on guard duty. The other on-duty officer had remained at Armstrong's house.

It was currently under discussion at the station whether or not to allot more officers to the task. There was also the option of taking Armstrong and his family and moving them out of Glasgow to a safe house until the killer had been apprehended. The downside of the latter, of course, was the possibility of the killer never being apprehended. As a short-term measure, however, it was currently favoured.

As ever with these things, with discussions continuing at a high level in Dalmarnock, it wasn't just about saving Armstrong's life. If someone wanted him dead badly enough, there was a chance it was going to happen at some point. It was about the police not looking bad if something did happen to him. For every article a journalist was poised to write about Police Scotland not making the effort to save the life of someone obviously under threat, there was the counter article talking about how much was being spent on the life of one individual.

Despite the weather, there was a band playing in the pavilion. Bluegrass. Not miked up, and Bain wondered if it was an official thing organised through the park, or whether they'd just pitched up for the afternoon.

Good spot. Lousy afternoon.

There was a drummer, with bass, snare and high-hat, two fiddles, three acoustic guitars, an acoustic bass, an accordion and a banjo. Despite the lack of power and therefore of a mixing desk, the mix sounded perfect, every instrument where it should be.

They were playing Red Hot Chili Peppers' *Dani California*, which sounded bizarre and wonderful to Bain in its bluegrass form, the violins electric, without the need for power. He stopped to listen, hands in pockets.

Looked to the sky, the afternoon set grim. The rest of the weekend too, by the sound of it, with talk of much heavier rain by Sunday afternoon. The way it was going, the cricket season would never be starting on time; or, more likely, they'd be playing the first few games of the season on fields that resembled marshland.

He was worried about Pereira. Knew how hard it was for her, juggling work and family, with no partner to help, totally reliant on her mother. Equally knew that it was her choice, and that she would want neither his help nor his pity. Still, she was the best partner he'd had in the last ten years, and his compassion for her wasn't going anywhere. If it came to it, he would need to try to take on the burden of the case the following day, and hope that she managed to spend some time with Anais and Robin.

As the tune came to an end, there was a smattering of applause from the few who had gathered around the pavilion. Bain stood for another moment, knowing that he really had to get on, but unable to drag himself away just yet. Would wait to hear the next tune. That was all, hear what it was, then move.

He looked away up the small hill, past some trees. There was the officer, standing straight, hands on hips, bulky waterproof jacket over her bulletproof vest, a man sitting glumly on a seat in front of her. *Glum, even from here*, thought Bain.

The band started playing what sounded like Madonna's *Like a Virgin*. He smiled to himself, listened for another few moments, and then turned up the hill and started walking.

*

"This is how it works," said Bain.

Armstrong had acknowledged him, but said little. He was sitting forward, elbows resting on his legs, staring at the damp grass. He looked annoyed.

"And that newspaper," said Bain, "the one that writes that

195

article complaining about how much money we're spending to protect you, they need to make out that actually you might not be that much worth protecting. And they can't do that by saying you're just a sales rep. Sales reps read the paper. Nothing wrong with being a sales rep. So they need to get something bad. They need to rake. They need to find the dirt. Then they can cry outrage, then they can be appalled on behalf of their readers because the police are spending money on a whatever… whatever there is to find. The liar. The cheat. The womaniser. That's their story. And that's what it's coming to."

Still nothing. Armstrong looked resolutely down at the grass, the rain falling on the back of his close-shaven head.

"I'm not in the room, Mr. Armstrong, and the Police Service are going to make whatever decision they do based on what they think is best for you, and it'll have nothing to do with what you do in your spare time. But if we're going to protect you, we need all the facts. If they're going to come after you, and us, for a decision we make on your behalf, we need to be ready for them. Whatever it is you're sitting there, staring at the grass, keeping to yourself, you need to let me know. And if there's a name, I need the name. We need to find out who killed Archie and Peters. Sure, it sounds like you should be next on the list, but what if you're not? What if there are others in the firing line? We're spending our resources safeguarding you, then some other poor sucker gets a–"

"I just needed to get away from Jan," he said, his voice shooting out, the head still down. "I just came here to get some peace. She's just always in my ear. It's like… you don't know what it's like, man. You just want to tell her to shut up."

"I don't need to know why you're here now," said Bain. "I think it's pretty obvious why. I need–"

"I'm saying," said Armstrong, "that I came here for peace. Jesus. Is that such a hard concept to grasp? Peace, that's all. And now you're here. I might as well be at home having her nipping my ear, as you standing over me with your sanctimonious bullshit."

"I think that came out wrong," said Bain.

"What?"

"Sanctimonious? I don't think so. But really, there's an easy way for me to be walking away from here leaving you in peace, Mr. Armstrong. Tell me the name of…"

"Hilton," he said. "All right? Lucy Hilton. A bit on the side.

The casual shag. There we are. Congratulations, you got me to say it. Her name's Lucy Hilton, and last night… I went out on my bike, just like I said, earlier in the evening. Then later, after Jan had gone to bed, I went back out. Jan never comes down the stairs, she's always asleep when I get up there, so I was safe. You know? I was safe."

He had turned to look at Bain as he spoke, then stopped at the look on his face.

"What?" he said, his annoyance seemingly renewed, even though it had never really gone away. "You're looking at me like… what?"

"There can't be that many Lucy Hilton's in Glasgow, I wouldn't have thought," said Bain.

"Fuck should I know?" said Armstrong.

"She's a lawyer at Bolden Associates?"

"So?" he said.

Underrated in surveys, thought Bain, if anyone actually did such a survey, but *so?* was probably the most frequently asked question that the police received. That, and its companion, *so fuck?*

"How d'you know her?" asked Bain.

"Seriously? What?"

"How d'you know Lucy Hilton?"

"How the fuck *d'you* know her?"

"How do you know Lucy Hilton?" Bain repeated. "Get on with it, and don't make me take you into the station, Mr. Armstrong, because that's where we're going if you don't start talking."

"Fuck's sake," muttered Armstrong, head shaking, looking away. "It was… I write this thing. Just a stupid blog about Scottish politics. My tuppence ha'penny's worth. Gets pretty brutal in the comments section sometimes, but what the fuck, eh?"

He stopped, still staring down the hill towards the band, his annoyance emanating from him like steam from a rugby scrum in the depths of winter.

"Go on," said Bain.

Another shake of the head.

"Lucy contacted me. She was actually nice, and I mean, that's pretty fucking rare. Usually I've got someone on there accusing me of being a wanker. Like I'm the bad guy. Like I'm the reason politicians are a shower of arseholes."

———

"We don't need the commentary," said Bain.

He got a sharp glance, and then Armstrong continued, his voice still full of outrage at having to talk.

"We worked out we both lived in Glasgow, agreed to meet for coffee one day. That was that. I mean, it happens sometimes, doesn't it? Like in a fucking movie. Call it a thunderbolt, some shite like that."

Armstrong's voice, thought Bain, was about as far away in tone from the notion of thunderbolt movie romance as he could imagine. He could have been describing himself and Hilton getting into argument at a pitbull-baiting arena.

"I'm sure you can get Hugh Grant and Julia Roberts to play you in the movie," said Bain.

"Fucking hilarious."

"What was the timeframe? When did she first get in touch?"

A moment, Armstrong bent forward, picked at a piece of grass. "Not long. Like four weeks ago... Don't you fucking tell, Jan, by the way. I mean it."

"You're not in a position to be demanding anything, Mr. Armstrong."

"The fuck shouldn't I?" he said, looking round sharply. "You think I'm just telling you this shit for biscuits?"

"What does that even mean?" said Bain, almost smiling. "Seriously? Two people have been murdered, and we're conducting an investigation. Did you ever discuss Mark Randall with Ms. Hilton?"

"What?"

"Answer the question."

Finally, having conducted the entire interview sitting down, the sergeant standing over him. Armstrong got to his feet. Braced himself, aggressive, jaw clenched. The constable behind Bain, who had been watching the surroundings, seemingly paying no attention to the interview, aligned herself a little more closely with Bain, getting ready to intervene.

"Now why the fuck would I have done that?"

"I don't know," said Bain. "I don't know why you'd go and meet someone who contacted you on the Internet either, but you did. Did you ever discuss Mark Randall?"

"Off course I fucking didn't!"

They were standing a few feet apart. Not much. Close enough that, at the raising of Armstrong's voice, Bain could smell the alcohol on his breath. He let the silence extend, waiting to see what Armstrong would do with it. A peculiar kind of a stand-off.

"What?" said Armstrong soon enough, unable to tolerate the quiet.

"Are we going to find you're lying again?" said Bain.

"Jesus."

"You're two out of two so far on not being truthful during interviews."

"Have you seen her? I mean, really, she's fucking gorgeous. That's it. God knows what she sees in me, but do I give I fuck?"

Bain held his gaze for a while longer, still didn't believe him, using the time to wonder if it was appropriate to take him into the station, but ultimately deciding that they likely weren't quite there yet.

He turned and glanced at the constable behind, nodded, and she returned the look, backing off slightly.

"I think maybe you should just go home for the rest of the day, Mr. Armstrong," said Bain. "Put on a movie, and maybe you and your wife can sit and watch it in silence."

Armstrong lowered his eyes, the snarl on his lips, then turned away and slumped back down onto the bench.

32

Pereira sat in the small room at the station with the papers from the inquest. The others in the team were all on the latest murder, but she felt it right that she and Bain stay on the Randall case. That was where the result was coming from, and she had the feeling. Something was close.

Usually she'd have some idea where it'd come from, but not this time. This time it was a strange, alien notion that she didn't necessarily recognise in herself. It was coming, that was all, and more quickly than had seemed possible.

Tobin, Parks and Somerville were doing the regulation legwork of Peters' murder inquiry. Last known contact with anyone – albeit that seemed to be Sergeant Bain – comparing the wheelbarrow tracks and the murder weapons, looking through all Peters' digital correspondence, the nuts and bolts of tying the two murders together.

Given the level of detail in the similarities between the two, including several points not released to the media, it seemed fairly safe to assume a common killer, but no investigation ever got anywhere by assuming anything. Everything had to be nailed down, as close to the time of the murder as possible, all part of compiling the case for conviction, assuming the perpetrator was to be apprehended.

Pereira was sure there would be something in the inquest papers. She was surprised, but also relieved, that the information hadn't been digitised. Not everything had, after all. Too big a manpower requirement. There were several large box files, and she'd been happy to take herself off to a small meeting room, a cup of coffee and a glass of water in hand, and to sit with a view of the Clyde as she worked her way through the boxes.

So much time these days was spent looking at monitors, tracing e-mails, looking at phones, all of modern life reduced to gigabytes and technical specifications. Like everything else that you remembered from a bygone age, no matter how long ago, there was a comfort to be had in doing paperwork, and jotting down notes in an A4 notebook as she went along.

She worked quickly, took everything in that was required, scribbled down anything she thought she might need to remember. So far it hadn't been much.

The day was dark grey outside, the room warm, but she wasn't tired. It was coming, it was in these pages. The testimonies and the list of daily attendees. People came and went. Lawyers and media, friends and family, of both the victim and the poor souls who'd been unable to save him.

When a name finally jumped out at her, after almost two hours, it was a name she hadn't been expecting. She couldn't, if asked, have said who she would have expected to see there, but not this one. Not the Reverend Dr. Thomas Melville, with whom she had felt strangely uncomfortable whilst sitting in Glasgow Cathedral.

Reverend Smith had been there, of course, that was entirely reasonable. He was the minister of the church through which the Chief Scout expedition had been organised. But Melville? There was no reason given for his attendance. And he had been there on just one day, that was all. A day not so different from any other.

Presumably he'd attended in an official capacity. Not unreasonable, given that the church and its organisation were under scrutiny. Nevertheless, his name naturally leapt off the page, and you didn't see coincidences like this in a case and ignore them.

"Fucking bingo," she heard herself say, and then she shook her head and smiled at the words, and the strange feeling of lift that the information had given her.

Did she really think Melville might have had something to do with it? A senior minister in the Church of Scotland? It didn't make sense, and not because of his position. The Church had been about to be the beneficiaries of a long-term deal with Wilson. Why kill him?

She read on, specifically looking for Melville now. Regardless of whether or not she found any other mention of him, she would need to return to the day of his attendance at the inquest, try to establish what might have been different about that day and if there was anything in particular that might have encouraged his presence.

She wasn't really looking for any other names to unexpectedly crop up. Finding the one seemed almost more than she could have hoped for. There was so much police work that involved doing what you had to do with little prospect of success, and this was definitely such a case. She could have imagined herself sitting here all day and finding nothing. But first there was Dr. Melville, and then, shortly afterwards, another name leapt even more glaringly and strangely from the page.

The phone was in her hand to call Bain when it started to ring. The Sergeant had got to her first.

*

Cooper was leaning forward, elbows on the desk. Both Pereira and Bain were in his office, but only Pereira had been doing any talking.

Bain had learned that Armstrong had been seeing Lucy Hilton, adding to the fact that she herself had admitted spending an evening with Archie Wilson; on top of this, they now had Pereira discovering that Hilton had been in attendance as a work experience lawyer at the Mark Randall inquest. It was one day only, but it was another connection.

"The affair, if that's what it is, with Armstrong is enough to bring her in," said Pereira, "so she's coming. Her presence at the inquest, however, that adds a new level."

"Yes," said Cooper. "But it doesn't put her hand on the knife, and it doesn't put her anywhere near either of the victims on the night they died. How d'you want to play it?"

"She was at the inquest acting for a company called Crevette & Parkin. We need to speak to someone there, try to establish if she played any part, or if she had any relationships there with other parties."

Pereira looked at her watch as she spoke.

"However," she said, "I'm pretty certain we won't get anyone until Monday morning… This angle points to her prior knowledge. She knew what had gone on with these people. When Archie Wilson suddenly appeared in the news with all that money, it allowed her to move straight in. She knew this guy's past. Other people weren't joining the dots, didn't even know that the dots existed. But she could make the connection straight away."

"She must have dealt with hundreds of cases," said Cooper. "Why remember this one?"

"We don't know yet. It was her first one, maybe. Perhaps there was something else significant going on we don't know about. I say we bring her in and ask her."

"Tonight?"

"Yes. We have guards on Armstrong," said Pereira. "For that, as well as so many other reasons, we need to work to bring this killer into custody as quickly as possible."

"Cost alone," said Cooper, staring at the floor. "That's what the boss'll say," he added. Then he looked up, glanced at Bain, back to Pereira.

"And the priest?"

"The minister, sir," said Pereira. "Again, we don't know. We're going to speak to him too, but in the first instance, we need to be concentrating on Hilton."

Cooper shook his head, eyes drifting away again.

"Jesus," he said. "Lawyers and the church. What a combination. It's just asking to be sued, buggered and condemned to the pits of Hell, all in a oner."

He stood up, turned his back on them, and looked out the window.

Not much to see. Raindrops streaked the panes, dark outside, his reflection staring back at him. He looked through, at the lights of the offices away to his left.

A Saturday evening in March, and this is where he was. What were other people doing in the world, out there, right this minute? Those other people who had started life in the same way as him, same school, same university, same degree, what had become of them? Were they stuck at work on a pishing wet Saturday evening, knowing that they were going to be utterly condemned by the following morning's newspapers? Where were the left/right forks in his path that led him to this? Which one could he go back to?

As ever, prosaically, he kicked himself mentally. It wasn't about the past. It was about identifying the forks in the future, and trying not to make the wrong choice. That was all.

The forks, however, always seemed much more defined once the decision had been taken.

His shook his head, shaking away the thought, and turned.

"Bring her in," he said. "Leave the vicar until tomorrow. Let me know what she's got to say for herself."

Then, as Pereira and Bain accepted the instruction and started to get to their feet, Cooper looked curiously at Bain, brow furrowed.

"And the other guy, Cobalt," he said. That was a name that had jarred since he had first been mentioned. "He was working with her, right? Different company, same ends."

"That's right, sir," said Bain.

"You think we should bring him in too?"

Pereira glanced at Bain, picked up on his agreement without a word or nod being exchanged.

"Yes," said Pereira, "we should. We bring them in separately, see how much their stories clash. Maybe we get something out of that."

She nodded, within the nod a slight self-reproach. She should have thought of that herself, shouldn't have needed Cooper to come up with it. The thought of Cobalt had crossed her mind at some point in the last half hour but she'd been thinking about too many things and the thought had been lost.

"Right," said Cooper, "get them in, let me know how it pans out."

And with that, Pereira and Bain were on their way.

33

Cobalt was having none of it. He was going through the usual bastardised version of the five stages of grief that came with being unexpectedly brought to the police station. He'd done surprise and annoyance, was currently at amusement, and had not long to go before moving on to anger and then silence, thought Pereira.

"Seriously," said Cobalt. "How many times? I'm good. People look me up. That's what happens. Look, I get it, I really do. How these things start. My name's Eston Cobalt. Deal with it. We're in Glasgow, and it sounds a bit, you know, whatever. You might think it sounds a bit wank. Out of place. Pretentious. But I'm telling you, when it comes to dealing with money, that's what people want. They don't want to be investing their money with someone called Big Malky, or Tommy One Ear or, I don't know, Billy The Fish. You know? No offence to Glasgow or anything, but they don't want to give their money to someone who actually sounds like they come from Glasgow. So they see a guy named Eston Cobalt, and they think, that sounds pretty cool. This guy, he's got a nice ring to him. Different. This could be the guy. It sounds New York, you know. It sounds like money."

He made the money sign.

Pereira and Bain stared deadpan across the table. At some point they had wondered about splitting up, but Pereira had decided she wanted to conduct both interviews. And in any case, the way in which Hilton had come to the station, kicking and screaming and already threatening legal action at the outrage of her Saturday evening being ruined, Pereira had been happy to leave her to stew for a while, now that they had her in the building.

Bain looked down at a piece of paper, raised his eyes and said, "Malcolm Pratt."

Cobalt smiled. "Yeah, sure, laugh, whatever, I don't mind. My parents called me Malcolm. Big deal. You know who my parents are? They're just a couple of people who live in Ayrshire, that's all. I call them at Christmas. That's all they need."

Oh my God, thought Pereira.

The indifferent smile on Cobalt's face vanished, as though he had offended even himself with his dismissal of his parents' importance.

"Look," he said, and now there was a new edge to his voice as he moved on to the next stage, "that might be how it started. The name. Got people curious. But the name's nothing without the talent behind it, and I'm good. I earn people money. You get a reputation for that. And that's how it went. Now people come to me because of who I am. The reputation. The ability. The knowledge that I'll leave them richer than when they came to me."

"So Lucy Hilton had no part to play in it?" asked Pereira.

"Seriously?" he said, the anger growing in his voice. "What is it with you people? You have to see connivance and collusion and, I don't know, underhand crap, you see underhand crap, everywhere you look."

"Two people have been murdered," said Pereira, "so, yes, we see underhand crap."

"Wait, now you've got me murdering Archie and, I don't know, this other guy who I've never even heard of? Holy shit. We're done here."

"You didn't answer the question," said Bain.

Cobalt looked at him, eyebrow raised, something in it to suggest that he needed the question repeated, even though he still would have no intention of answering it.

"Did Lucy Hilton have anything to do with you getting the Archie Wilson account?"

Cobalt held Bain's gaze for a moment, then he turned back to Pereira. The anger gone, a smile returned to his face.

"I have a question for you, Detective Inspector, or whatever it is you are. Given that we're done here, and I'm really not going to answer any more of your dumbass questions, can I go, or are you actually going to arrest me and force me to get a lawyer in here? Is that where this thing's going, because if that's what you want…?"

Pereira sat back, an obvious movement, her eyes on him, her right hand left resting against the desk. She drummed her fingers slowly, rolling them round, the quiet pad of her fingertips on the desktop the only sound. Finally, as she sensed the ejaculation of forced laughter from Cobalt was imminent, she nodded at the door.

"There you are," she said.

Cobalt rolled his eyes, shook his head, pushed the chair back from behind him, held the two of them one last time in a contemptuous stare, and walked to the door.

"Mr. Pratt?" said Bain, as Cobalt's hand went to the door.

He hesitated, then finally he turned, shaking his head.

"I know," said Cobalt, "don't suddenly take off to the Amazonian rainforest. You people are assholes."

He opened the door, he left, he slammed the door behind him.

Pereira laughed lightly, shaking her head.

"Mr. Pratt…" she said. "Nice."

*

Lucy Hilton had gone straight to the fifth stage. Sitting in sullen silence, staring at the table in the small room.

Pereira and Bain were sitting opposite, waiting. Occasionally speaking, but Pereira was more minded just to sit it out, wait for her to finally open up. She knew Hilton was going to talk, because she was still sitting there.

Having said all that – it was almost as though she and Bain were having the conversation by telepathy – this interrogation was not taking place inside a vacuum. Life was going on around it. Other strands of the case; Glenn Armstrong and his family living in fear, a police guard at their door; and her own family at home, a Saturday, usually a day for her and the kids – or her and Robin, to be more precise, with Anais lurking unhappily in the background – had continued now into evening, with her mother once more called to duty. Every such day, it seemed to Pereira, brought the day when her mother moved in that bit closer.

"Is it possible," said Pereira, breaking another long silence, "we'll discover that Archie Wilson was thinking of moving his business, so that you and Mr. Cobalt were forced to take swift action to ensure his money stayed where it was? Archie's dad seems a conservative type of man. One can imagine he would just leave the money where it was for quite some time, allowing you two to take your share."

"Oh, wait," said Hilton, finally plucked out from beneath her blanket of silence, "here was me thinking I was in here being questioned for murder. But no, it's what? Fraud? Embezzlement? Anything else you want to lay at my door, while we're here? You know how us lawyers love false police accusations."

"You'd've hardly needed to have been embezzling anything," said Bain. "Given the amount of money involved, Eston Cobalt's cut alone was going to be substantial. He wouldn't have had to defraud Mr. Wilson of anything, just hang on to the account."

"Well go and ask Eston then," said Hilton. "Seriously? You need me to explain this shit to you? I'm the lawyer. Someone asks me to do something for them, I do it. I either bill them by the hour, or I have a set fee for any particular piece of work. It doesn't matter how much my client is worth, because I'm not charging him a percentage of that worth. Am I?"

"Didn't say you were," said Pereira.

"Why am I here?" asked Hilton. "Really, I'm leaving in a minute, I've had enough."

"No, you're not," said Bain.

She flashed a glare at Bain, the threatening, *just watch me* look.

"What we're saying," said Pereira, "is that you remembered Archie Wilson's involvement with the death of Mark Randall. Maybe you had more knowledge than was revealed at the inquest, maybe not. Perhaps you'll tell us."

Hilton snorted. Pereira talked on.

"When Archie suddenly appeared in the news with all that money, you saw an opportunity. You joined forces with Mr. Cobalt, with whom you perhaps already had some sort of alliance – and that'll be easy enough to check out, so you can lie to us about it if you want, but it'd be stupid – and you approached Archie."

"Because people who win money are never approached by financial advisors," said Hilton.

"You had something the others didn't have," said Pereira. "You knew about Mark Randall. Maybe you knew more about Mark Randall than you're letting on. Maybe you knew enough to blackmail Archie into employing the two of you. Low-level black–"

"Wait, what? What would I be blackmailing him about?"

"Low-level blackmail," continued Pereira, as though Hilton hadn't spoken, "nothing too significant. Not actually taking any money off him, nothing that the police would be able to come after you for. Maybe not ethical, and bad for business if it got out, but it was just a bit of leverage, that's all."

"And what would I be blackmailing him about?" repeated Hilton.

"How about you tell us everything you know, and we can decide whether any of it would be serviceable blackmail material."

Hilton smiled, lifted her shoulders slightly.

"And what of it?" she said. "What if that was it? You've got me sitting here on a Saturday night because I paid attention at an inquest eighteen years ago? I'm sitting here because I'm good at my job? Seriously?"

"The Detective Inspector already outlined where we're going with this," said Bain, and Hilton shifted her contemptuous look across.

"Oh, you're speaking again, that's good. The minion. What was the point again, minion, I might have missed it in amongst the all-consuming haze of bullshit?"

"The point was that you and Cobalt were working together," said Pereira, "you used your prior knowledge to get Archie Wilson to take you on as lawyers and financial advisors, and then at some stage, when Archie had had a little more time to think it over, he decided that he didn't need you or want you, and that he was going to move his business. You went out for dinner with him, maybe tried to win him over that way. That didn't work, so you killed him."

"Oh, that's just beautiful," she said. "I mean, congratulations, that is magnificent. Really."

"Where were you on Tuesday evening?" said Bain.

Hilton turned back to him. "What?"

Her face still had the disdainful look, still the incredulity.

"Where were you on Tuesday evening?"

"Why?"

Bain and Pereira stared across the desk.

"Wait, you're being serious. Tuesday? The night Archie was murdered?"

"Yes," said Pereira. "Where were you the night Archie Wilson was murdered?"

"Jesus. What is it in this grand theory of yours, I mean, where…" and Hilton shook her head, the words no longer flowing coherently. Then she slapped her hand against the side of her head, as though she could literally knock sense into herself, then said, "Why is it you think I then killed Iain Peters? What's the motivation for that?"

"You knew Archie had something to hide from the Mark Randall death. You had enough to force his hand, but you wanted more. You started seeing Glenn Armstrong–"

Hilton snorted.

"–to try to get him to talk. You learned what you needed to. Then you set up the upcoming deaths of Wilson, Peters and Armstrong, as though they were revenge for the death of Mark Randall. Your own personal motive only required the killing of Wilson, but you wanted to make it look like someone else's motive. You hoped that at the end of it, you'd have this huge fund at your disposal, and you would find Mr. Wilson Senior easier to deal with and manipulate, particularly since he'd just lost his son. You would also then not have to concern yourself with the story getting out, via Archie, of how you'd come to have his business in the first place."

"That is some convoluted story," said Hilton. "You been making that up all day?"

"Where were you on Tuesday evening?" asked Bain.

As ever, Pereira thought, the slightly different angle of attack was of great benefit. Always hurt the interviewee, no matter how solid they might be in defence.

Hilton held his gaze for a few moments. Tongue ran across her teeth, though her lips were closed, then she glanced back at Pereira.

Bain waited another moment and then opened the thin folder in front of him, took out an A4 black and white photograph and passed it over to Hilton. "This was taken one block away from the entrance to the Garland Club on Tuesday, fifteen minutes before the last sighting of Archie Wilson."

Hilton looked at the picture. She was walking down Hope Street beside Cobalt, side by side, though at least not hand in hand. Not on Tuesday they hadn't been.

"Can you tell us what you were doing on Tuesday evening?" asked Pereira.

34

It was one of those days when Pereira would have liked a long commute on the way home. She needed the breathing space. Firstly, to think about the case, put together the information they had, file it away in the respective compartments, and park it for the following morning; then she needed the transition, the down period, the time that, to be honest, could well have lasted a couple of hours, following which she could switch back on to being mum and daughter. Thanking her mother, seeing her off without getting the lecture or the worry or the subtle hints about what they should be doing next, and then turning her attention at last to the children. Taking in Robin's babbling download of the day, trying to get through to Anais, trying to deal with her claims of favouritism and implied hurt at Pereira generally allowing Robin to run out of words before shifting her attention.

Today, as so often, she got just over twenty minutes.

They had done the necessary paperwork at the end of the day. They had decided to hold Lucy Hilton overnight. They had allowed Cobalt to go, but with the intention of bringing him back in the following day. They had applied to have surveillance placed on Cobalt and to have his calls monitored. How easily they took the decision, she sometimes thought, to pry on people's lives. They'd applied for the paperwork to be able to go to Lucy Hilton's office and home and remove papers pertaining to Archie Wilson, her computer and any other communication devices.

The officers still stood guard on the home of Glenn Armstrong, but otherwise the case had been parked for the night. Little to be done by that time on a Saturday, except to see what the Sunday papers were going to do with the latest murder, and how much the police were going to be vilified for allowing it to happen.

She walked in the door at twenty-four minutes to ten, quietly as ever, trying to gain those extra few seconds. Stood for a moment, staring at the stairs directly in front of her, wondering if both kids would be upstairs already. Robin should be in his bed by this time. When she was that age, her mother certainly would have had her in bed by nine thirty, Saturday or otherwise. Grandparents worked to a different clock, of course, she knew that much.

Silence. There didn't even seem to be the sound of the television coming from the sitting room, which was unusual. Her mother would normally be watching *Casualty*, although she couldn't think whether *Casualty* would still be on at this time.

And then the first thump, then the hurried footsteps to the door, she braced herself, the moment was over, then the sitting room door was flung open, and Robin charged out, pale blue dressing gown, Thomas The Tank Engine pyjamas, white, fluffy M&S slippers that Lena had given him for Christmas.

"Mummy called and Anais is crying!" he shouted, and he was straight into her arms.

She bent down, hugging him, looking over his shoulder at her mum, who always approached apologetically at these moments, as though it was her fault that Robin wasn't already fast asleep.

There it was, she thought, the thing that she'd placed in its compartment to be considered at another time. To be dealt with at another time. And Lena had gone and taken the timing out of her hands.

"Thank you, Robin, I'll call Mummy in a while. Have you had a good day?"

"Anais is crying!" he said again, as it didn't seem to have had as much an impact on his mum as he thought it might.

"I know," said Pereira, "I heard you the first time. I'll go and speak to Anais shortly. How was your day?"

"Boring," he said.

"That's a shame. How come?"

"Just was. D'you want to play Thomas cards?"

She smiled. The Thomas the Tank Engine card game. Kind of like *Top Trumps* multiplied by Wagner's *Ring Cycle*. Always an effort, she was ashamed to admit, but all she had to do was sit there, on the other side of the table, and keep him amused.

"Of course," she said, looking over his shoulder at her mother, who was shaking her head. "Tell you what, I'll have a quick word with Nanni, then I'll go and say hi to Anais to see why she's crying, then I'll be right down, OK? Give me five minutes."

"I'll give you double that," said Robin. "I'll give you eight."

He smiled at the joke, she smiled back, then he ran past his gran, back into the sitting room.

Pereira got to her feet, the look of apology already on her face.

"Sorry I'm so late," she said.

"That's all right," said her mum, as ever.

"When did Lena call?"

Her mum held her gaze for a moment, then looked at her watch, said, "About two hours ago. She spoke to Anais. Asked her what she was doing tomorrow when you came to see her with Robin. Anais, apparently, told her that wasn't the case. Lena told Anais that she'd spoken to you this afternoon."

"Shit," said Pereira, then dropped her gaze, shook her head, offered a quick hand of apology.

"I'll leave you to your mess," she said, rubbing her daughter's arm, but Pereira felt the rebuke in the tone.

Imagine if she finally conceded to her mother and got her to move in with them. That would be it, the end of her personal life.

Shoot me now, she'd once unadvisedly said to Anais, another comment that had further undermined the relationship between gran and granddaughter. "Always a bad idea," Lena had said to her later, "to let the kid know that you're in it together against the grandparent."

Lena forever seemed more grown up than her. How did that happen when Lena was eight years younger? When Lena worked in advertising, writing copy for wine labels and packets of coffee and pillows that would cure virtually every ailment currently known in human society, and seemed to work five hour days largely centred around meetings sitting on bean bags in an open-plan office, with a crowd of twenty-three-year olds, while Pereira was doing this. This! Bringing up two kids, and spending her working life dealing with serious crimeland, Scotland. Why did Lena always seem to her to be more responsible, more sensible?

213

Her mum stood at the door.

"Will you be at church?" she asked.

Pereira shook her head.

"Sorry, I need to work. I'll drop Robin off with Annie, she'll take him to Mums and Tots, then I'll just get Lena to pick him up at twelve from church."

"And what if she doesn't show up?"

Jesus, don't start that. Once! It had happened once!

"She's his mum," said Pereira, "she'll be there. She knows how much trouble it caused the last time."

A moment, a shake of the head, and then her mother was gone, the front door closed.

Pereira put her head into the sitting room, said, "Two minutes!" to Robin, as brightly and cheerfully as she could, then she walked slowly up the stairs. Giving herself the time. Giving up, as she walked, on the following day. It was done now. Ruined by her own procrastination.

It could be, of course, that tomorrow wouldn't be happening in either of the ways she'd planned. Work might take over completely. As it was, what option did she have now? Her daughter was crying, because once again, she'd found out that her mother, her awful, useless, obsessive, lovestruck mother, was putting her lesbian ex-partner ahead of her thirteen-year-old girl.

She didn't even think that she'd made that decision. She still held out some hope that in the end she'd have done the right thing. In the face of it, however, she'd been unable to tell Lena that she'd had other plans. And now, if she told Anais that Lena had picked up the wrong end of the stick, Anais would never believe her.

She knocked on the bedroom door, waited a second or two, then opened it and walked in.

SUNDAY

35

Robin had been miserable and very tired after staying up too late. He cried when she left him with Annie. Cried? Cried was a nice way to describe it. She'd left Annie's house with Robin on the floor throwing an all-out tantrum and Annie's daughter, Sarah, clinging on to her mum's leg, asking what was wrong. Pereira had remarked, consumed by guilt, that Annie's child looked scared, and Annie pointed out that, like every other pre-school child on earth, she looked at other children having tantrums as though it was completely alien and incredible, while being no stranger to one herself. Annie had shooed Pereira away, smiling, telling her to go and get on. Catch the killer that all the Scottish Sundays had on their front pages that day.

Pereira stopped at the small newsagents in Dalmarnock she occasionally used, just to look at the headlines. *Necropolis Killer Strikes Again*, mundane in itself, was used mundanely by more than one. *Horror of Bible John 2* was another. That almost made her smile. *Bible John 2*. Nice. Like serial killers were sequels. And there it was, the one she'd been expecting. *Clueless Cops Face Public Outrage as Death Toll Mounts.*

She walked away, head shaking. Could you really call two murders a mounting death toll? What do you call Syria and South Sudan, or migrant boats sinking in the Mediterranean?

She walked into the station, noticing a complete lack of public outrage directed at Police Scotland HQ in Riverside. Maybe public outrage was being expressed in a more modern way, on Twitter and Snapchat.

#tenwaysthepoliceruinedmylife

The team was assembled around the table in the small conference room in the usual formation, short of Parks, who was out, and Tobin, who had the day off. A Sunday, no one begrudged him it, or those who did were keeping it to themselves.

They hadn't spoken to Lucy Hilton again, and she'd been left to consider her position. They had until that evening to release her or charge her with involvement in the deaths of Archie Wilson and Iain Peters.

"We're a long way from that," said Cooper. "We can hope she tells us more, but if she's involved in these murders, that lawyer of hers isn't sitting down there at the moment suggesting she spills the beans. Where are we on the paperwork?"

"Oh, it's done." Pereira looked surprised. "Sorry, I thought you'd been told. Sergeant Parks is at Hilton's office at the moment, gathering up everything we need. She's got Payne and Cleveland with her."

"Good."

"We don't have a lot of time," said Pereira, "but we can get into all that stuff this afternoon, hopefully pull some things together. We've got more people back on the CCTV footage from Tuesday evening, starting from where we caught Hilton and Cobalt together on Hope Street. Then we're going to speak to Hilton's PA, and to a couple of the senior suits in her company. And before we go back in with her, we'll go and see Cobalt again. Might do that early on, actually, and if we need to bring him back in and keep him here, we'll do it."

"Busy day," said Cooper, nodding. "You think we need to leave the guard on Armstrong? Already getting muttering from upstairs."

"Definitely," said Pereira, eyes widening slightly at the idea that perhaps they didn't. "I mean, Hilton may well be guilty of nothing but opportunism. We're focused on this today, but easily, tomorrow we could be back trying to figure out a whole new line of inquiry."

He was reluctantly nodding in agreement, although as ever he would be thinking about budgets. Difficult though their relationship was, she understood that Cooper was a policeman, and he wanted to do his job. He wasn't a pencil pusher and he wasn't an accountant, but those were the people who held him

216

accountable, and so he held his staff accountable for the same things.

Cooper was staring at the desk, fingers tapping. Pereira was waiting, wanting to get on. Bain and Somerville contributed little so far, and were more there to be tasked with what was next.

"We just need to get on, sir," said Pereira. "If we could."

Cooper looked up, then quickly got to his feet. "Of course, Inspector." He looked out the internal window at the paltry numbers of the late Sunday morning staff. "Take what you need, or what you can get. Let's try and pin this down today, and if you can get something positive on Hilton or Cobalt all the better. Where's Cobalt now, do we know?"

"Still in bed, sir," said Somerville. "Far as we know, given that we're not actually in his house."

"OK," said Cooper, "OK…" and he let any further words drift away, as he nodded at Pereira and left the room.

Pereira didn't waste any time.

"OK, Colin, I'll need you to help Sergeant Parks when she gets back. We need to get into Hilton's files as quickly as possible. And even before she gets back, start tracking down Hilton's past, anything you can find on her. Make phone calls, make connections. Find us something we don't know, Constable."

"Yes, ma'am," he said, and he was up and gone.

Long breath from Pereira, just her and Bain left.

"I want you to speak to the PA. She'll be at Hilton's office making sure Parks and the others don't steal the coffee and biscuits. When that's done, identify others at the firm you think worth speaking to. Let me know how you're doing, and I can get into it later if needs be. I'm off to speak to Cobalt, and then…" and she let the sentence go for a moment as she looked out the window to make sure Cooper wasn't coming back, feeling guilty as she did it. "I'm afraid I have to go home and see Anais for a short time. Just need to do–"

"It's all right, boss," said Bain.

He smiled, she returned the smile ruefully, and then the two of them were up and out the door.

*

The rain was tipping down as she headed out on the Great

217

Western Road to speak to the police constable currently sitting in a parked vehicle, fifty yards from Cobalt's front door. A horrible, grey morning, dark and cold, water on the roads, the pavements deserted bar occasional people huddled beneath hopelessly inadequate umbrellas, small dogs in pink raincoats scuttling around, pointlessly marking territory, investigating discarded, sodden chip wrappers.

She brought up Lena's number and called. At least now that part was easier. There was just no seeing Lena today, not for a chat, not for a coffee, not for anything. The chat would have to wait, whatever it was, and it pained her to have to say it. Wasn't this job, the awful hours and the constant drag on her time, wasn't that one of the reasons Lena had given for leaving in the first place?

Who would want to be married to this life? Apart from Martin, of course. He'd been happy. Happy to wait, happy to look after Anais, happy to still be up when Pereira got home. Happy to have weekends ruined and holiday plans changed at the last minute. Always happy, always there.

And then what had she done to him? How had she rewarded his faithfulness and attentiveness?

"Hey," she said, as Lena answered the phone.

"Hi," said Lena. She sounded flat. As ever, with any kind of tone to Lena's voice, Pereira was only too ready to assume that it must be her fault. There be must some way in which she'd displeased her.

"You all right?" asked Pereira.

"Sure. Just out the shower," said Lena. "I'll do a little work before going to get Robin. Been reading the papers. I take it you'll be a no-show."

It wasn't even a question. Maybe that's why she was flat. She had a speech for Pereira, she had something to say, and she'd already realised it wouldn't be happening.

Maybe that hour she was going to spend with Anais could be redirected?

Sitting at traffic lights, Pereira closed her eyes for a moment, slowly shook her head. *God, don't even go there*, she thought. *Don't start. It's not happening, just let it go and go home and speak to your daughter.*

"Sorry," said Pereira. "Really, I thought I'd be able to–"

"That's OK, really. Don't worry about it."

"You had something to say," said Pereira. *Here we go.*

"Maybe we could meet for coffee later in the week."

"Might as well just tell you now," said Lena, and Pereira drove off at the lights, phone clipped into a holder on the dashboard, earpiece in, heart sinking. She didn't want the quick chat over the phone. She didn't want the casual words tossed down a line when she couldn't see Lena's face. She wanted to look into her eyes, she wanted to be able to lean across a table and hold her hand, she wanted to feel the squeeze of Lena's fingers in hers.

"I can do coffee," said Pereira, hating herself for the desperation as the words emerged, sadly, pathetically into the car, where she sat alone.

"I'm seeing someone else," said Lena quickly, brutally. "I just thought you should know."

The words clamped around Pereira's chest. Round her heart, round her lungs. She couldn't breathe, her blood couldn't move. She couldn't speak.

"She's an actress. You might have seen her on TV, but really… you don't need to know who it is, yet."

"How long?" asked Pereira, forcing out the words.

Yet? Why yet? What was to come?

"Couple of months."

"You never said," said Pereira. Driving on instinct.

"No," said Lena.

And then silence.

Silence. Another set of lights. Pereira could feel the tremble beginning inside her, like her insides were hurting so much they had begun to vibrate, and that it was slowly carrying through the rest of her body. She gripped the steering wheel. She wondered if maybe she was about to start crying.

For God's sake, Aliya!

The lights changed. How long had they been sitting in silence on the phone? What was the point of that? One of them should just say something, put the silent, tortured conversation out of its misery.

"I should go," said Pereira.

"Yes," said Lena, and Pereira could almost hear the relief in her voice. "Sorry, Ali," she added.

And the phone went dead.

Short and pitiless and functional. Job done. Information dispatched.

The phone returned to its home screen. Pereira stared

219

straight ahead. Forced, deep breath, hands rhythmically squeezing the steering wheel as she arrived at Cobalt's apartment block, pulling in across the road.

Keep it together, Aliya, she thought. It was inevitable, and it didn't have to mean anything. Not yet. Of course Lena was seeing someone else. Why wouldn't she be? She wasn't the obsessed one. She wasn't the one hung up on the past.

And Lena could be difficult, after all. Maybe the actress wouldn't put up with her for very long.

There was a knock at the car window, and she jumped, turned to see Constable Graham, waving apologetically.

Another deep breath. How many before one of them actually settled her down?

She got out of the car, clicked the door locked.

Time for her game face, even as her insides gurgled and spat and quaked.

"Sorry, ma'am," said Graham. "Everything all right?"

"Yes, of course," said Pereira. "He hasn't moved, then?"

Graham shook his head.

"'K, let's go and knock the door. We'll go together."

"Yes, ma'am."

They crossed the road, a short walk. A new apartment block, glass and steel, the builder's advert still to the side of the building. Luxury 3, 4 and 5 bedroomed apartments, from £750,000. It looked like a hotel.

Graham let out a low whistle. Pereira might have made a remark on some other day, at some other time when her insides hadn't just been kicked around. Stayed silent. It wasn't as though she'd have expected to find Cobalt in a single-bed terrace somewhere in Tollcross.

They pushed open the door into the reception area, where the similarity of the building to a hotel continued.

There were plants and a few comfortable chairs, the area was carpeted, and there was a reception desk, where a young woman stood awaiting visitors, checking a monitor.

"Good morning," said Pereira, and she held out her ID for the receptionist to see.

The receptionist's eyes widened slightly, and then she resumed her normal stance and expression. "Oh, hey," she said. "My name's Megan Lind. How can we help you this morning?"

Pereira took a moment, turned and looked around the reception area, and then turned back. "Do you get many visitors?"

"Not yet."

"How many of the apartments are occupied?"

"Three, so far."

"Have the others been sold?"

"I don't have that information right now. Perhaps I could put you in touch with–"

"We'd like to speak to Eston Cobalt."

Megan Lind stared at Pereira closely for a moment, as if trying to recall the name, and then she started nodding vigorously to herself, turned back to the monitor, brought something up on the screen and lifted the phone.

"I'll just give him a call," she said.

Pereira lowered her eyes, waited. Didn't have the spark to turn to Graham, to step away from the desk and chat to him about the absurdity of this place. The feel of the building, and the look of expense, and the fact that they likely hadn't been able to sell anything like the apartment space they'd obviously thought they could.

Or perhaps the developers had known all along that they wouldn't be able to sell the apartments, and there was something else going on. Some other deal, where shady money changed hands.

"I'm sorry, Mr. Cobalt doesn't seem to be answering his phone," said Megan Lind.

"We'll go up," said Pereira.

"I don't think that's possible."

Pereira stepped forward. She once again took out her ID card and placed it on the counter. "I disagree, Miss Lind," she said.

Megan Lind swallowed, took an involuntary step backwards.

"We're in the middle of a murder inquiry," said Pereira. "We don't know Mr. Cobalt's level of involvement, indeed if he even has any. But given that people have been murdered, there are two possibilities as to why he's not answering the damn phone. He's disappeared, in which case we need to know, or he's dead, in which case we need to investigate his murder."

"He could be in the bathroom," said Megan Lind uncertainly.

"Either you can take us up now, or we can call for a warrant, and by the time that arrives, so will the reinforcements.

And rather than just two plain clothes officers in your building, you'll have several squads of uniformed, armed policemen."

Megan Lind would have taken another step back, but she had nowhere else to go. She swallowed, she looked at Graham, she turned back to Pereira. "You want me to take you up to Mr. Cobalt's apartment?" she asked.

*

They stood in the corridor as Megan Lind knocked on the door of the apartment. The calm before the storm. The briefest of respites. Thoughts of Lena, and her new love, began to intrude.

"Worried?" Pereira said to Graham, forcing the word from her mouth, forcing the conversation. What if they got married, Lena and the actress? What if they wanted custody of Robin?

She tried to smile as she spoke, but it didn't work.

"Maybe he's just asleep," said Graham.

More likely, dead or gone, he thought. Just as Pereira was thinking.

"Which d'you suppose would be worse for you, Constable?" she said, and although she intended it with a certain amount of light-hearted teasing, there was none of that in her voice.

"Ma'am," he said, and he lowered his head.

"Sorry," she found herself saying. "Don't worry about it."

"He's not answering," said Megan Lind.

"You can let us in?" asked Pereira.

"I'm not sure I have the authority," said Lind. "I need to check with my boss."

"No," said Pereira, "you don't. You need to let us in. Given that you've called, you've buzzed him, and you've knocked on his door, I think it's safe to say that Mr. Cobalt will not be complaining about our entry. Please, Miss Lind, open the door."

Pereira took a deep breath. Keeping it together for the moment. Managing not to swear, which was something.

Megan Lind bowed her head, turned back, wafted a security card over the entry system, and pushed the door open. Then she stood back and allowed Pereira and Graham to enter.

A short entrance area, opening out to an open-plan sitting room and kitchen, large windows looking down the length of Great Western Road, back towards the city.

They walked into the middle of the room, which was

beautifully and simply furnished – as though Cobalt had taken over the show home – and had an airiness and brightness about it, despite the dark, miserable day outside.

"Cobalt?" said Pereira.

All the doors that led off were closed. Pereira turned and looked at Megan Lind, who had come in behind them, but was standing back, wanting to dissociate herself as quickly as possible should Cobalt appear.

"The doors?" asked Pereira.

Lind looked like she was considering not answering the question, as though to do so might perjure herself or leave herself open to a reprimand from building management.

"Megan," said Pereira.

There was nothing in her voice, no tone, no threat, barely any interest, and it was possibly all the more intimidating for its detachment.

"Washroom," said Lind pointing at the nearest door, before moving quickly round the room, picking the doors off as she went, saying, "closet, corridor to the auxiliary bedrooms and bathrooms, master bedroom with en suite."

"Thank you," said Pereira. "Right, Constable, here we go. Master bedroom…"

She lifted her eyebrows at Graham, then the two of them walked round the luxury four-seat Pearl Concorde sofa, past the Kleidek luxury P130 sound system, to the bedroom door.

Pereira stopped for a second, knocked sharply on the door, listened for a reply, and then opened the door and entered.

36

"Why?"

The word came out of nowhere. Pereira paused for a second, but did not turn. Standing over the kitchen counter, making a couple of sandwiches.

Anais had been sleeping when she'd got home, and Pereira had decided to get lunch ready before waking her up. In the silence of the kitchen she'd been trying to concentrate on the case. Trying to sort out the mess, trying to work out why it was that Cobalt hadn't been in his bedroom when she and Constable Graham had entered, why it was he hadn't been in any room in the apartment.

Not dead, not drunk. Just not there. He had run, that was all, evading detection as he went.

And as she thought about it, and as she thought about Archie Wilson and the possible part played in his death by Lucy Hilton or Glen Armstrong, Dr. Melville or who knew who else, it was as though she was looking at it all through the fog that Lena had created.

Whatever she tried to think about, there was Lena. Lena and the actress.

She finally glanced over her shoulder, then turned back to the orange cheddar she was slicing. Anais was leaning against the doorframe, arms folded.

"Just came to see you were all right," said Pereira. "Thought I'd make us a sandwich."

"I can look after myself."

"I know. I'd've asked you to make them if you'd been awake."

A moment. She didn't look back. Didn't want to see her

daughter's retreat, or the space where she'd been.

"Thought you were seeing Lena."

"Work, I'm afraid," said Pereira. "Had to…" No, she wasn't going to say she'd had to call it off, that would imply that she'd definitely been going. "I couldn't do anything today, not after the murder yesterday, and we've got someone in custody and someone else has done a runner."

"Why are you here then?"

Pereira took a deep breath, placed the second sandwich on a plate – cheese, ham, mustard, tomato and cucumber on brown bread – then turned and put the plates on the table.

"Just needed a breath. Been a bit of a day so far. You want a drink?"

Don't ask her to have lunch with you, just take it as a given, thought Pereira. *Maybe she won't notice she's still mad at you.*

"Coke."

Pereira took the bottle of Coke Zero from the fridge, poured two glasses, set them on the table, left the bottle on the side.

"I hate these big bottles," she said.

"Why? Saves money, doesn't it?" said Anais, her tone still edgy, as she sat down.

"They never quite fit in the fridge door, then when you leave them lying flat on the shelf, you have to put them at an angle or the door doesn't close."

"Get a bigger fridge," said Anais.

"Where are we going to put it?" said Pereira. "These bottles are designed for those huge American fridges you see on TV shows. We don't have fridges like that in this country. Maybe you do if you're rich."

"Get a smaller bottle."

Pereira nodded. "I know. Then you're in Tesco and you see the big bottle and it's the same price as something half the size, so you end up buying the big bottle anyway."

"How can it be the same price? How does that work?"

Pereira stared at the table. Still trying not to try too hard. Still trying not to think about the day. "I don't know," she said eventually. "I don't know how these things work."

She took a bite from her sandwich. Risked a glance at her daughter as she chewed, her eyebrows lifting slightly.

"Me neither," said Anais. "Doesn't make sense though, does it?"

Pereira shook her head. She shrugged slightly, she began to

relax for the first time since she'd woken up that morning.

She didn't have long, and she prayed the phone wouldn't ring. Not for the next twenty minutes. She'd meant to turn the ringer off before she came in, and she'd forgotten.

Eat and hope and don't say anything stupid, that was what she thought. A normal twenty minutes. Try to get through it without having an argument.

"I never understand how two-for-one works," said Anais. "If they're still making money from that, why don't they just make them half the price in the first place?"

37

Glenn Armstrong was not having a good couple of days. Jan had threatened to leave a couple of times, and the house had become so strained and uncomfortable that he'd begun to wish that she'd just go.

The phone hadn't stopped ringing, of course, not now that the media were in full flight with their vengeance of Mark Randall narrative, and with the phone calls had come the media circus to their front door, something that had at least been mitigated by the weather.

That was what he assumed, at least. Perhaps they just weren't that interested in him, or perhaps there just weren't very many journalists anymore. They'd all been laid off, or had their jobs taken by unpaid interns who sat at a computer all day rewriting news from the BBC and the Press Association.

Maybe if he'd just told Jan the truth, or some of the truth, she would be gone and he'd be done with her. It wasn't as though they'd had this great marriage in the first place. But, of course, if Jan went, then Tyler would go too, and he couldn't have that. He found it hard to imagine that Jan would be able to get anyone else, but then he himself had been sucked in, so why wouldn't it happen again? And then Tyler would have another father, and he'd possibly never get to see his kid.

This seemed better. Just getting out, getting away from the house. Didn't care about the weather. The main thing was not being stuck inside with Jan, having to listen to her, having to hear her ask if there was anything else he hadn't told her.

And yes, there was a lot.

He had driven down the Clyde, stopping finally in Greenock. He was down by the waterfront, past the games pitches. Bleak day, the hills on the other side of the firth completely obscured by low cloud.

He wondered why he bothered bringing his own car; he might as well just have travelled down in the police car that followed him. The copper hadn't seemed to like that idea, however. Obviously didn't want to be used as a taxi.

He was standing at the water's edge, leaning against the bonnet, smoking a Benson & Hedges Extra Mild, rain coming down in a fine drizzle. Not one person had walked past him in the twenty-five minutes he'd been here. Barely a sound. A car door closing, the car starting, driving away. Another car door. Another car. Another sound. He wasn't even turning to look.

It seemed so surreal. Him with a police escort. A guard. Like royalty or a presidential candidate. Quite possibly the stupidest thing he'd ever heard of.

He wondered how he could make more use of it, or, more likely, make more fun of the police officer. Take the piss out of her. Why not? She was just a kid, why not have some fun? She was standing back there, dutifully, next to her car. Not even sheltering in the rain.

He flicked the end of his cigarette away, towards the water, although it never got close. Checked his phone. Still nothing from Hilton. Maybe they'd been right, the police. Maybe she'd just been using him. Well, it had been fun being used, he wasn't going to complain about it. Maybe the other one was using him as well, but what did it matter?

He laughed at the thought, took the cigarettes from his pocket, flicked the lid open with his thumb, shook the packet as he lifted it, then pulled his next smoke out with his lips.

"Hey, you got a light, pal?"

He lifted his eyebrows in acknowledgement at the voice, then smiled. "About time," said Armstrong. "Freezing my balls off standing here."

*

Pereira's phone rang as she got in the car. Unexpected relief that she'd been saved from walking out prematurely on Anais, but now she wasn't to get the quiet drive back to work, the time to readjust, the chance to think through their next move.

"Boss," said Bain.

"What's up?"

228

"You near?"

"Just leaving the house. I'll be there in twenty. What'd I miss?"

"The constable watching Armstrong was drugged, Armstrong's gone missing."

"What? Seriously? Who was on duty?"

"Dobson," said Bain. "Not one of yours. Think they pulled her from Bridgeton."

Pereira inserted the phone into the holder, started the car, earpiece in, foot to the floor and drove quickly away, with a slight squeal of the tyres, a slight skid in the rain. Didn't notice Anais, standing at the window, waiting to wave goodbye.

"Dobson all right?" she thought to say.

"Yeah. Groggy. Hand over the mouth, stabbed in the arm with a syringe, didn't see her attacker coming."

"She was on watch, right?"

"Yes."

"Jesus. Whereabouts?"

"Greenock. Down by Battery Park."

"She was standing on open ground, with nothing within a hundred yards, and she didn't see her attacker coming? Seriously?"

"Haven't spoken to her, ma'am, but that appears to be the size of it."

"For God's sake. Who's down there?"

"Just heading there now, ma'am, you want to join me?"

"No," she said. "I'll go round and speak to Armstrong's wife, see if he told her anything else after we spoke yesterday. After that, back to see Hilton. I'll meet you back there. There's got to be one of these people knows something."

"Yes, boss."

She rang off. Driving too quickly, the car twitched on a corner, straightened up, she slowed, lights ahead turned red, and she braked heavily, the car sliding to a stop.

The phone rang again.

"Yep?"

"Where are you?"

Cooper. She didn't want to talk to Cooper.

"On my way to see Armstrong's wife, then coming in to talk to Hilton again."

A beat. The lights changed quickly, the car in front waited, and then slowly moved on, she inched to the right a little to see if there was an overtaking manoeuvre open to her, decided that it would be stupid, and sat in behind the old Volvo.

"Where have you been?" he asked.

"Had lunch with Anais."

She wasn't going to lie. Working on a Sunday, she wasn't going to excuse herself for having had lunch with her daughter.

"Speak to me before you speak to Hilton. I want to sit in on that."

He hung up.

"Shit."

Another deep breath. It was a day for them. One crappy thing after another. Was there anything else that could happen?

Don't think that, she thought, shaking her head. *There always is.*

*

"What were youse lot doing?"

"I wasn't there," said Pereira, "I don't know exactly what happened."

"Is that good enough? You think that's good enough? Why was there only one polis on him when there was an obvious threat to his life?"

"We applied the resources to the issue that we could afford at the time and which were deemed appropriate given the level of threat. What I–"

"Appropriate? Are you listening to yourself? Can we get some of the press in here? I want them to hear this pish."

Pereira agreed, to some extent. The police had not had a good morning. One man absconded, another seemingly nabbed from under their eyes. Yet, what had Armstrong been doing down by the Clyde in the first place? How hard would it have been for him to stay at home for a few days, until they had a better idea of where this was going?

Of course, she couldn't argue personal responsibility. No one wanted to hear about that, not when there was the Police Service to blame.

"There'll be plenty of opportunity for you to raise your concerns–"

"Oh, you think? Too right there will."

"For the moment, we need to concentrate on finding Glenn. It's quite possible that with Archie Wilson at least, he was taken some time before he was actually killed. We needn't assume that anything's happened yet to Glenn."

"You'd better hope not."

Something tells me you might not be that bothered, thought Pereira. But you couldn't beat a solid court case against the police. She was probably already fielding calls from lawyers.

"I need to know if he told you anything else after we spoke to him yesterday," said Pereira.

Armstrong snorted. "Like, I'm telling you lot anything."

"Seriously, Mrs. Armstrong? Your husband's missing. There will be a time for apportioning blame, but now, right now, we need to do everything we can to find him. I need you to talk to me."

Armstrong held her gaze, an angry stare, making sure Pereira felt the full force of her resentment.

"He didn't tell me anything about what he was doing on Friday night, if that's what you mean. If you think he had anything to do with that other eejit being murdered...."

"He saw a woman named Lucy Hilton," said Pereira. *Hardly the time for keeping secrets*, she thought. *Get it out in the open.*

"Who's that?" Armstrong shot back. No sign of recognition.

"She was Archie Wilson's lawyer."

"What the fuck was Glenn seeing her for, then?"

"Said he got talking to her online over some political blog he wrote."

"That shite?"

"Yes," said Pereira.

"So what had that to do with Archie Wilson?"

"We think Ms. Hilton was going to use Glenn for something, but we're not sure."

Armstrong tutted, rolled her eyes. "Just using him for a bit of shagging, I expect. Not that she'll have found him much use for that."

"You knew he was sleeping with her?"

A moment, she nodded. "Aye, whatever. I was covering for him, but I knew. He comes to bed at, I don't know, two in the morning or whenever, stinking of her. Stinking of perfume, stinking of... pussy. He couldn't even have a shower, the stupid arsehole."

"Right," said Pereira. "Well... all right, he was having sex with Lucy Hilton. Is there anything else? After what you learned yesterday morning about the death of Mark Randall, you must have asked Glenn about it."

Armstrong let out another heavy sigh. "Suppose," she said.

"And what did he tell you?"

Armstrong got up from the sofa, walked over to the window. She had one arm folded across her chest, the other resting against it, hand held out, as though holding an invisible cigarette.

"He said it'd been really hard at first. Living with it. But then, you know, time and all that. It was water under the old bridge by the time he met me, he says, so he didn't want to bring it all up again. Didn't want to talk about it. I mean, he told me the basics obviously, 'cause it'd been in the papers and stuff, but not the other thing. Not the thing he told youse yesterday."

"Did he think anyone else knew?"

A moment. Pereira kept her eyes on her, but wasn't pushing. If there was something to be told, it was coming, she just had to give her the time.

"Said he and Archie both told their dads. He and Archie were gutted, felt really shit. Peters, though, he was the bastard, and they just fell in behind him. Peters never told anyone. But Glenn had to tell his dad."

"How did that go?"

"Said his old man was supportive. Nothing to be done, nothing to be gained by telling the truth. Wasn't like they were actually going to be convicted of anything. They'd've looked bad, and maybe there'd have been some civil suit or something, he didn't know. His dad just told him to keep his mouth shut."

"Did he know if his dad told anyone else?"

She shook her head. "Didn't ask him. I mean, I didn't ask Glenn. And too late for youse to ask his dad, if you know what I'm saying."

"When'd he die?" asked Pereira.

Armstrong snorted again, a peculiar sound, like a bitter laugh squeezed out into the world against its wishes. "Night before we got married. Typical of the bastard. Hated me from the start, did everything he could to ruin the wedding."

38

Durban, Hilton's lawyer, was wearing probably the most expensive suit that Pereira had ever been in the same room as. Beautifully tailored, colour that seemed to shift from blue to grey, it wore the man, rather than the other way round.

Anyone would look good in a suit that well-made, she thought. *Even Martin, who never wore a suit.* Martin, of course, would have looked out of place as soon as he'd opened his mouth. Durban, of Durban & Shanks, however, had the words and the voice to go with the clothes.

His shoes were currently beneath the desk, but she expected no less of them.

Classic, she thought. Dissecting the guy's wardrobe. Feminists of the world would be turning in their graves.

"Before we go any further," said Durban, "in fact, before my client and I get up and walk out the building, why don't you actually tell us why we're all here?"

"We have Ms. Hilton near the scene of Archie Wilson's disappearance," said Pereira. "We have paperwork from Ms. Hilton's office testifying to the amount of money which Ms. Hilton and her partner, who has now gone missing, were making from this current arrangement. We have an e-mail chain from Ms. Hilton to this partner, Eston Cobalt, discussing Archie Wilson's determination to place the vast proportion of his money at the disposal of a trust fund, running an as yet unnamed mission around Scotland. It is also clear from this chain that there was, indeed still is, a romantic attachment between the two."

"You have copies of this e-mail chain?" asked Durban.

Pereira removed four stapled pages of A4 from a thin

brown folder and passed them over. While Hilton sat impassively beside him, Durban quickly read the four pages, and then turned them upside down and placed them to the side.

"There is proof that my client was worried that she would lose an account, and that she was romantically involved with Eston Cobalt. Is either of those things a crime?"

"We can at the very least build a case that shows your client had originally coerced Archie Wilson into taking her and Mr. Cobalt on as lawyer and financial advisor respectively. As is often so in a case such as this, there are many different strands to follow, and we don't know yet where they'll all lead. This one, however, is already leading to Ms. Hilton being under investigation for unacceptable legal practice."

She was looking at Hilton as she spoke, although Hilton seemed uninterested in returning the stare. A harsh look, directed at the table.

"There is, of course," said Pereira, "a deal to be done here. Archie Wilson is dead, and we're not especially interested in an act of coercion. We are interested in what was happening between your client and Mr. Armstrong. If your client tells us everything–"

"All right!" snapped Hilton.

"No," said Durban quickly. "I want to hear it from them first."

"We can't promise immunity from anything here," said Pereira, "because we don't yet know the full extent of Ms. Hilton's involvement. Certainly, if she's implicated in any way in either Wilson or Peters' death, or the disappearance of Glenn Armstrong–"

"I'm sitting here, aren't I?" snapped Hilton, at last lifting her head.

"No one said you were working alone," said Pereira.

"Jesus, all right."

"Lucy," said Durban. "It isn't all right. Let's just–"

"No, let's just… Jesus, there isn't much more to say anyway," she said. "Really. I didn't have anything to do with either of these people dying. I have absolutely no–"

"Lucy!"

She shook her head.

"We're good," she said. "If you don't want to hear it, if you think it'll look bad for you, leave the room. But really, you won't be missing anything."

"Ms. Hilton, I strongly recommend that you do not talk to the police at this stage," said Durban, his voice very formal, as though he was reading from a card. "If you choose to ignore my advice, then I can no longer act as your legal advisor in this matter."

Her eyes were on the table, then slowly she turned her head, held his gaze, then indicated the door with a slight movement of her head.

A moment, Durban glanced harshly at Pereira and Cooper, a silent but intimidating presence throughout, then he quickly got to his feet and lifted his briefcase.

"You should get another lawyer before you say anything," said Durban.

Hilton stared back at the table. Durban gave her a moment, and then walked quickly from the room.

The door clicked shut, silence returned. Hilton, Pereira, Cooper, Constable Wales at the door. Hilton's jaws were working, fingers tensing. *Containing the wrath*, thought Pereira.

"In your own time," said Pereira. "And don't lie. We won't like it if you lie. And we know more than you think we do, so we'll know if you're lying."

Hilton leaned forward, lifted her head. "There was something going on with Archie," she said. "Something to do with Mark Randall. I never knew what it was. He felt guilty, that was all. Said he'd lived with it all these years, and that it was time to bring it to an end. To face the guilt."

"That he hadn't been able to save him?"

She shook her head. "It was more than that. I mean, it was apparent at the inquest there was more than that. There was this undercurrent. You could feel it, but what did they have? There were no witnesses bar these three young boys, and they all told the same story. It felt like there was something more, but the only way it was coming out was if one of the three of them told it. But none of them did. They got them in separate rooms, but by then they'd had plenty of time to get their stories straight, even if there had been something to hide."

"So where did Iain Peters and Glenn Armstrong come into it? Why did you contact them?"

"I knew there were these two other guys, and I thought if I get close to them, maybe I could find out the missing link. Use it against Archie. Use it to make him stay onside with Eston and me."

"So what happened?"

"I got in touch with Peters first. We met for a drink. I was quite direct. I think he took it as a threat, told me to piss off. Walked out on me. Didn't want to know. So, I tried a different approach with Armstrong."

She lifted an eyebrow, pursed her lips.

"Which was?" asked Pereira.

"We're all women here, right?" she said, ignoring Cooper. It wasn't even clear that she was including PC Wales, even though she was in the room.

"You slept with him?"

"Yes, Detective Inspector, I slept with him. I mean, whatever… It was just sex."

"And did it work?"

Hilton smiled ruefully, shook her head.

"Yeah, funny joke," she said. "I got an orgasm out of it, so there was that."

"Did you try to talk about Archie Wilson?"

"Oh, we talked about Archie Wilson. We had a long talk about Archie Wilson. And I got nothing. Nothing that I didn't already know. So, I wasn't sure where else to go with that, and then Archie got murdered. Archie was dead."

"So why see Armstrong on Friday evening?" asked Pereira.

Hilton held Pereira's gaze for a moment, and then finally lowered her eyes.

Silence.

Pereira was aware that Cooper was becoming restless, and slowly placed her hand on the table beside him, hoping to get him to stay silent. They were getting there, but not with any unnecessary questions.

"Why did you see Armstrong on Friday evening?" repeated Pereira.

"I didn't."

"I think you did."

Hilton smiled, still not looking up. She seemed to glance to the side, then she looked up at Pereira. "Yeah, sure, of course."

"You saw him?"

"Yes."

"Really?" said Pereira. "Don't fuck around with us. This is on the record."

"Oh, I wouldn't fuck around with the police," said Hilton, the smile still on her face, and then it slowly died away and she shook her head.

"So, what happened?"

Hilton looked bored suddenly, as she prepared to settle in to telling her story.

This is like arguing with a teenager, thought Pereira.

"He got in touch with me, and I was going to blow him off, then I thought, whatever. Just… just, out of badness, I got him to come over. Fucked him. Scratched the shit out of his back with my nails. And his stomach. I mean, really hurt him. Scratched the shit out of him." She laughed. "You know, when he was close to coming and wasn't stopping for anything. So, that was all. He had that to take home to his wife."

Three feet apart across the desk. Pereira holding her gaze, Hilton finished talking and lifted her eyebrows. Finally unclasped her hands, laid them open on the table.

"That's it," she said. "That's all I've got."

*

"What d'you think?" said Cooper.

Back in his office, a quick chat before Pereira could head off. Absurdly, already dark outside, the sound of the rain against the window.

"Interesting," said Pereira. "I mean, they were tense on Saturday, the two of them, Armstrong and his wife. She already said she knew he'd had sex, but she never mentioned any marks. Still, he could have covered them easily enough. A thick t-shirt or pyjamas in bed. It's cold still, no reason not to. Weird that he didn't shower."

"Hmm…" said Cooper.

He was looking at his computer screen, becoming distracted.

"What now?" he asked.

"Need to speak to Bain to see if there's anything further on Armstrong's disappearance, and then I've got another appointment with Dr. Melville."

"You found out he was also at the inquest?"

"That's right. And then home, sir, back on it in the morning."

"Right," said Cooper, and without looking at her, indicated the door with a slight head movement.

She nodded, got to the door, fingers on the handle, to the

sound of the rain.

"Inspector," said Cooper.

She turned, and he was actually looking at her for once.

"You played that well. In there. With Hilton."

She wasn't sure what to say, as she couldn't remember him praising her before, on anything.

"Thank you, sir," she said, after a moment.

Another second, then a slight nod, and he turned back to his monitor.

39

The rain was hammering down, the roads and pavements awash. Already the police and the fire brigade were being called, in various parts of the city, to areas of local flooding, traffic hold-ups, cars stuck in deep puddles that had appeared in the last half hour.

Bain and Pereira were together in her car, stuck in that traffic, on High Street, on their way to the Cathedral. She hadn't been able to get hold of Melville, but had been told that was where they'd find him.

There was a sense of urgency now that there hadn't been previously in the investigation. It was quite possible that Peters had been killed as soon as he'd been attacked, but there had been the suggestion with Wilson that he'd been taken, held for a couple of hours and then killed.

While there was still the chance that the same situation could apply to Glenn Armstrong, they had to throw everything at the investigation. Would she go home after they'd spoken to Melville, as she'd told Cooper she would? There wasn't much chance of that. They needed to find Glenn Armstrong, be it alive, or strapped to a headstone, a small metal cross embedded in his skull.

"Tell me how it looked down there," she said.

Getting anxious, sitting in silence. Silence just allowed her to think about Lena, and now thinking about Lena meant thinking about Lena and the other woman.

"There are rocks along the water's edge. Tide was up, so mostly covered. Then there's a railing, grass, a tarmacked path that runs round, behind there's the big playing area. Played cricket there once. It was April. Day like today, in fact," said

Bain, nodding out at the choking wet darkness.

Pereira acknowledged the joke, couldn't quite bring herself to smile.

"So there's really a lot of open ground?"

"For a couple of hundred metres, either direction, except the Clyde at the front."

"And what reason did Dobson give for not seeing her attacker coming?"

Bain shrugged. Didn't really like to land a fellow officer in any trouble. However, she'd done a poor job, that was all, and someone was more than likely going to die as a result. "She was watching Armstrong, and got blind-sided. Ball watching."

"And what about Armstrong? Isn't it odd?"

Bain thought about it, began to nod. The car moved forward a few feet. They could see the cathedral less than half a mile up ahead, the spire in between buildings. They both knew that they were going to have to get out and walk, but were putting off the inevitable.

"You would have thought he'd have been twitchy. Looking over his shoulder."

"Not according to Dobson," said Bain. "Said he was chain smoking, standing at the water's edge, looking out to sea."

"You think…?" began Pereira, "you think he thought no one was coming for him? *Knew* that no one was coming for him? But then they did…"

"The sea's magnetic," said Bain, after a few moments. "You ever just stand and look at it? Or a loch or a river… Very easy to get lost."

"Yes," said Pereira, "you're right."

She sighed, a heavy breath, fingers gripped the steering wheel, looked out the windscreen, up at the rain. Up into the early evening, dark sky, nothing to see.

"Dammit," she said. "Come on, we need to walk."

She leaned to her left, looked out past the cars in either direction, and then cut across the road and slotted into a parking space fifty yards up, just as someone had started beeping their horn at her with outrage at the possibility she'd intended bypassing the queue of traffic.

Into the space, annoyed at the hold up, annoyed at the situation, annoyed at the noise and the rain, she slammed the brakes on, handbrake on, engine off, out the car, and then the two of them were walking quickly up the road, past fed up

---

240

motorists, on pavements awash with water.

*

They were wet and cold, and not all that much warmer in the great expanse of the cathedral. Bain was rubbing his hands together, Pereira was sitting formally, absolutely still, staring at Melville.

They were near the back of the choir. Melville was turned away, his bald head bowed slightly, staring up the length of the eastern section of the cathedral to the presbytery, where the minister was coming to the end of a short prayer.

At first Pereira had thought she would wait until the end of the service, but had quickly grown impatient, aware of the possibility that Armstrong, somewhere in this awful, wet, bleak, dark evening, might not yet be dead. It felt as though they were a hundred miles from finding out where that was, but it didn't mean they shouldn't be trying. And so she had walked more or less into the middle of the service, and she had tapped Melville on the shoulder, and she had stared back at the look of annoyance, which had bordered on anger. She had intended that they leave this section of the cathedral, and go into the larger, more open nave, but Melville had played his own part in the game, refusing to be drawn from the choir.

"You attended the inquest into the death of Mark Randall," said Pereira for the third time. Determined not to change her tone, or her statement, until he answered. If he was getting more and more annoyed, all the better. There was more chance that he'd let something slip.

She still didn't think he was hiding anything, as such, more than likely just not telling everything that he could.

That was the essence of police work, anyway, wasn't it? It wasn't necessarily the brilliant piece of deduction; it was working to get people to tell you everything they could, even when they had reason not to.

"Yes," said Melville, his voice low.

"You could have mentioned that when we spoke previously."

"You didn't ask," he replied.

"Come on, Doctor," said Pereira. "We're trying to solve a murder here, we need to know everything. Everything."

"Did you know Iain Peters was going to get killed?" he

241

snapped, his head whipping round, anger across his face. The fire died a little, but still, as he looked at her, it was with contempt.

"How could we have known that?"

"And how could I?" said Melville. "I couldn't possibly know that Archibald's death was related to the Taynuilt incident, so why on earth would I think to tell you about it?"

He angrily held her gaze for a few moments, then turned away. His knuckles cracked, as he worked his fingers, the sound loud in the vast space, as heads were bowed, the lone voice of the minister the only other sound.

"Why did you attend the inquest, Doctor Melville?" asked Bain.

He was sitting in the pew behind Melville, slightly to his right.

A deep breath, slowly exhaled. Fingers still being crunched together, the sound of the popping gas becoming less pronounced.

"The church was involved, Sergeant," he said. "It… the whole thing was done through the church, organised through the church. I was there as the Glasgow Presbytery's representative. It was my capacity at the time."

"You didn't know any of the boys beforehand?"

"I got to know them. I'd had no interest in that parish prior to those events."

"And, as far as you know, was the finding of the inquest a fair and true reflection of what had happened on the River Awe?"

A solo voice was singing at the other end of the choir, and then slowly, after the first line, the rest of the choir began to rise in accompaniment. The voices soared, the music seemed to fill the building.

"As far as you know, was the finding of the inquest a fair and true reflection of what had happened on the River Awe?" asked Pereira, repeating Bain's words, the question asked with a little more urgency.

"No," snapped Melville, spitting out the word. "No, it wasn't. Archie told me the truth. God knows, maybe that was what he needed. To talk to someone he barely knew."

His head was down. Pereira was looking at him side on, could tell that the story was coming. It might just have been the same story that Armstrong had told them, but somehow she had the feeling that it would be more. She noticed Bain move an inch closer from behind, and shook her head slightly. *It's coming, it's coming...*

"And I agreed with him to say nothing. I agreed... I was part of that lie. I didn't lie, I wasn't up there lying on oath, but I knew those boys were lying."

He turned again to Pereira. The music ascended around them, filling in the gaps in his speech and the holes in the walls, the spaces in between.

"There were no witnesses, no one there to tell a different story. As long as those three kept singing the same tune, they were going to be fine. No one could possibly claim anything different. Two of them even cried, they cried, up there on the stand, for all the world like they meant it."

"Which two?"

"Archibald, and that boy Armstrong."

"But not Peters?"

"No, not Peters."

"But..." began Pereira, then she shook her head. "I still don't understand. The boys were just messing about. They might have pushed him off, but that doesn't mean..."

She stopped at the snort, the further lowering of Melville's head, the scorn on his face, as he stared at the floor beyond the end of the pew.

"It would have been... it would've been a disaster for the church if it had got out. The truth. If the truth had come out."

"What was the truth?" said Pereira.

Please say it, she thought. *Say the line. Tell me I can't handle it. Bring some levity to the bloody awfulness of this day, this day that doesn't seem to know when to stop getting worse.*

"They killed him," said Melville. "He...killed...him..."

"Who? Peters?"

"What?" snapped Melville, looking at her with derision.

"Peters? It was Peters who pushed Mark Randall off the raft?"

"No," said Melville, the scorn now in his voice, as though both Pereira and Bain were stupid for not having worked it out. "Armstrong. That bloody... bastard... that bloody bastard, Armstrong. He had it in for Mark the whole weekend. Maybe he didn't mean to kill him. The kid died because he genuinely banged his head, but Armstrong pushed him off at the worst possible spot, knew that he'd likely get into trouble, and made sure that the other boys didn't try to help."

He paused, holding Pereira's gaze, ignoring Bain, ignoring the chorus that continued to fill the cathedral.

"Then when the police arrived, Armstrong was there, he started, right from the off, telling the story. The story he'd then make the others stick to. And… and damn us all, those three boys and me, we all knew, and we all stayed quiet. We let Armstrong call the tune. I thought…" His head continued to drop, his shoulders too. "What did I think? I wanted it to have been an accident. I wanted it to blow over as quickly as possible. I didn't want this on the church's watch. On the church's conscience. I didn't want the lawsuit. I didn't want the investigation into how we'd organised the boys. Accidents happen, Detective Inspector, but manslaughter like this, like that boy Armstrong was guilty of, that doesn't need to happen. I sit here, and… I quite literally hang my head in shame."

The fire had completely left his voice. Pereira and Bain shared a quick glance. Armstrong had lied to them the day before. But not the usual lie, not the one he'd been telling for years. A very specific variation, one that made Peters look like the guilty party. And now Armstrong had disappeared in what, under closer examination, were quite peculiar circumstances.

"And the story had resurfaced since Archie won all his money?" asked Pereira.

Melville nodded.

"Yes, yes of course. Archibald… he had never forgotten. Never been able to get it off his back. And then he won all that money, and he was still distraught. He came to me to ask for forgiveness, like I was in a position to bestow it upon him… He was going to confess. He intended putting the money, all the money I understand, into a fund to run mission churches throughout Scotland. For the good of the community. That was his penance. And he would go to the police and confess, tell them everything that happened. I've no idea what the consequences would have been for any of them, but certainly they would have been worst for Armstrong. Funny now that he's the only one of the three left alive…"

"Did Archie tell the others what he intended to do?"

"Yes. Neither of them were very pleased, as you can imagine. Archibald accepted that he was putting them in a difficult situation, and at least promised he would use his money to cover their legal expenses."

"When did he tell them?"

"Several weeks ago," said Melville. "He wasn't going to the police just yet, but it was coming. I think... I think he would have gone by now. He died just before he..."

He let the sentence drift off, staring at the floor. His shoulders began to straighten.

The music, soaring ever further and louder, came to a final, magnificent chorus, the voices converging beautifully and then slowly tailing off, growing quieter, the last chord held and released, the sound drifting away into the furthest recesses of the cathedral.

"How could one of them murder Archibald over that?" asked Melville. "Glenn? You think Glenn did this?"

"Glenn has also disappeared," said Pereira.

"What? I thought... I thought I read that he was under guard?"

"He was taken this afternoon."

Melville's mouth opened a little, but no words emerged. He shook his head.

"I don't know," he said. "I don't know."

The final benediction at the head of the choir came to an end, and organ music began to fill the cathedral, again the sound rising quickly, all-consuming, overwhelming, engulfing.

"I don't know," said Melville again, the voice small, at last every semblance of authority and defiance gone.

40

They walked through the cathedral towards the exit, their march slowing as Bain looked up at the great window above the west door. As people left, and sound drifted in from outside, it was apparent that it was still raining heavily.

They stopped, finally, Bain's head titled upwards. They were both still soaking, although water no long dripped from their clothing where they stood.

"I've never been to Evensong before," said Bain.

"I'm not sure that counts, under the circumstances."

"Not as boring as I thought it'd be."

He finally looked at her, lifted his eyebrows slightly, and then looked around the great space of the nave as he talked.

"So," he said, "do we think Armstrong might be behind this, even though it doesn't tie in with him disappearing today?"

Pereira nodded slowly, thoughts still running through the sequence of events.

"He lied to me yesterday," she said, "but then, he might not have wanted to tell the same story the doctor just told us. He hardly sounded great from what he said to me, but if he'd told me the truth – assuming Melville's story is the truth – then he really would be re-opening the case by volunteering the information to the police."

"He certainly had more to hide than the others, and if Archie told him it was time for him to get it off his chest... Perhaps that's when he started putting together his plan. Archie said he was going to do it in a couple of weeks, so Armstrong started sending the notes, knowing that he had the space to write a few."

"Yes," said Pereira. "It begins to come together. So maybe

Armstrong's not dead. Maybe this thing today, his disappearance, is part of the plan."

"That would explain why he didn't see his assailant coming. He already knew they were coming, didn't have to look."

"But how does it end for him, if not dead with a cross in his head?" said Pereira. "How does he walk away from this, still looking like a victim?"

"He escapes," said Bain. "Or he gets discovered. He and his partner contrive something, that standing here we can't see, but when it comes, when we get the call later today, or tomorrow, to say that Armstrong's been found, will seem perfectly normal."

A pause, while a couple of people walked past, chatting, ignoring the two sodden detectives. The service had been over for a while, but still the congregation drifted slowly out, as they and members of the choir lingered, hoping the rain might ease.

The door to the exit opened again, the sound of the rain once more entered the building. The door closed, the sound was turned off.

"So is this our call?" said Pereira. "That Armstrong hasn't been kidnapped. That he's currently holed up, waiting to pick the perfect moment, which will have to be pretty soon, to play the reveal and execute his plan?"

"Who's the partner, though?" said Bain. "The way we're telling this, he has someone working with him."

"Jan Armstrong?" said Pereira, then shook her head. "No, the timing doesn't work. She certainly couldn't have been down to Greenock today to take care of Dobson."

"Definitely not," said Bain.

"Cobalt," said Pereira. "They could have met through Hilton. If Archie had lived, then he was going to place all that money in a trust fund for this mission. It would have been taken out of Cobalt's hands. He loses his healthy commission he'd been intending living off for the rest of his life. He had a motive, Armstrong had a motive."

"But Cobalt's vanished," said Bain. "He's done something that implicitly makes him look guilty. How does he return now to working in his office on Monday morning, making money and standing at that damn window looking smooth?"

"He hasn't done anything wrong," said Pereira. "At least, not so that we know, so far. We have him and Hilton in the vicinity of Archie's club on Tuesday evening. Doesn't mean anything. And now, we had him under watch and he slipped away. Maybe he didn't like being followed. Maybe he just wanted to go and hole up somewhere for the day. Maybe he'll be back later, or will stay away for the night, and be at work tomorrow morning. He's just a guy. We never said he was a suspect, we never told him not to move, we didn't say, we're keeping you under watch and if you run away you'll be under even more suspicion. We can't actually get him on anything he's done so far. So he bolts, he goes somewhere to set up an alibi, he knocks out Constable Dobson, he implements whatever plan he has with Armstrong, and then he's back at work tomorrow, claiming to have spent the night at the Loch Lomond or something."

Bain was nodding by the end of it. "Sounds decent," he said. "We should get back to the station, ma'am, try to get working through this."

She looked at her watch. Almost six thirty. When had she told her mother she would be home? She could give it another hour, but she'd better call.

"D'you want me to run down and get the car?" said Bain.

"Thank you, but no. Come on, we should get on with it. Try and salvage something of the Sunday evening."

"Just going to nip to the loo, ma'am," he said, then turned away.

She sighed, stood for a moment, watched Bain walk away, and then looked round at the small gift shop, open plan, in a corner of the nave beside the entrance. The first thing you saw when you came in, the last thing you saw before you left. Classic.

Pereira found herself automatically moving towards it. Maybe she could get something small to give to Robin, if there was actually likely to be anything suitable for a four-year-old in a cathedral gift shop.

Is this what she'd come to, she thought, as she entered the shop and looked around at the books and CDs, the dishtowels and the small cuddly toys? Was she feeling guilty about the amount she'd been working the past few days? Was this who she was to be, the working parent, buying her son's affection?

She stopped. Stopped in her tracks. Stopped walking, stopped thinking.

She reached out and lifted the small metal object with which she'd become so familiar. She was still holding it as Bain walked in beside her and looked down.

"Jesus," said Bain, then quickly looked over his shoulder, fearing someone might have heard the profanity.

Pereira glanced at him, and then looked round and up, her eyes scanning the walls.

*

"I know, it's… it's embarrassing," said the Deacon, shaking his head. "It's what we've come to. The Church… I'm afraid the Church is dying. Quite literally. What is the Church, any church, if not its people, and everyone is getting older and not being replaced by the young. Membership is now under four hundred thousand, and how many of those d'you think actually attend the kirk on a Sunday morning?"

"We're not here to judge, Mr. Brodie," said Pereira. She held up the small metal cross, which she'd picked up a few minutes earlier in the shop. "We're interested in where these came from, how many you have, how many you've sold, and if you'd have a record of who bought them."

"Oh, I can tell you all that easily enough. And you might wonder, you might think, how would I have such information off the top of my head? Well, it's quite appalling. I know these are desperate times, and I know how much the church is struggling for money, but to be selling such piffle. Such piffling claptrap. It's shameful."

"Where did they come from, Deacon?" asked Bain, trying to move on from the commentary.

"All our stock is bought centrally. Through Edinburgh. What we stock in the shop here, and indeed in every such gift shop in all Church premises, comes from there. By diktat, you might say. It was them who decided we should sell such utter rubbish. Pet crosses in five different sizes… Did you ever hear of such nonsense in your entire life?"

"Where did they come from, Mr. Brodie?" asked Pereira.

"The States, of course, where else? They bought a job lot, high numbers I believe, that's how they think. A high numbers game. Buy 'em cheap, sell 'em high. Truly awful. I sometimes think, if this is what the church has come to, we'd be as well letting it go. Maybe we would…"

His voice trailed away. The sound of defeat. Everywhere you went in the church these days, thought Pereira. Wasn't the message supposed to be one of hope?

"How many have you sold here?" asked Bain.

Brodie laughed, smiled, made a small, dismissive gesture with his right hand.

"None," he said. "Precisely none. Are you at all surprised? Because I'm not, I'm really not. This is what we come to. We debase ourselves and our principles, and we debase our Lord. We have this American drivel in our churches and here in the cathedral, and it brings in not one penny."

He was shaking his head, talking, talking. *There goes the easy win*, thought Pereira. That anything could be that straightforward, on such a day, had been too much to ask.

"They would deserve the opprobrium… They? We…we will get what we deserve when some newspaperman is in one of our shops and notices this. When he prints a picture of it in his paper. When people ask why we do this, and someone takes the time to really look. To look in the faces of the churchmen and women of Scotland, to see the desperation. The sense of defeat."

"Oh, you're quite safe," said Pereira. "I don't think anyone cares enough to print this in a newspaper. And I don't think many would even share your feelings of the cross's inappropriateness."

"Well…" he said, and he let the thought and the words go again.

"But these crosses," said Bain, "they're on sale in Church of Scotland gift shops throughout Scotland?"

"Oh, yes. And elsewhere. The Church of Scotland extends beyond our borders. I'm quite sure we'll be infecting many other countries with this deleterious and poisonous tripe."

"But they're not on the website," said Bain, an observation as much aimed at Pereira. He knew she'd be wondering why Parks hadn't spotted them for sale, and while Bain didn't know for sure that they weren't, he was confident enough in Parks doing a decent job, that his question had really been more of a statement.

"I believe not," said Brodie. "They don't update the website as often as they might. Costs money, you see. Always comes down to money. I think there's another update due in the next couple of months. No doubt they will add them then, and then we'll see what happens. Maybe they'll sell out and we'll be done with them."

"Would you have a list of other premises in Scotland that

250

would sell them?"

"Everywhere sells them!"

"Yes, I get that," said Pereira. "But do you have that list? To hand?"

He nodded. "Normally, you know, the police, one is wary, and I'm sure you could find that information without getting it from me. But today, now, since you come asking about these awful things, I'm inclined to help you. I really am."

"Thank you. Could you get the list for us now?"

"Now?"

Pereira smiled. "Yes, Deacon, if that's possible."

"Yes, yes," he said, resigned to getting up from his seat, "I expect it is."

*

"OK, let's not start slapping ourselves on the backs here," said Pereira. "For a kick-off, we should have found out that the church was selling these things must sooner…"

"Not necessarily. If they bought them straight from America, wholesale, then the only way we were going to find out would be from the US company, and we can't force that information from them. Like he said, it's not on the Church of Scotland website."

"All right," she said, accelerating away from the lights, driving more quickly than she likely should have been, rainwater splashing up around them. "Nevertheless, it still might mean nothing. You get onto Church of Scotland central sales, tonight, now, when we get in, keep calling them until you can get someone into an office. Establish if we can identify if and when any of these things have been sold. It might well be that they haven't sold any, anywhere. I mean, really, what were they thinking?"

"Someone bought them, ma'am, and even if it's only two or three, that's all we need."

Long sigh, head moving slightly, almost with the weight and speed of thought.

"When Armstrong turns up, and I'm convinced he will, we need to be ready for him. I want CCTV footage of him walking into one of those shops and buying a cross. I want his hands on it. I want the guilty look up at the camera."

"Yes, ma'am," said Bain, smiling grimly.

41

"I'm getting my balls roasted here," said Cooper. "Did you follow that press conference?"

Bain stared across the table, feeling restless. He had something to do, and just wanted to get on with it. And it felt right, it felt like the thing that might help them make the breakthrough. Often enough with police work, you were methodically working through everything that needed to be done, the just-in-case and the due process. You knew that likely it would not lead you where you wanted to go. This, however, this felt at least like the path to the breakthrough, if not actually the breakthrough itself.

"No, sir," said Pereira. "We missed the press conference."

"Well," he said. "I suppose that's good. You'd have better things to do in this investigation than follow that garbage."

Hands thrust in his pockets, he turned away and stared out the window. Rain still drummed against the pane, if with less ferocity than before.

"Biblical," said Cooper, his voice moving down a gear. "The rain. I suppose that's fitting." He looked back at them. "This business with Armstrong. How sure are we? Scale of one to ten?"

"If ten is to be able to go to the press, then we're not near a ten, sir," said Pereira. "But I'm fairly certain. But we need to find Cobalt, or we need footage of someone involved in this walking into a Church of Scotland gift shop. So, I'm not sure what the number is, but–"

Cooper silenced her with a wave. "You should get on," he said to Bain. "You're right. We need to nail something down." He nodded at Bain when he didn't immediately get to his feet, and then he finally realised he'd been dismissed.

"Yes, sir," said Bain.

"And what are we doing about Cobalt, Inspector?" asked Cooper.

There was a knock and the door opened before Bain could get to it. Somerville. He acknowledged the DCI, then looked at Pereira.

"We need to get to Bellahouston Old Parish, ma'am," he said. "There's a body."

A moment. Silence in the room, bar the sound of the rain. Everyone waiting for someone to be the one to ask the question.

"Do we know who?" said Cooper. He withheld the dismissive and derisive *as if we need to ask* from the end of the sentence.

"Glenn Armstrong, sir," said Somerville. "He's dead," he added, unnecessarily.

Cooper leant forward on the desk with both hands, jaw clamped, then finally straightened up, swiped a hand across his desk catching an empty mug, and sending it flying against the far wall, where it broke noisily and fell to the floor in thirty pieces.

"Jesus fucking Christ," he said. "Inspector, get out there and fucking find me who did this."

"I should go and speak to Mrs. Arm–"

"Leave the serious stuff to the grown-ups, Inspector. Get out there and find me a damned killer. For fuck's sake."

Pereira got to her feet, and walked quickly from the office, pushing past Somerville and Bain as she did so.

Bain and Somerville followed, Bain closing the door just after another heavy thump of Cooper's fist on the desk.

"Sergeant," said Pereira, "I need you to come with me. Task Sergeant Parks with what you were doing. You've got forty-five seconds, then we're going."

She walked quickly from the office, head filled with anger and frustration, feeling stupid for having voiced her views so quickly, for having come to a rushed conclusion, for having trusted herself and her intuition, and for having taken that intuition to Cooper.

"Fuck it," she barked in a low voice, marching from the open plan.

*

———

They were all soaked. Few were dressed for the weather, many had rushed out from their offices, or had been called out from their homes on a Sunday evening to deal with the emergency.

Not that there was much of an emergency. Glenn Armstrong was dead, and there wasn't a lot to be done about it.

The rain had turned to smearing, miserable, dreadful drizzle, thick and just as soaking as the earlier torrential downpour. The scene at the bottom end of the graveyard was the same as before, the victim's body bound to a headstone, the cross embedded in his head. This time, however, the blood from his eyes had washed away.

"Do we suppose it was always the intention to place Armstrong here," said Pereira, "or had we just made the Necropolis out of bounds by placing officers on the gates?"

Bain looked at the graveyard around the old parish church, so small compared to the great cemetery beside the cathedral. He had no answer, but it had likely been a rhetorical question.

"Who found the body?" asked Pereira, looking round at a constable, dressed in huge waterproofs, but with her head uncovered, her hair soaking.

"Called in anonymously, ma'am," she said. "Sounded rough. Couple of druggies come in to shoot up, we think."

"Man or a woman?"

"Man, ma'am," she said. "But there's talking in the background. On first impressions, the call unit didn't think it was the killer. Pretty sure it was just a couple of folk who'd stumbled on the body."

"Thanks, Constable," said Pereira, then she turned back and looked down at the propped-up body of Glenn Armstrong, the pink flowers in his hands already battered by the rain, wasted, beleaguered and dead.

There was a noise behind her, the sound of waterproof clothing approaching. Pereira turned, and there were Corkin and Gayle, virtually the only two people there appropriately dressed for the weather. There was something comical about them, like some bedraggled, bastardised version of Laurel and Hardy, but they'd be dry to the skin, and there were few others there who would be able to say the same.

"Gentlemen," said Pereira. "Glad you could make it."

"I'd've preferred it if we'd been called at two in the morning," said Corkin, "but I can manage this all the same."

The two of them stopped for a moment, looking down at

the body.

"It's like watching a repeat," said Gayle.

"Aye," said Corkin, "a shite one 'n' all."

"I'm going to leave you to it," said Pereira. "Give us a call with any preliminary findings. And just one thing before we go. Can you check his torso, back and front, please."

"What are we looking for?" asked Gayle, bending down beside the body, alongside Corkin.

"Scratching," said Pereira.

They both looked up.

"Sexual scratching," she added.

"Not sure that'll tell you anything," said Corkin. "Most of us have that."

"Full of shite," muttered Gayle, knocking him slightly.

As with those who had gone before him, Armstrong's body was propped against the headstone solely by a rope around the neck, allowing them access to the torso without having to cut anything away.

They carefully lifted Armstrong's sweatshirt and t-shirt, examined his chest briefly, then held the clothing aside for Pereira to take a look.

"And the back too," she said.

Gayle eased the body forward as much as he could to look behind, lifting the clothing as he did so.

Pereira moved into position, shaking her head at the lack of light.

"Flashlight, anyone?" she said, and quickly one was being put in her hand, and she didn't even look to see where it had come from.

She shone the light on Armstrong's back, then looked at Gayle, who shook his head in return.

"Reports of this man's sexual predilections have been greatly exaggerated," said Gayle.

"Hmm," said Pereira, then she quickly got to her feet. "Tell me we didn't release Lucy Hilton," she said to Bain.

"No, ma'am," said Bain, "we have until ten this evening."

"Right. And we need to speak to Jan Armstrong, regardless of what state she's in. I'll call Cooper, see if we can get her to the station."

42

Pereira sneezed for the first time as they walked through the station, still soaking wet, seemingly having been wet all day, to the interview room. She had called ahead and placed an order for Hilton to be waiting in Room 3, like she'd been ordering pizza or drinks at the bar.

"Uh-oh," said Bain.

"What?" said Pereira, barely looking at him.

She was angry, still not recovered from the feeling of uselessness from having allowed herself to be convinced of Armstrong's guilt, from walking into Cooper's office so confident and bold.

"The sneeze," said Bain. "If this was a movie, you'd have been diagnosed with TB by the end of the evening. Dead by this time tomorrow."

She would probably have smiled under other circumstances, at another time.

"Inspector!"

She stopped a few yards shy of Room 3, annoyance exploding within her at every interruption, then she turned to look at Sergeant Parks, walking quickly down the corridor towards her.

"Inspector," Parks said again.

"Sergeant," said Pereira.

Bain recognised the tone, hoped for Parks' sake that she was bringing them something worthwhile. Parks, as usual, completely ignored him.

"We found what you're looking for. Five separate, individual sales of those crosses through Church of Scotland gift shops, three of them in the last two weeks."

"And?"

"We're in the process of accessing the CCTV at the moment. It's operated through G4S, in coordination with us, and–"

"Sergeant, I don't need the mechanics!"

"We've got the first one. Thought you should know. It's Glenn Armstrong, ma'am. He bought at least one of those crosses. We're trying to find the others now."

"Dammit," said Pereira, turning away. "I knew it." Long, exhaled breath, then she turned back to Parks. "Thanks, Sergeant," she said. "We'll be in Room 3, bring it in when you've got anything else."

"Yes, ma'am."

Parks turned, and they moved apart, all three of them quickly on their way.

In Room 3, Hilton was sitting, her back straight, handcuffed arms resting on the edge of the table. Constable Wales was standing by the door, staring straight ahead. Pereira did not acknowledge her.

"Don't lie to us anymore, Ms. Hilton," said Pereira. "Another man dead, a woman widowed, a child left without a father. We need this to come to an end, and–"

"Who's dead?"

"Glenn Armstrong," said Pereira.

"Hmm," said Hilton. "It's like *Ten Little Niggers*, or whatever you're supposed to call it these days. Who's next?"

"I need you to start telling the truth," said Pereira.

"I don't know about that," said Hilton. "Because here I am in here, and Armstrong was out there when he got killed, so I couldn't possibly have had anything to do with his murder, could I? So, what exactly is in it for me to–"

Pereira slammed the palm of her hand onto the table. "Just tell me the damned truth about Friday evening! You told us you had sex with Glenn. You told us you scratched his chest and his back. You told us you sent him home to his wife with something to hide."

Hilton smiled, moved her head from side to side. "Maybe I made some of that up."

"*Did* you see him on Friday evening?"

Hilton pursed her lips, stared at Pereira from across the desk, like she was giving the question some thought, but was unlikely to answer.

"We can add wasting police time to the list."

"I'm sure you can, Inspector. You've certainly kept me here long enough for having absolutely nothing on me. I'm sure you're more than capable of trumping up a few more charges to add to your imaginary list, my affirmative action friend."

Pereira felt the snap in her brain, the explosion, like she could reach across and grab Lucy Hilton by her pretty, blonde, dyed hair and slam her face into the desk.

Instead she turned away quickly, eyes closed, mouth clamped shut, jaws clenched, holding in the anger.

"Did you sleep with Glenn Armstrong on Friday evening?" said Bain, stepping forward, standing by the desk.

"Ah," said Hilton. "How nice. How subservient of you to play the foil. A thing of beauty."

"Did you sleep with Glenn Armstrong on Friday evening?" repeated Bain, his voice level.

"Jeez, you people really are no fun," said Hilton. "Look, if I, like, tell you what you want to hear, can you let me out? This really has been a total dr–"

"Did you sleep with Glenn Armstrong on Friday evening?" asked Bain again.

Pereira had turned round, but was now standing back from the table.

"No," said Hilton. "I slept with him once, which was quite enough, I can assure you."

"Did you even see Glenn Armstrong on Friday evening?" asked Bain.

She held his gaze for a few moments, then looked at Pereira. Obviously amused by the turn of questioning, toying with how far she could push it.

"Did you see Glenn Armstrong on Friday evening?" repeated Bain.

Same tone, refusing to rise to the bait. He knew that Pereira would likely be kicking herself for getting so angry.

"No fun," said Hilton again. "You really are no... whatever. I did not see Glenn Armstrong on Friday evening," she said, her voice a robotic monotone.

"Was there a reason why you lied, other than that you were taking the piss?"

"Just telling you what you wanted to hear at the time. Trying to do my bit."

"We wanted to hear the truth."

"You should have said."

A moment, as the conversation that had been flying back and forth, temporarily ended, Bain feeling himself getting as annoyed as Pereira.

"When did you see him last?" he said after a few moments.

"Last weekend," she said, her voice now that of the bored teenager again. Pereira recognised the tone. "We had plans, but I cancelled them soon as Wilson got murdered. It might not have been the answer to all our problems, but you know, we were about to have to transfer our attentions to Mr. Wilson Senior, and I don't think he had poor Archibald's guilt hanging over him. You can tell with these old people. Frightened by money and change. He was going to be just fine with Eston and me looking after his assets."

A moment, she turned back to Pereira, having been addressing herself to Bain.

"We still will be, in fact, I would imagine, what with neither Eston nor I having killed anyone."

"Where is he?" asked Pereira.

"Ha!" said Hilton. "Slipped the net, eh? With you people on the case, I'm a bit worried, I have to say. Rate you're going, everyone in Glasgow will be dead by the time you get around to working out who did it."

"Where is he?" asked Bain. Same tone as before.

"Nice, Sergeant," said Hilton. "Another nice interjection. This time, though…"

She shrugged, accompanied by the very slow blink, eyes open again, the superior look directed at Bain.

"Come on," said Pereira, and without looking at Hilton again, she was out the door, Bain close behind her.

Bain closed the door, another few quick paces up the corridor, and then Pereira slowed as they got to the stairs. Took a moment, looking out at the damp night, fingers working in her right hand, tapping against each other, thinking it through.

"That's it," she said.

"Is it?" said Bain.

"The woman, the one he saw on Friday night. Why lie about Hilton? That was careless. The fact that Hilton ended up covering for him feels like a… it's a fluke. She wasn't covering for him at all. She was just screwing with us, and it just so happened to help him out. We were right, Sergeant."

She started walking up the stairs, Bain beside her.

259

"Armstrong killed Archie when he found out he was going to tell the truth, then he killed Peters and faked his own disappearance to cover his tracks. Perhaps his partner did one of them, and they helped cover for each other. Armstrong obviously just didn't think he'd be getting killed at the end of it. At least, that wasn't his part of the plan."

"Who's he working with, then? Cobalt?"

"Cobalt's as bad as that one in there," said Pereira. "I would lay money he'll be walking into work tomorrow morning as though nothing was wrong. It was someone else who wanted those three dead. We need to speak to Jan Armstrong. She's here?"

"I think so," said Bain.   ·

"Right," said Pereira, and she quickened her pace.

*

Jan Armstrong was staring at the table in front of her. Face drawn, a numbness about her, yet with something not quite there. Pereira could tell. There was something incomplete about her grief.

She'd seen women whose husbands had just died. They didn't look like this. There were all sorts of ways they might look, but the ones who cared, the ones who were looking down a black pit of desolation, had something about them. Something that was missing from Jan Armstrong.

"Can you talk?" asked Pereira.

They were sitting in Room 7. Not an interrogation room. Softer. Calmer. They called it the Bereavement Room. In fact, they called it the Dead Room amongst themselves, but officially, it was the Bereavement Room, which seemed ghoulish enough for Pereira.

Cooper had been in the room too, and Pereira had waited for him to leave before trying to question Armstrong. Bain was there too, and Constable Payne was standing by the tray with the tea and the biscuits. As though there might, at any moment, be an emergency requiring one or the other.

"Sure," said Armstrong. "Why not?"

"Your son's at his gran's?"

"Aye. Has been all afternoon. Doesn't know yet. He'll be upset," she said matter-of-factly.

"And what about you?" asked Pereira.

260

Armstrong lifted her head, held Pereira's gaze across the room.

"Hmm," she said.

Pereira didn't speak. She recognised a talker, as ever.

"You're the clever one, eh?" said Armstrong.

"Why did you cover for Glenn?" asked Pereira. "Was there any point?"

"I was embarrassed." She shook her head. "You know, it's not like… look, we had a shit marriage, we really did. I know the life insurance is fine. We're made, me and the boy. I mean, not made like Archie Wilson was made, but we'll be all right. I'd rather this than Glenn just buggering off with that bird, whoever it is. Lucy Hilton, whatever her name was. Any of the others. And there were others, believe me. It's just, wee Tyler's going to be without a dad now, and where'm I going to find him another one? Who wants the likes of me?"

She looked at Bain, as though he might be interested, or possibly like she was looking for him to contradict her.

"You said he smelled of the other woman when he got in, early Saturday morning?" said Pereira.

"Smelled? He stank," said Armstrong. "And you know, that's the thing. See… I don't know, see two year ago. He'd have done the same thing, but he'd have went and had a shower at her place. He'd have taken a change of clothes or something. He'd have done something, you know, so that when he comes in he's not stinking of Chanel No.5 or some shite like yon."

She smiled ruefully, looked between them again.

"Now, see now… he didn't care. He was past caring, I was past caring. He went out, then later he came back in, stinking of I don't know what."

"Perfume?"

"Aye. Perfume."

"Did you recognise it?"

Armstrong laughed lightly, shook her head.

"I don't know who youse think I am? But no, it was just…" and she let the sentence go with a shrug.

"What did it smell like?" asked Pereira.

"Seriously?"

"Yes. Can you remember the smell?"

"Can I remember the smell? My bastard of a husband comes in stinking of some tart…? Aye, I can remember the smell. Jasmine," she said. "It was fucking jasmine, and, I don't know, something. Jasmine and something."

"Orange?" asked Pereira.

Armstrong considered this for a moment, though she more seemed to be considering Pereira for having said it. "I don't think so."

"Pomegranate?"

Armstrong laughed. "Don't know what that smells like, love."

"Cinnamon?"

"Hmm," said Armstrong. "Not sure."

"Apple?"

"Are you just running through fruits and spices? I mean, really…"

"Apple?"

"Maybe," she said.

"Right," said Pereira. Ran through the catalogue in her head. Crossing some off, working out the best available options, and then flicking the switch, changing the catalogue. Wanted to get it done quickly, not wanting to have to go out to find a department store still open, or have to wait until the following morning.

She also knew where she was going, and was trying to ensure that she did a proper job getting there, and didn't force the thought process into the box she wanted it to be in.

"Sergeant," said Pereira turning to Bain. "You know Mrs. Walker, works in admin, ground floor, far end of the building?"

"Think so," said Bain. "Blonde. Well, you know…"

"Yes. And Barry, second floor, accounts?"

Bain nodded.

"I need you to go and get something from them."

"They're not going to be here, ma'am. It's Sun–"

"Something from their desks," said Pereira. "The unlocked bottom drawer. You'll find a bottle of perfume in each. Will you get it, please?"

"Barry has a bottle of–"

"And will you ask Sergeant Parks for her bottle of Laundry, please?"

Bain hesitated for a moment, looked at Armstrong, who was staring at the floor, and then back to Pereira.

"Now, Sergeant," she said.

"Yes, ma'am."

43

"Where are we going?" asked Bain.

Pereira was driving again, too quickly, back into town.

"Shouldn't have left Melville alone," she said.

"What's up?"

"I'm not thinking straight," she said. "That's what's up. I'm tired. Rushing around. I had this need to get it cleared up as quickly as possible, and in the rush, missed the most glaringly obvious thing. We were in there with him an hour and a half ago. Shouldn't have left him alone."

"You think he'll still be at the cathedral?"

"I have that feeling," she said.

Bain was watching her, but didn't really understand. Still, he knew her ways, knew that they were coming to it.

"Who knew the truth?" asked Pereira. The wipers going full tilt, the air vents on full blast.

"The three guys," said Bain. "And the Doctor. Melville."

"Exactly," said Pereira. "And the first three are dead, which means someone is killing off the people who knew. The guilty ones."

"And you think Melville will be considered guilty by association?"

"Yes, Sergeant, I do."

Crashed a red light, took a corner too quickly. Someone, huddled under a large bright yellow mac, stepped back and howled as Pereira's car splashed them through a huge puddle.

It had been a long day. Anger always sapped the strength from her, like she was some sort of regular Hulk figure. Filled with rage, utterly exhausted afterwards.

Perhaps everyone was like that when they got mad.

Almost done, now, she thought. One more person she could save, and then they had to get her principal suspect into custody and hope that they could spin the flimsy evidence that had so convinced her into enough to charge her with murder.

"When you started talking about perfume," said Bain, "I suddenly thought, ah, bloody Frank. We just parked him, didn't we, and I suddenly began wondering if that's where this was going."

"It's not Frank," said Pereira, and she grimaced as she squealed around the corner into High Street, and then slowed to make sure she got the car completely back under control.

Bain didn't mind. Would have been enjoying getting thrown around under other circumstances.

"Jasmine," he said. "Yes… I feel like I've got the scent of it from somewhere recently, but then maybe that's just because you've put the suggestion in my head. I can't think."

Bain's phone rang, and he took it quickly from his pocket. Parks. Probably not calling for a date, he thought.

"Hey."

The road was much quieter now, and they were approaching the Cathedral. Pereira accelerated again, and then slammed on the brakes as she got close, the car skittering to a halt on Cathedral Precinct.

She wasn't paying attention to Bain, just wanting to get on and get this over with. She jumped out the car, round the front, heading straight to the door.

"Inspector!" called Bain, following, phone in his hand, hair almost instantly soaked in the rain.

"What?"

"The call. They found someone else buying two of those crosses. It wasn't just Armstrong."

"Yes," said Pereira. "Come on."

"But…" said Bain, unable to get out the name before Pereira had put her hand to the south side wooden door and pushed it open.

It hardly mattered, he thought. She already knew.

*

They entered at a rush, and then stopped in the great expanse of the nave, looking around in the low light. No one around, complete silence once the door had clicked shut behind them.

Aware that she was breathing heavily in the rush of the moment, Pereira took the positive step to slow down, take a breath. Bain walked a pace or two past her, looking up at the galleries on the second floor, wondering if that was where they were going to have to go, and how to get up there if it was.

Pereira looked along the length of the nave, up towards the great screen that separated the east and west ends of the cathedral. Wasn't it obvious, she thought? Where else would you go to in a cathedral to commit your final act of vengeance?

"Come on," she said, and she walked quickly towards the partition.

Up the stairs, and they entered the choir, where they had earlier sat and interviewed Melville. The light was low, a few candles burning, two or three small electric lamps also lit behind the presbytery.

The only other two people present were up at the front of the cathedral, behind the altar, by the large cross attached to the central pillar. Indeed, the Reverend Doctor Melville wasn't so much by the cross, as about to be suspended from it. He was standing on a chair, completely naked, a rope around his neck, the rope knotted around the centre of the cross. From where they stood, Pereira couldn't see how precarious the perch already was, but even if he was on firm footing, it wouldn't be lasting.

"Shit," said Bain, his voice low, as they started walking quickly down the aisle.

In the dark, the choir appeared cavernous, their footfalls loud in the silence. In the light of the candles, set up around the altar, Laura Kane was watching them approach. She was by the chair on which Melville was standing. It wouldn't be too long before she told them to stop.

As they neared, they could see that Melville was at least comfortable on the chair. He was standing absolutely still, the look on his face set firm. No contrition, no fear. A man who now seemed at peace with what he'd done in his life, and who accepted the onrushing end of it. *If nothing else*, thought Pereira, *that's going to annoy Kane. The killer usually wants to see fear, or at least regret and remorse, not a general acceptance of the punishment being meted out.*

"I think that'll do you, Inspector," said Kane, and both Pereira and Bain stopped.

They were still twenty-five yards away, although already closer than Pereira had been anticipating getting. Making the calculation. It was possible Kane could go nuclear, straight to whipping the chair away at the slightest sign of any further advance from either of them. More likely, however, there would be at least some warning, some instruction to not move any closer.

They could get to twenty yards. They run. Kane whips the chair away. Pereira takes out Kane, Bain supports Melville. Would he have the time before grabbing Melville, to get the chair and put it in position beneath Melville's feet? Or would he have to support him straight away, so that she would have to fight off Kane, allowing her to set the chair upright?

The thought of getting into a fight sounded so stupid. Like a cop on late night duty in the middle of town, dealing with drunks and halfwits outside a pub.

Keep talking, as long as possible, then take any other action as and when.

"Back-up's on its way, Laura," said Pereira. "We've got enough on you for this, for the killing of Glenn Armstrong, and at least being an accomplice to the murder of the others. Don't make it any worse for yourself."

"Nice try, Batgirl," said Kane. "Really. But you have no case."

A step forward. A silent step behind from Bain. Melville watched wordlessly from above, like he was already a ghost. There would be no pleading, no desperation. His skin looked cold and damp, his genitals shrivelled to insignificance.

"We know you saw Armstrong on Friday evening, we have CCTV of both of you buying the crosses used in the murders, we ha–"

"I don't mean that," said Kane scornfully. "I know you have *that* case. Jeez, I'll confess, I don't mind. Armstrong was just a stupid slut, only ever thought with his dick. Yep, a slut. And I know what you're doing, by the way, inching your way forward, making your judgement. I'm not getting into that, though. I'm not getting into the whole stop-or-I'll-pull-the-chair crap."

For the moment, Pereira and Bain stopped. What was it now? Twenty-two yards? Twenty-one?

"I'm going to pull the chair at some point. In five seconds, in five minutes. You're not going to be able to save him… and anyway, look at the man. He's getting what's coming to him. He knows. Nothing more than he deserves."

"What d'you mean we don't have a case?" asked Pereira.

"You don't have a case to stop me pulling the chair. Why wouldn't I do it? Listen. I've lived with it for eighteen years. I lived with the knowledge that those fuckers killed my brother. I lived with the cover-up by Mr. Messenger From God here, about to go and meet his maker. Archie told me, a few weeks after it was all over. Had to get it off his chest. And I just let him tell me, and did nothing about it.

"Then I watched it go on tearing my mum and dad apart, I watched them both wither and die. I tried to move on, I really did. And then the stupid, witless Archie went and won a hundred and thirty million."

"How did you come to get in touch with Armstrong?"

"Picked him up. He didn't remember me. Really, he had no idea who I was." She shook her head. "Just a slut. And really, that's all he was. Men, you know, they always get called a Lothario or a stud, Casanova, Don Juan. Women… we're sluts. Ha! Well, fuck you Glenn Armstrong. He was thinking with his dick. I bided my time for a week or two, and then Archie had got in touch with Glenn by this time, and Glenn was troubled, and he told me… Lies, of course, he told me lies, because he didn't know that I knew the story. And so, together, for all the world like we'd be played by Juliette Lewis and Woody Harrelson in a movie, we plotted murder. The end of his game plan was always the weak point for him. I was to tie him up, drug him, and then rescue him, claiming to have seen someone run away."

She rolled her eyes, watched the creeping movements towards her from both Pereira and Bain.

"Really. Like that was going to remove any suspicion. What an idiot."

"You all right, up there?" said Pereira, looking up at Melville.

A simple ploy. Sometimes those worked. Maybe Kane would look round, give them that extra half second. Her stare, however, never wavered.

"Death will come," said Melville, the voice unyielding. His mouth opened, as though there might be some other words to add to his epitaph, but he remained silent. Death will come. That was all.

"Still inching closer, Detective Inspector," said Kane. "Like a ninja. In a moment you'll look over my shoulder, your eyes wide, and I'll turn, and you'll charge, is that how this is going to play out?"

Less than twenty yards now, thought Pereira. Soon enough they were going to have to bring this to an end. Very soon. She didn't stop moving, Bain behind her. He had looked to the side, wondered about taking another angle of attack, but the only way to do that from here would be to go along the pew, pointlessly trapping himself in the confined space for several seconds. That wouldn't gain him anything. Why hadn't they thought to split up before they came in? Why *wasn't* there someone coming in from behind?

"Almost… almost…" said Kane, as if she were guiding Pereira in.

A moment. She was right, thought Pereira. Almost.

"You know how Judas died, Inspector?"

"Depends which book of the Bible you read," said Pereira. "Matthew says he hung himself, Acts says he fell in the field that he'd bought with his thirty pieces of silver, and…" and she paused, thinking of the line, then said, "*burst asunder in the midst, and all his bowels gushed out.*"

"Very good, Inspector, you know you're st–"

They made their move, Pereira at the front, Bain just behind. A couple of paces to the end of the pews, and then Bain bursting from behind Pereira to her right, heading straight to the hanging man. A few steps to the altar, just the low wooden partition between the altar and the cross to be negotiated.

And it was already too late.

Kane was ready for them, would have been ready if they'd been running from five yards, never mind twenty. With her left foot she flipped the chair, toppling it from under Melville. The body slumped with a grunt, and then she whipped the small metal cross from her pocket, and thrust it brutally, and perfectly, into Melville's abdomen, at the base of the ribcage.

Unlike the other crosses, this one had been amended. Sharpened. It wasn't just for thrusting in, it was for ripping and slashing. In the same stabbing movement, she pulled the knife down across his stomach, tearing a great, bloody gash, then she reached in and grabbed the viscera, a handful of blood and tissue and organs, and yanked them out as hard as she could.

Pereira was on top of her, pushing her aside, Bain was grabbing at the body, lifting it, easing the pressure on the neck, as the bloody, stinking mess of the insides of Melville's abdomen poured from the wound, then was compacted against

Bain's body, and poured in a tangle of coils and tubes and blood and bodily ooze down Melville's legs and Bain's jacket.

Pereira pushed Kane to the floor, both of them landing with a peculiar and almost comical oof. Pereira was ready for the fight, but there was nothing there, no fight to be had. Kane had done her job. Her final revenge had been taken. The sharpened cross in her hand had already been dropped. She had no interest in stabbing Pereira.

A moment, Pereira looked up at Melville's face, pushed herself up, off Kane and off the ground, grabbed the chair and set it beneath Melville, so that he could place his feet on it. A hopeless cause.

Bain struggled with Melville's body, the weight of it, the horror of it, the sheer lifelessness of it. But this was no longer Melville. It was a cadaver, that was all. Just an empty shell, devoid of everything that marked the human spirit.

*

A minute later. Kane was going nowhere. Indeed, she hadn't even got to her feet. Sitting on the floor of the cathedral, staring at the slumped, disembowelled body of Reverend Doctor Thomas Melville. Bain had fallen back, under the weight, as Pereira had reached up and loosened the rope, and he too was sitting down, covered in blood, his back against the altar partition.

Pereira was the only one still standing. Handcuffs from her pocket, she grabbed Kane's wrist, pulled her roughly towards the altar and attached her to the wooden latticework.

Pereira looked down at the blood on her hands, and could think of nothing else to do but wipe them on her own, soaking jacket.

They held each other's gaze for a short while. Why hadn't she been able to see that, thought Pereira? See behind the mask. She'd talked to her, and it wasn't just the talk of an alibi that'd fooled her. It was the look in the eyes. She hadn't seen it, hadn't been able to see the real person behind the lies.

"Who's the girl?" asked Bain. "Your witness, vouching for your whereabouts on Friday?"

Kane nodded, the first look of regret that they'd seen from her.

"Sandy," she said. "She'll just... really, she doesn't know

anything. You'll get her in, no doubt, you'll do all your police shit, but she had no idea who I was. I was just her mate. Told her I was involved in some low-level drug deal and needed her to cover for me should anyone come asking." She rolled her eyes. "She was a little, you know, *what the fuck is happening?* when you actually showed up, but then, you didn't push her, did you? You just asked the question, and she answered, and that was all."

Pereira and Bain glanced at each other. Who was it that had checked with Sandy, the alibi? Parks? Somerville?

"I don't think you need to kick yourself, Inspector," said Kane. "I did a pretty decent job. Quite enjoyed it. You noticed the graves that Wilson and Peters were placed against? Thought that was a nice touch."

"A thing of beauty," said Pereira, drily.

"Thanks."

"And Wilson, when did you pick him up?"

"Ach, that was nothing," she said. "Asked around. Waited for him in town one night, like I was casually driving past. Poor Archie, so fucking miserable. All that money, and no one to play with. He seemed happy to see an old face. A friendly face. Jesus. He was such a pussy."

She shook her head, rolling her eyes, as though Wilson had been a disappointment.

"Well, anyway… there we are," said Kane. "Now you've got your killer, and the right four men are dead… Judas will get his just deserts, won't he?"

"Judas," said Pereira, shaking her head.

"You'll never know," said Kane. "None of you. What Mark was like. The intricacies of the boy, the contradictions, the things he held dear. He was fascinated by the Judas story… Fascinated."

She looked off to the side, taken back all those years, to her teenage life with her older brother.

"What a weird kid," she finally said, looking round, smiling. "Good weird, but weird. He'll be happy now. He'll like the tale of revenge."

"And the cross in the skull?" said Pereira. "The flowers? Seriously?"

"Ha! Can't a girl employ a little flourish? An artisan at work."

Pereira shook her head. The phone was already in her hand, blood on the case, and she was about to make the call, when it

---

270

rang. She glanced at it, lifted it to her ear.

"Sergeant," she said.

"Inspector," said Parks, "thought you might want to know that Eston Cobalt just came back to his apartment. Walked in the front door like he owned the place. You want him brought in?"

Pereira stared down at Kane, who had watched her for a moment, before letting her eyes drift away.

"Yes," she said, "please do that. First, though, Sergeant, I'm at the cathedral. I'm going to need the full team." She paused. She looked at Bain, her face deadpan. "There's been another murder."

44

She got home at sometime between eleven and midnight. Had barely even noticed the clock. Closed the door quietly behind her, walked into the sitting room, wondering if everyone would still be up, Anais on her phone, Robin with his head in his grandma's lap.

She had no idea how long she would have needed the drive home this evening to be in order to get down off the thrill and the high and the awfulness of the case. The sight and the smell of the death of Doctor Melville. The feeling of helplessness and hopelessness. Just another death on her watch, and right in front of her.

"You look awful," said her mum. She was sitting in the armchair by the small electric fire. No television, no magazine, just sitting, waiting patiently for her daughter to return. "And your clothes are damp. How long have they been like that?"

"Are they asleep?" asked Pereira.

"Yes, I think so. They were an hour ago."

Pereira glanced up the stairs, then walked further into the room.

"Just go up and see them, I'll still be here when you get back down."

A moment, Pereira wondered if that was her mother indicating that she intended staying the night – and if there'd been a spare room, she presumably would have – and she nodded and turned back out the room.

She walked slowly and quietly up the stairs, wanting at least one of the kids to be awake. Someone to talk to. Someone to be on her side. And yet, she wanted them both to be asleep. A conversation at this time of night would inevitably be drawn out as long as they could manage, until Pereira was having to extricate herself from it, and feeling bad – again – about shutting them down when they still wanted to chat.

She opened the door and looked in. The light was on, as ever, but both of them were asleep. She walked quietly over and stood over Robin's bed. He was lying on his stomach, his legs bent at the knees, his feet in the air, creating a tent with the duvet. He was sound. She leaned forward, kissed him lightly on the top of his head, ran her finger gently through his hair.

Swallowed at the sudden thought she was going to start crying. The thought of losing him. There had been no mention of that, but she couldn't shake the idea of it, of Lena and the actress, the two of them settling down and wanting a family, and Lena deciding that the time had come to fight for her son. And she could never ask if that would be the intention. It was just something she would have to wait for, something that would happen or not.

She straightened up, quickly forced the thought away. They were a long way away from that. A long way.

Deep breath, she turned to the other bed, just a few feet away in this tiny room. As ever Anais had fallen asleep with her ear buds still in, the phone in her hand. The phone had now drifted quietly away from her fingers, and was nestling in the duvet. Pereira lifted it and placed it on the window ledge beside the bed, then took the earbuds out and laid them on top of the phone. Anais moved as she did so, her brow furrowed a little, her lips parted as though she was going to speak, and then she seemed to burrow further down into the pillow, her face relaxing.

Pereira bent over and kissed her, straightened again, still looking down at her. She used to be scared that Martin would come looking for Anais, trying to take her away, take her through to Edinburgh to live full-time, but it had never happened.

Maybe that possibility had passed. Or maybe Martin was just biding its time.

She turned, back out the door, closing it softly behind her, and down the stairs. Exhausted now that the end of the day was in sight. Work done, case solved – insomuch as she felt she had solved anything – nothing left but the time to wind down with a glass of wine and get to bed.

Her mum was already standing, her coat on.

"I'm really sorry," said Pereira. "Been an horrendous day."

"That's all right. We had a nice time. They missed you, but we played Monopoly, and Anais got her homework done."

"That's good, thank you."

"You should change out of your damp clothes."

As if in confirmation, Pereira sneezed again, and smiled as she reached for the tissue box on the small coffee table.

"Going for a shower in a minute," she said.

"And straight to bed," said her mum. "Don't be coming back down here, drinking and thinking and staring at the wall like you usually do."

"I won't," she lied.

A beat. Her mother held her gaze for a moment, then reached out and rubbed her arm.

"Things have to change," she said, her voice soft.

Yes, thought Pereira. She could feel the choke of a tear at the back of her throat, and she swallowed and smiled.

"I know," she said.

Her mother nodded, let her hand rest lightly on her daughter's face, smiled and turn away.

"Get to bed," she said as she got to the door, and then she was out into the hallway and on her way, the front door opening and closing quickly.

"Things have to change…" said Pereira to the empty room. "Of course. I'll pick one of the many options open to me in the morning."

*

An hour later. Maybe more. The middle of the night, and now the wind had picked up, and the rain was swirling.

The house was quiet. Pereira had had her shower, she'd put on her heaviest pyjamas, she'd got the bottle of wine from the fridge, and a small bag of crisps. She was on the sofa, her legs curled beneath her. Ella was playing, down low, *Stars Fell on Alabama*, with Louis Armstrong. And Bain was right. They sounded like they were having so much fun, no matter the subject matter of the song.

There was no post-case wrap-up going on in her head. There was still work to be done, there was still a conviction to be sought and won, indeed doing a good job now was possibly even more important than the one done in identifying the perpetrator of the crime.

That was for tomorrow and the days after. Now there was just the music, and the wine, and the quiet of a house at rest, and the wind and the rain outside.

All that, and the worry of what was to come next.

She took a sip of wine, she let the music engulf her, she stared at the swirling orange light of the fire. This was the moment when she cried, right? This was the moment when all the stress and the crap and the work and the worry got the better of her, and she could give in to it. The middle of the night. No one around, time to weep for her bloody life.

The familiar buzz of an incoming text sounded beside her. She closed her eyes for a moment. The time to cry would be nice, she thought, and smiled ruefully, her head shaking.

She lifted the phone. Cooper. Maybe he was actually going to say something nice to her for once, to compensate for the fact that he had been surly and unimpressed on their return to the station that evening which, given the death of Melville, had not really surprised her.

And after all, what had they achieved for their six days of investigation? Laura Kane had set out to kill four people. Kane had been, as Lena would say in her American way, four of four for her objectives. The Serious Crime Unit had achieved nothing. If they had sat back and not bothered, if they'd actually been as indolent and useless as people wanted them to be, what difference would it have made?

Perhaps, if they'd done nothing, Laura Kane would have walked off, disappearing into the sunset, never to be found. Perhaps that was all they had to show for their efforts. They'd caught the perpetrator. But then, how did they know that she hadn't just been intending to sit there, revelling in the spilled viscera of Reverend Dr. Melville, until someone arrived at the cathedral the following morning?

Not now, she thought, shaking her head. Don't have the personal inquest now, sitting here, melancholic and alone, at the end of such an awful day.

For a moment she contemplated not opening the text, then eventually she turned her eyes down to the phone and looked at the message.

Front pages look bad
Be here @ 0730

She stared at it for a short time. Be there at 07:30. She had no way to be there at 07:30, not without running around trying to make other arrangements at 06:30. Just as the boss would know.

She closed the message, placed the phone back on the seat beside her. Staring into the fire, she lifted the wine and placed the cool glass against her forehead.

Printed in Great Britain
by Amazon

27634295R00162